The Tree of Liberty

The Tree of Liberty

A Lawson Holland Thriller

M.P. MacDougall

DYSFUNCTIONAL DOZEN PRESS
Subsidiary of
DTwelve Media, LLC

The Blood of Patriots

For information, inquiries, or updates on new editions, contact: mp@mpmacdougall.com

ISBN: 9798782547837

For all who stand in the breach

Recreari aliquando lignum libertatem patriae sanguinis tyranni.
Est sua naturalia stercore.

The tree of liberty must be refreshed from time to time with the blood of patriots and tyrants. It is it's natural manure.

- Thomas Jefferson, in a letter to William Stephens Smith
November 13, 1787

CHAPTER ONE

Congregatio Tempestate

"Bursts as a wave that from the clouds impends,
And swell'd with tempests on the ship descends;
White are the decks with foam; the winds aloud
Howl o'er the masts, and sing through every shroud:
Pale, trembling, tir'd, the sailors freeze with fears;
And instant death on every wave appears."

~ Homer, The Iliad

PROLOGUE
15 Days After the Crash of AIR FORCE ONE

The United States of America was a country in chaos.

Only fifteen days had passed since a freak accident had caused *Air Force One* to crash in an Idaho wilderness. Within twenty-four hours of the accident, terrorists had coordinated hundreds of attacks on civilian locations across the country, resulting in thousands of deaths and mass panic. Many of the victims were civic leaders and governmental officials, a fact that contributed heavily to the rapidly spreading sense of fear and uncertainty.

The American government had quickly proven itself incapable of wringing order from the chaos. Vice President Aron Reese had been sworn in as the new president within hours of the downing of *Air Force One*, but glaring inconsistencies in reports about the causes of the accident, as well as the presence or absence of survivors, had fed conspiracy theories and wild speculation. Some people at the highest levels of government suspected, and others whispered, that Reese might have played some part, either active or passive, in removing his former boss.

Those whispers grew to shouts several days later. Shocking video footage surfaced of President Tolliver, very much alive hours *after* the crash, being shot to death by a single assassin in a remote mercantile near the Montana-Idaho border. Having already reported that Tolliver's body had been found, burned in the plane crash more than fifty miles away from that mercantile, Reese was backed into a corner, his role in the assassination and his legitimacy as president overshadowed by a fast-growing cloud of suspicion.

Then, Secretary of Defense David Coleridge had turned up dead in his home, dangling from an upstairs railing by his own necktie. Speculation started growing about Coleridge's potential involvement with Tolliver's assassination, and how close his ties had been with the new president, Aron Reese. Coleridge was potentially the second assassination victim in less than two weeks, and his death only served to increase pressure on Reese and his already stumbling transition.

Unable to explain away his role in the events, Reese had withdrawn, eventually cancelling all press briefings and eliminating his public appearances altogether. Aides agreed that the new president seemed mentally unstable at best, and completely unhinged at worst. Most people believed the country had just suffered a coup, but no one seemed to know what to do next.

With his enemies and opponents circling, Reese became more and more isolated and less in charge of the day-to-day events of the country. Drastically weakened at home and abroad, America suddenly found itself a ripe target for foreign opportunists.

The significance of America's sudden vulnerability was not lost on the rest of the world. Terror attacks continued to break out around the country, executed by sleeper cells of radical Islamists and home grown radicals alike. Reprisals by civilian groups spread as well, resulting in a general disregard for the rule of law, growing vigilantism and an increasingly realistic fear that the entire nation might collapse under the strain.

Overseas, the Russians saw an opportunity and began moving men and equipment to their Far East. Their eyes were on Alaska, and they were gambling that the United States would not have the resolve or the resources to respond to the threat.

In Europe, the NATO powers scrambled to find a solution, knowing that the wholesale collapse of America both economically and militarily would soon lead to a similar fate for them.

And in China, the Communist Party leadership also saw a golden opportunity as they watched the developing situation. It quickly became obvious to them that the time was ripe to manipulate events to further their own gains.

America was gravely wounded, its enemies were circling, and time was running out.

CHAPTER TWO

Patientes Nulla

**Beijing Capital International Airport
Beijing, China**

Day 15

Gao Jianli was sweating, in spite of the air conditioning. The four blank-faced soldiers escorting him to his departure gate had mostly kept the crush of people in the terminal at a wary distance, but Gao still had to pause when the crowd waiting at his gate got too dense. He turned slowly and looked at the scowling Guoanbu agent following behind him.

Gao had been in the custody of the Guoanbu, better known as the Chinese Ministry of State Security, for the past seven years. His crime had been to speak out against the Chinese government at an international symposium on human rights, and the government had responded by arresting him, seizing all his assets, and sentencing his wife to life in a forced labor camp. She had died there two years later.

In the years that followed, Gao had had plenty of time to wish that he had died in her place. The Guoanbu had not been gentle. When he wasn't in solitary confinement, locked in a four foot by four foot cell with no room to lay down, he'd been subjected to a never ending variety of torture and interrogation. He had been constantly sleep deprived, sick and repeatedly beaten. He wasn't certain any more how he'd survived, much less why.

He was even less sure about why he was now standing at a gate in the largest airport in China, under a departure board indicating a non-stop flight to Los Angeles, California. He didn't know if he should be happy or if this was just another method of torment the Guoanbu had come up with - tempting him with freedom and then dragging him back to his cell at the last moment.

The agent scowled at Gao, shoving his way past and pushing through the crowd to the boarding agent. He flashed his ID and spoke to her in hushed tones, pointing behind him at Gao, who watched the exchange with dread.

The woman's eyes widened slightly, then she motioned Gao forward. "Your ticket, please."

Gao glanced at the Guoanbu agent again, then handed over his ticket. His hand was shaking. The woman scanned the ticket, then disconnected the nylon strap blocking access to the jetway entrance. Gao looked at her, but she averted her eyes, so he started to move forward.

He jumped when the Guoanbu man clamped a hand on his shoulder and spun him around. The man had eyes like a snake. He stuck his face close to Gao's and spoke through clenched teeth.

"You are fortunate, traitor. The Party has decided that you are of more value alive than dead. I have no idea why - I would have preferred to see you executed for your crimes against the state, but that was not my choice." He glanced over Gao's shoulder out the window. "Take a good, long look. It will be the last time you ever see China." He leaned in close and hissed into Gao's ear. "If you try to come back, I will happily kill you myself."

Gao nodded once, and the man released his grip. Gao took a deep breath, squared his shoulders as much as he could, and shuffled through the gate into the jetway. He had no idea what awaited him at the other end, but he was certain the Guoanbu man was right.

There was nothing left for him in China.

Fourth Military Medical University
Department of Biomedical Engineering
Xi'an, China

"How does it work?" Colonel General Ma Yong's eyes were wide as he stared through the thick glass into the bright lights of the Level Four biological containment laboratory on the other side.

President Zhao Shen started to answer. "As I understand it, this gene…"

"The ZC3H12 gene," the doctor interrupted.

Zhao glared at the man before continuing. "As you say. This gene is essentially a protein that is crucial for the efficient growth of a variety of organisms, but most importantly for our purposes, for several types of deadly viruses."

The doctor sniffed. "That is a simplification, but yes, it is accurate enough."

Zhao glared at the doctor again, but the man seemed oblivious. "At any rate," Zhao said, "the presence of this gene helps these viruses to grow. And we have developed a method for encouraging the gene itself to grow unchecked."

"But how?" Ma was still staring through the glass at the half dozen people working in HAZMAT gear on the other side, as if he was afraid some horrible pathogen would burst through the window and kill them all.

Zhao looked at the doctor. "Perhaps you would like to explain it more clearly, Doctor."

The man nodded and turned to Ma. "You recall the MERS scare several years ago, when many Western governments panicked and pushed through experimental mRNA vaccinations?"

"Yes, of course."

"We had people working on the research teams at two of the American companies that produced those vaccines."

Ma's eyebrows went up. "You're saying they laced their vaccines with a virus?"

"Not at all," the doctor sniffed again. He didn't seem capable of hiding his disdain for less intelligent people - even when those people were the two most powerful men in China. "What they did do," he continued, "was alter the mRNA the vaccine was built around. People who received the altered vaccine would experience rapid overgrowth of the ZC3H12 protein gene, but would have no outward indication of that overgrowth."

Ma shook his head. "Forgive me - if there is no effect, then what would be the point?"

The doctor frowned, looking down his nose at Ma as if he was an idiot. "The point is, that when a host carries a protein gene that has been instructed by the altered mRNA to replicate on a massive scale when exposed to a certain viral agent - and the viral agent itself thrives *because* of that protein, you have a perfect storm for spreading an infectious disease. The subjects get the vaccine and then go about their lives, completely unaware that they have willingly received the first half of a binary biological weapon into their bodies.

"The second half of that weapon is a genetically modified version of the Marburg virus that is even more contagious than the naturally occurring strain - because we have discovered how to make it airborne - but it is mostly benign in any host who lacks the modified gene protein. In those cases, it would present as nothing more serious than a common cold. We have completed extensive research on fruit bats, which are the natural hosts of the Marburg virus. These animals show no outward symptoms of the disease, even when blood tests show they are clearly infected. We used that knowledge to work backward and perfect a method - "

"Wait," Ma interrupted, holding up a hand to stop the flood of information. "You're saying we had people on the American R&D teams that developed the MERS vaccines?"

The doctor scowled. "Yes, I said that, but that is not the interesting part. Now, as I was saying about the fruit bats - "

Ma ignored him, looking back through the window into the laboratory. "And those people inserted the modified mRNA into the vaccines, but the mRNA is essentially invisible…"

"Until the vaccinated person is later exposed to our similarly modified Marburg virus," the doctor said, exasperated that Ma seemed uninterested in his line of explanation. "Once that happens, the Marburg virus runs its course. The mortality rate is incredibly high, and all known treatments are mostly ineffective."

"How high?"

"I'm sorry?"

"The mortality rate," Ma said. *"How high?"*

"Ninety percent, in our live trials." The doctor folded his arms across his chest and let slip a thin smile.

Ma looked at Zhao. "And this is ready to deploy?"

Zhao smiled slightly. "It has *already* been deployed."

Ma's jaw dropped. "When?"

"This morning. As soon as our friend Gao Jianli boarded his flight to Los Angeles." He looked at his watch. "Another carrier should be landing in Moscow within the hour. Two more have already arrived in Irkutsk and Khabarovsk."

"The Russians developed their own vaccines during the MERS outbreak," the doctor explained. "But by the time they did, we had already infiltrated their laboratory as well. The same modified mRNA was added to their stock that we added to the western nations' vaccines."

Ma was stunned. He looked at Zhao, then the doctor, but

words escaped him. It was all he could do to maintain his composure as he turned away, staring dumbly back into the lab.

"Time of incubation from first exposure runs from a week to ten days," the doctor went on. "We should be getting reports of multiple outbreaks within that time frame. The first deaths will follow immediately after.

"Computer simulations show the secondary infections from the aircraft passengers on the Los Angeles flight alone will reach most of the population centers in North America. Tertiary exposure, people contacting those who contacted the passengers, will be exponentially higher. The spread will be more rapid in Russia, since we are going in with three hosts, all of them diplomatic attachés with wide contacts in the Russian government. The outbreak will be global in a month."

Ma felt bile rising in the back of his throat. He could feel his own pulse pounding in his head.

"You have done well, doctor," Zhao was saying. "We look forward to the success of the project."

"Thank you, sir." The doctor bowed slightly and backed out of the room.

Zhao stood next to General Ma and clasped his hands behind his back, following Ma's gaze into the lab. "Are you unwell, my friend?"

Ma turned and faced him. The man before him had been his friend since they were young boys. They'd risen together in the Party, but Ma had no illusions that his own ascendance had been anything more than a reflection of Zhao's. Ma had pursued promotion as a means to privilege and luxury, but Zhao had always been more driven, more ruthlessly focused in his pursuit of advancement, and that drive had won him the most powerful position in China. Ma knew that Zhao was capable of -*no, guilty of* - brutality, but until now he'd been able to rationalize it away as a necessary evil, an unfortunate corollary of the incredibly powerful position his friend held.

But *this?*

This was too much. Zhao had unleashed biological warfare on the entire planet apart from China. If that smug doctor was even halfway correct in his projections, millions - *no, billions,* Ma corrected himself - would die as a result. A sudden impulse welled up within Ma, screaming out at him that the man he had thought was his friend, the person whose coat tails he'd ridden to his own success, was actually a genocidal monster.

He had to do something. He had to stop him; stand up to him, even if it meant just reaching out and taking him by the throat, choking the life out of him right then and there, for the greater good of mankind -

"General Ma." The hint of menace in Zhao's voice startled Ma, who realized with a start that he'd been staring blankly.

"I - ah, forgive me," Ma stammered. "My mind was… elsewhere." He quickly lowered his eyes, afraid that Zhao would somehow discern his thoughts. "No, *lingxiu*. I am not unwell. Thank you for asking."

Zhao sniffed. "You look sick to me." He motioned toward the door. "Shall we go, then? We both have much to do. Perhaps you should make time to see your doctor?"

Ma found that his good intentions were not enough to overcome his own weaknesses. He wasn't strong enough to take matters into his own hands, to reach out and kill Zhao, even if it would be for the greater good. It was all he could manage just to nod and meekly follow his leader out of the building.

Someone else - *anyone* else - would have to stand up to Zhao.

Gao tried to relax as the plane lifted off and turned to the east. He could feel his pulse racing. As the aircraft climbed through ten thousand feet and the cabin crew started moving around, passing out drinks, he felt tears welling up. A thousand thoughts and memories flooded his mind, but especially he thought about his wife, and the last time he'd seen her, crying as the Guoanbu had dragged him from their home. Even though she'd been dead for five years now, he felt a sense of betrayal in abandoning her this way, leaving the country of their birth like some common criminal going into exile.

It was irrational, he knew, but he still couldn't ignore it. She had *wanted* him to stand up to the Communists, to speak out and risk everything in the hope that his voice might change something. But still, Gao knew beyond a shadow of a doubt that his actions had led directly to his wife's murder at the hands of the Chinese government.

Even worse, *he* had somehow survived. For whatever reason, he was still alive, and was finally escaping from the brutal regime he and his wife had opposed throughout their marriage. He was alive, and she was not.

He tried to hide his tears as the flight attendant came to his row, but she didn't look at him, much less offer him a drink. After serving the two people on his right, she moved on. Gao knew she did it out of fear. He knew she was afraid that if she showed him kindness, another member of the crew or one of the passengers would report it to her superiors. He knew that was the case, but deep inside, his self-loathing told him it was just confirmation that he was beneath even the simplest act of compassion.

He turned his face to the window and watched his homeland recede below him. He was alive, but try as he might, he couldn't think of a single reason to want to be.

Irkutsk International Airport
  Irkutsk, Russia

Georgy Toporov snaked his cab through the crush of traffic in front of the terminal, cutting off another cabbie and stopping next to an Asian man dressed in a cheap suit. Georgy hopped out and walked around the cab, grabbed the man's case without asking if he wanted a taxi, and tossed it into the trunk. The man opened his own door and climbed in the back seat. "Marriott," he said simply, then busied himself with his cell phone, ignoring Georgy.

Perfect, Georgy thought. Twenty minutes out, another twenty back. He'd have time to grab a bite to eat before picking up one more fare, then he could go straight home. He'd had a busy day today, and he wanted to go home early. After a couple of failed attempts at small talk, Georgy left his passenger to himself and enjoyed the drive. He barely noticed the two times the man sneezed on the way to the Marriott.

Los Angeles International Airport
Los Angeles, California

The Boeing 787 Dreamliner that brought Gao to Los Angeles had been packed to capacity. The nationwide flight restrictions imposed by the Americans immediately following the crash of *Air Force One* two weeks earlier had only been lifted for a few days, and the backlog of travelers was still immense. About two thirds of the passengers on Gao's flight were Chinese nationals, but the other third were Americans, with several Canadians and two Mexicans mixed in. The close seating made it a foregone conclusion that the latent, modified strain of the Marburg virus that Gao was carrying would spread to the people seated around him, and the thirteen hour flight time made it even more certain.

Gao didn't know it, but he was the delivery system for a weapon the Chinese government had been working on for years. Prior to releasing him from prison, Gao's captors had given him a variety of injections, telling him they were vitamin shots and basic vaccinations. He hadn't believed them, but he'd been in no position to argue, and now that he was safely away and hadn't become sick, he'd forgotten the episode altogether. He didn't know that they had injected him with a deadly virus, and that throughout the flight, he'd been unwittingly infecting his fellow passengers with it.

None of the Chinese passengers were in danger - they hadn't been injected with the hastily developed American MERS vaccine years before that had carried the necessary mRNA trigger. The Western passengers were a different story. One of the Mexicans, all of the Canadians, and ninety-five per cent of the Americans on board the flight had received the MERS vaccine with the modified mRNA. When one of them inhaled even a microscopic aerosolized particle of liquid that Gao breathed out, the ZC3H12 protein they carried would recognize it as an instruction to reproduce on a massive scale. In turn, the modified virus would feed on the growing proteins and then reproduce rapidly, and it would tear through their bodies like a wildfire.

The lucky ones would die quickly.

Gao emerged from the jetway and into the terminal in Los Angeles, and started to follow the crowd as it shuffled toward the customs area. He noticed a man coming toward him against the flow of people, and he stopped, suddenly fearful again. The man's suit and manner told Gao clearly that he was a police officer or government official of some sort. Gao glanced around, but there was literally nowhere to go, so he simply stopped and waited. If they had allowed him to come this far, only to return him to custody now, they were even more sadistic than he'd imagined. His knees felt weak as he watched the man approach.

"Mr. Gao?"

Gao looked at the man. "I am Gao Jianli."

The man smiled and thrust out his hand, causing Gao to flinch. "Dave Proctor, U. S. State Department. Welcome to America, sir."

Gao looked dumbly at Proctor's outstretched hand. He couldn't bring himself to respond.

Proctor withdrew his hand, looking uncomfortable. "I apologize that we had no one else here to greet you, Mr. Gao. Things around here have been, well, chaotic to say the least, and your arrival wasn't made known to us until the very last minute.

They sent me over as soon as we heard you were on the flight. Normally, we would have arranged for a more, uh, appropriate welcome, but under the circumstances, I guess I'm it." He stuck his hand out again, this time raising an encouraging eyebrow.

Gao slowly took his hand. He struggled to respond, since he hadn't spoken English in years. "No need to apologize, Mr. Proctor," he finally said slowly. "I did not expect to survive, so *any* welcome is appreciated."

"You must be exhausted," Proctor said. "If you'll come with me, I think we can dispense with the need to wait at immigration. We'll set you up with a temporary place to stay for the time being, until we can work out where you want to settle down." He gently ushered Gao toward a doorway off the main corridor. "Is this your first time in America?"

"No." Gao stopped abruptly, caught off guard by a sudden mental picture of the first time he'd been to America. He'd come on a business trip with his wife shortly after they were married. They had both been arrested and interrogated by the Guoanbo after they returned to China from that trip, and after their release, both of them had found they had plenty of reasons to think more critically of their government. In a way, it had put Gao on a path to this very moment.

"Mr. Gao?" Proctor was looking at him. "Is everything all right?"

Gao blinked back the tears that had welled up again. "Sorry. I was just remembering someone." He straightened up and forced a smile. "It is fine. I will come with you now."

Proctor escorted Gao through a maze of hallways before they finally made their way into the main terminal, and then out to the parking garages, where Proctor had left his vehicle. He hurried to open the passenger door for Gao, who looked embarrassed by the attention. As Proctor got in and started weaving the car through traffic toward the exit, Gao stared vacantly out the window.

"Why 'chaotic'?" he asked.

"Excuse me?"

"You said inside, that things were 'chaotic.' Why?"

Proctor glanced over at him. "Sorry. I forgot you've been... out of the loop, so to speak. When *did* they let you out of prison?"

"This morning," Gao said softly. He half turned his head toward Proctor. "I thought they were taking me to a firing squad." He looked back out the window. "But they took me to the airport instead."

Proctor shifted uncomfortably in his seat. "I guess that explains a lot. You wouldn't have heard about everything going on here. We can catch up on that later, though. I don't want to dump on you right now."

"Please," Gao said. "I would like to know what has been happening. I have not had much information since I was sent to the prison. Any news would be better than being kept in the dark."

"That might depend on the news," Proctor said. "But if you really want to hear it, I'll do my best to bring you up to speed. Just stop me if it gets too much, all right?"

Gao nodded, continuing to stare out the window.

"All right," Proctor said, taking a deep breath. "So, a couple of weeks ago, President Tolliver's plane crashed in the mountains up in Idaho..."

"Sorry," Gao interrupted. "President who?"

"Tolliver. Galen Tolliver?" Proctor caught himself again. "Oh, right, you wouldn't have known that he was even elected. So, Galen Tolliver was only about two years into his first term as president, okay? He was on a trip across country and his plane flew into a storm and crashed. He survived, but then he was assassinated the next day as he hiked out of the mountains. They haven't caught the assassin yet.

"Then, on the same day as the assassination, a bunch of Muslim terrorists staged attacks against civilian targets all across the country. Killed lots of people, including quite a few members of Congress, Supreme Court Justices, you name it."

"Oh, my. I am very sorry to hear."

"Yeah. So Aron Reese, who was Tolliver's Vice President, takes over. There's rumors going around that Reese had something to do with Tolliver's death, but you didn't hear that from me, okay?" Proctor chuckled.

Gao looked at him in horror. "In my country, even joking about such a thing would get you arrested; most likely shot."

Proctor's grin evaporated. "Sorry. We're a little freer with our gallows humor over here, I imagine."

"You are freer in many more ways than you appreciate, I think."

"Probably. You want me to go on?"

This time Gao managed a slight smile. "You mean there is more?"

"Oh, yeah," Proctor said. "It's mostly along the lines of civil unrest and economic disaster, though. People have been really nervous since the attacks, and nobody in the federal government seems to have a good handle on what to do. You ask me? This country is on the brink of collapse. Not to detract from what you went through in prison, but this might not be the best time to come here. You're not exactly catching us at our best."

"Believe me, Mr. Proctor," Gao said. "Even at its worst, America is better than China at its best. I wanted to make China more like America, and they imprisoned me and murdered my wife for it. You have great freedom here. That may be a vulnerability - it makes it easier for terrorists to attack you, for example - but in my country and others like it, freedom is seen as a threat to those in power. They wouldn't have tortured me and killed my wife if they weren't frightened by what we had to say."

Proctor nodded, accelerating as the airport exit road finally merged with the freeway. "I understand your point, but forgive me for asking - if they saw you as such a threat, why let you go now, after what, seven years? That doesn't make sense."

Gao thought about that for a moment, then shook his head slowly. "It may make no sense to me or you, Mr. Proctor, but do not be deceived. The Chinese Communist Party does nothing - *nothing* - without having very good reason for doing it. I do not know how they think my release will benefit them, but if *they* did not think it would, they would *not* have let me go." He fixed his eyes on Proctor. "They would have put a bullet in my head and saved you a trip to the airport."

Proctor fixed his eyes on the road. He believed Gao was right, and the thought gave him no comfort.

CHAPTER THREE

Ponam Aereas

Anadyr-Ulgony Airbase
  Chukotka Autonomous Okrug, Eastern Russia

Day 15

"Fools!" Colonel Pavel Karpov stormed out of the operations building, into the cold light of a subarctic midday. He was supposed to be planning an assault schedule, but every day brought another setback. The original war plan - more than twenty years old and rushed into use in response to the ongoing terrorist attacks and political crises in America - had called for a widespread airborne assault against multiple targets in Alaska, with fifteen thousand airborne troops deploying in the first wave. Karpov had known that plan was overly optimistic, since it was based on the total number of heavy lift aircraft in the Russian Air Force's inventory. In reality, less than half that number of planes were actually combat ready - the other half were victim to mechanical failure, incomplete maintenance or parts cannibalization.

Karpov had just ended a conference call with his superiors at Air Force Command in Moscow. They had blithely informed him that he would have to execute their original plan with still *less*; they were only able to provide him four Antonov AN-124 heavy transports, and twenty-seven Ilyushin IL-76 medium transports. Even if they made good on that much smaller number, which Karpov was beginning to doubt, it would leave him with the ability to deliver little more than three thousand troops in the first wave.

One fifth, Karpov thought. He was required to carry out the original war plan as written, with only one fifth of the troops allotted in that plan. High Command had tried to reassure him that additional troops would be landed from amphibious assault ships which were already enroute. Still more were to be transported in successive waves as the transport aircraft returned from their initial sorties, but Karpov knew that wasn't good enough.

Overwhelming force, he'd argued. They needed overwhelming force in the first wave, not a piecemeal buildup over the course of several hours or even days. Alaska was immense, and with no less than fifteen military, industrial and port facilities designated as critical targets, Karpov had been concerned that fifteen thousand troops were barely enough to accomplish Moscow's goals. But three thousand? It was a logistician's nightmare.

Karpov fumed all the way back to his office, a tiny room at the back of an ancient cargo terminal that felt more like a janitor's closet. He pulled up his operations order on his computer, going over it line by line and trying to determine which targets he could ignore until the second or third wave, and which ones he could bypass altogether. Karpov mentally eliminated every Alaskan Coast Guard station on his list, since those facilities were geared mostly for search and rescue rather than combat operations - they posed minimal threat. Their runways would need to be targeted by cruise missiles in order to deny their use to the Americans, but Karpov couldn't justify using any of his limited personnel to take those sites.

Fairbanks, a thousand miles east of Anadyr-Ulgony, had three major airports that the Russian forces would need to control right away. There were another three in Anchorage. The first priority would be to take Elmendorf and Eielson Air Force bases, as well as the Army installations at Forts Wainwright, Richardson and Greely. Those bases housed the majority of the American military personnel in the state, so neutralizing them would go a long way toward ending the campaign.

Each of those installations would be targeted by cruise missiles first, then assaulted by airborne troops immediately afterward to secure their airfields and whatever infrastructure survived. The amphibious ships would land more troops and heavy equipment that would support the airborne forces, but the landing ships had to cross nearly two thousand miles of ocean before they could bring their equipment to bear. Anything could happen during the week it would take to make the journey; for them to arrive in time to correspond with the airborne assault was, to Karpov, little more than a fantasy.

Karpov's other major consideration was capturing intact the Alaskan oil production facilities. Spread over eight hundred miles of mostly wilderness from Point Barrow in the north to Seward in the south, those facilities accounted for almost one quarter of all domestic American crude oil production. The Alaskan refineries were smaller and had a much lower production capability than their counterparts in the continental U.S., with the majority of their output being jet fuel rather than automotive gasoline or other products; but the Russian forces would desperately need that jet fuel, as well as the crude oil it came from, in order to press their conquest further into North America. Taking those resources would not only bolster the Russian position in Alaska, it would make it even more difficult for the Americans to fight back.

Three thousand men, he thought again, shaking his head. Even with the severely diminished strength of the American armed forces in Alaska, thanks to the massive drawdown under the late President Tolliver, Karpov was still almost certain that it couldn't be done.

And yet, he had no choice.

Lemhi County Sheriff's Office
Salmon, Idaho

"Sheriff Ferrara." Lemhi County Sheriff Sam Ferrara held the phone loosely to his ear as he tried to stir powdered creamer into his cold coffee.

"Sheriff, it's FBI Special Agent Marsden with the Salt Lake Field Office."

"Agent Marsden! I was beginning to think you'd forgotten about us. How're Dumb and Dumber holding up to questioning?" Ferrara was referring to the two Air Force Office of Special Investigation agents he'd arrested several days earlier in connection with the cover-up of President Galen Tolliver's assassination. Ferrara had turned the men over to Marsden and the FBI.

"That's what I'm calling about," Marsden said. *"When I first took those two off of your hands, I figured Coakley would be a hard sell, but Ford looked like he was close to spilling the whole story."*

"Were you right?"

"Not exactly. Ford clammed up, but Coakley? After sitting in a holding cell for twenty-four hours, we laid out how many years of hard time he was looking at. Told him he was headed for the supermax prison down in Colorado. Twenty-three hours a day of solitary confinement for the rest of his life. He started crying, you believe that?"

Ferrara chuckled. "Actually, yeah. I can picture it. When the loudmouths break, they usually break pretty hard."

"Well, he broke hard, all right. It was pretty embarrassing, actually. Guy blubbering and crying all over himself, begging us to cut him a deal."

"He give you anything worthwhile?"

"Quite a lot. You ever hear of a private security contractor called Hydra Security International - HSI?"

Ferrara let out a long breath. "Can't say as I have."

"Well, it turns out these two were working as independent contractors on the side for HSI. They were both recruited by that Air Force General you told me about."

"Pope."

"The very same. Apparently, Pope was using his position at the Pentagon to line his pockets as a headhunter for this HSI company. Trolling the military to find willing subcontractors."

"What - for assassinations?"

"Among other things. Apparently, HSI has operatives all around the country. Mostly ex-special forces types, guys with specialized military training. When they had a job that required a tactical team, they'd call those guys in."

"Let me guess. Pope handled logistics, transportation, that sort of thing."

"You got it. So our boys Ford and Coakley get a call from Pope shortly after Air Force One turns into a smoking hole in the mountains. He sends them out to the Trail's End Mercantile as a sort of clean-up crew. Tells 'em to collect one of the bodies, and make it disappear."

"They strong-armed the medical examiner up there. Threatened him."

"That lines up with what Coakley told us. They came in and collected the body of this supposed John Doe, then took it to a local funeral home that had access to an incinerator and an owner willing to look the other way."

"So now we know what happened to President Tolliver's body."

"We do."

"Pretty good chance that the three 'independent security consultants' that were executed at the crash scene were one of HSI's teams, then?"

"We think so," Marsden said. *"Seems like HSI covered its tracks pretty well as far as employee records, but we're making some headway. One of those guys in particular we were able to connect to HSI right away."*

"Which one?"

"The one with the bullet hole behind his right ear, Teodor Skizak. Went by the alias of 'Teddy Skeet.' Second generation Polish immigrant. Did two years in the Navy before getting kicked out for punching a training supervisor during SEAL selection, of all places. That was right before Tolliver drew down the military. Looks like our Mr. Skizak was an adrenaline junkie of sorts. Couple of arrests after he left the navy, for base jumping off of several prominent buildings without permission. Then he ended up working at HSI."

"How'd you find that out, if they were so careful about their records?"

"They were careful; Skizak wasn't. His apartment was full of news clippings showing different major events that he claimed to be involved in through HSI. He'd written on them with a magic marker a bunch of stuff about how he was a hero, saying 'my company, HSI' did this or that. Real ego trip, that guy must have been. We put together a lot of pieces just from what we found at his place.

"The other two victims at the Air Force One site were basically just what you said they were before we took over the investigation. Both special forces vets, pushed out of work by Tolliver's foreign policy. They both listed their occupations as 'independent security consultants', just like Skizak and Newill."

"So, what about HSI itself? You said Pope worked for them?"

"Indirectly. We've started digging into that as well. Found something pretty interesting, too. It looks like the company was formed by several investors, but they aren't specifically named on the company's filing documents. We had to dig through a bunch of shell parent companies to find out who was really behind HSI."

"You're killing me, Agent Marsden."

Marsden laughed. *"Sorry. It was Coleridge."*

Ferrara almost choked on his coffee. "The late Secretary of

Defense?"

"*Yes, sir. Turns out, Coleridge started HSI in response to the years of military downsizing. He figured there was still a demand for some of the personnel who got the axe, and he could hire them and get their old jobs done for much less than Uncle Sam. He did that, and was still able to make millions in the process, using his position in government to ensure that HSI got the most lucrative contracts, but he managed to stay out of the limelight in doing it.*"

Ferrara sighed. "And then when Tolliver gutted the military, Coleridge was already in position to pick up the slack."

"*That's right,*" Marsden said. "*They did all kinds of stuff, all for a premium. Hostage rescue, hits on cartel bosses, midnight snatch and grabs on violent criminals, you name it. They'd activate whatever operatives they needed, use military transport to get them to the job, then send them back to their normal lives after it was over. Their teams would just vanish back into society, and nobody would be the wiser.*"

"A lot easier to hide a paramilitary group if you hide 'em in plain sight, I guess."

"*That's a fact.*"

"So, do you think Reese had Coleridge killed? To cover up his involvement?"

"*That's certainly an angle we're exploring,*" Marsden said. "*If I had to bet, I'd lay good money on it.*"

"What a mess." Ferrara yawned. "Sorry. I had a long day yesterday."

"*You've had more than your share of those lately, I gather?*"

He laughed. "Yeah, more than I'd like."

"*The crash recovery team isn't giving you too much trouble, I hope?*"

"Oh, no. They pretty much stick to the airport and their hotel, when they're not flying back and forth to the crash site. No, we had a big structure fire in town last night, so I'm pretty much on no sleep right now."

"*Not terrorist related, was it?*"

"No. Drunk teenager related. Small town, kids get bored,

sooner or later something gets set on fire. This time it got out of hand."

"Anybody hurt?"

"Just the parents' pride. The building was abandoned, and the fire department was able to keep it from spreading. We're trying to track down the property owner now so we can notify them."

"Well, I'll let you go then. I just wanted to fill you in on what we found so far."

"Hang on - what about Pope?"

"Oh, yeah. I almost forgot. Looks like he's in the wind. He went AWOL a couple of days ago, right around the time that Coleridge turned up dangling from his own balcony rail. That's the first time I've ever heard of a general going AWOL, unless you count Benedict Arnold. Nobody's heard from Pope since, but we'll smoke him out eventually. We figure there's no way that Coleridge was running HSI by himself, and we have a lead on a guy we think could be at the helm now, but we just uncovered that today. We'll check into that, and I'll let you know as soon as we know something more conclusive."

"What about Lawson Holland? Did you find out anything about him?"

"A little more than you had, maybe. Retired SEAL, exemplary service record. Lots of stuff that we haven't been able to access yet, but we'll get a judge to open what we can. For all intents, it looks like he was just a guy caught up in events. I really doubt he had anything to do with the assassination."

"What about the footprints and shell casings at the crash site?"

"Can't tie those to Holland, or anybody else for that matter, if we don't have the actual boots and pistol that left them there."

"Hmm. That's what one of my deputies reminded me of. Any idea where Holland got to, then?"

"No. Honestly, we don't have the manpower to chase that lead, what with everything else going on. You can feel free to look into it, if you like."

"Ha. Manpower problems are my middle name lately. Tell you

what - Holland comes back here and breaks any traffic laws, I'll put him in a cell for ya."

"Fair enough. I'll find you a good lawyer between now and then, unless you can come up with some real evidence against him."

Ferrara laughed. "Thanks a lot. Pleasure doing business with you, Agent Marsden."

"You too, Sheriff. Take it easy up there."

"You do the same." Ferrara ended the call, shaking his head. He raised his voice, shouting toward the outer office. "Grant! Come in here!"

Deputy Grant Davidson came in, eyebrows raised in question. "What's up, Sheriff?"

"I don't want you to go getting a swelled head or anything, but it looks like the FBI agrees with you."

"Really? About what?"

"Lawson Holland. Specifically, whether or not he was involved in Tolliver's assassination."

"They have evidence that he wasn't there?"

"Well, no. Agent Marsden just said the same thing you told me the other day. That without the gun and the boots to prove it was Holland at the crash, it could have been anybody. So this is me saying you were right."

"Oh. Well, thanks, Sheriff." Davidson couldn't force the grin off of his face.

"What's so funny, Deputy?" Ferrara tried and failed to sound severe.

"I was just thinking that you could have saved your breath."

"How so?"

"I already knew I was right." Davidson turned to go. "But, it *was* nice to hear you say it."

"This episode will be reflected in your performance report, Deputy." Ferrara called after him.

"I'd settle for a pay raise," Davidson shouted back from the outer office.

Ferrara picked up his phone again and dialed, leaning back in his chair and plunking his feet on his desk. He noticed his abandoned coffee cup and took an exploratory sip as the phone was answered.

"*Nikki Nikkanen.*"

Ferrara succumbed to an involuntary coughing fit, his face screwed up in disgust. "Miss Nikkanen…" <cough> "Sheriff Ferrara here…" <cough> "Sorry - I got some nasty coffee down the wrong pipe."

"*Hello, Sheriff,*" Nikki said, letting him catch his breath again. "*Assuming your coffee drinking doesn't kill you before the end of this call, how are things in Idaho?*"

"Peachy," Ferrara said, sliding the cup out of reach. "I thought you might like to know that I talked to the FBI a few minutes ago. They didn't have much that I can pass along to you at the moment, but you remember I told you about that local guy that I thought might be working with the assassin?"

"*Yeah, what was his name again?*"

"Holland. Lawson Holland."

"*That's right. What about him?*"

"Well, it doesn't seem likely that he was working with the killer, and all we have tying him to the scene of the plane crash is circumstantial at this point. He's still interesting to me, mostly because I can't untie how he fits in to all this. If he had nothing to do with it, why did he just disappear, for example?"

"*Good question. What about the actual killer - Newill?*"

"No trace of him. We know from the video that he was the trigger man, but I still have no way of knowing if he was working alone or not. One interesting thing did come up about who Newill was working *for*, though. Have you ever heard of a private security company called Hydra Security International?"

"*I don't think so. Sounds sinister, though.*"

"It appears to be. Apparently, all the commando types, including Newill and the two OSI agents I busted are all tied to this HSI in one way or another. Also, and you *cannot* print this part, it looks like HSI was started by none other than the late

Defense Secretary, David Coleridge."

"Whoa."

"Yeah, 'whoa' is right. Let's just run through this. The Secretary of Defense runs his own private army on the side. Then the president's plane goes down, and three of SecDef's private goons end up dead at the crash site. The next day, Newill, who is probably another HSI employee, turns up out of nowhere and murders Tolliver in cold blood, and the whole thing is caught on camera. Then Coleridge ends up dead, too, under suspicious circumstances.

"Add to all that this Holland character, who lives in my town, and fits all the criteria to be another HSI employee. FBI and one of my own deputies seem to think he's not involved though, at least not beyond innocent bystander status."

"Something's still missing," Nikki said.

"Yeah. I can't for the life of me figure out why Holland would be at the scene if he *didn't* work for HSI, and if he did work for them, why wasn't he in the video of the killing, or dead at the crash site like the others?"

"Maybe you're not asking the right questions, Sheriff."

"How do you mean?"

"Well, let's say Holland was a subcontractor for HSI. You have boot prints and shell casings that point to him being at the crash site, but his body wasn't there. You also have three dead guys who almost certainly worked for HSI, who were at the scene also, but were found very dead as a result of several well-placed rounds from the mysterious .45 pistol."

"Which leads me to think that Holland was their killer."

"Probably, but not concrete."

"Yet."

Nikki laughed. *"You're not gonna let this go, are you?"*

"Nope. Holland did those three contractors, or I'm the pope."

"All right, Your Holiness. I'll humor you. You say Holland killed those three, without a doubt."

"That's what I think."

"And in your theory, Holland, as well as the three gunshot victims, all worked for HSI."

"I'm not as certain about him, but he fits the profile."

"But Sheriff, if he worked for HSI, and they worked for HSI, then why would he shoot them?"

"They had a fallout, maybe. That's part of what's bothering me."

"But if that was the case, Holland would have had no reason to walk Tolliver out of the woods, just so he could collude with Newill to kill him the next day."

"Occam's Razor," Ferrara murmured.

"Excuse me?"

"Oh, sorry. It's just something I was lecturing my deputy on the other day. Basically, it means the simplest explanation is usually the right one. I think you just turned my own argument against me. You're right, Holland walking Tolliver out makes no sense, if Holland was originally sent there to kill him."

"Maybe he was sent, but he changed his mind."

It was Ferrara's turn to laugh. "Now you're playing the other side of the argument?"

"No, not really. I admit, it's confusing. You know what bothers me about this?"

"What's that?" Ferrara reached for his coffee cup, then caught himself and yanked his hand back.

"Who dropped the surveillance video on the doorstep of the BBC?"

Ferrara thought for a moment. "Had to be Holland."

"That's what I was telling my boss the other day."

"Which lines up with the theory that Holland had nothing to do with the murder. So if he just happened to be in the area when the plane came down, killed the three hitters out of some sense of chivalry or whatever, then tried to rescue Tolliver by walking him out of the wilderness…"

"- and ran into Newill at the mercantile."

"Right. Newill pops Tolliver, and Holland escapes? But that doesn't follow, either. Holland took out three guys at the crash site; why would he run from Newill?"

"Do you know for certain that Newill was alone?"

"No. He was the only one caught on video, but I suppose there could have been other team members off camera."

"Maybe they got separated, and Newill got to him before Holland could get him back."

Ferrara thought about that. "Ok. What if Holland witnesses the shooting from a distance, or can't stop it for whatever reason, then retrieves the video footage before the place goes completely up in flames?"

"But he would have had to have been close by, judging by what I saw in that video. Newill torched the place after the video ended, remember?"

Ferrara sat up in his chair. "It ended, or it was cut off?"

"What?"

"How do we know we saw the entire video? You said he torched the place after the video ended, but why would the video have cut off *before* he started the fire? If Newill stopped the recording, then why wouldn't he have just destroyed it? If he didn't stop it, then it would have continued recording until the fire destroyed the cameras, and *we should have seen that in the clip.*

"Whoever got their hands on that tape at the BBC may have cut some of it, or it may have been already cut before it came to them. Wouldn't be the first time that somebody creatively edited video footage to elicit a desired response. I'll bet my house that there was more to that video than they released."

"I wonder…" Nikki's voice trailed off.

"What is it?"

"I'm going to try to answer that question, Sheriff. I need to make a couple of calls, but I'll get back to you as soon as I can."

"Good luck," Ferrara said, but Nikki had already ended the call. Ferrara leaned back in his chair for a moment, staring at his coffee cup. Then he got to his feet and grabbed his jacket, heading for the front door.

"Where to, Sheriff?" Deputy Davidson asked.

"To get some real coffee. I think I might have poisoned myself with that industrial solvent that passes for coffee around here."

"I'll take a tall Americano with a half inch of cream, since you're offering," Davidson said, grinning.

Ferrara stopped halfway out the door and looked back at him. "Ah, what the hell. You earned it." Then he turned and left. Davidson stared at the closing front door, surprised that the sheriff had agreed to his not-so-subtle suggestion.

"'I earned it'? What did I do?"

Xi'an Satellite Control Center
Weinan, Shaanxi Province, China

"Why was I not informed of this earlier?" Wei Ming looked again at the report his subordinate had just shown him. "This is *days* old!"

"Forgive me, sir," the man said, bowing his head. "With the recent focus on our three malfunctioning communications satellites, this information... escaped our notice. Until now, sir."

"You are a fool!" Wei hissed. "Your ignorance will likely get both of us shot!" He stood up and waved an arm at the terrified man. "Get out!"

The man backed hastily out of Wei's office, closing the door behind him. Wei sat down hard in his chair, staring at the pictures on his monitor. A shipyard, with several empty berths. Berths that had contained ships a week earlier. Ships that had been the focus of an unusual flurry of activity.

Ships that had now vanished.

Net News Daily Headquarters
Silver Spring, Maryland

"Charley, I need a favor." Nikki walked in to Charley Carter's office without knocking. She knew he didn't mind, and she was in a hurry to chase the thread she'd found while talking to Ferrara.

"Sure thing." Carter leaned back away from his keyboard. "What do you need?"

"I need an in with the BBC."

Carter frowned. "You're not looking to improve your lot in life already, are you? How long have you been here, a week?"

She shook her head, realizing how she must have come across. "No, no. That's not it at all. I want to find out who took in the Tolliver assassination video, and where they got it from."

Carter shook his head. "They won't give that up, Nikki. They'll want to protect their source."

"I know. But I was just on the phone with Sheriff Ferrara, and I got to thinking - who gave the video to the BBC, and was the video redacted at all?"

"Redacted? What for?"

"To hide whatever they didn't want people to see."

"Now you're sounding like me," Carter chuckled. "What 'they' are we talking about here?"

Nikki shook her head and sank into a chair next to Charley's desk. "I don't know, to be honest. But the Sheriff got me to thinking about the content of the video. If you remember, the feed ended right after Newill shot Tolliver, right?"

"Yeah…"

"But *why* would it end there? We don't see Newill move further into the building like you would expect if he was looking for the camera controls, and you don't see the place go up in flames, like you'd expect to see if the fire caused the recording to end. If the video had run until the fire destroyed the cameras, you would have seen it, but we only got up to the point where Newill shot Tolliver. Somebody redacted the last portion of that recording."

Carter's eyes widened slightly. "Ah, I must be getting old. How did I miss that?"

"You see what I mean? There's got to be more to it, between the shooting and the *actual* end of the tape."

Carter was nodding furiously, but already had his phone out and was scrolling through his contacts. "Hang on," he said, "I know a guy who might be able to help."

Lemhi County Sheriff's Office
Salmon, Idaho

Ferrara backed through the front door of the office, balancing the four-cup drink carrier and a box of doughnuts in his hands. Deputy Davidson looked up from his paperwork, his eyes widening with hunger. "Coffee *and* doughnuts?" Davidson asked, coming around his desk. "Is it Christmas already?"

"No," Ferrara said, plunking the drinks and pastries on Davidson's desk. "But it *is* half-past breakfast." He pulled a coffee from the carrier and was reaching for a doughnut when Davidson grabbed the box and slid it out of his reach. The deputy leaned over the doughnuts with a theatrical lick of his lips. Ferrara was reaching for the box again when the phone in his own office started ringing. He grimaced. "You just happened to be in the right place at the right time, Grant. Save me an apple fritter, or you're fired." He took his coffee and went to answer his phone.

"Ferrara." His tone was harsher than he intended, but he chalked it up to his constantly interrupted hunger.

"Nikki Nikkanen again, Sheriff. You sound like you need some breakfast."

Ferrara scoffed. "Don't remind me. I'm getting hangrier by the minute, and my deputy is drooling all over my apple fritter as we speak. You find the answer you were looking for?"

"I might have. I talked to my boss about the missing footage, and he called the head of the foreign desk at the BBC. An old friend. I guess when you've been around as long as Charley, you get to know a lot of

people."

"I hope this story has a point," Ferrara said, leaning over to look out his door at the abandoned fritter on Davidson's desk, wishing he hadn't left it there.

"Sorry. Yes, it does. So this foreign desk guy told Charley that he couldn't give out the name 0f their contact that gave them the tape, but he did make some cryptic allusions suggesting that the tape was routed through Brussels."

"Belgium? Don't tell me the Belgians planned this whole thing. That's a bit of a stretch."

"It would be, if that were the case. But it's not. Brussels isn't significant if you're thinking of who ordered the hit on Tolliver, but it is significant if you're thinking of organizations that might be able to do something with the knowledge of who did *order it."*

Ferrara closed his eyes. "You completely lost me, Nikki."

"NATO headquarters is in Brussels, Sheriff."

"So? Why should NATO care about…" he trailed off. "Oh…"

"Exactly," Nikki cut in. *"They'd care about it, because they're looking at the potential fallout on a geopolitical scale. They're concerned about their position vis-a-vis a completely weakened United States. And it would be considerably weakened, if it had suffered a coup orchestrated at the highest levels, and if the deposed president had already done everything possible to weaken the country at home and abroad before he got himself assassinated."*

"NATO's afraid that the U.S. is vulnerable."

"I think they are. I think they also know what's on the rest of that tape, and they're sitting on it for their own reasons. The BBC guy told my boss that they got the tape from a 'good Samaritan' who happened to be in the area at the time of the killing."

"Nonsense."

"Maybe not. It couldn't have been some random farmer just driving by, but it might be that they're referring to your guy, Holland."

"So how would they know whether he was a good actor, or a bad one?"

"I'm guessing that whatever was on the redacted portion of the tape

was compelling enough evidence for them." Nikki took a deep breath before continuing. *"Look, Sheriff. Holland's the only one who fits the profile for both ability and proximity. I'd bet he's front and center on that video, running into the building shortly after Newill left. I'd also bet that NATO edited the footage to protect him for some reason, and then fed the BBC the good samaritan line. But what I can't figure out, is why would NATO take such an active interest? I mean, I get it, if the U.S. goes belly up, it'll have a direct impact on world events, but we're not even a NATO member anymore. Tolliver put an end to that."*

"Yeah, but think about it," Ferrara said. "If you were NATO, and things were running full speed toward another world war, would you want America on your side, or would you want to face Russia on your own?"

"America isn't the military power it was three years ago, Sheriff."

"I know that, but if you were facing a bully, would you rather have a weakened, but experienced old bodyguard, or no bodyguard at all, and a big 'kick me' sign taped to your back?"

Nikki laughed. *"You have a funny way of putting things, Sheriff, but I see your point. It'd be better for NATO to try to coax America back into the organization, and from their perspective, there's probably no time like the present."*

"So, we agree that Holland probably brought the tape to NATO, and NATO released it to the press… but why?"

"Well, think about the confused narrative Reese was pushing right after the crash. First, Tolliver was killed in a tragic plane crash. Then, the crash was the work of terrorists. Then Tolliver was burned beyond recognition. But then, the real terrorist attacks happened, and the tape surfaces proving Tolliver didn't burn in the crash. Finally, Reese stops talking about the crash altogether. He had to have something to do with it, Sheriff. Now, if hard evidence proving that comes to light, his mandate to ascend to the presidency goes right out the window. He'd be an accessory to murder, at the least. It could bring down his presidency - and replace him with someone more likely to support NATO against Russia."

"Crazy," Ferrara said. "This has to be one of the most

unbelievable stories I've ever heard."

"Unbelievable, but not impossible. I just never thought this sort of thing could happen in America."

"Well, there are plenty of examples of countries that seemed secure, but ended up collapsing almost overnight. We're not immune to it here."

"You think we're really on the brink of collapse?"

Ferrara took a deep breath. "At the risk of sounding all fatalistic - yeah, I do. Up 'til now, politics in this country has just been a figurative bloodsport. This makes it literal, and that's not often a step you can reverse, once you take it. I'm old enough to remember when the United States was the undisputed super power in the world. But the problem with being number one is, everybody else is growing and progressing and learning from you, and they're all looking for a way to tip you off the top of the hill."

"Wow," Nikki sighed. *"Makes me want to move someplace where it's safer."*

"Yeah. Only I'm not sure that place exists any more."

Ministry of National Defense HQ
Beijing, China

"Gone?" Zhao Shen asked. "How could they be gone? More importantly, Admiral, *where* have they gone?" Zhao, who held the offices of General Secretary of the Chinese Communist Party as well as President of the People's Republic of China, was not known for asking questions lightly. Any query from him carried behind it the force of law - as well as the implicit threat of strict punishment if the answer was not to his immediate satisfaction.

Admiral Qin Hua fixed his eyes on a point on the far wall. "We have re-tasked a satellite to pass over the Sea of Japan and the Sea of Okhotsk, sir. After that, it will continue over the Aleutian Islands. It will take time to analyze the camera footage, but we *will* locate the Russian ships."

Zhao glared at the admiral. "You did not answer my question."

Qin stiffened. "Forgive me, sir. As to their location, I gave you the information I have at the moment. We simply do not know where they went, but we are looking. As to the first part of your question, it would appear that the Russians sortied under cover of darkness and cloud, some time in the past week; the weather conditions in that area have been terrible for visual surveillance. The ships had been laid up at Petropavlovsk for some months, with no indication that they were ready for sea. Our analysts at Xi'an were assisting with a developing software malfunction causing control problems with some of our satellites, and they failed to monitor the status of the Russian ships."

"They are to be shot." Zhao was unblinking and furious, but he kept his voice low. "Then you are to focus *all* of your attention on finding out what the Russians are about, before they surprise us with anything else!"

"Yes, *lingxiu*. I will see to it at once." Qin bowed and backed out of the room.

Zhao waited until the admiral left, then took a deep breath. He wanted to vent his rage, but knew that now was not the time. The disappearance of the Russian naval vessels from Petropavlovsk was potentially disastrous, but he could not allow it to distract him. By sending Gao Jianli to the United States and three low level diplomats to different cities in Russia, all of them infected with the new virus, he had completed a critical phase of his overall plan. The unnoticed departure of the Russian ships was a failure, to be sure, but he couldn't reasonably expect everything to go his way, could he? *No plan of battle survives first contact with the enemy,* he reminded himself.

The larger question was, *why* had the Russians sailed? Had they somehow found out about the virus, and set their own plans in motion as a response? He considered that for a moment, then dismissed the idea. It didn't matter - the virus was already loose in Russia, and every MERS vaccinated person they came in contact with would only help to spread the sickness. Even if the Russians knew about it somehow, they could no more stop the spread than they could stop the sun from rising.

This is a minor setback, he told himself. *Nothing more than a fly in the ointment.*

But still, it was galling to think that any part of his plan could begin to unravel before his forces had even fired a single shot.

CHAPTER FOUR

Vinctus

Rud, Afghanistan

Day 17

Daoud Farouq walked across the compound, eyes sweeping from the shot-up barracks building on his right to the destroyed wall next to the gate on his left, cursing to himself as he went. The remaining idiots who had survived the assault on the compound couldn't even seem to clean up the aftermath adequately. Everything had gone wrong since the Americans had attacked under cover of darkness and escaped with Khan and their hostage two nights earlier.

Faced with no other choice, Daoud had assumed command of the group in Khan's absence, but he knew he had little to offer the men beyond harsh discipline. Khan had always been the natural leader because Khan had brought in the money, and he had possessed a charismatic confidence in everything he did that would have been out of place had he not been in charge.

Daoud, on the other hand, had no access to the funds they

would need to find Khan and bring him back, or to carry on the struggle without him, if it came to that. He was also about as charismatic as a mad dog. He was best used in barking, not in holding the leash. Daoud didn't know what to do next, and that realization only made him angrier.

He changed direction and headed for the hole in the compound wall, intending to take out his wrath on the hapless fools milling around the spot, playing at effecting some kind of repairs. He drew a breath to shout, but was interrupted.

"Daoud! Daoud!"

The terrorist turned, fixing the speaker with his most wilting glare. The man didn't notice.

"Daoud! You must come! The infidels have killed Khan!"

Daoud's face fell. "What?!? When? How do you know this?" He grabbed the man by his collar and shook him.

"It was on Al Jazeera, Daoud. Just a moment ago - they threw him out of a plane into the sea!"

Daoud forgot all about upbraiding the work crew at the wall. "Show me." He held on to the man's collar and half-dragged him back to the barracks.

He needed to see this for himself.

British Army Garrison - Stirling Lines
Credenhill, Herefordshire, England

Lawson Holland opened the front door to find his best friend, Boone MacAulay, waiting on the step. "You're louder than a full toolbox falling down a concrete staircase, you know that?" Holland hissed, trying and failing to sound indignant.

Less than forty-eight hours earlier, Holland, Boone and six other men had been in an intense running gun battle in the remote village of Rud in eastern Afghanistan, where they'd successfully rescued Holland's son, Tony, from a group of terrorists. Tony had been a hostage for more than two years, passed from one group to another; beaten, neglected, tortured - and at one point early in his captivity, even forced into prize fights for his captors to gamble on. During the rescue, Holland had been shot in the right buttock and one of their friends, Cal Hodge, had been killed.

The rest of the team had escaped under fire with Tony, who was weak but healthy in spite of his long captivity. The team had also managed to capture Akhtar Khan, the charismatic leader of the terror cell that had held Tony. They'd stopped over in Cyprus where they handed Khan off to British authorities, and Lawson and Tony had received medical care for their injuries. Now, Law was walking with a limp. Tony was malnourished and weak, but otherwise healthy considering his ordeal. They'd only arrived safely back in England late the previous night.

Characteristically, Boone seemed unfazed by the whole affair. Except for the loss he felt at the death of his friend Cal, he was mostly back to his good natured, irreverent self. He pushed past Holland and into the room.

"Still sleeping, is he? I guess I'd stay in bed 'til the crack of ten if I could get away with it, but some people still have to make a living."

"Whatever." Holland couldn't help smiling. "He's been out since we rolled in here last night. I'd like him to get some more sleep, if he could manage it with all the racket from unwanted guests."

"There's gratitude for ya," Boone said. "He'll sleep like a baby while we're gone."

Holland closed the front door. "Oh yeah? And where is it you think we're going now?"

"Put some shoes on. General Reardon wants us to sit in on an interrogation with GQ at some prison in London. Helicopter's already warming up at the airfield." Their extraction team had assigned the moniker 'GQ' to Khan, owing to the man's appearance being more like a male model than a terrorist mastermind.

Holland shook his head. "Pass. We'll be fine right here."

"Speak for yourself, Dad."

Both men turned to see Tony standing in the entrance to the hallway, wearing a pair of gym shorts and looking haggard.

"Morning, sunshine," Boone quipped. "You're just in time to catch *Days of Our Lives* on the tube. Or whatever passes for a soap opera in this country. Your old man and I need to run an errand."

Tony shuffled into the tiny kitchen and poured himself a cup of coffee. "If I was deaf, I'd still be sleeping, Uncle Boone. But since I'm *not* deaf, I did hear you beating the door down, and I heard what you were saying to Dad, too." He blew steam off of his coffee and stared at them over the rim of the cup. "I'm going with you."

Boone glanced at Law. "You think he's up for it?"

Holland was about to answer when Tony beat him to it. "He doesn't get a vote, Boone. He didn't have to play trained monkey to those terrorists for two years, and neither did you. I did, so I'm going." The expression on his face didn't allow for much argument.

"Look, Younger," Boone said, raising a questioning eyebrow in Law's direction, "I'm OK with it, but Reardon didn't mention you coming along. He just asked for your dad. No offense, I'm sure."

Tony took a careful sip of his coffee. "None taken, 'cuz I'm going anyway. Gimme a minute to put a shirt on." He set his cup on the counter and disappeared back down the hall. As soon as he was gone, Boone aimed both raised eyebrows at Holland.

"Don't look at me," Holland said, pulling on his shoes. "He's right - he's a big boy. I don't necessarily get a vote anymore."

"Doesn't mean you don't have an opinion, though."

"Opinions are worthless if you force 'em on people. They usually just resent it, then they ignore your opinion anyway. Better to wait 'til he asks for advice."

"You say so. But he isn't the only one here who's been a POW.

You might just have a nugget or two of wisdom to offer on the subject."

"I don't know about that. I wasn't a prisoner near as long as he was."

"True, but would you have wanted to confront the people who took you, so soon after your release?"

"You forget, Boone. None of those people survived long enough to be confronted."

"Oh, yeah." Boone feigned shame at the decades-old memory. "Oops."

Holland grinned. "Even if you guys hadn't come in and blown everybody up, I think I would have wanted to face those scumbags sooner rather than later. Otherwise there wouldn't have been much resolution to the whole thing."

"Huh. Makes sense, I guess."

Tony emerged from the bedroom again, now fully dressed. "We going, or what?"

"We're going," Holland answered, handing Tony his coffee.

"Don't blame me if Reardon doesn't let you in the room, Younger," Boone said as they followed him outside. "You might be committing some horrible party foul by showing up uninvited. The Brits are picky about manners like that sometimes."

Holland chuckled. "Then we should definitely leave Boone behind."

"Don't care about manners," Tony said. He opened the back door of Boone's rental car and climbed in. "I just need to see how that sucker likes being the prisoner for a change."

HM Prison Belmarsh
Thamesmead, London, England

Boone called General Reardon during the helicopter ride to London, letting him know that Tony had tagged along. As the chopper touched down on a prison soccer field surrounded by twelve foot concrete walls, General Reardon emerged from a door in the nondescript block building at the north end of the field and walked over to meet them.

"Morning, lads." He looked at Tony, extending his hand. "You must be Tony. Max Reardon, Director Special Forces. Boone and your dad have told me a lot about you, lad. I've heard you acquitted yourself well under fire during the escape. Well done, and welcome back to the world."

Tony shook his hand, but couldn't help looking uncomfortable. "Thank you, sir. I appreciate all the support you gave in getting me out."

"Not at all. Leave no man behind, right? We're just pleased we had an opportunity to help."

Tony nodded and managed a slight smile. "So am I, sir."

"I take it you know why I asked Boone and your father here this morning?"

"Yes, sir. I want to be in the room when you interrogate Khan, General."

Reardon nodded, considering. "I thought that might be why you came. Let me ask you, lad: What do you hope to gain by being there?"

Tony's eyes flashed. "Khan took a lot of pleasure in making me squirm while he had me." He shrugged. "Shoe's on the other foot, now."

"Indeed. Correct me if I'm wrong, lad - but weren't you only in Khan's custody for less than two weeks, before your father and Boone's band of merry men came for you?"

"Yes, sir, I think that's about right. His boys took me from a group of ISIS terrorists. I'm not sure why. All I remember is an apple orchard, and then some explosions, and when I woke up I was with Khan's group. Later, I overheard them talking about wiping the other group out."

Reardon nodded. "Turf war."

"That's what it sounded like to me, sir."

44

"So if Khan's crowd wiped out the men who had held you for the lion's share of your captivity, why so much animus toward him?"

"He's no different than they were, sir. Might be he's worse. He told me straight out that I was nothing more than livestock to him. He said was gonna use me to get in good with the American government. He didn't say what he hoped to get in return, though. Bottom line is that he didn't rescue me. He *bought* me. Paid for me by killing a bunch of other terrorists, who'd made me a slave before that. Just because Khan only owned me for a few days, doesn't make him any better than the ones who had me for two years. He killed all of them and just took their place, is all. Sir, all I was to him was a pawn. I want him to know that I'm not, anymore."

Reardon turned to Holland. "You're all right with that?"

Holland looked at his son and grinned. "Tony already told me that I don't get a vote in the matter, sir. But even if he hadn't, I'd still be all right with it. I think it'll do him some good to see Khan as he is: just another powerless thug, once he's separated from his buddies and his cash."

"I couldn't agree more." Reardon looked back at Tony. "But understand something, young man. If you disrupt the process or attempt anything other than observation, I will not hesitate to clap you in irons and drag you out. Are we quite clear?"

Tony nodded, but he looked like a boxer waiting for the opening bell. "We're clear, General."

"Lovely. Let's get inside then." He looked at his watch. "They'll be bringing him out in a few minutes."

The interrogation room was a featureless cube, without even a table to break up the emptiness. The only piece of furniture was a backless stool, slightly taller than the average barstool. It had three legs, but no horizontal bracing, so anyone of average height or less sitting on it would be forced to have their legs dangle uncomfortably short of the floor without support. The room was cold enough that a person could easily see their own breath.

Tony watched from a video monitor in an adjacent room as they brought Khan in. Two soldiers wearing black balaclavas marched him through the door and roughly forced him to sit on the stool. They didn't bother to unshackle his hands from behind his back, and they left the thick black hood over his head. Unspeaking, they stepped back to the corners and waited.

Reardon glanced at Tony. "You are welcome to wait in here, if you think this is far enough. There's no shame in it."

Tony shook his head. "No, sir. I want him to see me. See that he didn't break me."

"As you wish, lad. You will remember what I mentioned about interfering, won't you?"

"I will, sir."

"All right, then. Would you two like to be masked, then?" Reardon offered balaclavas to Boone and Holland. Boone waved him off and Holland shook his head.

"No, sir," Holland said. "He's already seen my face. I don't think I'm much interested in hiding from the likes of him, anyway."

Reardon tossed the balaclavas on a table. "Just so. Shall we get to it?"

Khan was sitting quietly when they filed into the room. He tilted his head to one side, trying to position his ears in such a way as to discern what was happening beyond the bag over his face. The sounds were muffled, but he could at least tell there were multiple men in the room with him now. He wondered what that meant, and where it would lead. He worked his jaw, trying to wet his lips in spite of the gag stuffed in his mouth.

He tried to steel himself for whatever might be coming. Ever since the commando team that captured him had turned him over to the authorities, no one had spoken a word to him. He'd been gagged and blindfolded every time he'd been moved from place to place, so he had no idea where he was. His sense of time was completely destroyed. He knew all this was done to disorient him, make him feel uncertain and afraid, but he resolved to stay strong in spite of the growing sense of dread in his gut.

Holland and Boone took up positions against the wall facing Khan, while Tony moved over and leaned against the wall behind him, folding his arms. Tony could feel his face getting hot with anger; he wanted to step forward and beat Khan senseless, but he didn't want to let his father down. He'd made a promise to keep his cool, so he would keep that promise, even if it wasn't easy.

Reardon stepped in front of Khan, waiting as one of the guards reached beneath the bag on the prisoner's head and removed the gag, leaving the bag in place. "Good morning, Akhtar."

"Is it?" Khan replied, doing his best to sound bored as he flexed his sore jaw. "I wouldn't know. And who are you, might I ask?"

"You might," Reardon said. "But I wouldn't hold out hope of getting an answer."

"British, obviously," Khan said, ignoring Reardon's answer. "That tells me a great deal."

"Oh? And what would that be?"

"I was illegally kidnapped and taken from my homeland against my will by a team of special forces soldiers, mostly Americans but one of whom had a strong British accent - Birmingham, if I'm not mistaken. Not like you. I detect a hint of Suffolk in your voice. Ipswich, I think. So I have at least two Englishmen now, involved in an illegal military operation which was undertaken in concert with mostly American soldiers. That tells me that Britain and America are colluding again. Meddling in the sovereign affairs of other nations, as they so often do."

"You assume a great deal, based only upon hearing a few voices."

"I am an observant man," Khan said.

"Yet for all your powers of observation, you have still failed to address the reason you're here."

"Not at all. I told you - I was kidnapped, and illegally brought here against my will."

"What a tragic story."

Khan nodded. "Tragic, and true."

Reardon started to pace slowly back and forth. "Hardly. You were captured during the rescue of an American Marine; a man you were holding hostage while attempting to use him as a bargaining chip with his government."

Khan cocked his head to one side, following Reardon's pacing by the sound of his voice. "I know nothing of any of this. I know nothing of this American Marine you speak of. I am a simple farmer…"

"My, Akhtar, but you are a terrible liar. You expect me to believe that a simple Afghan farmer would naturally possess a perfect Oxford accent, would be able to identify the hometown of a total stranger - a foreigner no less - by the sound of his voice, and would be as well versed in international politics and military tactics as you seem to be?"

"We Afghans are a resourceful people. As I said before, I know nothing of what you claim against me. I don't know why you have brought me here; I don't know any American Marines. Now, I demand to speak with a lawyer."

In response, Reardon moved behind Khan and yanked the bag off of his head.

Khan blinked rapidly, trying to acclimate his eyes to the intense light in the room. As they slowly came into focus he found himself looking directly into the eyes of Lawson Holland.

"Hello, Akhtar. Remember me?"

Khan involuntarily leaned back, trying to put some distance between himself and Holland. This was the same big American who had terrified him on the plane ride out of Afghanistan; Khan had been stripped naked, wrapped in a flag with a serpent on it, and dropped out the back of the plane to what he thought was his certain death, only to be yanked back inside by a cable that they'd fastened to a belt around his chest.

In his terror right before they had dropped him, Khan had involuntarily emptied his bladder all over himself. This big American had facetiously claimed then to be his lawyer, but he had given Khan no illusions about his chances of ever seeing the inside of a court of law. Now, here he was again, leaning relaxed against the wall as if this was something he did every day.

Reardon put a hand on Khan's back to prevent him falling off of the stool. "I assume you two know each other?"

"This... this person tried to kill me!" Khan leaned backward again, and again Reardon pushed him back upright. "He tortured me! I demand his arrest and prosecution under international law!"

Holland scoffed. "Now, Akhtar, that's no way to talk to your lawyer. Remember what I told you on the plane. We own you now. There'll be no trial for you - you've already been found guilty. All that's left is the small matter of your sentence."

"I have committed no crime!" Khan protested. "You have arrested the wrong man! I told you, I'm just a farmer. I..." His voice trailed off as the young American he knew as Tony Holland slowly moved into view from behind him. Khan looked up at the young man, who glared down at him as he walked past and took up a position next to the big American. Khan looked at them both, then took a sharp breath. Despite the obvious differences in their skin color, there was an unmistakable resemblance between the two. The older man spoke.

"I believe you've already met my son. Haven't you?"

Khan was getting a bad feeling. "You cannot keep me here."

"We can do whatever we want."

Another soldier wearing a balaclava walked in, carrying a laptop computer. He held it up so Khan could see the screen. It was showing a video capture from an Al Jazeera news program playing footage taken from inside the cargo bay of a large aircraft. The chyron across the bottom of the screen read in English:

FREEDOM FIGHTER AKHTAR KHAN MARTYRED BY UNKNOWN STATE AGENCY - AMERICANS SUSPECTED; NO COMMENT FROM US GOVERNMENT.

Khan was shamed to see himself on screen, wrapped in the hideous yellow flag with the snake on it. The video, censored to obscure his nakedness, still caught the humiliating moment when Khan's bladder had given out. Even though he knew what was coming next, he still felt the tension almost as acutely as he had when it had actually been happening. His heart was in his throat.

On screen, the aircraft deck tilted precipitously. Khan watched in horror as his on-screen self screamed, fell and shot out the back of the aircraft, his body dropping out of sight below the end of the extended cargo ramp.

Khan was breathing rapidly now, but he caught his breath at what came next. He had expected to see on the screen what had *actually* happened; him being hauled back over the ramp and into the relative safety of the aircraft. But in the video, the angle of the aircraft changed slightly, and then Khan looked on in shock as his body inexplicably came back into view, flailing in the wind and cartwheeling away toward a massive body of water far below, shrinking rapidly into nothing more than a speck. When it was no longer visible, the video ended.

The man holding the laptop closed it and stepped back. "You're dead, pretty boy."

Khan's stomach sank even further. "That... that did not happen." His ribs were still sore from the belt that had arrested his fall after he'd dropped out the back of the plane. The video had been very realistic - so much so that he found it hard not to believe, even though the fact that he was sitting here was enough to disprove it.

The Americans must have doctored the video. Somehow they had hidden the safety cable that had prevented him from falling to his death, and then added CGI footage of a body falling after the real camera had been switched off and he had been dragged back inside the plane. He had to admit it was an impressive fake. "No one will believe that," he said, but he wasn't really convinced of it.

"They already believe it, Akhtar." The big American said. "We sent that footage to Al Jazeera, and they were only too happy to broadcast it worldwide. They're calling you a martyr. You should thank us."

Khan had already started shivering due to the cold in the room, but now his shaking became more intense. What did these people want? If they wanted him dead, why had they not allowed him to simply fall from the aircraft? Why this deception?

The British man that Khan had pegged as being from Ipswich stepped in front of him again. "There will be no extradition for you, Akhtar. No prisoner exchange. No release. No one will come looking for you, because you're now nothing more than an unpleasant memory."

"This will do you no good." Khan tried reverting to bluster. "There are many more like me. I have many friends in powerful places. They will come for me, and you will be punished for this."

The Englishman shook his head. "Your friends won't be coming. Not now, not ever. Did you think the Americans wouldn't apprehend at least some members of your suicide squads? That they wouldn't take at least some of them alive?"

"That makes no difference."

"Actually it makes a world of difference. They didn't catch just a few, Akhtar. They captured *dozens* of the buggers within hours of the attacks. The Canadians and Mexicans caught several more after they fled the States, as did we. Do you imagine that all of those individuals will be able to hold out under interrogation?"

"They are true believers. They will not break."

"They already *have* broken, Akhtar. And I'm not talking about one or two. I'm talking about *most* of them. Your ring is falling apart already."

"You think you've won, by capturing me?" Khan snapped. "This is only the beginning. We will not stop until the decadent West bends the knee to the true path." He took a breath, then smiled. "There are too many of us. You cannot fight us with armies. We'll vanish when you come, and reappear where you're most vulnerable. You'll exhaust your resources chasing shadows, and when you least expect it, we'll be there to cut your infidel throats."

The Englishman returned the smile. "You go on and believe that, lad. You can talk all you like about jihad and cutting throats, but that's all outside this room. Soon enough, you'll understand that for you, there is *nothing* outside this room. There's just you, and us, and your pain."

Khan scoffed. "Why? Why go to such lengths for one man? Why pretend to kill me - why not actually do it? You're bluffing!"

"Well, now, that's the beauty of it. Even though many of your men have already cracked, there are still those who haven't yet. Seeing your failed attempt at unpowered human flight may help break their will to resist. Besides, this way we don't have to deal with the unpleasant delay of waiting for a court to decide your fate.

"And finally, you also have information that we want - information on your organization that only you are privy to. You are going to give us that information, Akhtar. All of it. If you lie, we'll know it. We won't kill you for that, but you will certainly wish we had. We're going to keep you alive, and you are going to suffer. I promise you that much, lad. I don't bluff."

"I don't believe you."

"You will." This came from the young Marine, whom Khan

had intended to use as capital to leverage against the Americans. *That may have been a mistake*, Khan thought now. He looked on, as the Marine turned his palm toward Khan to reveal a tattoo on his forearm. It read *Semper Fidelis*. "You know what that means?"

Khan scoffed. "Of course."

"I doubt it," the young man said. "You may know the words, but I really doubt you understand the meaning. You think we don't have the stomach to do the sort of things you do? You just wait. You have no honor. You don't even know what honor is. You torment the helpless, and prey on the innocent, but when someone stronger comes along, you crawl back into your hole and hide. We're always gonna fight your kind, because we're 'always faithful.' Faithful to our families and our country, and to our way of life. You're only ever faithful to yourself. You hide behind your religion and use it as a lever to get power. You're a weak, selfish little excuse for a man."

Khan glared at him. "You don't frighten me."

"I don't really care. That's not my job. I'm only here to tell you that you messed with the wrong people." He nodded toward the guards behind Khan. "I'll leave it to them to frighten you. Judging by how fast you wet yourself on the plane the other day, I'd say they're gonna have short work."

Khan flushed at the reminder of how his fear had so easily undone him. His eyes involuntarily flicked away from Tony's.

"We know you planned the terror attacks in America, Akhtar," the Englishman said. "You're going to tell us how you contacted your people and how you passed the orders to carry out those attacks. Then you will identify every remaining splinter cell you have in the west."

Khan shook his head. "I will not."

The Englishman smiled. "The amount of pain you endure is entirely up to you, Akhtar. You give us accurate information, you will suffer less pain. It really is that simple."

"I have rights…" Khan's body convulsed as one of the men behind him jabbed him in the spine with an electric stun baton.

He twisted to get away, only succeeding in falling off of the stool and cracking his head on the floor. He landed hard on his right side, the impact dislocating his shoulder. He screamed in pain through gritted teeth.

"Gentlemen," the Englishman said, "it seems Mr. Khan has opted for more pain rather than less. Perhaps we should leave him to his handlers now?"

"I have money," Khan gasped. "I can make you all rich - AAGHHH!" He let out a guttural scream as the man with the baton shocked him again.

The Englishman dropped down on his haunches next to Khan's head. "To be precise, lad, you *had* money. We have it now, all of it, and to be honest, it wasn't all that much. We've seized all your assets because, well - you're dead, remember? You won't be needing money now, will you?"

Khan whimpered, still writhing in pain. The Americans moved toward the door, but Tony paused next to where Khan lay and looked down at him.

"I spent the last two years thinking I was dead. Thinking everyone I knew and loved had forgotten about me and moved on. Nothing to look forward to but pain and fear. Two years, living like that." He leaned down. "Your turn. Rest in peace, coward."

Khan's reply was lost in screams as the man with the baton hit him again.

Reardon escorted them back out to the soccer field and the waiting helicopter. "You lads get some rest," he called over the noise of the engines. "We still have a great deal to discuss."

Tony turned around. "Swear to me he never sees the light of day."

Reardon wore a grim smile. "Believe me lad, his days of playing petty warlord are over. We'll drag every shred of information out of him, and then he *will* disappear. That's why we doctored the video footage. As far as the world is concerned, he's already dead. Nobody's going to expend much energy trying to free a dead man. He'll be forgotten by whatever allies he has, and then he'll die once we're truly finished with him."

"And somebody else will take his place."

Reardon nodded. "More than likely, yes. But we can only kill the snakes we can see. His cronies will think twice about coming into the light when they see what happened to him."

"But they'll still come." Tony looked bleak. He'd held up well, facing Khan, but now doubt was creeping in again.

Holland put a hand on his son's shoulder. "That's why people like us exist, son. We're protectors. It's what we do. There're always gonna be people like him, but there're also always gonna be people like *us*. We fight the good fight because it's *good*, not because it's easy or a guaranteed win."

"There's two kinds of dangerous men, Younger," Boone added. "The first kind is like GQ in there, who'll hurt and kill anybody for pleasure, money or ideology. Second kind's like us. We can be every bit as brutal, but only when we're dealing with the first kind. You get it?"

Tony nodded slightly. "Yeah. I guess so." He didn't sound convinced. He shook Reardon's hand, then turned and climbed aboard the helicopter. Reardon stopped Holland as he moved to follow. "May I ask what your plans are now, lad?"

"To be honest, I hadn't thought that far ahead yet, General."

Reardon nodded, glancing at the chopper. "Give me a day or two, would you? I need to coordinate with the chaps inside who'll be wringing Khan dry, but when that's sorted I'd like to help you and your son, if you'll allow me."

"I appreciate that, sir. I think we could use a few days before we head home anyway. It'll give us a chance to get rested up."

Boone chuckled. "Not sure restin' on your laurels is such a good idea in your case, Law. Especially since the bad guys shot a hole in your laurel the other night." With that, he smacked Holland on the backside and climbed aboard the helicopter, grinning like a lunatic.

Holland winced and took a deep breath, shaking his head. Medics in Cyprus had removed the bullet from his butt, finding that it hadn't done any serious damage. Even so, the recently stitched up wound was still very sore.

Reardon was shaking his head. "He's a good lad, Boone is. Just don't turn your back on him. He's like a teenage boy, most days."

Holland allowed himself a rueful smile as he shook Reardon's hand. "Yeah. You'd think I'd have learned that by now, wouldn't you, sir?"

CHAPTER FIVE

Arcticum Venti

Anadyr-Ulgony Airbase
Chukotka Autonomous Okrug, Eastern Russia

Senior Sergeant Eduard Voronin watched the faces of his men in the cargo bay of the Antonov AN-124 heavy transport as it lumbered toward the runway end. Theirs was the second aircraft in line for departure in a group of two AN-124s and ten smaller Ilyushin IL-76 aircraft. A second, similar assault group would be departing simultaneously from the new airbase at Provideniya, followed closely by fighter escorts from bases at Mys Shmidta and Pevek.

Voronin was a veteran of the Russian annexation of the Crimea in 2014, and he had little doubt of his own abilities or those of his men, but deep inside he knew that Alaska was *not* the Crimea. Several years earlier, he had fought alongside American soldiers in Syria, when Russia and the United States briefly found themselves both supporting Kurdish YPG rebels. Within months of that operation, he had found himself on the other side, fighting against the Americans in a four-hour pitched battle that was mostly brought on by poor communication and mistaken identities, resulting in massive Russian losses. That incident had taught Voronin that the Americans could be formidable enemies.

But less than a year later, they had inexplicably pulled all their forces from overseas locations, and the Russians had moved quickly to fill the void. It started with small territorial grabs in Georgia, followed by border incursions into the Baltic states of Lithuania, Latvia and Estonia. The subsequent American departure from NATO had all but ensured that there would be no tangible response to these moves; the best the Western European nations could do at the time was strongly worded protests on the floor of the United Nations, which fell on deaf ears.

Following those early gains, Russia had focused on building up its forces in the Far East in anticipation of larger objectives. Alaska, with its massive size and vast natural resources, would give Russia an economic and strategic foothold in North America.

An isolationist America only invited conquest, and Voronin tacitly accepted that reality as part of the natural order of things. He believed that if Russia did not take this chance, other nations would, and soon. But that didn't mean it would be easy. He had been around long enough to know that the propaganda fed to him and his men by their superiors was mostly wishful thinking. The Americans would not go down without a fight, in spite of the demobilization of their military. Many Americans civilians would fight; in groups or on their own if need be. The reality was they were invading a country with a heavily armed populace, a condition that would lend itself to partisan attacks and guerrilla warfare.

As Voronin scanned his mens' faces, he wondered how they would respond in the face of that type of enemy. He also wondered how many of them would live to tell about it.

* * *

The Russian air armada climbed out, making a gradual turn to the northwest to gain altitude. Each transport aircraft was flanked by two Sukhoi SU-57 fifth-generation stealth fighters, flying in close formation, just off each of the transport's wingtips. All the aircraft had their transponders turned off, preventing them from transmitting any identifying data to air traffic control facilities. As each three-aircraft element approached its enroute altitude, it drew alongside a single civilian airliner, flying under a standard international flight plan filed for a destination in Alaska.

As the flights of three drew close, the airliners switched off their transponders and began a rapid, spiraling descent to land at the closest Russian air base. At the same time, the cargo planes switched on their transponders, which were meticulous clones of the equipment aboard the civilian airliners they had just replaced. To air traffic controllers, the change would be unnoticeable, and the flight of three would look exactly like a single civilian aircraft, until it was too late to do anything about it.

Using the SU-57s as escorts was a bonus, since their stealthy characteristics gave them a radar cross section equivalent to a small flock of sparrows. With their transponders off, they simply would not show up on civilian or military surveillance radars. They would stay with the transports until they reached their objectives, then hold overhead to provide air cover while the assault forces landed.

Following parallel routes to the transports were ten Tupolev TU-160 Blackjack long-range bombers, each carrying twelve KH-101 air launched cruise missiles with conventional payloads. The bombers were spread out across a thousand mile front, flying at barely a hundred feet above the waves to avoid radar detection. With an effective range up to three thousand miles, the KH-101s were targeted to hit military installations and civilian infrastructure targets all along the west coast of North America, from as far south as the Oregon/California border all the way to

Point Barrow, on Alaska's northern coast.

The bombers would launch their supersonic missiles from well behind the transports, allowing the missiles to overtake the slower aircraft and strike their targets roughly at the same time as the airborne troops made their combat jumps. While the Americans were still reeling from the massive explosions of 120 cruise missiles hitting a wide variety of targets, airborne Russian special forces troopers would be dropping out of the sky to complete their own mission objectives.

But unknown to Colonel Karpov, who had drawn up the original assault plan, leaders at High Command had decided not to hit the major American military bases in Alaska with the missiles. Elmendorf and Eielson Air Force Bases, and Army Forts Wainwright and Richardson were taken off the target lists for the cruise missiles. High Command had decided that those bases were best taken intact by airborne troops, while the more remote installations and targets along the American West Coast would be destroyed by the KH-101s.

Had he known, Karpov would not have approved of the change.

Vasiliy Trushin
Ivan Gren-**Class Landing Ship**
Cook Inlet
Eight Miles Southwest of Anchorage, Alaska

Captain Ivan Sukhotin stood on the bridge, worrying. The tide was just past slack, meaning it would be almost another three hours before high tide. Sukhotin didn't need high tide to get in to the Port of Anchorage, but it would allow him more maneuverability. More water under the keel was never a bad thing, either.

The *Vasiliy Trushin* was a highly modified *Ivan Gren*-class landing ship. The superstructure had been re-worked to disguise it as an ocean-going salvage vessel. Three large cranes had been added forward of the bridge, making Sukhotin's beautiful ship look like a perch for several giant steel insects. The cranes also ruined his forward visibility, but it couldn't be helped. The combination of ungainly cranes, a filthy paint job, strategically faked rust stains all over the hull and the false name *MV Ascension* stenciled across the stern was necessary to maintain the charade, at least for another few hours.

What worried Sukhotin wasn't the tide, or what the engineers had done to the appearance of his ship. He was more concerned with the amount of traffic blocking the approach to the port. There were several ships maneuvering for positions along the mile long concrete quay. Sukhotin was concerned that they would still be in his way when his time came. In about three hours, timed for just after high tide, Russian Airborne troops would parachute onto Elmendorf Air Force Base, little more than a mile east of the port. His landing needed to be timed to match theirs, so the heavy equipment and extra troops on board the *Trushin* could assist the paratroopers in taking the American base in a surprise pincer movement.

There were four other *Ivan Gren*-class ships coming up the Cook Inlet behind Sukhotin, all disguised as factory or salvage ships, a mile or more apart. The second ship would land fifteen minutes after the *Vasiliy Trushin*, with the others following at fifteen minute intervals.

They didn't need the concrete quay, though; the *Ivan Gren*-class ships all had unusually high, overhanging prows, beneath which were sets of massive clamshell bow doors. A captain could drive his ship right up onto a beach, open the bow doors, and disgorge his cargo of armored personnel carriers, trucks, tanks and soldiers in much less time than it would take to unload quayside with standard cargo cranes.

Captain Sukhotin wanted these container ships in the channel ahead out of his way so he could better maneuver to beach the *Trushin* at the bulk yard just north of the main quay. That low-lying section of the port was used for loading and unloading barges, and temporarily storing large bulk items such as industrial piping, gravel, and logs. The water side of the yard was protected by a low seawall, but that was pierced in three places by inclined gravel ramps that allowed the barges to be pushed partly up on shore for loading and unloading. The middle of those three openings was Sukhotin's destination, but he had his doubts that the seven large container ships blocking him - three at the main quay and four more anchored in mid-channel - would be out of his way in time. He poured himself another cup of coffee and glared down at his watch, willing the ships to hurry up and move.

METEOR 55
Russian Air Force AN-125 Transport
Twenty Miles East of Anadyr

Colonel Pavel Karpov sat in the navigator's seat in the cockpit of the AN-125, listening to the radio traffic on the invasion force's scrambled frequency. So far, everything was progressing as planned, in spite of the nearly crippling aircraft shortages they were dealing with. Because of the lack of transports, this first wave would drop its cargo, then reverse course back to Russia to pick up more troops. The second trip would necessarily be conducted without the element of surprise, but Karpov tried not to worry about that. The first wave was mostly made up of Spetznaz commandos and battle-hardened veterans of the conflicts in Syria and the Crimea. It would have to be enough.

"How long to the drop zone, Captain?" Karpov asked the pilot. Captain Yevgeny Markov suppressed a sigh, knowing that Karpov knew exactly how long they had to go, since he had planned this phase of the mission to the last detail. He was nervous, Markov thought, but he answered the question anyway.

"Two and a half hours, sir."

"Very good." Petrov nodded. "Any mechanical issues? Any aircraft drop out?"

"Negative, Colonel. Everything is functioning as it should be." He turned slightly in his seat, risking the wrath of his superior officer by offering advice. "If I may, Colonel - your plan is not perfect." Karpov's eyes flashed, but Markov forged ahead. "No plan is perfect. But if you were to ask my opinion, sir, this plan is as *close* to perfect as one could hope for under the circumstances. It will work, sir. You have done everything you can to ensure that. Now, please - trust the rest of us to do our parts."

Karpov gave the pilot a fierce glare for a few moments, but he knew the man was right. He leaned back in his seat and passed a hand over his eyes. "You're right, of course. Carry on, Captain."

Vasiliy Trushin
Three Hours Later

Sukhotin was very late. The traffic jam of container ships blocking the channel ahead of him hadn't eased, and it was putting him well behind schedule. He was holding position in the channel under minimum power to counter the now-receding tide combined with the flow of the Knik River, but he hadn't dared move any closer to his assigned landing spot. They were scheduled to have landed ten minutes earlier. Major Yuri Cheremisin, commander of the Special Operations troops aboard the *Vasiliy Trushin*, could barely contain his frustration.

"Captain, we *must* maneuver around them!" Cheremisin said through clenched teeth, waving an arm out the windscreen. "Our airborne troops will be overhead by now!"

Sukhotin glared at the ships ahead. A major portion of his country's assault plan was unravelling, because his ship was unexpectedly stuck in traffic. He had finally had enough. "Thirty degrees left rudder!" he barked. "All ahead two-thirds!" The big ship shuddered to life and the bow slowly came around to the left with help from the current, but coming from a near stop as they were, the *Vasiliy Trushin* was sluggish and slow to respond to the helm.

The channel at this point was almost two miles wide. The container ships ahead of them were anchored in a line abreast with roughly fifteen hundred feet between each ship. There was a wider channel to the left of the westernmost container ship. If Sukhotin powered around to the left of the ships, he would have plenty of room to make a hard right turn back to his landing spot on the eastern shore. He knew the channel was shallower on the west side, but with the tide still this close to high, it was a risk he was willing to take. Just in case, he planned to pass as closely as possible to the left hand ship, which he could now see was named *MV TransAtlantic*.

But as often happens, even the best laid plans don't survive first contact with the enemy. As the *Trushin* gathered speed and started to draw closer to the group of ships, the bow of the vessel on the far left of the group suddenly started slewing around further to the left and directly into their path, slowly picking up speed as the river and the falling tide took hold.

"All back full! Left full rudder!" Sukhotin shouted, seeing the danger. Cheremisin swore. The *Trushin* responded painfully slowly, but for a moment, it looked as if they would be able to reverse their movement in time to avoid smashing into the other ship. Then the *Trushin* shuddered violently as its keel dragged in the mud of the river bottom, and the bridge crew was thrown to the floor.

They had run aground.

MV TransAtlantic

"We're dragging the bow anchor!" Captain Teddy Garcia jumped from his chair. "Port bow thrusters to full, give me a hundred percent on the main engines!" At three hundred thirty feet long, the *TransAtlantic* was small by container ship standards, but as it drifted at the mercy of the current, it seemed to the bridge crew as though the whole world was moving under their feet. Garcia snatched up the radio handset, keyed to the local Vessel Traffic System frequency.

"All vessels vicinity of Anchorage, *MV TransAtlantic* is dragging anchor a half mile south of the quay, drifting with the tide to the southwest. Attempting to arrest with bow thrusters until main engines come online. All vessels maintain safe distance and steerageway."

Vasiliy Trushin

Sukhotin grabbed his own handset, shouting in English. "*TransAtlantic*, this is *MV Ascension*. We're aground off your port quarter! Power up and turn hard astarboard!" Sukhotin watched in horror as the container vessel continued to swing toward them. He switched to the intercom and shouted into it in Russian. "All hands, brace for impact, starboard side!"

MV TransAtlantic

Garcia ignored the urgent radio call from the *MV Ascension*, instead rushing to the left bridge wing to look out. He saw the ungainly looking salvage vessel that had followed them up the inlet, now dangerously close and listing to the port side, the falling tide rushing around its hull from bow to stern and pushing the ship broadside into at least a twenty degree list. He guessed the ship was larger than his by at least sixty feet, and long experience told him there was not enough room for the *TransAtlantic* to complete its turn downriver without crashing into the *Ascension's* stern, which was jutting out into the channel.

Still, he had to try.

"All back full, belay port bow thrusters, starboard bow thrusters to a hundred percent, brace for impact!"

Vasiliy Trushin

Sukhotin watched as the huge container ship drifted inexorably toward them. He saw the roiling water at its bow calm slightly as the ship's port bow thrusters shut down, and he guessed the captain had switched to the starboard thrusters in an attempt to speed his ship's bow through the turn. He probably would have done the same, but Sukhotin knew it wouldn't be enough. They were doomed.

The forward third of the *TransAtlantic* slammed into the *Vasiliy Trushin* amidships with enough force to heel the grounded ship over another twenty degrees. Now the *Trushin* was in very real danger of capsizing, if the collision hadn't been bad enough. Alarms were blaring on the bridge, men shouting and grasping for handholds as the deck tilted crazily under their feet. Several men who had been out on deck had fallen overboard on the port side, and were now floundering in the freezing water.

Sukhotin dragged himself up in time to see both of the hundred foot tall deck cranes mounted on the port side of the *TransAtlantic* snap off and collapse across the *Trushin's* deck. At least thirty cargo containers broke loose and followed the cranes overboard, smashing into the side of the *Trushin's* bridge superstructure before continuing across the deck like giant tenpins, crushing everything in their path. The *Trushin's* false cranes had toppled in the collision as well, tangling with the remaining containers and cranes aboard the *TransAtlantic* and locking the two huge ships together. Smoke was curling upward between the two hulls in multiple places.

"Engine room, damage report!" Sukhotin called over the intercom. Flooding alarms were lighting up the master control panel, showing the main cargo compartment had been breached, as well as two compartments forward of it. If they couldn't get the flooding under control, and quickly, the *Vasiliy Trushin* was going to be a permanent part of the river bed.

The chief engineer came on the intercom. There was a high-pitched shrieking noise in the background, forcing him to shout. "Captain, the turbocharger is seriously damaged! It sounds like the bearings are gone - recommend shutting the engine down!"

Major Cheremisin was slowly pulling himself off the floor, his face covered in blood from a gash on his forehead. "We cannot shut the engine down, Captain!" he slurred. "We must land, now!"

Sukhotin looked at him. Cheremisin was staggering, clearly disoriented and struggling just to stay on his feet. Outside, ragged clouds of smoke boiled up between the two tangled ships. Sukhotin simply shook his head, then keyed the intercom. "All stop, Pasha. Leave us enough power in the engine to run the pumps." He switched to the ship-wide channel. "All hands, fire control stations! Fire on the lower decks amidships!"

CG6002
U.S. Coast Guard HH-60 Helicopter
Providence Alaska Medical Center
Anchorage, Alaska

Lieutenant Joy Rollinson and her crew had just brought in a heart attack victim from a fishing boat thirty miles southwest of Anchorage. Hospital staff had barely wheeled the victim off the helipad when Rollinson heard the radio call from the ships near the port, less than five miles away. "Strap in!" Rollinson shouted at her crew over the aircraft intercom. "Two ships collided, at least one is aground!" She increased the power as her crew checked in ready to go, then lifted off.

The copilot, Lieutenant Dan Kennedy, was already on the

radio. "Merrill Tower, Coast Guard Six Zero Zero Two, just off Providence, northwest bound responding to a distress call in the Cook Inlet near the port of Anchorage. Request to cross over the approach end of runway Three Four en route."

"Coast Guard Six Zero Zero Two, Merrill Tower, roger. Proceed across runway Three Four at the approach end, traffic is a Cessna departure roll on Three Four straight out."

Kennedy quickly scanned the municipal airport ahead of them. "Coast Guard Six Zero Zero Two, traffic in sight, we'll pass behind him, and we'll report leaving your airspace."

"Coast Guard Zero Zero Two, roger."

Kennedy pointed at the Cessna traffic. "He's going straight out, pass behind him."

"In sight," Rollinson replied, adding power and lowering the nose of the big chopper as she accelerated. "I got smoke."

Kennedy followed her eyes out beyond the city to where the Knik River emptied into the Cook Inlet. In the dim early morning light, he could just make out two large ships side by side slightly south of the main pier. The downstream vessel was pressed hard over into a serious list by the weight of the other vessel against it. "That's gonna leave a mark," Kennedy said. He reported out of Merrill Field's airspace and contacted the tower at Elmendorf Air Force Base, which was only two and a half miles north of Merrill. He coordinated with Elmendorf to operate off the departure end of their runway Two Four, then switched frequencies to raise the tangled ships. Rollinson swung the helicopter out to the south of the wreck, and they saw the name on the container ship first.

"*MV TransAtlantic*, this is Coast Guard Helicopter Six Zero Zero Two, coming up off your stern. Can you give us a status report?"

"Coast Guard Zero Zero Two, this is TransAtlantic. *We have some topside structural damage and several minor injuries, but nothing requiring medical attention. We have power to all three engines, and some minor flooding below decks. We're tied up pretty good to this*

other ship; we didn't want to try to forcing a separation, in case we do more damage."

"Roger, *TransAtlantic*, we'll get back to you shortly. *MV Ascension*, Coast Guard Six Zero Zero Two."

A slightly accented voice replied. *"Go ahead, Coast Guard Zero Zero Two."*

The rescue swimmer in the back of the chopper interrupted. "I got a man overboard, nine o'clock, hundred yards downstream!"

Kennedy told the captain of the *Ascension* to stand by as Rollinson banked the chopper hard to the left, diving for the surface of the inlet. Now they could all see him, a single man in dark clothing, struggling in the water and being swept rapidly away from the ships.

"Swimmer's ready!" rescue swimmer Chris Taylor called out. He had swim fins on his feet and a snorkel mask on his face, and was looking eagerly toward the figure in the water. Rollinson pitched the Jayhawk's nose up at the last moment, bringing the big chopper to a smooth hover ten feet above the water. The rotors churned the water into a white froth all around the man, and Taylor jumped.

He hit the water twenty feet from the man, and was swimming powerfully toward him before he regained the surface. On reaching him, Taylor could see that he was almost out of gas. He swam up behind the man and wrapped an arm around his chest, kicking with his oversize flippers to drive both of them higher out of the water. Suddenly, the man spun halfway and almost knocked Taylor's mask off with an elbow.

Taylor backpedalled slightly, letting go his grip. "Calm down!" he shouted over the noise of the hovering helicopter. "I'm here to help you!" With that, he kicked closer to the man again, but the man instantly started flailing his arms, trying to punch at Taylor while shouting something unintelligible.

Taylor knew that time was critical. Despite his sudden burst of aggressive energy, the man was already showing signs of hypothermia. It was not uncommon for people lost at sea to panic when a swimmer tried to help them, but Taylor didn't have time to waste trying to convince this guy that he was trying to help. He kicked twice, propelling his body about a foot higher in the water and driving close to the man, who was still flailing. From his new height advantage, Taylor came down on the man's temple with a wicked right hook that knocked him almost senseless. Then he got behind him and re-wrapped his arm under the man's left armpit and across his chest, before waving at the helicopter to lower the rescue basket.

As Taylor stuffed the nearly unconscious man into the basket, he noticed his clothing. He was wearing camouflage from head to toe, and what looked like a ballistic vest on his torso. He also had a pistol in a holster on his left hip. Taylor took that and waved it at the winch operator above him as the basket ascended toward the chopper.

Darnell Hulse flashed a thumbs up at Taylor from the open side door of the chopper as he raised the rescue basket. Whoever this guy in the basket was, he'd been carrying a pistol. Normal enough in Alaska, but they couldn't risk a near delirious man waving a pistol around inside their helicopter, and they also had to prepare for the possibility that he had more than one weapon. Forewarned by Taylor waving the commandeered weapon, Hulse would take no chances. He pulled the basket inboard, quickly securing the passenger with straps across his chest and arms. Then he disconnected the basket from the cable and sent the hook back down to Taylor.

Hulse waited until Taylor had clipped the cable to his safety harness, then hoisted him quickly back into the chopper. As Taylor clambered back aboard, Hulse took a closer look at the man they'd rescued. He was semi-conscious, but all the fight seemed to have gone out of him. He was wearing a Kevlar vest and camouflage tactical clothing with no insignia visible. Hulse searched him quickly, finding a combat knife in a sheath at the man's ankle. He stowed that and covered the man with a Mylar blanket to hold in his body heat.

"What's a soldier doing on that piece of junk?" Hulse asked.

Taylor was pulling off his mask. "I dunno. Anybody else in the water?"

"Nope." The helicopter was moving in a slow arc downstream of the tangled ships, searching for other people overboard. "Hey Lieutenant," Hulse called. "This guy is some kinda armed military. Should we know anything about that?"

"That's news to me," Rollinson answered. "Is he stable?"

"Yeah, he's good for the moment. He's trying to say something, but it sounds like nonsense to me."

"Okay, let me know if his condition worsens. We're gonna drop in for a closer look at that ship before we head back to the hospital." She spun the helicopter ninety degrees right and powered toward the stern of the *MV Ascension*.

Vasiliy Trushin

"Helicopter inbound!" the first mate called from the starboard bridge wing. "They picked one of our troops out of the water!"

Captain Sukhotin was on the radio, warning the following landing ships about the blocked channel. Those ships still had the option to land further south, but that would put their forces on the south side of Ship Creek, which would block a direct approach to Elmendorf and the U.S. Army's neighboring Fort Richardson. Landing north of the pier allowed them a straight approach to both, without having to work their way through crowded city streets and across bridges.

The remaining captains had decided to risk sailing through the narrow spaces between the anchored container ships in order to hit their primary landing zone. Everyone in the assault force knew by now that speed was the most important consideration.

Sukhotin put the handset down and glanced out the window at the orange and white American helicopter, now in a slow orbit on the far side of the *MV TransAtlantic*. The chopper pilot was calling him, asking if his firefighting equipment was operational and if he was carrying any hazardous materials. Sukhotin reached for the handset to respond, then noticed a soldier scrambling up the steeply canted foredeck below him. The man made it to the railing, and lifted something to his shoulder.

CG6002

"GUN GUN GUN!!" Taylor yelled. Rollinson reacted immediately, dropping the Jayhawk's nose and diving behind the right side of the *MV TransAtlantic,* putting that ship between them and the shooter on the deck of the *MV Ascension*. The man had fired both shots from his DP-64 Nepryadva double-barreled 45 mm grenade launcher in rapid succession, missing both times as the chopper dropped below his line of sight.

The grenades sailed over the chopper and dropped into the water beyond, detonating underwater several seconds after they hit. Unfortunately for the shooter, the DP-64 was intended to protect ships against enemy combat swimmers, and so fired a grenade that was detonated not on impact, but like a depth charge - by water pressure. If he'd hit the Coast Guard chopper anywhere but directly in the rotors, he'd have caused nothing more serious than a small dent.

That didn't matter at all to Kennedy. He was instantly on the radio, reporting the attack on maritime and aviation emergency frequencies, warning others away. Taylor was furious. "That sucker just shot a couple of grenades at us! We pull his guy out of the water, and he tries to shoot us down? What the hell?!?"

"Hulse!" Rollinson shouted. "Get on that Two-Forty!"

Hulse stepped over the man in the rescue basket and unpinned the M240 machine gun from its bracket, allowing it to swing outboard on its swivel mount. The fact that Coast Guard rescue choppers go out armed is less testimony to their war preparedness than it is to simple reality; plenty of people on boats in international waters who are engaged in illegal activities will not hesitate to fire on a Coast Guard chopper if it starts sniffing around too closely. So the rescuers are sometimes forced to show their teeth.

Rollinson turned the chopper around, bringing the starboard door to face the starboard side of the *TransAtlantic*. Then she side-slipped the aircraft away from the two ships, bringing their altitude up at the same time. They could see the shooter, struggling to reload his launcher while clinging desperately to the side railing of his ship.

Kennedy keyed up the chopper's loudspeakers, his amplified voice booming over the water. "DROP YOUR WEAPON! YOU ARE UNDER ARREST!"

The shooter kept fiddling with the weapon, fumbling one grenade and dropping it, where it rolled down the deck and lodged under a wrecked shipping container.

"Convince him, Darnell!" Rollinson ordered.

Hulse responded by opening up with the M240, lacing a long burst of 7.62 mm rounds within five feet of the man, who ducked and dropped a second grenade to the deck. The fire below decks on the *Ascension* was growing, filling the air between the two hulls with black smoke that roiled and swirled in the wind from the Jayhawk's rotor. The shooter vanished momentarily behind a veil of smoke, only to reappear a half second later when it cleared, this time pointing a pistol at them.

"Bad idea," Hulse muttered, as he cut loose another long burst. This time, the bullets impacted the hull directly below the shooter and stitched rapidly upward, catching him with five rounds from pelvis to collar bone. The man toppled backward down the sloped deck, slid between the wires on the port side railing, and disappeared overboard.

That should have ended the confrontation, but suddenly a hatch on the superstructure of the ship opened, and more men poured out amid a cloud of black smoke, all of them armed.

Most of them were ignoring the helicopter, just looking around in confusion, but Hulse could see several who looked to be in charge, waving their arms and pushing men into positions on the rail. One of the men raised a light machine gun to his shoulder, and Hulse fired again.

"Back off, back off!" he shouted into his headset, but Rollinson had already yanked the aircraft into a hard left turn and was racing away from the ships while Kennedy reported to their base on Kodiak Island, 250 miles to the southwest, asking for further instructions.

"We're gonna need a bigger gun, guys." Rollinson said, deadpan.

Taylor was checking the vital signs on their 'victim', and he raised his head after the now-smiling man said something to him. "You got that right, Lieutenant. I think this guy just insulted me. In *Russian*."

CHAPTER SIX

Frigida Re Vera

METEOR 55
Ten Miles West of Anchorage

The red light lit the cargo bay in an eerie glow, giving the paratroopers' faces a menacing cast beneath their helmets and balaclavas. They were all on their feet, each quickly checking the kit of the man in front of him, making sure that nothing was out of place at the last minute. Colonel Karpov was closest to the door, eager to lead his men into this historic battle. To lead the force that would expand the Russian Empire's territories into North America was a greater honor than he could have ever hoped for. He was thrilled.

The aft cargo ramp was already lowered. Karpov knew that in keeping with their disguise, the aircraft would be on approach to land at Ted Stevens International Airport, seven miles southwest of their drop zone at Elmendorf Air Force Base. Captain Markov had requested a straight in approach to runway Seven Right, and Karpov knew that once they descended to five thousand feet and were established on final, the pilot would only need to level off and make a slight left hand turn to take them over their target instead.

Karpov felt the deck shift beneath his feet as the big aircraft started its turn. He smiled, knowing the controllers at Ted Stevens would be scrambling to figure out what was happening. Urgent phone calls would be made, other traffic would be vectored away, all in the belief that something had gone wrong with a civilian airliner's normal approach. Karpov knew the reality of it, though. Everything was going exactly as it was intended.

The green light suddenly flicked on, and now Karpov was running down the ramp, his men close on his heels. Off the end of the ramp, a blast of icy wind, and they were falling, their parachutes snapping open seconds after they were clear of the aircraft. Karpov steadied himself under his canopy and looked around. He could see that Markov had done an outstanding job. They were floating directly toward their objective, the transient ramp in front of the control tower at Elmendorf. In the glow of street lamps below, Karpov could see several people in the parking lot south of the tower pointing up, caught off guard by the sudden appearance of paratroopers in the sky. Their inaction wouldn't last long.

But something was wrong. Karpov knew that there should have been multiple explosions across the base and at Fort Richardson several miles to the east, but he saw nothing. *Surely, all of the missiles couldn't have failed to detonate?* he thought. But Karpov knew better. He knew the great temptation for high ranking officers to change military plans in mid-stream, often times for no reason other than to put their own fingerprints on it and thus be able to claim any future accolades for themselves. The only problem was that this type of meddling in an operation of this size usually did more damage than good.

Karpov swore as he slid his AK-104 rifle on its sling to a better position across his chest, where it would be ready to fire as soon as he touched down. From what he could see, the surprise they had hoped for appeared to be complete, but that advantage would vanish within seconds of his feet hitting the concrete. Perhaps earlier. Without the destruction he'd counted on from the cruise missiles, his airborne forces would be forced to carry more of the battle themselves, and more of them would pay for that decision with their lives.

People on the ground were running now, and further off to his right Karpov saw the flashing emergency lights of an approaching military police vehicle. The Americans were already responding, and they were as yet unhurt.

Karpov pulled on the control toggles to arrest his descent, allowing him to touch down with less force than if he had just stepped off a city bus. He quickly collapsed his canopy, marshaled the next several men as they landed behind him, and took off at a run for the control tower. They had work to do - and thanks to some armchair generals who were safe at home in Russia, it would be much more work than he'd anticipated.

METEOR 56
Five Miles West of Anchorage

"Cathay Pacific Thirty-two Ninety-eight Heavy, you're well left of course. Turn twenty degrees right and verify you still have the airport in sight." Captain Sasha Orlov couldn't help smiling. The tower controller at Anchorage International sounded rattled, with good reason. What he must have thought was a regularly scheduled Cathay Pacific Airlines 747 coming from Japan was actually the second of four Russian AN-124s, at the vanguard of an airborne invasion. Moments earlier the controller had watched helplessly as the first Antonov had veered off course and headed directly toward Elmendorf. Other controllers were scrambling to sort that out, and now it was happening again. Orlov found the American's confusion funny.

"Standby," he told his copilot. Orlov could see the lights of his lead plane already over the air force base several miles away. The early morning light was too dim yet to make out the paratroopers in the air, but he knew they must be falling already. He checked his instruments as they drew closer to the jump zone, making sure everything was correct before he flicked the switch to notify the men in back that it was time. *"Do svidaniya!"* he said, his smile spreading wider.

Senior Sergeant Eduard Voronin bolted for the end of the ramp as soon as the green light came on. He was full of a familiar adrenaline, the same feeling he'd had so many times before when going into battle. But this time, it was something different. This time, he was finally going to face off against his country's old nemesis in something other than a case of mistaken identity. Voronin looked at it with a mix of eager anticipation and dread.

Would the Americans be ready for them?

His parachute jerked him upright in the air, and he looked ahead and below him. Already, he could see muzzle flashes and small explosions on the ground. Something was wrong. The Americans were already fighting back against the first assault element, which meant his element would be landing under fire. That was not completely unexpected, but he had also expected to see major destruction already inflicted by a wave of cruise missile attacks. There were no collapsed buildings, no smoking craters left by massive warheads.

The cruise missiles had either missed their targets, or they had not been fired at all.

Something snapped past his head, and Voronin realized with irritation that he was being fired on. He looked around below, trying to pinpoint the shooter, but the situation on the ground was extremely chaotic. His landing zone was north of the control tower, on the far side of an east-west runway. His objective was a command and control building near a large concrete cargo ramp, which once taken would serve as the Russians' command post at the base.

He was floating toward one of several C-17 cargo planes parked on the ramp south of that building, and he could see maintenance and security vehicles racing around between the parked aircraft in apparent confusion. He saw a muzzle flash from near the tail of the plane he was approaching, so he raised his AK-104 and fired a burst in response. A figure slumped to the ground, and then Voronin was past the fuselage and touching down on the other side.

He quickly cut loose his parachute and looked around for other threats, but there seemed to be no enemies close by. Gathering his men into assault teams, he directed them to their objectives. The Russians spread across the ramp quickly and efficiently, only slowing to respond to what sporadic resistance the base security forces could manage. So far, American resistance was light and mostly ineffective.

Perhaps the cruise missiles were unnecessary after all.

Elmendorf Air Force Base

Staff Sergeant Clay Kirkpatrick looked out the windshield of his police cruiser and did a double take. "What the…"

His partner, Senior Airman Lucy Hume, followed his eyes. "Are those… paratroopers?"

"Yeah," Kirkpatrick said. "I didn't know the Army was still doing practice jumps. Even if they are, they're way off course. They're west of the dang drop zone by a couple of miles."

"Guess they're a little out of practice." Hume craned her neck to see better. "Looks like they're coming down right on the flight line, Sergeant."

"Perfect. This is gonna be a long day." He shifted the car into gear and hit the overhead emergency lights as he headed toward the runway.

Hume got on the radio and reported what they'd seen. The dispatcher asked her to repeat it twice before he believed what she was telling him. "That guy never listens to me on the radio. Next time I see him I think I oughta whack him over the head with the handset, see if that improves his hearing."

Kirkpatrick chuckled, but his mood instantly soured as they rounded a corner and saw muzzle flashes coming from the cargo ramp in front of the control tower. Several muffled explosions followed. "That doesn't look like an exercise to me!"

Hume was back on the radio as Kirkpatrick mashed the accelerator. "Dispatch, Car Two-Three, shots fired, southwest flight line at the base of the control tower! Request immediate armed response, Two-Three is on scene!"

The car slid to a stop and both officers grabbed their rifles and were out and running around the west side of a generator building next to one of the large hangars before the dispatcher could respond. Kirkpatrick pulled up in a crouch just short of the corner of the building and peered around. He could see dozens of soldiers on the wide concrete ramp between his position and the runway, cutting themselves free of their parachutes and moving toward the hangars and control tower. He plucked his radio handset from the clip at his shoulder. "Dispatch, Two-Three has multiple armed paratroopers on the ground south of runway Six, moving in force toward Base Ops and the control tower! Can you verify if they're ours?"

"Negative, Two-Three. We have no ongoing friendly exercises anywhere in the state. Multiple casualty reports are coming in - this is no drill!"

"Roger, dispatch. Two-Three is engaging." Kirkpatrick waved Hume forward. "Alright, Lucy, here we go. You set up here. I'm moving to that truck." He pointed at a parked vehicle fifty yards to their left. "I'll shoot first. Any of those guys start keying on me, you hit 'em. We'll set up a crossfire. Okay?"

"Okay, Sarge." Hume took a knee and braced the forestock of her rifle against the corner of the building. Kirkpatrick slapped her shoulder and took off running for the truck.

The ramp was brightly illuminated by spotlights on tall poles set along the south edge of the pavement, but the area where the two Security Police officers were setting up was still mostly in shadow. Kirkpatrick stayed low as he moved, making it to the truck safely. Coming around the west side of it, he spotted a single paratrooper less than thirty yards away, running east.

"SECURITY FORCES! GET ON THE GROUND!"

The soldier spun immediately and brought his rifle around. Kirkpatrick dropped to a knee and fired three rounds, smashing the man's right kneecap with the first and slapping into the chest plate of his body armor with the other two. The man screamed and fell. Bullets smashed the windows of the truck next to Kirkpatrick and he ducked back, unable to see if the man he'd shot was out of the fight.

He heard several shots from Hume's direction, then her voice over the radio. *"You're clear for now, Sergeant."* She was all business.

Kirkpatrick poked his head out again and saw that the man he'd shot was no longer moving. Forty yards to his right was another soldier sprawled on the concrete, also motionless. *Kid's a great shot*, he thought. He scanned the area once more. "Cover me, Hume. I'm moving." He sprinted from cover and slid to a stop next to the man he'd shot. He was dead, one of Hume's bullets having caught him directly under his chin. *Jeez, she dropped both of these guys in less time than it took me to wound one of them*, he thought. *She's good to have around in a pinch.*

He quickly went through the man's gear. Top-end battle dress and body armor that could have come from anywhere, but the helmet gave it away. It was flared wider around the rim than helmets in use most everywhere in the west; this one just *looked* characteristically Russian. Add to that the man's AK-104 rifle and Glock 17 pistol, and it became more than just an outside chance that he was a Russian paratrooper. The Russians had been grabbing up little bits of territory around their own borders for the past two years, but invading *Alaska?* Suddenly, Kirkpatrick felt like he was living in a bad dream.

90th Fighter Squadron Alert Hangar
Elmendorf Air Force Base

The klaxon blared throughout the alert facility, followed by a disembodied voice coming over the loudspeakers in the hallway leading from the ready room to the hangar. *"Enemy aircraft overhead, numbers unknown. Airborne troops on the ground inside base perimeter. Use caution for multiple civilian aircraft in the vicinity of Anchorage. Weapons free."*

Captain Ray 'Sweep' Broome shot a questioning look at his wingman, Captain Gregg 'Bus' Driver, as the two men ran across the hangar floor to their aircraft. Driver looked just as confused and surprised as Broome felt. *Enemy aircraft overhead? Troops on the ground?*

As the men climbed into the cockpits of their Lockheed F-22 Raptor fighters, the hangar doors finished opening. The engines on their jets were already turning. Both of the two alert jets' systems were constantly kept warm by auxiliary warm air fans and electrical carts, so they could be started and launched within two minutes of receiving an intruder alert. Broome kept thinking this must be a mistake, as the Russians had been uncharacteristically quiet over the previous couple of months. The alert birds hadn't had to do an actual air defense intercept in at least six weeks, and now this?

Broome allowed the crew chief to strap him into his seat, gave him a thumbs-up, and keyed his radio. *"Sweep* flight, check."

Driver answered him immediately, even as both pilots released their brakes and started taxiing toward the runway. *"Sweep Two."*

Broome keyed the mic again. "Tower, *Sweep One*, flight of two Raptors, taxiing from the north alert hangar on an active intercept."

"Sweep One, Elmendorf Tower, use caution for parachute activity

overhead and multiple heavy cargo aircraft in the pattern to runway six, NOT on my frequency. Two AN-124s have landed so far, but neither rolled as far as the runway one-six intersection. Use caution for multiple unauthorized personnel on the movement area. Departure from runway one-six at your own risk. Change to departure - go get 'em, guys."

"*Sweep One* flight's rolling, thanks tower. *Sweep Two*, push button six." Both pilots pushed the radio selector for the Alaska Region Air Operations Center, the air defense controllers responsible for directing them to any airborne threats in the airspace over Alaska. Then they both pushed their throttles to the stops and raced south down the runway and into the morning sky.

MV TransAtlantic
   Cook Inlet

Captain Garcia couldn't wait any longer. The growing fire on the *MV Ascension* was bad enough; now its people were firing on the Coast Guard and massing on the *Ascension's* starboard rail, looking like they might try to jump across to his ship. His crew of thirteen was in no way equipped to repel boarders, so he had only one choice.

"Engine room, all back full! Hundred percent on the port thruster, right full rudder!" He could feel the pulsing of the three big diesel engines below decks as the *TransAtlantic* scraped and shuddered against the other ship. Men on the rail of the *Ascension* were shouting and waving, trying to avoid losing their footing as Garcia backed his ship off. "Deck crew, weigh the stern anchor! If it's not aweigh by the time we swing around, cut it loose!"

There was a deafening screech, and the forward cargo crane wrenched free of the deck. The *TransAtlantic's* bow started to come around as the current worked against the stern, pivoting her away from the other ship. Several men on the *Ascension* fired bursts from their rifles, breaking glass in the bridge windows, but Garcia and his bridge crew were uninjured.

"What the hell's going on, Skipper?" the first mate asked, his voice panicked.

"No idea." Garcia watched the receding shape of the *Ascension* as the *TransAtlantic* floated away with the current. "Nothing good, though." He checked his chart plotter as he waited for the bow to come all the way around to the south. "Let's get this thing down to Homer and make sure we didn't break anything serious below decks. Coast Guard can handle a shipload of terrorists without us. Rudder amidships, all ahead full!"

Vasiliy Trushin

As the *TransAtlantic* pulled away, the *Vasiliy Trushin* shuddered, then slid slowly backwards into the current as if it were trying to follow the other ship. The *Trushin* was free of the mudbank, but now had almost no engine power. The fire below decks was out of control, and the list to the port side had not improved much when they came off the shoal.

Captain Sukhotin needed to give the order, but still he hesitated. Abandoning his ship at this point would mean the certain deaths of almost everyone on board. Part of their disguise did not include carrying enough lifeboats to accommodate all the troops on board; they only had two small boats with room for thirty people total. And now, as he tried to maneuver the ship under minimum power, he found that the helm would not answer. He picked up his radio.

"*Vladimir Andreyev, Vasiliy Trushin*."

"*This is the* Andreyev."

"The *Trushin* is off the shoal now, but I have no steering, and only idle power. We are taking on water and our fire fighting equipment is not keeping up with the fire. Request you either come alongside and take our people off, or take us under tow and continue with the mission."

There was a long pause before a new voice answered. "*Unable, Trushin. We cannot risk the loss of another ship. Suggest you beach your vessel and evacuate as best you can.* Andreyev *out.*"

Sukhotin was stunned. "Did you not hear? *Andreyev!* We have no steering, and not enough engine power to overcome the current! We are adrift! *Andreyev!*"

There was no reply, only the soft hiss of static. Sukhotin grabbed his binoculars and scanned the water to his south, quickly spotting the *Trushin's* sister ship almost a mile off, despite the weak half light of early dawn. The *Vladimir Andreyev* was northbound at full speed, her bow roiling the water into a froth on a course that would pass wide to the east of the stricken *Vasiliy Trushin*.

Sukhotin swore.

Sweep One
Climbing Through 10,000 Feet
Two Miles South of Elmendorf

"Kodiak Control, *Sweep One* is with you, climbing through one-zero thousand, request vectors to target." Broome had already activated his aircraft's powerful search radar, but his screen was lit up with a confusing multitude of civilian transponders. He swiveled his head from side to side, trying to pick out individual aircraft in the pre-dawn light.

"*Sweep One flight, Kodiak Control, we have no confirmed targets for you. Multiple reports of airborne troop landings at Elmendorf, as well as multiple air carrier flights scheduled to land at Ted Stevens that appear to have diverted to Elmendorf, can you confirm that?*"

"*Sweep One*, affirmative, those are *not* air carriers, Kodiak - the first two at least were Russian AN-124 cargo aircraft dropping paratroopers. Do we have permission to engage any aircraft diverting to Elmendorf?"

There was a long pause before the weapons controller came back on frequency. *"Ah, negative, Sweep One. Climb to one-five thousand and hold over Elmendorf, observe and report all aircraft landing at Elmendorf."*

"You gotta be kidding me," Broome said on the plane-to-plane intercom.

Fort Richardson
Four Miles East of Elmendorf
Anchorage, Alaska

"No, sir, it's not a drill!" Sergeant First Class Larry Nugent had to force himself not to shout. The Second Lieutenant blocking the gate to the vehicle park technically outranked him, but Nugent knew the man was barely out of college and had almost no experience. Nugent was a lifer, coming up on twenty-nine years in uniform. Early in his long career, he'd learned that Second Lieutenants were a nuisance to everybody, officer and enlisted alike. The lowest of the officer ranks, they still outranked every enlisted man in the Army, even though their youth and lack of experience often led them to make foolish decisions.

Like right now.

"Sir," Nugent tried again. "Elmendorf is under attack. We don't know if the enemy is coming here next, but it's a safe bet. These vehicles are not safe if they're concentrated here, and besides, we need them if we're gonna respond to the threat. Now open the gate. Sir."

The lieutenant hesitated, looking back and forth at the troops with Nugent. "Sergeant, you are off duty. You know I cannot allow off duty personnel access to combat vehicles." He set his jaw and tried to sound determined. "I will not open this gate without proper written authorization."

Nugent sighed, then raised his M4 carbine and aimed it

through the chain link at the lieutenant's forehead. "Lieutenant, I do *not* have time to go over to the Command Post and sign in, just so you can adhere to the letter of your orders. So you will open this gate, or I *will* open your skull, and we'll climb the fence anyway. Your call."

The young officer's eyes widened dramatically, but a natural aversion to a violent separation from his frontal lobe won out. He hurried to open the gate.

Sweep One

"Missile launch!" Driver shouted, though Broome couldn't have possibly missed the piercing tone in his headset. They'd barely been in the air for two minutes, and somebody was already shooting at them.

"Tac split, pop chaff and flares!" The two Raptors broke away from each other in opposite directions, both releasing flares and chaff to throw off the incoming missile. Broome kept his aircraft in a tight turn until he'd reversed course completely. There it was; at the head of a rapidly growing smoke trail and a sun-bright rocket plume was a narrow missile, about three feet long. Broome's heart was racing, even though he could already see that the missile had been fooled by either their chaff or their flares; it was driving straight at the point where the flight had split up seconds earlier.

He followed the smoke trail with his eyes, looking for the launch aircraft, but Driver saved him the trouble. "Two bandits, your eleven and two o'clock, going low!" Broome looked where Driver had said, and finally spotted the Russian fighters. They had a look about them that was common to many Russian designs; an odd combination of menacing beauty mixed with a certain awkwardness, depending on which angle you saw it from. The twin engined SU-57s (NATO code name *Felon*) had a broad, blended wing design and twin vertical stabilizers that looked almost ridiculously undersized for the aircraft. Both design features increased the SU-57's stealth characteristics as well as its maneuverability, making it a dangerous enemy under any circumstances. The good news was that Broome and Driver's F-22s were still more than a match for them.

"*One's* got the west bandit, *Two,* take the east." Broome said.

"*Two, Wilco.*"

Broome pushed the throttle forward and felt his aircraft respond almost as if it had anticipated the command. The F-22 was designed for stealth and maneuverability, but its high thrust-to-weight ratio made it extremely fast as well. Broome had read reports about the SU-57 having an even better thrust-to-weight ratio and higher top speed, but he knew that reports of Russian technical prowess were often wildly inflated. He'd also read reports from other sources claiming that the Russians had run into difficulties with the engines originally designed for the SU-57, forcing them to retrofit the fighters with older, less powerful engines. Those reports, at least, appeared to have been accurate.

"You see any other missiles?" Broome asked.

"*Negative,*" Driver replied. "*Looks like these guys want to run.*" The Russian fighters were speeding away to the north, skimming the treetops in an attempt to confuse the Americans' search radar.

Broome went to full power, and felt the force of the engines pressing him into his seat. He had visual contact on his target, but his radar still wasn't getting a solid lock. He switched to his video-assisted targeting system and steadied the SU-57 in the sight, then allowed the computer to take over. The solid tone came a moment later as the missile acquired a radar lock, and Broome pulled the trigger.

The AIM-120 missile dropped out of the internal weapons bay and accelerated rapidly away from *Sweep One*. Quickly reaching its top speed of Mach 4, it closed the distance to the Russian fighter with shocking speed. The Russian pilot reacted immediately, pulling his aircraft into a maneuver known as Pugachev's Cobra, in an attempt to confuse the targeting radar on the missile. The pilot pulled back hard on the control yoke, pulling the nose of the aircraft up so sharply that it would normally cause a stall; but thanks to thrust vectoring and computer assisted control surfaces, the SU-57 was able to maintain its altitude while bleeding off almost all of its forward motion. The pilot held that position for a brief moment before lowering the nose and increasing power to speed away again.

The intent of the maneuver was for any missile using radar tracking to lose its target lock as its computer classified the target as no longer moving fast enough to be an aircraft. Anything moving less than about fifty miles an hour is normally filtered out as ground clutter by most radars, allowing a clearer presentation of fast moving objects, such as fighter jets. The downside of Pugachev's Cobra is that it forces the aircraft into the undesirable combination of low speed and low energy - making it vulnerable to visual attack - and Broome still hadn't lost sight of the SU-57.

The Russian pilot had gambled, and he had lost. Broome watched as the SU-57's nose pitched up suddenly and the aircraft seemed to almost stop in mid-air, and he heard the steady tone of the missile's radar lock change to the warbling sound indicating the radar was again searching for a target.

Recognizing the change in the situation, Broome immediately switched to his 20mm Vulcan rotary cannon and chopped his power, simultaneously deflecting the ailerons up, the flaperons down, and the rudders outward; all of which acted to slow the speeding aircraft and keep it from overshooting the SU-57. Broome pressed the trigger, sending a burst of 20mm rounds streaking toward the enemy fighter as the Russian nosed over and tried to escape. The heavy cannon rounds tore through the Russian's right wing, smashing control surfaces and severing wires and cables. The aircraft went into an uncontrolled roll and corkscrewed into the trees, a huge fireball leaping into the air as

Broome pulled up and away.

He quickly scanned around him, searching for his wingman. Pulling the aircraft into a tight right hand turn, he saw a black smoke cloud six or seven miles to his east, tendrils of dirty smoke reaching toward the ground where bits of flaming wreckage had fallen from the sky. *Wreckage from whose plane?*

"*Sweep* flight, check." Broome flew toward the smoke cloud, keeping his eyes peeled for the other Russian fighter and hoping it had ended the same way as its partner. "*Sweep* flight, check," he repeated, still getting no answer. He crossed over the Glenn Highway, then over a line of low forested hills that climbed away to the east, marking the westernmost reach of the Chugach Mountains. Then he saw the wreckage, a line of flaming junk spread across a narrow valley floor. There was no way for him to tell for certain if the plane was American or Russian…

The missile warning alarm startled him, but his training kicked in like second nature, and he yanked his jet hard to the right, popping more chaff and flares as he did. He twisted in his seat, looking behind and to his right. He saw the missile coming, saw the smoke trail pointing the direction it had come, but this time the missile wasn't fooled by his countermeasures.

Broome reversed course, pulling the Raptor into a hard left hand turn followed by series of half rolls that had him coming out on a heading almost directly back at his attacker. As he rolled out, he fired another AIM-120, hoping the radar seeker would get lucky and pick up the other aircraft. His missile had barely left the rail when the Russian Vympel R77 missile passed twenty feet below his aircraft. Its laser proximity fuse detected the Raptor and detonated its 22.5 kilo high explosive warhead. The fragments ripped through the belly of the Raptor, tearing into the landing gear, weapons bay and both engines.

Broome survived by a fraction of a second, the closest fragments passing just six inches behind his seat. The aircraft shuddered and wallowed, suddenly displaying the flight characteristics of a thrown brick. Broome just had time pull his ejection handle and clear the aircraft before it came apart around him.

As his parachute opened, Broome looked around. He knew the standby alert crews would be trying to get airborne, but he couldn't make out anything in the direction of the airfield. He tried to twist around in his harness to get his bearings, and was startled as the SU-57 that had shot him down passed close alongside, circling him from barely a hundred yards away. The pilot slowed the aircraft, pulling the nose up almost as high as his wingman had right before Broome had killed him. Then the Russian snapped Broome a crisp salute before dropping the nose and racing away again toward Elmendorf.

So much for our aerial defense mission, Broome thought. He kept watching the SU-57 speeding away, until his parachute snagged in the thick trees below. He was left dangling from his harness like a marionette, helpless and alone.

CHAPTER SEVEN

Semper Paratus

Vladimir Andreyev
Cook Inlet

The Special Forces Major replaced the handset in its cradle and stared placidly out the windscreen as the *Vladimir Andreyev* continued to race northward, leaving the *Vasiliy Trushin* to its fate. "It is sometimes necessary to make sacrifices for the greater good, Captain."

Captain Bogdan Tsyganov clenched his jaw in fury, not daring to protest. It went against everything in him to abandon fellow mariners in danger, especially when they were aboard the twin of his own ship. Captain Sukhotin had been his friend since they had attended the naval academy together twenty years earlier. He wanted to shoot this arrogant commando and turn the *Andreyev* back around, but he knew he would never do such a thing. He would knuckle under and follow orders, even when those orders meant the loss of his friends.

Because at heart, Tsyganov was a coward.

MV TransAtlantic

Captain Garcia looked through the binoculars at the onrushing ship a thousand yards off his port bow. It was going to pass closer than he would have liked, but it wasn't the proximity that bothered him. It looked like the same ship he'd just disentangled his own vessel from, only... it wasn't. The superstructure looked slightly different, it was painted a different color, and the flimsy looking cranes on the foredeck were shorter. But the lines of the hull couldn't be disguised. He had noticed it on the *MV Ascension*, but it hadn't sunk in until now. That strange, diving board-looking prow... Garcia steadied the binoculars a moment, and then it hit him.

"That's an amphib!"

His first mate looked over at him. "What?"

Garcia pointed. "That! That's an amphibious assault ship, or I'm Captain Kirk!" He handed the glasses to the mate. "Look under the prow, right at the center line."

"Are those doors?"

"Yeah. They can drive that sucker right up onshore and offload troops through those doors. The ship we just tangled with was a carbon copy of that one, just with different plumbing bolted to the deck for camouflage. That explains why those characters were shooting at us."

"It does? I just figured they were some kinda terrorist nutbags."

"I did, too, until now. But terrorists don't usually put that many of their fighters in one place at one time. They also don't have navies. The only people who do are countries."

"So? Which country?"

"I don't know. Let's see if the military does." He picked up the emergency radio. "Coast Guard helicopter vicinity of the Port of Anchorage, this is the *MV TransAtlantic*."

CG6002
Providence Alaska Medical Center
Anchorage, Alaska

"This is Coast Guard Six Zero Zero Two, Go ahead, *TransAtlantic.*" Kennedy had spoken to his dispatcher, who had directed them to proceed without delay back to Providence to drop off the man they'd rescued. That man was being wheeled off the helipad under police guard at the moment.

"Yeah, Zero Zero Two, we just passed another ship northbound in a hurry toward Anchorage, and it's almost a twin of the one we just tangled with."

"Did you see a name, *TransAtlantic*?"

"Yeah, it was the MV Sagamore, *out of Dover. But that's not why I called. Both of those vessels are disguised amphibious landing ships. They have the exact same lines, and we just got a clear look at the bow doors on the* Sagamore - *if that's even its real name."*

Rollinson reached over and smacked Kennedy on the shoulder. "Dan, are you hearing this?" she was staring at the radio console.

Kennedy was about to tell her that of course he had heard it, when he noticed that her radio was tuned to an air traffic frequency, not the maritime channel he was on. "Standby, *TransAtlantic.*" He looked at Rollinson, whose eyes had gone wide. "What?"

"Everybody's screaming about an airborne assault at Elmendorf. Happening *right now.*"

He looked at her. "I'm talking to the captain of the *TransAtlantic.* He says the ship he tangled with is a disguised amphib, and he just passed its twin coming this way fast, a couple miles south."

Realization dawned on the pilot's face. "Oh, I can't believe we missed that! I was too busy looking at the wreckage, but that tub *did* have a cantilevered bow. I think we just watched the start of a war, Danny." She started flipping switches, prepping the chopper to lift off again. "Let's go see if we can slow that second ship down a little, shall we?"

Fort Richardson

"Come with us, Ell-Tee." Nugent called down as he climbed aboard the eight-wheeled Stryker Armored Fighting Vehicle. "We're gonna need all the help we can get."

Lieutenant Chad Leggett had only just recovered from the shock of having a senior NCO aim a loaded rifle at his head. Now he watched, helpless, as Nugent's group of thirty-plus soldiers fired up five Strikers and loaded them with supplies and ammunition, as well as additional weapons such as several Carl Gustaf M4 Recoilless Rifles. The Carl Gustaf was an anti-tank weapon - Leggett knew that much.

"I thought you said paratroopers were assaulting Elmendorf," he said. "What do you need anti-tank weapons for?"

Nugent looked down at him. "There's bound to be armor supporting them, Ell-Tee. None of these vehicles has anything bigger than a fifty-cal machine gun on board. We were supposed to get a few last year fitted with the 105 mm cannon, but you know the Army. Hurry up and wait, right? Well, we're still waitin'. Until then, we're gonna need the Gustafs." He dropped into the top hatch, then stuck his head back out as the driver revved the engine. "You comin', sir?"

Leggett looked around him, lost for a moment, then looked up at the sergeant. "You sure you want me? After..." He waved at the open gate. "That?"

"Lieutenant," Nugent hollered over the noise of the engine. "Everybody makes mistakes. You been here for what, less than a year?"

Leggett nodded, looking shamefaced.

"Everybody's gotta start somewhere, Ell-Tee. You'll figure it out. But if you stay here, and there really *is* an airborne assault going on down the road and you don't do something about it, you'll never forgive yourself. We'd like you to come with us."

"All right," Leggett finally said. He went around and climbed in the rear of the vehicle, and the small convoy rolled out of the yard.

CG6002
Over the Cook Inlet

"There it is." Rollinson inclined her head to the south. The light was improving slowly, and visibility with it. They could just make out the outline of the disguised ship ahead of them.

"He's in a hurry," Kennedy said. "Must be pushing twenty knots."

"If the *Ascension* was supposed to be the first to land, that collision will put them behind schedule. Maybe they don't want to be late to the war."

Kennedy snorted. "We're about to find out. You boys ready in the back?"

"Ready." Hulse's voice was grim. He had learned from their earlier encounter that he didn't appreciate being fired on. Taylor was next to him, strapped to a safety tether and holding a fifty caliber Barrett M82 sniper rifle, which was suspended from the overhead by a two-point sling.

"Good to go," Taylor said.

"All right then, here we go." Kennedy keyed the maritime radio as Rollinson positioned the chopper a hundred feet off the water and directly in the path of the onrushing ship, less than a thousand yards away and closing fast. "*MV Sagamore*, this is United States Coast Guard Helicopter Six Zero Zero Two. You are in violation of United States territorial waters. Shut your engines down and muster your crew on the foredeck, or you will be fired on. Acknowledge."

They only had to wait a couple of seconds. A loud bang

sounded from the right engine housing, and alarms started going off.

"We're hit!" Rollinson banked the helicopter hard left and away from the ship. Hulse and Taylor both started firing, but with the sudden movement of the chopper, it would have been a miracle if they'd hit anything.

Rollinson was doing everything she could to gain altitude, but they had lost one engine, and the second was straining under the added load. "I'm gonna try for the beach at Point Possession," she said. Kennedy called out their status to Coast Guard Station Kodiak, while Taylor and Hulse secured their weapons and strapped in for the landing.

At least, they *hoped* it would be a landing.

Vladimir Andreyev

"Well done," Major Vaslav Flyorov told his sniper, as the man lowered his Degtyarev 12.7 mm anti-materiel sniper rifle. They both watched with satisfaction as the American helicopter sheared away. Flyorov turned to the captain. "Now, as I was saying. There is a small boat launch on the south side of Ship Creek." He looked down at the chart, his finger hovering over it briefly before stabbing down. "There. That should suffice."

"What about the rest of the assault force?"

"There is only room for one ship. The rest will have to run the gauntlet and land north of the port, as originally planned. By the time they arrive, those container ships may have dispersed. But it is absolutely critical that we get on shore quickly, especially now that the Americans have been alerted."

Captain Tsyganov nodded. "And the *Trushin*?"

Flyorov stared at him, unblinking. "Casualties of war. We must avenge them."

"I see." The captain had a sudden urge to do whatever was necessary to get this man off his ship. "You should prepare your men in that case, Major. We are getting close."

CG6002
Over the Cook Inlet

Rollinson wrestled with the controls as the helicopter approached Point Possession. The Russian sniper's bullet had smashed into the right engine air intake with crippling efficiency, shredding the compressor blades and sending broken pieces into the engine. This caused a simultaneous catastrophic failure known as a compressor surge, where the smooth airflow into the engine becomes so interrupted that the engine can no longer overcome the force of the compressed air already inside, resulting in an overpressure situation that in this case blew a hole through the side of the engine housing.

All this happened in the split second after the 12.7 mm round struck the compressor vanes. Suddenly overloaded, the remaining engine started to race as it was forced to compensate for the power loss. That increased load burst an oil line, and the resulting loss of oil pressure in the number two engine was rapidly nullifying all of Rollinson's considerable efforts to keep the aircraft aloft.

They were several thousand yards off the beach at Point Possession, roughly twenty miles southwest of Anchorage on the south side of the Turnagain Arm of the Cook Inlet. Rollinson needed to get the chopper as close to shore as possible before they ran out of altitude. The entire crew was wearing survival suits, but even with the added protection the suits offered, the frigid waters of the Cook Inlet would still kill them within a couple of hours of exposure. There were only three other Coast Guard Jayhawk helicopters based at Kodiak, and they were all currently operating out to sea or in the outer Aleutian Islands, too far away to be of any immediate help.

This area of the Cook Inlet saw fairly heavy maritime traffic, but Rollinson didn't want to bet the lives of her crew on the chance of being plucked out of the water by a fishing boat or commercial vessel, so she was pushing the remaining functional engine well beyond its limits. Smoke boiled out of the wrecked right engine, leaving a dirty smear across the sky behind the chopper. There was also a disturbing noise coming from the main rotor gear box; a sort of random pop mixed with an irregular grinding noise. Rollinson knew their time was running out.

Kennedy was on the radio, broadcasting a mayday to air traffic control, when the number two engine abruptly died. Rollinson quickly lowered the collective pitch, allowing the forward speed and sudden descent of the aircraft to keep the main rotor spinning. Carefully watching her descent rate, she waited until they were less than two hundred feet above the water before she pulled the nose back up, flaring the helicopter and arresting their descent.

The maneuver was done so neatly that the helicopter's wheels barely made a splash as they touched the surface. The chopper settled into the water gently at first, but as water started flowing into the cargo bay, it became unbalanced and rolled over onto its left side. The huge main rotor smashed into the water and came apart with several violent cracks.

"OUT OUT OUT!!" Rollinson shouted. Taylor had already shoved Hulse out through the right side door and was helping Rollinson with her buckle before she could release it herself. The cockpit was filling with icy water at an alarming rate, and Rollinson was almost submerged before Taylor got her free. Kennedy had forced his door open, and climbed halfway out. Taylor bodily hoisted the pilot out of her seat and shoved her toward Kennedy's outstretched hand. Kennedy hauled her out the door after him as the helicopter sank beneath the surface and disappeared.

"Taylor!" Rollinson shouted, coughing out a lungful of water and looking around frantically for the rescue swimmer. He hadn't made it out with them.

Kennedy was treading water next to her. "Chris!"

Rollinson spun in the water, frantic now. Taylor was like a brother. The idea of losing him was terrifying. She started to call out again, but he suddenly surfaced right behind her, gasping for air.

"You all right?" Rollinson asked.

"No problem, Lieutenant," Taylor answered, coughing and treading water. "I was half standing in the back when it went under, so once I got you loose, I just backed out the side door. It was easier than trying to climb over the seat and follow you guys out the front."

"You scared the crap outta me," Rollinson said, forcing a smile.

"Sorry about that," Taylor nodded past her. "But we should probably get going."

Rollinson turned around in the water and was relieved to see that the beach was only a couple hundred yards away now. She had been so focused on getting the chopper safely down that she'd lost track of their forward progress. At least she'd managed to get them close to relative safety.

"You're right," she said. "Let's get to shore before we all turn into popsicles."

The Oval Office
The White House
Washington, D. C.

"Mister President, the Acting SecDef is on line one."

His assistant's nasally voice somehow seemed to remind Reese of a catatonic nun from a comedy routine he'd seen as a much younger man, but he could never seem to remember exactly where he'd seen it. He shook his head, trying to get rid of the mental picture so he could focus. "Thank you." He punched the button for the speaker phone. "Reese."

"Mister President, Avery Bassett here, I -"

"You do realize that my assistant tells me who's calling me *before* I pick up the phone, don't you?"

Bassett was caught flat-footed. *"Uh, sir, I ah…"*

"It's kind of like having an audible caller ID with a nasally nun's voice. Ha!" Reese started chuckling.

"Mister President, forgive me, but I have some unpleasant news. Sir, the country is under attack."

"Hmph. You're a little slow on the uptake, Avery." He abruptly raised his voice. "Of course we've been attacked! We've had terrorist attacks in every state and most major cities, not to mention riots and reprisals for the past two weeks! Where have you been, hiding under a rock?"

"I'm aware of those issues, sir!" Bassett had to raise his voice to get Reese to stop talking. *"That's not what I'm referring to!"*

"Well, what *are* you referring to then?"

"Sir, a few hours ago, the Russian military launched an amphibious and airborne assault on various targets in Alaska. We have reports of airborne landings in Anchorage and Fairbanks at least, with amphibious assault ships coming ashore in Anchorage, Valdez, Seward and several other ports. We've lost at least one Coast Guard helicopter, as well as four F-22 alert fighters out of Elmendorf Air Force Base. Reports are fragmented, but they're coming in from across the state, sir. We have to treat this as legitimate."

"The Russians?" Reese couldn't keep the disbelief from his voice. "Why would the Russians attack Alaska? That makes no sense."

"I can't speak to their motives, sir," Bassett said. *"All I know is that we've lost contact with the military commanders in the state. Whatever the Russians did, they did it quickly enough to isolate our military command and control. Whatever assets we have in the state are cut off, if not destroyed out of hand."*

Reese stood up and took a couple of tentative steps around the desk. "This can't be happening…" There was an uncomfortably long pause, before Bassett finally spoke again.

"Sir, may I suggest you convene the service chiefs and your cabinet at the earliest possible time? We need to work out a response."

"Response," Reese repeated. If Bassett had been in the room, he would have seen Reese staring blankly at the far wall of his office, his eyes suddenly unfocused.

Bassett waited another few moments, then tried again. "Sir? Are you still there, Mr. President?"

"What?" Reese turned around, almost surprised by Bassett's voice coming from the speaker behind him. "I'm sorry - what did you say?"

"Mr. President, we need an emergency meeting of the Chiefs of Staff and the cabinet. We have to do something!"

Reese was tapping his lower lip with two fingertips. "Yes. Do something… What would you suggest?"

"Sir, I've already suggested it -"

"Then suggest it again!" Reese exploded. "I can't be expected to keep track of everything every blathering idiot tells me over the course of the day, can I?"

Bassett couldn't believe what he was hearing, and he had a sudden sense of impending doom. "Sir. The Joint Chiefs, and your cabinet? We should probably have them all meet as soon as possible?"

"Ah. Yes," Reese said, brightening. "That makes sense. Get that set up for me, will you, David?"

"Uh, yes. Yes, sir," Bassett said. "I'll have them convene in the Situation Room as soon as I can, if that's all right with you."

"Fine, fine," Reese said. "Thank you for the call. Let me know when they're ready for me." With that, he hung up.

Avery Bassett sat in stunned silence for a few moments after the connection had been broken, just staring at his phone. *What the hell was that?* he wondered. *He called me David. Surely he doesn't think I'm Coleridge?*

Bassett shook his head in disbelief. Then he picked up the phone and started making the necessary calls.

Vladimir Andreyev
Anchorage, Alaska

"All hands, brace for collision!" The captain's warning blared from loudspeakers all over the ship as the *Vladimir Andreyev* bore down on the Ship Creek Small Boat Launch. There were two fishing vessels tied up at the wooden dock, neither longer than fifty feet. Warned by panicked shouts from people on shore, several men on the closest boat looked up. The sight of the nearly four hundred foot long ship, pushing a significant bow wave so close to shore, was enough to send them scrambling over the rail and running for the safety of the landward end of the dock.

The massive cantilevered bow of the *Andreyev* loomed over the two little boats, even as its bow wave lifted them and bashed their hulls against the dock. The boat launch area was less than a hundred feet across at its widest, bisected by the single floating dock. Small boats could tie up on either side of the dock during launch or recovery, but most of the boats that used the launch were less than eight feet wide.

The *Andreyev* had a beam more than six times that, and now as its bulk filled the little channel, the two fishing boats were lifted by the bow wave and dashed on the gravel of the sloping ramp, before the bulk of the assault ship caught up to them and crushed them to splinters. The wave pushed landward by the *Andreyev's* bow had barely started to recede when its massive bow doors cracked open.

Four Russian T-14 Armata main battle tanks were first to disembark, followed by twenty-four Bumerang next-generation armored personnel carriers. The Bumerangs each carried a crew of three, plus ten infantrymen, and bristled with 30mm auto cannons and anti-tank rockets. The Armata tanks would offer additional, heavier firepower with their 152mm cannons.

As the ship disgorged its cargo, fishermen milling around the boat launch stared in disbelief. The men who'd barely escaped their boat were shouting angrily, and several people were on their cell phones, either calling 911 or taking pictures. A crowd started to coalesce at the head of the parking lot, but one of the lead Bumerang commanders ordered a burst from the 7.62mm machine gun mounted on his vehicle, dispersing them in a panic. Then the entire force slowly started to move, lumbering up the entrance road for the short drive to the southwest gate at Elmendorf Air Force Base.

Frostbite One
Stryker Assault Vehicle
Elmendorf Air Force Base

"Frostbite One, Frostbite Two."
"Go ahead, Two."
"You ah… you got a plan here, Sergeant?"
"Standby."
It had taken the five Strykers less than ten minutes to cover the distance between Richardson and Elmendorf, and now they were parked at the intersection of the Davis Highway and Talley Avenue, directly off the approach end of Runway 24. They had a clear view across the middle of the airfield to the control tower, and the view was not encouraging. Sergeant Nugent was looking through high-powered binoculars, trying to formulate a plan. He swore and handed the glasses over to Lieutenant Leggett.

"I don't see any heavy equipment yet, Ell-Tee," Nugent said. "But it looks like an awful lot of ground pounders running around, and that smoke coming from the control tower can't be good, either."

"That's an Antonov," Leggett said, his voice subdued. "With Russian markings. Looks like another one turning final right now."

"What do you want to do, Lieutenant?"

Leggett looked surprised. "Why ask me? I was guarding the vehicle park until about ten minutes ago."

"You're the officer, sir. That means you're in charge."

Leggett continued as if he hadn't heard him. "Do you know why I was guarding the vehicle park, Sergeant? 'Cause I got popped for driving under the influence last week, that's why! They had to find something for me to do to remind me of my duty, so they stuck me out in that lot. Just because the war starts when I'm doing my penance doesn't put me in charge. There are lots of other officers around."

Nugent half turned in the cramped compartment. "Lieutenant, let me tell you something. The fact that you came along with us tonight tells me you're not a complete screw-up. Now, what I see here is a young man whose pity party is getting rained on by real life." He pointed out the viewport. "I don't think those guys would care one way or the other that you got a DUI - they came here for a war, and they're gonna get one, regardless of who's on duty or why, when the shooting starts. And by the looks of it, it's already started, so wipe your nose and do your job!"

The men in the back of the Stryker traded glances. Leggett stared at Nugent in disbelief. He looked back out the viewport as the massive Russian plane touched down and rolled out toward them.

"You are the ranking man here, Lieutenant," Nugent's tone was moderated now, but still urgent. "This is your call."

Leggett swallowed, then nodded. "All right... If it's my call, then I guess we should cripple their aircraft. They're already fueling the first one; probably going to rotate back to wherever they came from as soon as they finish. Will those Carl Gustafs do any damage to something that size?"

"HEDP rounds will, Ell-Tee. Those planes aren't armored."

"All right." Leggett gave Nugent an uncertain look. "Unless..."

unless you have a better idea… I think we should do that."

Nugent grinned. "Then let's go get some, sir."

CHAPTER EIGHT

Ecce Venient Apportant Ruteni

Susan Nightingale McKay Playground
Anchorage, Alaska

The massive Armata tank rolled into the small park at the end of Bluff Drive, crushing a large piece of playground equipment and several picnic tables before coming to a stop on the grass at the edge of a small bluff, overlooking the Tesoro Alaska petroleum storage facility on the bank below and the waters of the Cook Inlet beyond. The Armata's turret swung slowly to the right as the massive 152mm cannon rose slightly higher. It had barely stopped moving when the entire tank rocked violently with the recoil of the powerful gun. Evergreen bushes on the slope below the tank were smashed flat by the muzzle blast, and car alarms started going off up and down the quiet residential street.

The projectile the Armata fired was a High Explosive, Anti-Tank, or HEAT, round. The general idea for the ammunition's design had been around since World War II, with improvements in range and destructive power coming over the years. The Armata gunner in this case didn't need it to penetrate heavy armor, because he was shooting at a fairly thin-skinned container ship - but it would still have the desired effect.

A little more than a mile away in the middle of the channel was a cluster of container ships, in a knot of panicked confusion following the collision of one of them with the *Vasiliy Trushin*, and the subsequent exchange of fire with the American rescue helicopter.

The remaining container ships were still blocking the deep water channel, and it didn't look as though they would sort themselves out any time soon. The Russian landing force had more reinforcements inbound, and unless one or more of the container ships moved, the Russian ships could not get to their planned landing area just north of the quay. Major Flyorov had been adamant that something be done right away to get the ships moved, so the Armata had been split off the main force to do just that.

The first HEAT round struck the easternmost ship just behind its bridge superstructure. When the detonator mounted in the tip of the round impacted the bridge bulkhead, the explosive inside the round went off, forcing a conically shaped metal liner to collapse and become a superplastic mass, which was then expelled in a concentrated jet out the front of the round. The result was that the superplastic jet of collapsed metal transferred massive amounts of kinetic energy from the explosion into whatever it hit, causing catastrophic damage to the inside of a tank, concrete bunker, or in this case, a ship.

The explosion blew out all the windows on the bridge. Tiny bits of shrapnel shredded the bridge crew as smoke billowed from the shattered windows. Aboard the other moored ships, lookouts gaped at the stricken vessel as emergency radios came to life. One lookout had the presence of mind to look past the ship, and was scanning the shoreline when he saw the muzzle flash as the tank loosed its second round. It came from a hill above an oil storage farm, and the lookout watched in morbid fascination as the round smashed into the ship next to his. Smoke and flames were pouring out of the ship's bridge now, and the man snatched up his emergency radio and gave a hasty report before calling his captain to the bridge.

The tank commander watched with satisfaction as the first two rounds struck home. The autoloader had already loaded a third HEAT round, but the commander didn't fire, instead using the Armata's radar targeting sights to inspect the damage they'd done. There was a good deal of smoke and flame around the bridge superstructure on the closest ship, and he could see a frenzy of activity on all of the other vessels. Crewmen were running around frantically, mustering at their emergency stations. He scanned the water at the stern of each ship, and saw the telltale roiling that indicated the huge propellers starting to turn. They were getting ready to move, but the tank commander decided that a little more encouragement would not be misplaced.

"Gunner!" he barked out. "Anti-tank missile."

"Ready!" the gunner replied.

"Fire!"

The incoming missile was clearly visible to the naked eye. It streaked over the oil tanks and across the water toward the cluster of helpless ships with frightening speed. The lookout who had initially spotted the Armata found that he couldn't look away as the missile slammed into the starboard side of the neighboring ship. The explosion sent a shock wave across the water in an expanding circle, and flames shot up the side of the ship, curling around the superstructure and licking at the containers secured on the main deck.

The lookout didn't wait for the captain to get to the bridge. On his own initiative, he ordered the anchor cut loose and the engines brought to full power. He had no desire to stay here and become the next target for that tank.

Petr Morgunov
Cook Inlet, Alaska

"Captain, ground forces report the blocking container ships are moving away from the port facility. One is disabled, but the others are scattering in a panic."

"Very good." Captain Oleg Belanov said. "Increase to flank speed."

The *Petr Morgunov* was the third landing ship in the amphibious force, and it was currently far behind schedule. Belanov was furious at the mechanical problems that had plagued his ship since they'd sailed, but those were behind them now. With the *Vasiliy Trushin* out of commission and the *Vladimir Andreyev* forced to land at the secondary beachhead, Belanov felt it was up to him and his ship to save the operation from total failure. He was determined to bring the Morgunov to shore as planned, with no further delays.

On the *Morgunov's* massive well deck, Major Mikhail Dorogoi walked between the tanks and assault vehicles, encouraging his men. He was as frustrated with the delays as Captain Belanov, if not more. He had been angry to find that his assault element was to be the third to land, taking the assignment as a slight against him and his men, and the mechanical problems they'd had enroute had only added to his sense of frustration.

But now he found his team in a position to pull victory from the jaws of defeat. He knew the airborne troops must already be on the ground at Elmendorf, and that the element from the *Vladimir Andreyev* would be delayed linking up with them due to the *Andreyev* landing further south than they had planned. Dorogoi had no intention of letting this opportunity slip through his fingers.

"Major!" Dorogoi's aide waved at him from the port side of

the well deck, where he was replacing a phone in its cradle. "Five minutes!"

Dorogoi smiled and climbed to the catwalk overlooking the well deck. He waved his fist in a circle over his head, and the vehicle commanders began starting their engines. It reminded Dorogoi of an American auto race he'd seen on television once; the exhaust and roar of all the engines coming to life at once, all of the drivers eager to be first off the line.

Well, this is a race of a different kind, isn't it? he thought. *A race we are going to win.*

Frostbite One
Elmendorf Air Force Base

"*Frostbite Three, Four* and *Five*, spread out behind these hangars about a hundred meters apart, then proceed straight to the flight line on my mark, be ready to engage."

"*Three.*"

"*Four.*"

"*Five.*"

"*Frostbite Two*, with me, be ready on your Mk44."

"*Two, roger.*"

The five Strykers had driven onto the east end of Elmendorf's flight line, then looped around the northeast corner of the airfield. Nugent waited as the three vehicles he'd split off moved into position.

"Raines!" Nugent said. "Open that rear roof hatch and get ready with the Carl Gustaf."

"I'm on it, Sergeant." Private Raines popped the hatch and stuck his head and shoulders out while another soldier handed the anti-tank weapon up to him. Meanwhile the other three Strykers were reporting in position.

"Two, you ready?"

"*Two's ready.*"

"Follow us. The rest of you, standby. Let's go, Lieutenant." Leggett, now in the driver's seat as the best means to make him useful, started the vehicle forward, bringing the pair of Strykers along the east side of a large operations building. As they moved into the open, they could clearly see the first Antonov transport being fueled by a commandeered American fuel truck.

"Raines, hit that plane - engines or cockpit, I don't care!"

"On the way!" There was a loud crack as Raines touched off the Carl Gustaf. Nugent watched through the thermal camera on the Stryker's video periscope as the round impacted on the outboard left engine of the big cargo plane, exploding on contact and blowing off most of the wingtip in a big ball of flame.

"*Frostbite Two*, hit that fueler; *Three, Four* and *Five*, advance!"

The second Stryker opened up on the fuel truck with a long burst from its Mk44 Bushmaster chain gun. The 30mm rounds tore through the tanker truck, spilling jet fuel all around the parked aircraft, which added to the intensity of the fire burning at the aircraft's destroyed wing. A column of thick black smoke shot through with angry red flames billowed around the scene while secondary explosions started going off.

The other three Strykers emerged onto the tarmac in a line perpendicular to the first two and immediately started engaging troops on the ground with their chain guns. Russian airborne troops were cut down across a wide front while their luckier comrades ducked behind buildings and vehicles for temporary cover. A soldier with a Carl Gustaf popped out of a hatch on *Frostbite Three* and fired a missile at the second Antonov, which had stopped on the taxiway halfway between the ramp and the runway. The missile ripped into the fuselage at an oblique angle, penetrating just below the cockpit on the right side. The resulting explosion caused the big aircraft to shudder before it slowly veered to the left and drove off the taxiway into the muddy infield, where it finally came to a halt, smoke and flame licking around the gaping hole left by the explosion.

Small arms fire was pinging off the Stryker's armor now, and

Nugent decided he'd seen enough. "All *Frostbite* elements, recover to the secondary rendezvous!"

They spun around and retreated across the concrete to the northeast, barreling across the perpendicular runway and veering behind the hangars that housed the diminished squadron of F-22 Raptors. But *Frostbite Four* was slow to disengage, and a Russian trooper stepped into the open with a shoulder fired SA-25 missile launcher as the vehicle turned to retreat. *Frostbite Four's* vehicle commander saw the launch through his thermal sight, but had no time to rotate his Bushmaster around to meet the threat. Without the standoff slat armor installed around their vehicle to force the warhead to detonate before it touched the vehicle itself, they were already dead.

"Frostbite Four's *hit!*" The commander of *Frostbite Five* shouted over the vehicle radio net.

"*Frostbite Four*, roger, are you still mobile?" Nugent called, mistaking *Five's* call as coming from *Four*.

"*They're gone*, One," *Five's* commander said, collecting himself with an effort. "*Took a missile hit; I saw all their hatches blow out.*"

Nugent took a breath. "Roger that," he said. He suddenly felt very old. He'd known every one of the kids that were on that vehicle, but there was nothing he could do about it now. "Everybody stick to the plan - this is why we can't be stationary for too long. Let's regroup and find a way to hit these suckers back."

Vasiliy Trushin
Cook Inlet

Captain Sukhotin would have liked to discuss options with Major Cheremisin, but the blow to the head the Special Forces officer had suffered had rendered him unable to stand, much less to carry on an intelligent conversation. He was lying under a blanket in the corner of the bridge, glassy eyes staring up at the overhead without registering anything.

The *Trushin* was being carried seaward on the ebbing tide. The risk of floating onto another sand bank was very real, since they had no steering, but it was the least of Sukhotin's worries. They had almost been able to get the flooding under control, but then the fire had pushed the damage control parties away from the section of the hull that most needed their attention. By the time the flooding had checked the spread of the fire, it had destroyed the engine room. With nothing left but basic battery power, the *Trushin* was dead in the water. It was only a matter of time.

Sukhotin briefly considered how to get people off in the few lifeboats they had. The motor lifeboats were not meant for landing, but for keeping people alive at sea long enough to be picked up by other vessels. If he tried to use the boats to ferry his people to safety, they likely would capsize when they got close in to shore, and even if they didn't, they wouldn't be able to get back to the ship to take more people off. It would be just as effective to draw lots and fill the boats with the winners, leaving the rest to die on board the *Trushin*.

But Sukhotin knew he couldn't do that, either. He kept running through his options in his head, but kept coming up with nothing.

"Captain?"

Sukhotin turned to see Captain Gontarev, Major Cheremisin's second in command. "What is it, Captain?"

"Sir, I wish to suggest a course of action."

Sukhotin shook his head, his fatigue evident on his face. "Captain, if you're about to suggest to me that I should scuttle this vessel, I can save you the trouble. I will *not* scuttle the *Trushin*. He has been a good ship to me and to all of my crew. Besides, he will probably sink on his own in an hour or so, no matter what we do."

"Captain, please," Gontarev said. "That is not what I meant. I understand your problem with the shortage of lifeboats, but we don't need more lifeboats. We can use the Bumerangs."

Sukhotin looked at him for a moment, then dismissed the idea. "They are in the aft part of the well deck. The ship is pitched upward at the bow by almost fifteen degrees, so we cannot open the stern gate, or we will flood even faster than we already are. If we open the bow doors, the Bumerangs cannot get around the Armatas at the bow, and I don't think I need to remind you, the Armatas are not amphibious like the Bumerangs. If we take them off, they'll sink like stones."

"Which is precisely what I'm suggesting, Captain," Gontarev said.

Sukhotin looked at him in surprise. "Their drivers will not get out in time. You'd be sending them to their deaths."

"Possibly. But if we stay on board, more will certainly die. This is a risk we must be willing to take."

"And the loss of the Armatas? Is that a risk your superiors would be willing to take?"

"War is loss, Captain. Besides, if we do nothing, it is likely we'll either sink or be captured, neither of which is an option that has any chance of pleasing my superiors. This is the best bad choice."

"Very well, Captain Gontarev. I think we may still have enough power to open the bow doors."

Elmendorf Air Force Base

Sergeant Kirkpatrick felt like his lungs were going to burst. He had joined back up with Airman Hume and the two of them had tried to work their way closer to the control tower, but more Russians kept landing all around them. They'd fought their way through more than ten paratroopers in the process of touching down, but had been driven further from their goal with each firefight. Now they were running low on ammunition, and Kirkpatrick knew the only choice they had left was to get away, fast. They'd tried to get back to their patrol car, but had found it engulfed in flames. Running was their only option.

Hume was several strides ahead of him, running with apparent ease. They weaved between buildings and ducked behind trees, trying to shake any pursuit that might be following. They'd tried to contact dispatch on their radios as they ran, but the channel had gone dead. Hume seemed to sense that Kirkpatrick was lagging, so she slowed and looked back.

"You still with me, Sergeant?"

"I'm with you, Airman," Kirkpatrick gasped. "Keep going." She slowed her pace to match his, and Kirkpatrick noticed she barely seemed winded. He gave her a pained look.

"I used to run cross country in high school," she said, reading his mind.

"I guess baseball wasn't the best choice I could have made, then."

"It's not exactly an endurance sport, Sergeant." She looked over her shoulder. "I think we're in the clear for now. Where are we headed?"

"I'd *like* to go over to the Class Six and pick up a half rack of beer, but we should probably try to link up with the rest of the watch instead."

"Okay," she said. "Where do you think the rest of the watch is about now?"

He stopped and bent over, hands on his knees. "I have no idea."

Vasiliy Trushin

Captain Sukhotin stood on the catwalk above the well deck, watching as the *Trushin's* huge bow doors slowly swung open. Gontarev had found four volunteers to drive the Armatas off the ship into the water, and they were all sitting in the driver's stations with their tanks idling. Sukhotin had a bad feeling about this, but he knew Gontarev was right. Faced with only bad choices, they had to choose the best of them.

The *Vasiliy Trushin's* stern was sitting lower in the water than the bow, giving the bow ramp an upward incline of fifteen degrees, and the ship was also listing to the port by about ten degrees. The combination made the well deck a treacherous place to try to move around. Sukhotin watched as Gontarev ordered the cables holding the first tank in place removed. He almost expected the huge machine to slide backward and crash into the other vehicles behind it, but it somehow stayed in place.

Gontarev, standing on the deck alongside the tank, waved his hand forward. To his credit, the tank driver didn't hesitate. He applied power to the accelerator, and the Armata shifted and rumbled up the sloping deck toward the open doors. From his vantage point, Sukhotin could tell the man was trying to gauge his moment, trying to keep pressure on the accelerator long enough that the tank's forward momentum would carry it overboard, but also trying to leave himself enough time to climb out of the driver's hatch and jump off without going overboard himself.

As the tank approached the end of the ramp, the driver applied more power, then started clambering out of the hatch. The Armata slowed as soon as he let go of the accelerator, and he hesitated, unsure whether he'd given it enough of a running start. The momentary hesitation killed him. The tank had slowed considerably, but it was still going to make it off the edge of the well deck, and the driver had waited too long. He tried to heave his hips clear of the hatch, but the tank reached the edge and pivoted sharply downward, the sudden motion forcing the driver to lose his grip. Tank and driver disappeared over the edge and into the water with a huge splash, disappearing below the surface immediately.

The remaining three Armata drivers watched Captain Gontarev, who had climbed to the open bow and was looking overboard. He turned and shook his head once, then brusquely waved the next tank forward.

The next driver fared better, getting his tank almost to the edge before scrambling free of the hatch like it was on fire and leaping off the side, only to break his ankle when he hit the deck. But he was alive, and Gontarev slapped him on the shoulder, helped him up, and motioned for the next tank.

It had just started to move when the entire ship lurched suddenly. The forty-eight ton Armata slid sideways and backward, smashing into the fourth tank, which was still secured to the deck with thick cables. Three of the cables snapped, the fourth serving as a pivot that allowed the tank to slew around to the left, where its main gun smashed into the side of the ship. The driver of the other Armata saw the danger and added power, but the ship lurched again, its port side list increasing to nearly twenty-five degrees and pinning the two tanks against the bulkhead.

For the second time that day, the *Trushin* had run aground.

Elmendorf Air Force Base

Senior Sergeant Voronin was almost knocked to the ground by the explosion from the refueling AN-124, even though he was more than a hundred yards away. Shielding his eyes from the fireball, he scanned the area to his east for the threat the he knew must be there. He thought he saw the outline of an armored vehicle through the smoke, but he couldn't be sure. He was straining his eyes to see better when he was almost run over by an American Stryker. The big combat vehicle seemed to appear out of nowhere, racing onto the flight line with its 30mm cannon barking.

Voronin rolled out of the way, expecting the American gunner to turn the big gun on him, but somehow he hadn't been seen. He looked quickly around for someone with a missile launcher, but his men had scattered in disarray when the plane exploded.

Voronin cursed the planners who thought it would be a good idea to have the armor landed by amphibious ship rather than air dropped; if they'd had even a couple of Bumerangs on the ground, the fight would be very nearly even at this point. Instead, they would have to wait for the mechanized elements to arrive from the port.

The sergeant took cover behind a concrete barrier at the edge of the ramp as another Stryker fired a missile at a second Russian cargo plane that had just turned off the runway. The big freighter took the hit, then rolled slowly into the infield and stopped, already burning.

Having hit both of the Russian planes on the ground, the Stryker force abruptly stopped firing and turned to race away. Just as suddenly, another missile streaked across the ramp and struck one of the vehicles dead center, right between the second and third tires on the right side. The resulting explosion blew several hatches off the Stryker, and the vehicle itself tipped over onto its left side. Voronin knew everyone inside would have been killed instantly, but he couldn't help shuddering at the idea of dying that way, blown to bloody pulp inside a rolling metal coffin.

Now Voronin saw another Stryker further to his east, also retreating, and realized the Americans were either re-deploying for another attack, or had realized they were outnumbered and decided to withdraw completely. He got up and ran across the ramp to the man who had killed the Stryker.

"Do you have more missiles?" Voronin shouted.

"Yes," the man said, "but I can't carry them by myself." He pointed at the wrecked Stryker. "That thing killed my spotter."

"I'll take them," Voronin said, shouldering the case. It held only two more missiles, since the man had fired one and already loaded a second into his launcher. "We need to move that way and protect the perimeter from another incursion."

"Where is our armor?" the man asked bitterly. "They should've been here at the same time as we were!"

Voronin shook his head. "I don't know. We'll just have to hold until they get here. Come."

Vasiliy Trushin

The entire ship was shuddering and bucking now like a living animal. The outgoing tide had pinned the Trushin against a solid mud bank, and it was now in danger of rolling over. The last two Armata drivers had disentangled their vehicles and gotten them off in spite of the difficult angle of the deck. One driver had almost fallen in the sea, but had instead smacked down hard on the edge of the ramp as his tank went overboard, cracking several ribs. Now the Bumerangs were being loaded with nervous troops who wanted nothing more than to be off of this floating death trap, but who still felt that climbing into another windowless metal vehicle in order to escape was somewhat counterintuitive.

The Bumerangs were equipped with twin water jets at the back, which allowed the vehicles to maneuver in the water like a boat. They could travel over the water for as long as their fuel held out, and drive up on any shore with less than a forty-five degree slope, ready to fight. They would serve as lifeboats in this case, with the remaining tank crews and the naval personnel from the crippled *Vasiliy Trushin* crowding aboard wherever they could.

The two actual life boats would take only thirty people off, including Captain Sukhotin and the nearly comatose Major Cheremisin. That left another seventy naval personnel, plus the eleven surviving tank crewmen; all of whom were unceremoniously drafted into mechanized infantry service by Captain Gontarev.

Three of the Bumerangs sank on launch. The erratic motion of the beached ship being pounded by the waves made it next to impossible for the drivers to time their departure out of the bow gate properly. If they exited as the bow came down, they would go into the water relatively level, and motor away from the ship safely. But three of them either missed their timing, or the ship was hit by a random wave as they debarked. The bow was too steeply elevated as they exited the ship, and each of the three vehicles tumbled end over end, landing upside down in the water. Jammed to capacity with extra personnel, each sinking Bumerang took thirteen or fourteen men down with it.

Captain Sukhotin was reluctant to leave his vessel, but by the time the last Bumerang launched, it was clear that the *Trushin* was doomed. Sukhotin ordered his remaining men into the life boats, and followed the group of swimming Bumerangs toward the eastern shore of the Cook Inlet.

Elmendorf Air Force Base

Kirkpatrick and Hume had worked their way south along the flight line adjacent to Runway 34. There was less enemy activity here, but the lack of movement meant they could work their way closer to the Security Police headquarters without attracting attention. Hume tried to call the dispatcher again, but got nothing. They were about to cross a wide lawn between the flight line and their building when a rocket streaked across the open space from their right, driving straight into the north side of the Security Police building. Two more rockets followed in close succession, impacting each wing of the large building that was shaped roughly like a capital letter 'E', with the middle wing longer and broader than the other two.

Fire immediately broke out inside the building where the rockets had struck, and Kirkpatrick pulled Hume down next to some bushes.

"I guess they know where we work," Hume whispered.

"We need a vehicle," Kirkpatrick said, scanning the lot in front of the burning building.

"Troops coming this way, Sergeant."

Kirkpatrick followed her gaze to the north, where he could see at least a dozen men spread out in a line and moving toward them on foot. Now they knew where the rockets had come from.

"Come on, Lucy," Kirkpatrick hissed. "Time to leave." He took off to the southwest, angling for the furthest corner of the police lot. He kept as many bushes between them and the Russians as he could, but the cover was sparse. A police cruiser raced toward the building from the northwest, lights flashing. The Russians halted their advance toward the building and keyed on the approaching cruiser, opening up with automatic weapons.

"Oh, no…" Hume stopped to watch in horror.

"Move, Airman!" Kirkpatrick grabbed her arm and propelled her along toward the parked cruisers.

She tried to shrug him off. "We gotta help them!"

Kirkpatrick got in her face. "They're gone! Even if they weren't, I'm down to three rounds, and I doubt you have much more." He pointed toward the bullet-riddled cruiser, which the Russians were approaching now with caution. They were too far away to hear anything being said, but it was clear the occupants were dead. "The best thing we can do now is *not* end up like that for no good reason! Now move!"

Hume took one last look, then reluctantly followed. Kirkpatrick ran to a cruiser parked at the far end of the lot and got in. He started the engine and had the car rolling as Hume climbed in. They skidded around the corner leaving the lot, drawing fire from the Russians, but they were three hundred yards away now and accelerating.

"Where *is* everybody?" Hume asked, her voice cracking slightly.

"They must have been responding at the same time we were," Kirkpatrick said. "Think about it - at any given time we have several cars on patrol, and they're usually dispersed all over the base. Day shift hasn't come on yet, so staffing is low anyway."

"But I didn't see *anyone* at headquarters, did you?"

"Nope. Can't figure that, either. There should have been at least a few people around."

Hume was looking behind them at the burning building. "Maybe they were all inside."

Colonel Karpov climbed the last flight of stairs to the tower cab, looking around at the people gathered there. There were six of his own troopers, plus two combat controllers who were already setting up their tactical radios. Kneeling in the center of the room with their hands locked behind their heads were three Americans in U.S. Air Force uniforms. Karpov glanced at them, then jerked his head toward the stairs. Three of his men yanked the Americans to their feet and prodded them out of the room, while Karpov walked over to the north windows and looked out.

"Report."

One of the combat controllers looked up from what he was doing. "Sir. The first transport was destroyed by a missile while it was refueling, and -"

"I have eyes in my head, Lieutenant." Across the ramp from the tower, smoke from the burning AN-124 cast a pall across the sky.

The lieutenant caught himself. "Of course, sir. It appears there was a force of American Stryker combat vehicles that attacked the airfield before withdrawing."

"Withdrawing where?"

"We, ah... we don't know that yet, Colonel."

"They had to come from Fort Richardson," Karpov said. "Where is our armor?"

"We're just trying to raise them now, sir."

"'Trying?'" Karpov turned. "You mean you haven't been in contact with them at all?"

The lieutenant stiffened. His sergeant continued working on the radios, pretending not to hear. "We have had... technical issues, sir. We think the mechanized force is on the wrong frequency."

"Don't you have a data link to their computers? Contact them through that!"

"Yes, sir, we were supposed to be able to connect to their command and control computers, but there is no connectivity as of yet." He lowered his eyes. "Soon, Colonel."

Karpov growled and waved the man off, turning back to the windows. To the west, he could just make out another cloud of smoke, this one coming from a large container ship in the channel abeam the port. Several other ships were maneuvering around it. Karpov picked up a pair of binoculars and took a closer look. Just to the south of the burning ship, he saw another vessel rapidly approaching. It was one of the landing ships.

Karpov handed the binoculars to the lieutenant. "Perhaps if you had thought to look out the window, young man, you might have saved me the trouble." He pointed to the west. "Our armor is late, but it will be here soon."

CHAPTER NINE

Frigus Manus a Mortuis

Port of Anchorage
  Anchorage, Alaska

Major Dorogoi watched with satisfaction as the last of the Armatas rolled through the *Petr Morgunov's* open bow doors. From his position standing in the open commander's hatch on his Bumerang, he raised a hand in salute to Captain Belanov, who was watching the unloading from the overhead catwalk. Belanov returned the salute, grinning with satisfaction. Dorogoi's driver took them out close behind the Armatas, and the group sped across a gravel loading area toward the bluff several hundred meters distant.

Dorogoi dropped down into the seat, closing the hatch behind him. He checked his command console and radios, but couldn't seem to raise the airborne force at the airfield. Sending a secure message to the rest of his vehicles, he warned communications were down and the situation ahead was unknown. The Bumerang jolted as it crested the first of two bluffs between them and the base. Dorogoi checked his video periscope and saw several large columns of smoke rising from the air base several kilometers distant. He keyed his radio.

"All *Strelka* elements, expect enemy resistance, unknown strength. Eliminate all threats."

Elmendorf Air Force Base

"Where are we going, Sergeant?" Hume asked as Kirkpatrick drove the cruiser onto a sidewalk to avoid two wrecked cars blocking the road.

"My place."

Hume braced a hand on the dashboard. She shot him a sidelong look and raised an eyebrow. "Hardly the time for that, even if you *were* my type."

"That's *not* what I had in mind, Airman." Kirkpatrick yanked the car around a corner, sliding sideways before correcting. "I have some weapons in my room."

"That's against regulations," Hume said, smiling. "'Personal weapons are to be securely stored at the Security Police armory,'" she quoted. "I'm shocked at you, Sergeant."

"Stupidest regulation there ever was," Kirkpatrick said. "Military personnel living on a military base aren't allowed access to their own firearms? We might just be glad that I broke that particular rule before the day is out."

"What kind of weapons are we talking about? You don't have a main battle tank in the parking lot, do you?"

"No, but I do have a .338 Lapua Magnum with plenty of ammunition. Got a really nice spotting scope for you, too."

"What were you saving those for?"

"Moose."

"Did you ever get one?"

"Never even saw one, in three years of hunting. Saw plenty of bears, though, which made me glad I bought the rifle." He turned the car in to a lot in front of a large dormitory building and slid to a stop next to the curb. "Let's go."

Inside, several people were just milling around in the hallway, talking excitedly. Kirkpatrick looked at them for a moment, then raised his voice. "What are y'all doing? The base is under attack! Get your gear and report to your duty stations! MOVE!"

One young airman wearing shorts and sandals spoke up. "What are we supposed to do about it? We don't have any weapons. I'm a mechanic, for crying out loud! What, you want me to threaten 'em with an oil change? We're better off staying in our rooms."

Kirkpatrick stepped up and got in the young man's face. "You didn't join the military to stay in your room and watch a war on TV," he said. "Get your butt to your duty station. Your supervisors will give you instructions when you get there. I'm going upstairs for a couple of minutes. If you're still here when I come back down, I'll shoot you myself." Kirkpatrick glared at him, and the young man backed away. The rest of the people followed suit, vanishing into their rooms to get dressed or heading for the exits if they already were.

"Come on." Kirkpatrick headed up the stairs, and Hume followed. Her partner might be slightly out of shape, but he certainly didn't seem to lack anything where determination was concerned.

Twenty minutes later, they were on the roof of the base fitness center, covered by a camouflage blanket, watching the control tower through their scopes.

"Seems kinda crowded up there," Hume said, adjusting the focus on her spotting scope.

"I can't make out too many details, but I can tell those are *not* American uniforms. Same stuff the guys we tangled with on the ramp were wearing."

"So? What do we do? You start taking pot shots, they're gonna pinpoint us up here right away."

Kirkpatrick had to admit that he hadn't thought that part through. He couldn't very well take on the entire Russian Army with one rifle. They could observe and report - if they could reach anybody on the radio to report to. So what were they *supposed* to be doing? "You're right," he said. "But there has to be somebody mounting some kind of defense, and they're gonna want to know what these guys are doing. So we sit here a while, and try to figure out what they're up to."

Hume turned to look at him. "All due respect, Sergeant - I think it's pretty obvious what they're up to."

Kirkpatrick kept looking through his scope. "I know. But beyond just watching them take over the base, we can estimate their strength, maybe keep an eye on their movements, get an idea what they're planning next. Maybe then we can pass that info along."

"To who?" Hume unclipped her radio handset from her shoulder and waggled it at him. "Nobody home, remember?"

Kirkpatrick took his eye away from the scope. "We're gonna have to cross that bridge when we get to it, all right? Let's just keep our eyes open."

Frostbite One
Elmendorf Air Force Base

The group of Strykers had retreated back to the east, but had been forced to turn around when they ran into more Russian airborne troops who had dropped on Fort Richardson behind them. Things were getting very much out of hand. Nugent had taken his small force to the south, where they were now hiding in a thick stand of trees south of the Davis Highway. He knew they couldn't stay there for long.

"We need a plan here, boss." Nugent eyed Lieutenant Leggett, sitting quietly in the driver's seat. He was afraid that the nervous young officer might be slipping back into indecision, but protocol still forced him to defer to the man's higher rank. "Ell-Tee?"

Leggett looked up. "Sorry, Sergeant. I was just thinking - we didn't see any armor. Just ground troops, not even any APCs, right?"

"That's right, sir. But at least some of those troops are carrying missiles that can obviously penetrate our reactive armor. That levels the playing field some."

"Roger that. But we still need to go back and take the fight to them. How many of those missile teams do you think they'll have?"

Nugent shook his head. "Ballpark? Four or five teams, maybe more, depending on the size of their invasion force. Enough to be a very real threat."

"What if we just keep moving - hit and run tactics?"

"They'll tweak to it pretty quick - all they have to do is get a missile team up high someplace where they have a clear shot at us in the open. We'll get our licks in, but they're gonna hit back."

"What's the alternative? Running?"

"Pretty much. We already hit 'em pretty hard, Ell-Tee. Two cargo planes, plus a bunch of troops out of the fight. We did good."

"You saying you think we're done?"

Nugent realized that a change was coming over Leggett. The officer seemed less willing to just give up than he had been at the vehicle park less than an hour earlier. Whatever problems he'd had with the Army before today, he was starting to forget them. He just might rise to the occasion. "No sir, I don't think we're done. I just think our odds are gonna get progressively worse the longer we stay in this fight. It's my job to point out both sides of the issue to you, so you can make an informed decision. We stay and fight, it might be the last bad decision we ever make."

Leggett nodded. "I get it, Sergeant. But you were right earlier, when you told me I'd never forgive myself if I didn't do something. None of us will. I'd at least like the chance to do something worthwhile, even if it's a lost cause."

"That works for me," Nugent said.

"Good deal. So - if you have suggestions for how to go about this, I'd sure appreciate it."

Nugent nodded. "I might have one idea."

The *Frostbite* vehicles had split up, each Stryker taking a position well east of the runways at Elmendorf, yet still hidden in the trees. They were in line abreast, about a half mile apart. Nugent's plan was to attack as individual vehicles across a wide front, hopefully spreading panic and confusion over as large an area as possible. The control tower was the ultimate goal, since the Russians seemed to be concentrating there earlier, but each vehicle commander was given discretion to engage other targets at will on the way.

While they had been regrouping, several additional transports had dropped their paratroopers and landed to refuel. These were all smaller IL-76 aircraft, but they were inviting targets nevertheless. Nugent, still in the vehicle commander's seat, checked in one last time with the other Strykers.

"All *Frostbite* elements, report ready."

"*Two.*"

"*Three.*"

"*Five.*"

"All elements, advance. Good hunting, troops." Leggett mashed the accelerator and the big vehicle jumped forward. Capable of speeds approaching seventy miles per hour, the Stryker was faster than most every other ground combat vehicle in the world. They accelerated across a road, bouncing through a drainage ditch on the other side and lurching up onto the airfield. Bullets started smacking the vehicles as they crossed the north-south runway, and Nugent tensed as he saw a soldier touch off a rocket propelled grenade, the exhaust plume showing bright on Nugent's thermal camera. But the soldier hadn't compensated for the speed of the vehicle, and the grenade detonated well behind them, sending chunks of broken concrete airborne in their wake.

A tactical ATV with three troops on board rounded a hangar in front of them, the man standing in the back firing a light machine gun mounted on its roll cage in their direction. Nugent selected his Bushmaster auto cannon and cut loose a long volley, smashing the little vehicle in a hail of 30mm bullets. Leggett didn't even need to slow down. They turned north onto the parallel taxiway and raced toward the tower.

The pattering noise of light ammunition impacting the Stryker's hull was joined by a deeper, intermittent thunk that Nugent assumed was caused by a heavy sniper rifle. He scanned his command console, letting the thermal camera pick out heat signatures for him.

He could see at least ten silhouettes in the tower cab. The smoke they'd seen earlier had vanished, and there were clearly people using the cab, so it couldn't have been too badly damaged. He could make out two heat signatures on the roof of the tower as well. *There's your sniper,* he thought. "Raines, hit the tower cab with that Gustaf! Possible sniper on the roof!"

"Roger," Raines called from behind Nugent. The rear overhead hatch popped open, and the unmuffled noise of the Bushmaster suddenly filled the vehicle as Nugent fired a long burst at the tower to keep the sniper's head down.

"Keep it nice and steady 'til he fires, Lieutenant."

"Roger."

"On the way!" Raines sounded positively elated as he pulled the trigger. The missile streaked away, climbing with deadly speed toward the top of the tower.

Colonel Karpov looked just in time to see the missile launch from the approaching Stryker. He knew as soon as he saw it that he was a dead man. There was no time to run, or hide, or even to duck. Not that any of those things would have helped if there had been time.

Karpov swore under his breath, watching in morbid fascination as death sped toward him.

The missile entered the tower cab through a shattered window and impacted on the ceiling inside. The explosion killed Colonel Karpov and everyone else in the cab while violently lifting the entire roof upward a couple of feet. The sniper and spotter on the roof were both catapulted over the low parapet. The sniper was killed outright by the concussion of the explosion, but the spotter survived, only to be killed by the long fall to the roof of the base building more than a hundred feet below.

"All *Frostbite* elements, control tower is out of service; watch for snipers on the other rooftops. Keep moving!"

"Frostbite One, *this is* Three, *we just took out a guy with an SA-25; he was looking your way and didn't see us until it was too late. There's gotta be more of these guys out there, though.*"

"Frostbite Five *just took a missile hit in the right rear wheel! We're still mobile, but the shooter got under cover.*"

"Frostbite Two's *engaging the aircraft on the ramp - we got a lotta ground pounders in the open, we could use some help!*"

"*Frostbite Two, Frostbite One,*" Nugent called. "We're south of you, coming up the ramp below the tower. Keep your speed up all the way to the west end of the field and disengage to the south, we'll bring up the rear. *Frostbite Three* and *Five*, disengage ASAP. We'll meet at Point Bravo in an hour."

"*Frostbite Five, wilco.*"

"*Frostbite Three, wilco.*"

In less than two minutes, the force of Strykers had wreaked havoc on the Russian landing forces, taking out three IL-76 cargo aircraft and at least a hundred troops, not to mention knocking out the tower and killing the ground force commander and most of his staff in the process.

It was more than they had hoped for - but still, it wouldn't be nearly enough.

Strelka One
Elmendorf Air Force Base

Major Dorogoi watched the magnified camera on his command and control console as the Bumerang crested the second bluff, and was shocked to see that the smoke he'd spotted earlier was coming from several aircraft burning in the distance. *The airborne units were supposed to avoid destroying the American aircraft - but, no - at least two of those planes are Russian.* The reality of that caught him off guard as he tried to figure out what was happening.

He spotted the speeding American APC at almost the same moment that it spotted him. The vehicle swerved off the runway to the south, as a man at the rear hatch fired a missile directly at them.

"Missile launch, twelve o'clock!" Dorogoi shouted. The driver jerked the Bumerang to the left and accelerated, but the only thing that saved them was the sudden turn of the Stryker in the opposite direction, which caused its vehicle commander to miss the Bumerang with his laser designator. Without the laser to guide it, the American missile had nothing to home in on and simply flew a straight path from the end of the launcher. It barely missed the turret of an Armata that was just cresting the hill behind Dorogoi's Bumerang, then streaked across the top of the bluff and out over the water of the Cook Inlet beyond.

Frostbite One

"Enemy armor inbound from the west; Frostbite One, break off now!"

The panicked call forced Nugent to drag his attention away from a group of Russian troops fleeing from his Bushmaster across the ramp to his right. Checking his front, he saw *Frostbite Two* veering away to the south. The telltale smoke trail of a missile pointed away to the west, directly over the top of an approaching Armata main battle tank, its cannon traversing in the direction of the retreating Stryker. What looked like a Russian Bumerang APC was veering away northward.

"Raines! Target, tank, twelve o'clock!" Even as he spoke, the Armata's big gun recoiled, rocking the tank backward against its suspension. The shot went slightly high, but the 152mm shell clipped the rear right corner of *Frostbite Two's* roof, right behind the soldier holding the Carl Gustaf in the rear hatch. That soldier simply vaporized from the chest up, and the force of the shell knocked the Stryker into an oblique cartwheel over its front left corner like a cheap toy in a whirlwind. The vehicle came to rest on its side, with its nose pointing back the direction it had come. The Armata was already traversing its turret back around to engage *Frostbite One*.

"HIT THAT SUCKER, RAINES!" Nugent shouted. Leggett had the accelerator mashed to the floor, and they were closing the distance to the tank alarmingly fast. This time, Raines didn't bother to call out the shot before he fired. He just screamed in defiance as he pulled the trigger, certain that he was seconds from death himself; but he needn't have worried. It was a perfect shot.

Nugent held the laser designator at the base of the Armata's turret, right where it mated with the body of the vehicle. The 84mm missile struck just to the left of the cannon, beneath the edge of the turret. The force of the explosion was so great that it knocked the turret out of alignment with its track, effectively locking it in place. The greater effect was that the warhead had detonated directly on one of the Armata's few weak points, and the blast forced an opening between the turret and the body, penetrating inside the crew compartment. The entire crew was killed instantly by the overpressure and superheated explosive of the shaped charge, and the big tank lurched to a drunken stop at the end of the runway.

"Break left, Ell-Tee!" Nugent called out. "Close on Two, look for survivors!" Leggett wrenched the vehicle to the left, even as another Bumerang came over the top of the bluff at the edge of the airfield. One of the soldiers in the back was swearing and trying to pass another round up to Raines, who was shouting at him to hurry up.

"You see anybody moving, Sergeant?" Leggett asked, straining to see *Frostbite Two* through the pall of smoke hanging in front of them.

Nugent switched to his thermal camera. "I got a couple of survivors climbing out of the back hatch, Lieutenant. We're eighty yards out, don't run over 'em!" He glanced back at the men behind him. "You boys get ready for a hot evac - we're gonna roll up and grab these guys and then bug the hell out!"

Elmendorf Fitness Center

"So, you must be some kind of terrible hunter."

Kirkpatrick pulled his eye away from his rifle scope and cocked an eyebrow at Hume. "What makes you say that?"

"Well, you said you'd been hunting moose for three years, and never even saw one. We chase them off the runways at least three times a week. Shoot, they graze on people's front lawns in the middle of base housing. So how come you couldn't find one out in the woods?"

Kirkpatrick turned back to his scope. "Because moose are evil, spiteful animals that love to torment me, that's how come," he grumbled.

Hume grinned. "Well, I hope you're better at hitting your targets than you are at finding them."

"Shut up, Airman."

"Shutting up, Sergeant." She swiveled her spotting scope on its tripod.

"Is that a Stryker?" Kirkpatrick was looking to the east.

Hume pointed her scope in that direction and saw one of the vehicles racing westbound on runway 24, half a mile from midfield. "Whoa!" she flinched as a sudden explosion ripped into the control tower to their right. She saw one body fall from the roof of the tower, twisting in a surreal free fall until it hit the base building.

"Look at that!" Kirkpatrick said. "That's what I'm talking about!"

Hume swung her scope to follow Kirkpatrick's, and watched as the westbound Stryker's roof mounted machine gun ripped through a group of Russian soldiers. Another Stryker emerged from behind the control tower, following the first down the runway at high speed. Hume swung her scope all the way to the west end of the runway, looking for more American vehicles. She was surprised to see another vehicle cresting the bank off the west end of the runway. It looked different than the first two.

"Here come the Russians," Kirkpatrick said, as the lead Stryker veered wildly to the south. A soldier standing in the rear hatch fired a missile that sailed away above the Russian APC, missing it by twenty feet. A Russian tank appeared at the top of the bank and swung its cannon around, firing a quick shot at the Stryker. As the big cannon round struck home and flipped the American APC end over end, the second Stryker bore down on the tank. The soldier in its rear hatch fired off a missile that detonated at the base of the tank's turret, which froze in position as the tank veered off like a wounded animal. The second Stryker swerved south and raced toward the damaged one.

"We need to get out of here," Kirkpatrick said, as another Russian APC crested the hill. "Those guys are gonna get wiped out, and that'll be it." From their vantage point on the roof, they could see a line of Russian vehicles crossing the open area west of the airfield about a mile away.

"Where are the rest of our guys?" Hume lamented.

"I'm surprised the Army managed to even get two Strykers moving. They hardly ever take those things off the lot since the drawdown. They just don't have enough people to do much large unit training any more." He collected his rifle and started moving in a crouch to the roof access ladder with Hume following behind him. As they started down, the Stryker crew disembarked to look for survivors from the other vehicle.

Kirkpatrick led the way back to their cruiser at a run. They got in the car and headed south, away from the fighting.

"Doesn't feel right running away like this, Sergeant," Hume said.

"I know," Kirkpatrick said. "But either we pull a tactical retreat now, or we commit suicide by trying to fight a heavy mechanized force with a deer rifle. Sometimes, discretion is the better part of valor."

Hume slumped in her seat. Admitting defeat felt like a betrayal. She felt like all the life had gone out of her, and she wasn't sure how she'd ever get it back.

Strelka One

"All *Strelka* units, the airfield is under attack by enemy mechanized force, strength unknown. APCs in the open; engage at will!" Dorogoi was furious at the lack of communication with their airborne force. If the radios had been working, they could have warned his column of the American vehicles. Dorogoi had no way of knowing that the airborne force had been given the wrong frequency during their mission brief; one of the many things that could have gone wrong in an operation with thousands of moving parts. *Fog of War, indeed*, Dorogoi thought.

He was about to direct his driver to turn around when he saw another vehicle flash through the gap between two large hangars, heading north. Dorogoi quickly targeted the fleeing Stryker with his 57mm auto cannon and let loose a quick burst. Capable of firing a hundred and twenty rounds per minute, the roof-mounted cannon ripped off ten rounds in half as many seconds, missing the Stryker by a couple of feet as it disappeared behind another building.

"Driver, continue north! Enemy infantry fighting vehicle, two o'clock, one thousand meters!" The driver responded by accelerating and turning slightly to the right to join a taxiway northbound. Dorogoi spotted the Stryker again, now bouncing across a parking lot past several static displays of Vietnam-era fighter aircraft. If the vehicle got past one more building, it would be through the perimeter fence and into the trees beyond.

"Faster!" Dorogoi shouted, and they broke into the open. Dorogoi had a clear view as the Stryker slowed to climb an embankment just inside the fence. The Russian officer squeezed the trigger on his weapons control joystick, and a line of white-hot tracers reached out for the American.

Frostbite Five

Strykers are very resilient, capable combat vehicles, well loved by most of the soldiers who serve on them. But nothing is completely indestructible, and the crew of *Frostbite Five* were acutely aware of that fact as they tried desperately to escape the firefight. The driver was struggling to keep the big vehicle moving in a straight line, as something around the damaged right rear wheel was dragging and scraping, causing the steering to feel sluggish while constantly pulling the truck to the right. *Must be damage to more than just the one wheel,* the driver thought.

"We've got company!" the vehicle commander shouted. "Something's behind us on the left, looked like an APC! Get us into the trees!"

The driver had to slow slightly to climb a steep embankment before they smashed through the perimeter fence and into the cover of the trees beyond. As he did, the vehicle commander spotted their pursuer emerging from behind a hangar, moving fast.

"Enemy APC, seven o'clock!" The commander swung his Bushmaster around and tried to engage the enemy. He was just depressing the trigger when the 57mm Russian projectiles ripped into his vehicle. The reactive ceramic armor on the Stryker stopped the first dozen rounds, but the Russian kept hitting the same spot in the hull, and his heavy bullets quickly pulverized the ceramic and penetrated into the troop compartment.

Strelka One

Dorogoi kept squeezing the trigger, watching through his video sight as the Stryker shuddered under the barrage. He could tell when the American armor gave out, because the dust and shrapnel at the point of impact lessened as the rounds suddenly found their way through the weakened hull and expended their energy inside. The Stryker shuddered and stopped, just short of the fence at the top of the embankment.

"Check for survivors," Dorogoi said as the driver brought the Bumerang to a halt next to the wrecked APC. "I want one of them for questioning!" Three infantrymen clambered out the rear door and ran toward the rear of the smoking Stryker.

Frostbite One

"GET A MOVE ON!!" Nugent shouted. They couldn't stay here. More Russian APCs were climbing the rise to the airfield. Raines had managed to disable the first Bumerang as it crested the rise, temporarily blocking the narrow cut the Russians had been coming up in single file. Nugent knew it wouldn't last - the enemy would spread out and take the steeper bank around the cut all at once, and that would end it.

Three of Nugent's men were out of the vehicle now, dragging and carrying four survivors from the overturned wreck of *Frostbite Two*. Nugent watched as the nose of another Armata tank crested the bank several hundred yards away, and he lit it up with his laser designator. "Raines! Target, enemy tank, FIRE!"

The crack of the Carl Gustaf filled the air, followed by the fabric-ripping sound of the missile as it streaked away. The warhead hit under the front of the Armata as it tilted upward cresting the lip of the rise, and smashed into the inside of the track on the left side. The tread snapped and came off, and the tank slewed wildly around to the left. The turret started rotating toward them as the tank ground to a halt.

"Hit 'em again!" Nugent shouted as he opened up with the Bushmaster. His rounds had no effect on the tank's armor, but he was targeting the tank commander's sensor array, which housed all his cameras. If he could wreck that, the commander would be blind and the tank considerably less dangerous.

Raines touched off another missile from the Carl Gustaf as the tank fired its main gun. But because of the awkward angle of the tank body, the gun couldn't traverse quite far enough to reach *Frostbite One*. Instead, the round shrieked overhead and smashed into the roof of a three story barracks building half a mile to the south. Nugent's crew came back at the same time, staggering from the shock of the barrage so close at hand. In spite of that, they dragged the four survivors from *Frostbite Two* on board.

"Time to go, Ell-Tee!" Nugent shouted at Leggett. "Head southwest, keep those trees on our right as you go over the embankment!" Nugent wanted to rejoin with *Frostbite Three* and *Frostbite Five,* but turning immediately back to the north in the face of the arriving Russian mechanized force would be suicide. They had to survive first.

The Stryker's passenger compartment was jammed to capacity with the four extra soldiers, and they were all thrown around and jostled as Leggett drove the vehicle off the embankment and tore across an open field to the southwest. A copse of trees shielded them from view of the approaching Russian forces until they were a quarter mile from the airfield; then they broke into the open and were exposed for three hundred yards.

Several of the Bumerangs spotted them and tried to bring their weapons to bear, but the speeding Stryker was across the gap and under cover again before any of the Russians could get a solid bead on them. Two Bumerangs fired Kornet anti-tank missiles at them without waiting for a target lock, and both missiles streaked into the thick trees between the vehicles and exploded there without doing any damage. After that, the Russian forces kept going toward the airfield, not bothering to pursue the single fleeing Stryker.

Frostbite One had escaped - for the moment.

CHAPTER TEN

Et Nuntiaverunt Observe

Frostbite Three

Staff Sergeant Blanca Trujillo, in command of *Frostbite Three,* had ordered her vehicle away to the north as soon as Nugent called the retreat. They hadn't gone far before they ran into heavy resistance from a cluster of Russian ground troops near a command and control building on the north side of the runway. They'd taken one glancing hit from a shoulder-fired missile that had failed to detonate properly before Trujillo had used her Bushmaster auto cannon to shred the Russian shooter.

Now they were moving toward the north base perimeter again, but the brief delay had allowed *Frostbite Five,* which had been slightly behind them and several hundred yards to their west, to pull away northbound and lose contact. *Frostbite Three* sped between two parked C-17 cargo aircraft, racing for the cover of the forest outside the perimeter fence. Then Trujillo saw bright flashes to her northwest that could only come from a heavy machine gun of some type. She ordered her driver to angle that way, keeping buildings between them and the source of the gunfire for as long as possible.

"*Frostbite Five*, say position." Trujillo's call was met only with static. They emerged from behind the last building and saw what they had feared; *Frostbite Five* wrecked and smoking on a steep embankment, with a Russian Bumerang parked several yards away, its big auto cannon pointed at a gaping hole in the Stryker's left side. The Bumerang's rear hatch was open, and three Russian soldiers were running toward the Stryker, weapons raised.

The sight made Trujillo feel like she'd just been kicked. Centering the Bushmaster's crosshairs on the Bumerang's open hatch, she fired a burst directly into the interior of the vehicle. The three dismounted soldiers all dove for cover, but Trujillo quickly found them and cut them all down with the Bushmaster before they could hope to fight back.

"Booth, Meyers and James - go look for survivors, and be quick about it! Ortiz, give 'em cover; there's bound to be more bad guys close by!" Trujillo watched her video screen for threats as her three soldiers dismounted and ran to the wreckage of *Frostbite Five*. They opened the rear hatch and climbed inside, disappearing from her view.

"Come on, come on," her driver muttered, as the seconds dragged on.

Trujillo kept her eyes on her periscope cameras, but couldn't shake the feeling that they were sitting ducks. The urge to get her crew away was visceral and almost overpowering. By the time her guys started backing out of the disabled Stryker, carrying an injured man between them, she thought that she could hear her own heart pounding. "Ortiz, help 'em out!"

Ortiz slung his rifle and sprinted across the open space between the vehicles, helping his buddies carry the bloodied driver of *Frostbite Five* back to their own Stryker. They scrambled over the lowered rear ramp, laying the injured man on the deck at their feet as the door closed behind them.

"He's the only one," Private Carroll Booth said. His face was pale and he looked stunned.

"Let's go!" Trujillo ordered. The driver spun the Stryker around to the northeast, accelerating away from the scene. They smashed through the perimeter fence and plunged into the pine forest beyond, following an overgrown logging road that helped to conceal their passing. Trujillo glanced back to see Meyers and Ortiz working on the injured man, who looked more dead than alive. "You guys sure he was the only survivor?"

Corporal James looked up. "I'm surprised *he* made it, Sergeant," he said. "The inside of that truck looked like a slaughterhouse."

"Roger that," Trujillo said. She went back to scanning her cameras for threats, but she couldn't shake the feeling that it wouldn't ultimately make a difference. The fact was, they were hugely outnumbered and outgunned. They could continue to run - but for how long? Eventually, they would run out of fuel, ammunition, or food; or even more likely, the Russians would catch up to them, and they'd all end up blown to shreds, just like their friends on *Frostbite Five*.

Frostbite One

"More armor, straight ahead!" Leggett shouted.

"Turn left!" Nugent shouted back. "Down that little track!" They'd inadvertently driven right into the teeth of more vehicles coming up the hill from the port. Now Leggett veered off the road onto a narrow gravel track leading south through some trees, as several Russian vehicles fired at them, all missing as *Frostbite One* vanished into the woods. The trees ended fifty yards further on, and the Americans found themselves roaring through Cherry Hill, a neighborhood of mostly vacant, run down two-story apartments that had once been housing for military families stationed at Elmendorf. Now the buildings were derelict except for a few units that had been converted to low-income government housing.

There didn't seem to be any residents around. Leggett accelerated down the residential street, leaving the pavement where it came to a tee and continuing south across a wide lawn before jumping back onto the asphalt on the other side.

Nugent had the uneasy sense that they were painting themselves into a corner the further they went. As they approached the long entrance road that led to Arctic Warrior Drive and Elmendorf's southwest gate, he checked the cameras behind them, but they weren't being followed. Even so, his inner voice was screaming at him.

"Lieutenant, turn right! Pull in there!"

Leggett did as he was told, steering the Stryker down a narrow maintenance road that led to a small concrete cul-de-sac in front of a utility building surrounded on three sides by thick trees.

Leggett pulled up close to the trees on the south side of the cul-de-sac. "What are we doing, Sergeant?"

Nugent was frantically looking at the scrolling map on his video display. "Take a look at this, sir." He highlighted an area on the other side of the trees, a quarter mile to the south. "That gate is a choke point. We need to get through it if we want to get to the highway without having to cross the rail yards, here. But I'm afraid if we go through there, we'll run into more of the enemy, because it's a natural attack route into the base, too."

"It didn't look to me like the Russians were coming that way," Leggett said doubtfully. "Aren't they all behind us?"

"Some are, yeah," Nugent admitted. "But we have no way of knowing if that's all of them or not."

Leggett scowled. "You're the resident expert here, Sergeant - I've never been in combat until today. If you ask me, I think we need to get the heck outta Dodge, and sooner rather than later. But I'm deferring to you as to how we go about it. What do you think we should do?"

"I think we should go, but I think we should go carefully,"

Nugent said. "Racing onto the airfield like we just did worked fine, until the Russian armor showed up. We do that again, we're likely to run right into the middle of a bigger fight than we can handle."

"We almost did that already." Leggett flashed a tired grin.

Nugent nodded. "So, let's be a little more cautious. Now that we know the Russians didn't just bring infantry, we need to really watch our backs. We only have so many anti-tank missiles for the Carl Gustaf, and if we get into a slugging match without the element of surprise, they're gonna hammer us."

"We need to hide this vehicle. It sticks out like a sore thumb."

"Yes sir, but the first problem is getting out of the combat zone with it."

"Hey Sarge," Raines called from the back of the Stryker. "We aint givin' up, are we?"

Nugent rolled his head around, trying to stretch his neck. "No," he said. "We're not giving up. But we can't hurt the Russians if we're dead, so we're gonna figure out how to stay alive before we do anything else." He turned in his seat and looked at the four men they'd rescued from the wreckage of *Frostbite Two*. They all looked like they were in shock.

Leggett followed his gaze. "We could go back to the truck park," he said. Grab another Stryker, more ammunition. Then bug out north and hook up with the others."

Nugent swore under his breath. In the confusion of the attack, rescue and escape, he'd forgotten about the other two Strykers in their force. He checked his command and control screen, trying to locate them on it, but their icons didn't show up. Either they'd been destroyed, or his equipment wasn't working. He keyed his radio.

"*Frostbite Five, Frostbite One*. How do you hear?" Nugent let his hands drop into his lap. There was no response. "*Frostbite Five, Frostbite One*." Again, static. "*Frostbite Three, Frostbite One*, acknowledge."

Leggett watched him. "Maybe they're out of the fight."

"If that's true, then grabbing another Stryker may not be a bad idea. We're too crowded in here, and -"

" - One, Frostbite Three." The call was broken and faint. *"We're not picking up your location on our system. Where are you?"*

Nugent sighed in relief. *"Frostbite Three,* we got driven south of the airfield by a large number of enemy vehicles. *Two's* out of the fight; we picked up four of their crew. We're laying low right now - looks like our vehicle network is down for some reason. What's your status?"

"Frostbite Five's *destroyed. We got there in time to take out an APC crew that was trying to take prisoners from the wreck, but there was only one survivor, and he's in really bad shape. We're about a mile away from Point Bravo. Haven't seen any enemy activity since we crossed the wire."*

"Understood. We saw a lot of those Bumerang APCs, and at least two of the new Armata main battle tanks. We barely got away."

"Roger. What do we do now?"

Nugent looked across at Leggett. "Ell-Tee?"

Leggett looked back in the passenger compartment at the remainder of *Frostbite Two's* crew. "You guys good to go?"

The four men looked at each other before a corporal spoke up. "We're still in it, Ell-Tee."

Leggett nodded, then keyed his own radio. *"Frostbite Three,* is there any way you can get your casualty to a hospital?"

"Unless you know of someplace else, the closest one to us is back at the base. I'm pretty sure the Russians are between it and our position. You want us to try and go there?"

"Can you stabilize him, *Three?"*

"Affirmative. We got his bleeding stopped and got an IV going. He should be OK for now."

Leggett nodded, then looked at Nugent. *"Frostbite Three,* roger. We're not gonna make Point Bravo; we're too far in the wrong direction already. Go ahead to the hide site we agreed on and wait for us there. We'll come to you, but it may take us some time."

"Frostbite Three, *roger. Good luck.*"

Leggett looked at the men in back. "I need a volunteer."

Post Road Gate
Elmendorf Air Force Base

"Looks like we found where everybody went." Kirkpatrick slowed the cruiser as they approached a long line of civilian vehicles backed up inside the gate, trying to leave the base via Pease Road. He hit the rooftop flashers and maneuvered onto the shoulder. Closer to the gate itself, they could see several people involved in an altercation centered on two vehicles with crumpled fenders. Two Security Police officers were desperately trying to separate the people and restore some kind of order.

Kirkpatrick hit the siren, stopped the car and got out. "You people break it up! Get back in your vehicles and clear this road, right now!"

One of the drivers involved in the accident cursed at him, then took a wild swing at the other man, who was dressed in Air Force fatigues. Kirkpatrick had seen enough. Pulling his sidearm, he fired two quick shots into the gravel at the feet of the first man. The man stumbled backward and tripped, landing on his backside in the grass at the side of the road. Kirkpatrick was moving forward quickly, his weapon up and trained on the man's forehead.

"I said, break it up! You idiots realize we're under attack? You gonna stand here and throw down until the Russians come and shoot you all?" He glanced at one of the SPs. "Airman, escort this jerk to his vehicle, and see that he moves it out of the road. If he gives you any trouble or does anything besides *exactly* what he's told, you *shoot him*, do you understand?"

"Got it, Sergeant." The visibly relieved airman stepped over and hoisted the man off the ground by his elbow, propelling him back to his car. Kirkpatrick turned to the man in uniform, only then noticing that he was an officer.

"Major, where's your duty station?" Kirkpatrick was annoyed to see an officer in the middle of a crowd of fleeing military dependents, and obviously away from his post.

The major was flustered, but answered the question. "I work in supply and logistics. I was just getting off shift…"

"Fine," Kirkpatrick cut him off. "You're back on shift now, sir. We need to clear this mess out of the road and get these people moving off base. The Russians aren't gonna be long behind us, and we don't want them to show up and start shooting."

"What… what do you expect me to do?"

Kirkpatrick glared at him. "You're an officer, sir. Act like one. You don't get to be at the front of the line. You stay here and help us direct traffic, so these people can get away. When they're gone, we'll follow."

"You can't talk to me that way, Sergeant. I'm -"

Kirkpatrick stepped closer, putting his nose almost against the major's. "You're either going to help us, Major, or I'm going to place you under arrest, handcuff you, and leave you sitting by the side of the road while the rest of us evacuate. It's been a really rough morning for me, sir, and at this point I don't much care what rank you're wearing." He pointed with his pistol at the major's dented car. "First off, move that wreck off the road. Then you can walk back down the line and start splitting half the cars off into the inbound lanes. Nobody's gonna be using them. Let the traffic merge up as they get closer to the highway and away from this bottleneck."

The major stared for a moment, then got back in his car and did as he was told. Kirkpatrick watched him to be sure he wasn't going to try to force his way out, then turned to look for Hume. She was already moving down the line of cars, giving instructions and getting the tangled traffic to start moving.

Fifteen minutes later, most of the cars were through the gate, and the line of traffic was dwindling as it spread out along Pease Road, when Kirkpatrick thought he heard diesel engines approaching. He paused to look, and his heart dropped as three Russian Bumerang APCs crested the hill a quarter mile away, coming fast toward the gate.

"Lucy!" Kirkpatrick shouted. "Let's go!"

Hume turned and started running toward him. The two gate guards were already in a civilian vehicle, tires kicking up loose gravel as they accelerated through the gate and away. The major, his own car too damaged to drive further, was running after them, waving his arms. Then the lead Bumerang opened up with its auto cannon.

The first rounds went high, just over their heads, shredding the roof and windows on the gate house. "Down! Get down!" Kirkpatrick yelled at Hume, knowing they would never get in their car and away before they were cut to pieces. "Get on the ground!" Hume dropped on her face on the pavement and extended her hands ahead of her. Kirkpatrick was on his face too, but the fleeing supply officer didn't listen.

The 30mm rounds ripped him into a bloody ruin as he ran. He flopped to the ground, dead before he slid to a stop. Kirkpatrick didn't see it, but the sound of the barrage was enough. He felt his skin crawling as he waited for the next burst to tear into him, but it didn't come. Face down, he heard the Bumerang's engine noise getting uncomfortably close, then an accented voice boomed over a loudspeaker, making him flinch.

"Hands on head! If you move, we will shoot you! Hands on head!"

Kirkpatrick's head was turned the wrong way, so he couldn't see if Hume had been shot or not. There was nothing for him to do but comply. Very slowly, he moved his arms out wide, then bent his elbows and clasped his hands behind his head. Heavy footsteps approached, and somebody dropped a knee between his shoulder blades, driving the air from his lungs. As he gasped for breath and the Russian on his back wrenched his arms around, he could hear Lucy's gasp as another Russian gave her the same treatment.

They were prisoners of war, but at least they were both still alive.

Government Hill Elementary School
Elmendorf Air Force Base

Raines and Leggett were crouched in a thicket of evergreen trees just inside the base perimeter fence, looking at an elementary school on the other side. Just to the east of the school they had a clear view of Arctic Warrior Drive and the Government Hill gate leading onto the airbase. Leggett had left Nugent in command of *Frostbite One* on the other side of the trees and decided to take charge of the reconnaissance himself.

He was scared out of his mind, but he knew he had to step up. Nugent had been right; as the only officer, it was his duty and responsibility to lead, and this was the best way he could think of at the moment. He'd never imagined himself in combat, yet today he'd been right in the thick of a very intense running gunfight. What really surprised him, though, was that he had actually enjoyed it.

The rush of adrenaline he'd felt as the Russian vehicles were firing at them, as small arms fire pinged off the hull of their Stryker, even as Nugent had shouted out directions and curses at him in their desperate run for safety; all of it had been exhilarating in a way he couldn't have imagined before today. He was still terrified, no question about it, but he was terrified in a good way. He was becoming part of a team, part of a shared, desperate fight for survival, and that carried with it a strange mix of deep satisfaction and bowel-loosening terror.

For the first time, he felt like his decision to join the military after college hadn't been a huge mistake.

"How we gonna get past *them*, Ell-Tee?" Raines was asking.

They watched as a line of Russian Bumerangs and Armatas sped past the gate and onto the base. From what the two Americans could see, there was no opposition at the gate at all.

Leggett watched the enemy column through his binoculars. He counted three Armatas and twenty-four Bumerangs. The last Bumerang came through the gate at the rear of the column, spun around in the road, and parked next to the empty guard house as the rest of the column continued over the hill. Leggett watched for a few moments longer as several Russian soldiers climbed out of the last Bumerang and took up positions astride the road.

"Okay," Leggett said quietly. "That's their rear guard. We'll have to take them out to get by them, but at least it's just the one vehicle. Lets get back to the truck." He backed away, into the deeper cover of the trees, with Raines following.

Back aboard *Frostbite One*, Nugent considered their report. "Just the three tanks?" Nugent asked.

"Just three," Leggett said. Raines nodded.

"But two dozen APCs," Nugent continued, almost to himself. "That makes sense. They weren't expecting heavy resistance, so the tanks are just insurance. They brought mostly APCs so they could bring more troops with them. Troops that they'd need in order to occupy an airbase."

"We're sort of painted into a corner here, Sergeant," Leggett said. "If we want to get away, we should go now. We can take that one APC crew, but they might have another wave coming. If we wait, we're gonna get caught."

Nugent looked at the young officer and nodded. "You're right, Ell-Tee. How many troops did you say dismounted?"

"Just four. They set two up on each side of the road, with the APC parked right in the middle."

"We should take 'em out, and steal their ride," Raines said. We could use some more room, not to mention a little more firepower."

"That might work," Leggett said hopefully.

"No." Nugent shook his head. "It's a good idea in theory, but the reality is, their vehicles are probably data linked, just like ours. The rest of their force would be able to track exactly where we went with their APC, and we wouldn't want that. We're gonna have to take it out."

Leggett glanced at Raines and shrugged. "Ok. How do you want to do it?"

Nugent looked at the crew members they'd rescued from *Frostbite Two*. "I need a driver."

A corporal raised a bandaged hand. "I can do it, Sergeant." He had another bandage wrapped around his upper thigh, and dried blood on his forehead.

"You sure?"

"I'm sure. Just don't expect me to get out and push." He grinned weakly and dragged himself out of his seat, moving with difficulty to the driver's seat.

"Ell-Tee?" Nugent said. "You up for leading a fire team on foot?"

Leggett's heart went into his throat. Just leaving the relative safety of the Stryker earlier with Raines had been nerve-wracking. Did he *really* want to do that again?

He forced a nod. "What'd you have in mind, Sergeant?"

"I'm thinking a fire team goes through the trees south of the school, sets up to hit those guys outside of the APC. Meantime, the rest of us will loop around in the Stryker and run up on the road from behind them. They're facing out, expecting resistance to come from Anchorage, so they may not see us coming 'til it's too late. As soon as they do see us, your fire team will hit the ground troops while we engage the vehicle with the Carl Gustaf. Then we pick you guys up and hit the road. All right?"

Leggett thought about it. "Sounds good. I'll need Raines," he looked around at the rest of the men. None of *Frostbite Two's* crew were fit enough to move quickly on foot, but they could still shoot. "One of you guys will need to man the Carl Gustaf.

You two help with passing ammunition up to him." He pointed to two of his own crew. "You two, grab your rifles and come with us."

The four man team hurried through the trees and up to the fence, where Raines cut the chain link with a pair of bolt cutters he'd grabbed out of the Stryker. He stuffed them back in his pack and they all filed through the gap and onto the grounds of the elementary school, running in a crouch for the cover of trees on the west side of the building.

Once there, Leggett raised a fist and they all dropped down inside the tree line. Leggett left Raines with Private Winman, taking Private First Class Noble with him through the trees further west. They only had to go about fifty yards before they could see all four Russian soldiers on both sides of the entrance road, their APC parked in the center, facing out. Leggett clicked his radio.

"*Frostbite One*, *Frostbite One-Alpha* is in position."

"Frostbite One-Alpha, *roger. We're moving, standby.*"

Leggett used hand signals to alert Raines and Winman, even though they'd heard the same transmission. They all watched and listened, taking aim at each of the soldiers around the Bumerang while waiting for the Stryker to show itself.

Out in the open, the Russians heard it first. One man turned his head slowly to look at the road leading toward the gate from Cherry Hill. He cocked his head slightly, then his whole body tensed and he turned around as he realized what was speeding toward them.

"Take 'em!" Leggett shouted, and the four Americans opened fire. They'd waited a breath too long, allowing the Russians time to start moving. Their first volley struck two of the soldiers, but the other two dove for cover, one ducking behind a column supporting the roof over the gate, and the other diving behind the Bumerang. As they took cover, *Frostbite One* burst from behind the trees to the north, its 30mm auto cannon firing a long burst and raking the entire gate area. Corporal Gabriel Hudson was standing in the rear hatch with the Carl Gustaf. He fired just as the Stryker jumped the curb and cut the corner between Arnold Avenue and Arctic Warrior Drive.

The missile struck the edge of the gatehouse roof, detonating above the Bumerang and showering the area under the roof with hot shrapnel and debris, killing the soldier behind the column but leaving the Bumerang undamaged. The Russian APC lurched forward, its turret swinging around to bring its 12.7mm machine gun to bear.

Leggett and his men were firing wildly now, trying to pin down the remaining foot soldier, but he was running next to his vehicle, keeping it between him and the Americans. Nugent opened up again with the Bushmaster, sending rounds ricocheting off the Bumerang's armor, buying time for Hudson to line up another shot.

The Bumerang commander finally got his machine gun swiveled around and started spraying the tree line where Leggett and his men were hidden, but the movement of his vehicle forced his shots to go high. In the Stryker, Hudson got another round loaded and fired, this time hitting the Bumerang above the right front wheel. The explosion rocked the vehicle, but it kept moving, the commander traversing the machine gun back along the tree line. This time, his rounds found a mark.

PFC Noble was standing behind a tree, resting his rifle against the trunk and trying to get a shot on the single dismounted Russian soldier. The 12.7mm rounds from the Bumerang ripped through the trees around him, one of them smacking into the tree he was sheltering behind, hitting less than three inches from his head. The impact of the round shattered the trunk and drove splinters and bits of shrapnel into Noble's face. He collapsed to the ground, screaming.

Leggett ran to his side and dragged him by his body armor further back into the trees, shouting into his radio as he went. "Noble's hit! *Frostbite One*, you guys gotta kill that APC!"

Raines and Winman had shifted their position slightly to the east to get a better angle, and finally were able to bring down the dismounted Russian with combined rifle fire. The man collapsed in the road unnoticed next to the Bumerang, which just kept rolling. Nugent had brought *Frostbite One* around onto the road fifty yards behind the Bumerang, and was hammering the rear panel of the fleeing APC with rounds from the Bushmaster. Then Hudson stood up in the hatch again, and fired a third round from the Carl Gustaf.

The explosion lifted the rear of the Russian vehicle three feet off the ground. When it came down it looked like it had been slammed in a giant door and bent almost double. Smoke and flames poured out of several openings, but there were no further signs of life.

Nugent keyed his radio. *"Frostbite One-Alpha*, hold position, we're coming to you."

Leggett clicked his mic twice in response, unable to speak. He was kneeling next to Noble, trying to clear his airway. Noble was groping wildly at his wounds, hyperventilating and making noises like a dying animal. He suddenly started choking, thrashed for a few more seconds, and went still. Leggett sagged back against a tree, breathing hard and staring at Noble's body in shock. He was still clutching Noble's collar with one hand.

Raines ran up with Private Winman close behind. He looked at Noble, then at Leggett. "Come on, Win. Help me get 'em up." He laid a tentative hand on Leggett's shoulder. "Hey, Ell-Tee? Let's get Noble outta here, all right? This is gonna be a popular place for Russians any minute now, so we need to go." He knelt down and gently loosened Leggett's grip on Noble's collar. "Come on, Ell-Tee. It's time to go. We'll bring Noble with us, okay?"

Leggett looked up, seeming to have just noticed Raines for the first time. "Okay."

Raines nodded. "Help me out, Win." The two men lifted Noble's body between them and stood up. "You hurt, Ell-Tee?"

Leggett slowly dragged himself to his feet, shaking his head. "I'm not hurt. Not a scratch."

The thought struck Raines that the young officer suddenly looked a lot older.

Inside the Stryker, Nugent keyed the radio in frustration. "Let's go! We're gonna get cut off if we don't move, right now!" They'd run the vehicle as close to the trees as they could, but they couldn't see what was taking the fire team so long to get back to them.

Then Raines' voice came over the radio, slightly out of breath. "Frostbite One-Alpha's *inbound with one KIA. Don't leave without us.*"

Nugent swore, scanning his video monitor for signs of movement nearby. Switching to infrared, he picked up the team's heat signatures almost at the tree line, about twenty yards farther west. "Corporal Mullen, take us forward twenty yards." The vehicle lurched forward, then came to a stop as the three men emerged from the trees next to it, Raines and Winman dragging Noble between them. A hollow-eyed Leggett brought up the rear. Nugent opened the rear door, and the men clambered aboard, laying Noble on the deck between the seats in the already crowded passenger compartment.

Nugent hit the control to raise the rear door before the returning men had time to sit down. "Let's go, Mullen! Just head south over the overpass, then take 4th Avenue to the east. We'll figure the rest out from there."

"Roger." Mullen wheeled the big vehicle away from the trees and onto Arctic Warrior Drive, giving the mangled Bumerang a wide berth. Black smoke was still pouring out of the APC, and they could hear small caliber rounds cooking off from the heat inside. As he maneuvered the Stryker around the wreck, Mullen couldn't help thinking how close he'd come to ending up the same way, in *Frostbite Two*. He shook his head, trying to get rid of the thought, then steered the Stryker back onto the pavement and south toward Anchorage.

CHAPTER ELEVEN

Belli Captivus

673d Security Forces Squadron
Elmendorf Air Force Base

Sergeant Kirkpatrick looked up as the door opened, revealing a lean man in a Russian uniform with a deeply lined, scowling face. Kirkpatrick watched the man as he closed the door behind him. The Russian pulled up a chair and sat down opposite Kirkpatrick, staring at him across the bare table.

"Unsettling, no?" the Russian asked in heavily accented English.

"You mean your face?" Kirkpatrick said. "Yeah, if I'm honest, that is a little bit disturbing."

The Russian grinned, showing two gaps where he was missing teeth. "You will have to try harder than that to insult me, Sergeant. I am not so sensitive as you may think." He leaned back in his chair and nodded at Kirkpatrick's hands, cuffed together on the table between them. "No, I was referring to your present situation. Chained to a table in your own police station. Yesterday, you were the law, today you are the criminal. That, it seems to me, would be unsettling."

"Maybe," Kirkpatrick said. "But maybe '*I* am not so sensitive as *you* may think.'"

The Russian smiled again. "I admit, this is possible." He wrinkled his brow and looked up at the ceiling, deliberately looking speculative. "I wonder, how sensitive do you think your pretty friend might be?"

Kirkpatrick stiffened. *He's trying to goad you,* he thought. *Don't let him.* He said nothing, just staring at the man.

"I am not such a fool to think that you have no concern for her," the Russian said. "So. I have questions for you. You will give answers. If you do not?" He shrugged. "No harm will come to you, but I *will* allow my men to entertain themselves with her. You understand?" The gap-toothed smile was back.

Kirkpatrick glared at him, but forced himself to nod. "I understand."

"Very good."

"Will you guarantee her safety in exchange for my cooperation?"

"No." The Russian's tone was flat. " I will not. But I can tell you her chances will be greatly improved."

Kirkpatrick shrugged. "Fine. It's not like I have any earth shattering information anyway. I'm just a stupid noncom. They don't tell us anything."

"Excellent!" the Russian said, suddenly smiling again. "I am Major Vaslav Flyorov. Now, although I admire your pragmatism, Sergeant, I do reserve some doubts about your 'stupidity'. I am well aware that you Americans place much greater responsibilities on your enlisted men than we Russians - it is one of the things I admire about you. Now, can I get you anything before we begin?"

"A plane ticket to someplace else would be nice."

Flyorov laughed. "I couldn't agree more! Unfortunately, you and I are both far removed from our next holiday. I would offer you coffee, but I am afraid my troops were somewhat...

enthusiastic in their assault of this building; one of their missiles appears to have destroyed your kitchen facilities. They had a bit of a time getting the fire out. Water, perhaps? Or a cigarette?"

"Water would be fine."

Flyorov nodded, but showed no indication of getting up. Instead, he opened a pocket on his combat fatigues and produced a pack of Russian cigarettes and a lighter. He lit one, pausing long enough to blow a thick cloud of rank-smelling smoke across the table into Kirkpatrick's face. Kirkpatrick rolled his eyes and leaned back. He hated the smell of cigarettes, and this one was particularly nasty. Flyorov appeared to relax, reaching a lazy hand up to remove the cigarette from his lips between two horizontal fingers, all the while staring at his prisoner. After two drags, he waved the cigarette at Kirkpatrick.

"Are you certain you wouldn't like one?"

"No, thanks," Kirkpatrick said. "I never developed the taste."

Flyorov took another long pull on the cigarette. "How unfortunate for you. They are wonderful. And relaxing at the same time."

"Reminds me of Iraq," Kirkpatrick said.

Flyorov brightened. "Ah, you saw combat in Iraq?"

"Some."

"Who would have imagined that a simple cigarette could bring back such memories, eh?"

Kirkpatrick shook his head slowly. "Not too hard to imagine. The whole time I was over there, no matter where I went, the smell was the same."

"And what smell was that?"

"Burning garbage."

Flyorov blinked, then barked out a laugh. "Still trying to insult me, my friend?"

"I wasn't aware we *were* friends."

Flyorov leaned forward, crushing out his cigarette on the surface of the table. "We could be, if you would allow it. Of one thing I can assure you, Sergeant, you do *not* want to be my enemy." He spat out the last few words with venom. He flicked the crushed cigarette butt across the table, bouncing it off of Kirkpatrick's chest. He stood abruptly, glowering down at the American. "Perhaps your pretty partner will be more friendly, hmm?" He turned on his heel and left the room, leaving Kirkpatrick to wonder if he'd just caused Lucy Hume a world of hurt.

Two doors down the hall, Hume was cuffed to a similar table. A single soldier stood against the wall, facing her. He had an unsettling leer pasted across his face that made Lucy uncomfortable - to the point that she was entertaining fantasies about punching the man in the face until he stopped looking at her. He winked at her and grinned, then quickly snapped to attention when the door opened and another man entered.

"Good morning, Airman Hume," he said, sitting down in the chair across from her. "I am Major Vaslav Flyorov. I hope my men are treating you well?" Lucy shot a glance at the man by the door, but said nothing. Flyorov half-turned in his chair, then said something to the other man, who quickly scuttled out of the room.

"Is that better?"

"It is, yes."

"If that man - or any of my men - have mistreated you in any way, Airman Hume, you must report it to me, do you understand? Your safety is of the utmost concern to me."

Hume looked at him. "Since you mention it, there is the small matter of my patrol cruiser being lit on fire and my post being overrun, not to mention all the good people your men killed this morning. Would you classify that as 'mistreatment'?"

Flyorov grinned. "I do admire the American sense of humor. Your sergeant has a similar… what is the word…" He snapped his fingers. "Irreverence! Yes, Americans are very irreverent. I enjoy that about you, but you must realize that I am being serious."

"So am I."

"You think that we have mistreated you?"

"You *did* attack us. So, yeah. I do."

Flyorov leaned back and folded his arms across his chest. "I assure you, Airman Hume, we are here only as a stabilization force. Your country is on the verge of collapse. Our objective is to prevent that collapse and help restore order."

"Oh, please," Hume scoffed. "You can't expect me to believe that."

"What you believe is not my concern. The information you can give me, however, *is* my concern."

"What information?"

"What were you and your sergeant doing this morning at the checkpoint?"

"You mean the main gate?" she laughed. "We were retreating."

Flyorov nodded. "I see. Retreating, with a precision rifle in your car? Do you not mean you were moving to a prepared sniper hide, with the intention of killing Russian troops?"

"If you had been there, Major, you'd know that we were captured in the act of directing traffic. Pretty heinous stuff, I know, but there it is." She glared across the table at him. "We were trying to get non-combatants off of the base."

"What about the rifle? Or the spotting scope we found with it?"

"Personal hunting gear. Sergeant Kirkpatrick is a moose hunter. He figured you guys would steal his rifle and scope if he left them, so he grabbed them from his dorm room before we headed for the gate. Too bad, because if we'd have left them, we wouldn't be here right now."

Flyorov regarded her with a blank stare. "Moose."

"That's right."

"You are allowed to have your personal weapons in your barracks?"

"No, that's actually against regulations. But it doesn't mean people don't do it."

"Hmph," Flyorov scoffed. "You Americans have no discipline."

"I thought you said you admired that."

"I said I enjoyed your irreverence." He got up. "I enjoy it because it betrays your lack of discipline, and that will be your undoing. Now, I think I will go and discuss moose hunting with your Sergeant Kirkpatrick." He paused by the door. "If his story does not agree with yours, I may have to send Private Davydov back in to keep you company. He is also rather undisciplined. You should get on well together."

As the door closed behind Flyorov, Lucy repressed a shudder.

West Building, Zhongnanhai
Beijing, China

Zhao Shen stood with his hands behind his back, staring out the window at the thick layer of smog blanketing the city. "You doubt our ability to succeed, General?"

General Ma lowered his eyes. Zhao had become more irritable than usual over the past several days. Ma knew he had to tread carefully. "Not at all, my *lingxiu*." Ma's careful use of the reverent Chinese term for leader was meant to flatter and appease Zhao, but it had the opposite effect.

"Stop your groveling," Zhao snapped. "It is unbecoming. We *will* succeed in this endeavor, General. Do you understand?"

"Of course," Ma said, hurrying to agree. "It is my duty, however, to point out potential difficulties. To ignore them would be to do you and the nation - the Party - a disservice." He kept his eyes lowered as the president turned toward him.

Zhao glared at his top general for a moment, then took a deep breath. "Forgive me, General." Ma's eyes flicked upward warily as Zhao stepped closer to him, placing his hands on the general's shoulders. "I do not doubt your loyalty, Yong. To me or to the

Party. Stand at ease, my friend, and tell me what is bothering you. Honestly."

Ma finally allowed his eyes to meet Zhao's. "I do not disagree with the objective per se, sir. You know that. I simply state my concern for the timing. The Russians are fully mobilized and already on a war footing. In addition, their troop strength in the east is substantial, and growing by the day. Striking them now could touch off a conflagration that will be difficult to end."

"'The opportunity of defeating the enemy is provided by the enemy himself,'" Zhao said, quoting from Sun Tzu's *Art of War*.

"Again, I agree," Ma said. "But please, forgive my failure to *understand*. How do the Russians provide the means of their own defeat when they are at their strongest?"

Zhao walked across the room and opened a liquor cabinet, pouring himself a glass of expensive Scotch. He didn't bother offering one to Ma. "You disappoint me, General."

Ma's heart skipped a beat. Disappointing this man had proved fatal for many in the People's Liberation Army. The fact that Ma had been Zhao's closest friend since they were boys mattered little, and he knew it. "It... grieves me to hear that, *lingxiu*."

Zhao waved his drink dismissively. "It is my fault as much as yours. I appointed you to command the army. Perhaps I should have elevated someone with actual military experience, rather than someone I thought I could *trust* to learn on the job." He turned his back on his friend and went back to staring out the window.

Ma took a hesitant step toward him, then caught himself and stopped. "It was *not* a mistake, Shen. You can trust me, completely. I admit, my understanding of military tactics is less comprehensive than it could be. But the years I spent with you in the National People's Congress were not wasted. You know that. You always say that loyalty is more important than skill."

Zhao nodded. "I do." He looked sideways at Ma. "Political maneuvering is not completely unlike military maneuvering,

Yong. You simply need to understand the similarities and differences, and apply the principles accordingly. Political action often requires careful planning and execution, and it is conducted with words and intrigues. Military action requires the same care, but the application requires physical rather than intellectual maneuvers. The Russians are on a war footing, yes. They have massed their forces in the east, yes.

"But the piece you are missing, my friend, is that those forces must be maintained and supplied. The majority of Russian industrial strength is concentrated in the west of their country. Eastern Russia is vast and largely underdeveloped. Their troops conducting operations in North America are dependent upon very long, very vulnerable supply lines back to the west." He turned all the way to face Ma. "Do you begin to see my point?"

Ma allowed himself a small smile as understanding dawned. "They have overreached."

"Yes."

"If we cut their supply lines, their troops in Alaska will be stranded."

"They will. The Russians have no more desire to fight a war on two fronts than the Americans ever did, and less ability to do so. Besides which, we also have the biological element to consider. Once the virus takes hold, the Russians will be in no better shape to fight than the Americans are, regardless of any threats to their flank."

"If that is so," Ma asked quietly, "why bother with conventional tactics at all?"

"The American special forces have a saying: 'Two weapons equals one, and one equals none.' Only a fool would place all his hope on just one option, General." He sipped his whisky. "I am no fool."

"Of course not *lingxiu*, but are you not concerned that the Russians will escalate in the face of a biological attack? What of the threat of nuclear missiles - especially if they are backed into a corner and can see no other alternative?"

Zhao shook his head and sipped his drink. "They will never seriously consider that. Our missile batteries alone are enough of a deterrent, but we have also secured the cooperation of the North Koreans. Their *Hwasong-15* missiles can easily reach Moscow, and they have agreed to target as many major cities in western Russia as we need, in order to convince the Russians of the foolishness of a missile exchange. They will *not* escalate."

"Will the North Koreans also commit troops?"

"They will. They have promised us an entire Army Group, which will be useful in taking Vladivostok, and Khabarovsk immediately after. That will allow our own troops to focus overwhelming efforts on every other major Russian city from Khabarovsk to Chita."

"But, *lingxiu*..." Ma protested. "That would create a front more than two thousand kilometers long!"

"Yes, it would," Zhao seemed unconcerned. "But the extreme distance means the Russians cannot defend it."

Ma was almost apologetic. "The Russian Army outnumbers ours, Shen."

Zhao scoffed. "They outnumber us in total, my friend. But do not forget that their forces are more than two to one reserves, while ours are more than four to one active troops. If they have to rely on ill-prepared and poorly trained reserves, they will have already lost. What is more, their troops are spread out, trying to cover and defend the largest country on earth." He half-smiled. "Having the most territory is not always an advantage, Yong. Especially when most of your troops are dying from a virus they cannot fight. Trust me, old friend. This war will be over before it even starts."

Ma took a breath. "Are you certain the Koreans can be trusted, *lingxiu*? Their General Secretary is -"

"A complete fool," Zhao interrupted. "*Of course* they cannot be trusted, but they have no choice. They only have enough food for their people because of us. If they do not give us the troops, we will let them starve. It will be a simple enough thing for their

Army Group to cross the Tumen River from Chongjin and drive north into Vladivostok. That will be another compelling argument for the Russians to consider, and it will cost us nothing but grain for the Koreans."

Ma nodded slowly. "So, the Koreans will strike Vladivostok and Khabarovsk while we focus further inland." He looked at Zhao. "What of our forces massed along the Strait of Taiwan?"

"They will remain in place, for now. We will deal with our wayward province when the issue with Russia and America is settled. We wouldn't want a two-front war of our own, would we?"

"No, *lingxiu*. It is wise to focus on one front at a time. Still, the Russian operation will not be without great cost."

"Initially, no doubt," Zhao said. "But it is a cost we must bear. As I said, the North Koreans will absorb many of the initial casualties along the east wing of that front. Our conventional missile forces will strike Russian railheads and supply depots before we commit ground troops. Once we have softened their defenses, our shock troops will deal with their command and control elements, and the 78th Group Army will mop up and hold such territory as we require until we are certain that they pose no further threat."

Ma nodded, following his president's gaze out the window. "Very well, *lingxiu*. I will consult with my theater commanders and have more detailed war plans to you by the end of the week."

Zhao finished his drink, then shook his head. "We have war-gamed this exact scenario more than once, and the results have been favorable each time, without even allowing for the effects of the virus. There is no reason for further delay. Time is critical, General. I want to be *executing* this plan by the end of the week, not still dithering over the particulars.

"When the Russians slipped their landing ships out of Petropavlovsk right under our noses, it put us well behind. I do not like being caught on the back foot, as the Westerners say, but our hand has been forced. We *must* move, before the Russians gain too strong a foothold in Alaska. They must be struck, while they are still stretched to their utmost." He turned and gave the general a hard look. "Is that clear?"

Ma nodded quickly. "Absolutely, sir. Forgive me. With your permission, I will go and see to it at once."

"Inform me if you have any trouble, Yong," Zhao called as the general moved to the door. "I will not tolerate further hesitation. If any of your theater commanders resist, arrest them, shoot them, I don't care. But find replacements immediately and get on with it."

"Yes, *lingxiu.*" Ma pulled the door closed behind him.

Zhao went back to the liquor cabinet and refilled his glass before returning to the large window. He looked outside at the pall of smog hanging over the city, swirling the amber liquor in his glass in contemplation. Authentic Scotch whisky had to be aged for a minimum of three years in oak barrels. The drink he held had been aged for thirty-two, and it showed in the smooth, smoky, nearly perfect taste. Time and patience were required for greatness, Zhao thought.

Like a great whisky, his country's aspirations had been locked away for decades, just waiting for the proper timing; waiting for the right combination of ingredients. Timing and conditions had now finally coalesced, and he was the one who would open the barrel.

Zhao knew only too well that history had been unkind to many ambitious men who had reached for greatness, only to fail in their attempts. A lesser man might have been discouraged by that truism, but then, he was not a lesser man. The specter of potential failure only served as a goad, driving him harder.

I will not *fail in this,* he thought. *I* will *bend history to* my *will. The Russians won't know what hit them.*

The Situation Room

The White House
Washington, D. C.

"Where *is* he?" Secretary of State Sidney Black couldn't hide his frustration.

Avery Bassett shook his head. "I've called him twice. His assistant hasn't seen him. I just called his chief of staff, and he said -" Bassett's phone rang, and he plucked it off the table in front of him. "Bassett." He paused to listen, then let out a frustrated breath. "Thank you, Mr. Beckerdite. Tell him we're all ready for him." He disconnected the call. "They're on their way down."

"Where was he?" Black demanded.

"Beckerdite said he found him watching TV in the residential wing."

"You've got to be kidding," General Fader, the Commandant of the Marine Corps, growled. "We're at war, and the President wants to watch it on CNN?"

"No," Bassett said, obviously embarrassed. "He was watching *'The Price is Right'*."

"Oh, Good Lord." Black dropped his head into his hands.

"Look, I don't really think this line of conversation is appropriate at the moment." Joint Chiefs Chairman General Joel Mercier had a pained look on his face.

"Not appropriate?" Black was incredulous. "You imagine that the commander in chief watching a game show during an invasion *is* appropriate in some way, general?"

"Gentlemen, please!" Tom Shin, the director of Homeland Security said. "This is unseemly, really!"

"What would you know about it, exactly, Tom?" Black shot back. "How's the response to the terror attacks coming, by the way?"

Shin started to protest, and the rest of the people in the room all started talking at once, each angrily defending their positions or shouting their opinions. Then the door swung open, and

President Reese walked in, followed closely by Chief of Staff Will Beckerdite.

"Well, well!" Reese said, casting a predatory look around the room. "What could possibly have all of you fighting each other with such energy, when we should be figuring out how to fight the Russians? Anybody care to explain that one to me?" The room fell silent. "Nobody?"Reese walked around the table and took his seat at the head. "Fine. We'll start with you, General Mercier. Explain yourself."

"I… beg your pardon, Mr. President?" Mercier asked.

Reese gave him a withering look. "Beg all you like, there's no pardon forthcoming, General. You're the Chairman of the Joint Chiefs, or so I'm told. This country is under attack by a foreign power, and you apparently have done nothing about it, so if you're expecting my pardon, you're going to be disappointed."

"I… I…" Mercier spluttered. "Sir, with respect, I am *not* in the direct chain of command in any other capacity than as *your* advisor on military matters. The individual service chiefs might better be able to offer explanations…"

"Passing the buck, are you?" Reese cut him off. "Useless." He swiveled his head and glared at the military service chiefs, sitting in a row down the left side of the table. "How about you four? Any one of you have a better explanation than your future former boss here?" Mercier reddened, but held his tongue.

General Fader spoke up. "I can explain it, Mr. President."

Reese looked at him as if the man was a leper. "Can you. Well then? I'm waiting, General."

Fader glared right back. "Mr. President, this attack is the direct result of more than two years of a reckless isolationist foreign policy combined with an outright assault on military staffing and funding across all branches. It was bound to happen, sir. You drop your wallet in the middle of a bad neighborhood, somebody's gonna make a grab for it." Another hush fell over the room. Secretary Bassett's mouth was hanging slightly open, and all eyes turned to Reese for the inevitable explosion.

But it didn't come.

Reese's expression had gone momentarily blank. He blinked several times, as if he had something in his eyes and couldn't quite clear it. Then in a quiet voice, he said, "What - what was I saying?" He glanced around the room, his expression transformed instantly from fury and disdain to complete confusion.

Black cleared his throat. "You were discussing options for dealing with the Russian invasion, sir. In Alaska?"

Reese looked at Black in surprise, and Black noticed for the first time how red the man's eyes were. "Invasion? Oh yes, of course. The invasion." He hesitated. "Then, ah, I assume we're all in agreement?"

Black glanced around the room, noting the confusion and alarm on each face. "We... haven't quite worked out the finer details, sir."

"No?" Reese stood suddenly, momentarily losing his balance and almost upsetting his chair. He looked around, clearly embarrassed. "Well. I'd better let you all get back to it, then." He picked a pen off the table and fiddled with it. "I uh, I have a meeting." Abruptly, he dropped the pen and walked out of the room. Will Beckerdite cast a nervous look around, spread his arms in resignation, then followed him out. The click of the door behind him seemed unusually loud.

Black looked around at the military chiefs. "I'm going to optimistically assume that the president just gave you gentlemen a great deal of leeway in crafting your response."

"Is that what just happened?" Fader asked. "I could have sworn we just spotted an escapee from the local looney bin."

"General Fader!" Mercier snapped. "That is completely unprofessional, sir!"

Fader did nothing to hide his contempt. "No, General. What's completely unprofessional, is all of us sitting around this table, watching that man fiddle while Rome burns! Ten minutes ago, he was watching *a game show*, unless you've already forgotten.

Then he comes in here pointing fingers at the military for the colossal cock-up that *he and his* predecessor brought about, and then he demands that *we* explain *ourselves?* That's like punching somebody in the nose for no good reason, and then punching them again for getting blood on the floor!"

"You will limit your comments to military matters only, sir," Mercier said through clenched teeth.

"If you think an incompetent Commander-in-Chief isn't a pressing military matter, General, you might want to re-examine your understanding of the chain of command."

Black cut in before Mercier could respond. "General Fader makes a good point." Everyone turned to look at him. "The president has been under an enormous amount of stress since taking office -"

"Emphasis on *taking*," someone muttered *sotto voce*.

Black lowered his eyes and nodded slightly. "As I was saying. Under the circumstances, we may not be able to rely on the same level of support we might reasonably expect from the executive branch."

Bassett scowled. "What exactly are you saying, Mr. Secretary?"

"Only that the military has a responsibility to defend this nation from all enemies, foreign and domestic."

"Yes, but under the direction from the commander in chief!" Mercier protested. "Are you advocating that we come up with policy, absent his input?"

"Not at all." Black looked at Fader. "General?"

Fader hadn't taken his eyes off of Black. "Sir?"

"Tell me, if you were a junior lieutenant, serving in combat under a senior captain, and that officer was killed or incapacitated, where would your duty lie?"

"My duty would lie in completing my mission to the best of my ability."

"And would that duty include an honest assessment of the new situation to determine if the original mission parameters were still viable?"

"Absolutely, sir. The mission comes first. In a nutshell, if you take casualties, you reassess in real time. If you can still accomplish the mission, you press on and get it done. If not, you work out the best way to withdraw, fight another day."

Black folded his hands on the table. "That, Secretary Bassett, is what I'm saying. Thank, you General."

"But the president hasn't been… killed," Bassett said, clearly uncomfortable. "He's still here."

"That depends on your definition of the word 'here'," Fader grumbled.

Black stifled a grin. "All I'm saying, is that he needs his people to do what they're paid to do. He needs a break. I seriously doubt that the Russians would be willing to call a time out so he can get it." He looked at Bassett. "Avery, you would not be overstepping your bounds if you simply direct the service chiefs to implement war contingencies to deal with the immediate threat. Look, I know I'm just a State Department puke. But for what it's worth, the clock's ticking. I think you should let the warfighters go ahead and fight the war, before it's too late."

"Due respect, Mr. Secretary," Fader cut in. "I agree with you in principle. But even our most recent war plans were developed and war gamed more than three years ago. Our manpower is a shadow of a shadow of what it was back then. I don't doubt the commitment of our troops, sir, but with our present numbers, any military action we undertake is gonna look a lot like three hundred Spartans at Thermopylae. High inspiration, low survivability."

Black looked around the room. Every person in uniform lowered their eyes in silent agreement.

Bassett looked desperate. "What do we do, then? General Mercier?"

Mercier scowled. "I am *not* comfortable discussing this without the president."

Black sighed as he stood. "Well then, General, I suggest you find a way to get comfortable with it. Either that, or we can all start learning to speak Russian." He pushed his chair aside and left the room.

Frostbite One
South of Eagle River, Alaska

"Turn right at the next intersection, Ell-Tee, then pull off at the first building on the right." Leggett did as Nugent said, pulling the Stryker into the empty lot in front of Eagle River Volunteer Fire Station Number Three. There were two fire trucks parked outside next to the lone building, which had three large overhead doors across the front. As Leggett brought *Frostbite One* to a stop, the right side door started opening, and Staff Sergeant Blanca Trujillo poked her head out. She waved her arm, directing Leggett to pull the Stryker inside. There was another Stryker already parked in the adjacent bay. Trujillo closed the door behind them, and Leggett shut the engine down. Nugent hit the rear door release and the crew started filing out.

"Good to see you guys," Trujillo said, meeting them as they left the vehicle. She shook Nugent's hand as he stepped out, and was stunned to see how tired he looked. "You okay, Sergeant?"

Nugent nodded. "I'm all right. It's just been a long day already." He turned as Leggett came slowly down the ramp. "Meet Lieutenant Leggett. He's our new CO. For now."

Trujillo saluted Leggett, and he returned it half-heartedly. "You can probably knock that off now, Sergeant," he said. "I get the idea we're going to have to start blending in from here on, and saluting is sort of a dead giveaway."

"Roger that, sir." Trujillo dropped the salute and shook his hand instead. "Glad you decided to come with us."

"I'm not so sure I feel the same way." Leggett said.

Trujillo noted the hollow look in the young officer's eyes, and the blood on his uniform. *This guy's gonna be in charge?* She thought. *He looks awfully rattled.* "You hurt, sir?"

He looked down at his chest. "No. That's not mine." He looked away.

"We lost Noble," Nugent explained.

"Oh, man."

Leggett changed the subject. "How'd you swing this place?"

"My husband's in the volunteer fire department here," Trujillo said. "I know the door code."

"You don't think they'll mind, us sticking their trucks outside and hiding ours in here?"

Trujillo shook her head. "No, sir. Every one of them is either retired military or they're married to somebody who's active duty. They're gonna be feeling the pinch of this invasion as much as anybody. Sergeant Nugent figured we'd need a place to hide if we survived the night, so I called my husband from the base before we even broke in to the vehicle park. The trucks will be safe here for the time being."

Leggett looked at Nugent. "You didn't mention we might not survive the night."

"I figured that was need-to-know information, Ell-Tee."

"Right," Leggett said, "and I didn't need to know." He took a deep breath. "All right, so we made it this far. Now what?"

"Well sir," Nugent said, "now we see how well we all can hide in plain sight."

CHAPTER TWELVE

Interitus

Chugach Mountains
Six Miles East of Elmendorf AFB

Ray Broome struggled for almost fifteen minutes to get free of his tangled parachute harness, then nearly broke his leg falling out of it when he was finally able to get to his knife and cut the straps. He'd been dangling ten feet in the air, and when he dropped onto the steep slope below, he rolled head over heels for thirty feet before coming to rest against the trunk of another tree. He was scratched and bruised, but mostly unhurt except for a badly twisted ankle.

He immediately pulled his emergency radio from his survival vest, and was about to turn it on when he caught himself. He knew the radio was encrypted, but how certain could he be that no enemies were listening, or even if any friendlies would be able to come for him? If he was honest, he really had no idea how the fight had gone with the Russians. He and Driver had been shot down within minutes of getting airborne. What about the standby aircrews? Had they even made it off the ground?

He looked around, wondering if the Russian pilot who'd beaten him had called in ground troops to pick him up. It wasn't as if he was behind enemy lines in a foreign country, but because he didn't know the Russian strength and dispositions, he couldn't be completely certain where safety might lie. He knew he was about a half mile from Arctic Valley Road, a narrow two-lane that wound up the mountain about seven miles from the valley floor to the little ski resort of Arctic Valley. There was still snow on the ground, but not enough left for skiing, so traffic wouldn't be heavy on the road; if he followed it he could be off the mountain relatively quickly.

He could also be spotted just as quickly.

The other option was to bushwhack straight downhill, keeping under cover of the trees and brush until he got to a house or building where he could hide and figure out his next steps. Carefully, he pulled himself to his feet, easing onto his twisted right ankle, testing its strength. It didn't seem too bad, so he put his radio away and slowly started down the hill to the west.

He'd gone less than half a mile when he realized that he hadn't noticed where his ejection seat had come to earth. Stored beneath the seat was a larger survival kit, with emergency rations, first aid, and - possibly more critical if he ran into Russian ground forces - a Sig Sauer MCX Rattler compact rifle in .300 Blackout. The only firearm he had now was his 9mm Sig Sauer M18 pistol. Hardly comforting, if it came down to a firefight against a Russian infantry unit.

He was standing at the edge of a wide west-facing clearing near the top of a low saddle. From there, he could clearly see three columns of smoke, each marking the final resting place of a multi-million dollar aircraft. He could hear jet engines, and after a careful search, he located three fighters, orbiting high up in the vicinity of Elmendorf. They were too far off to tell what type they were, but Broome was pretty sure they weren't American.

So much for the standby alert crews.

Looking around to be sure he was alone, he started across the clearing, limping slightly. He had the uneasy feeling that he was being watched; he couldn't shake the thought that another SU-57 might streak over the tree line and riddle him with cannon fire before he could make it to cover on the other side.

He picked up his pace, trying to ignore the pain in his ankle.

Texas Medical Center
Houston, Texas

Thomas Behan looked up as the door opened. Cooney walked in, nodding at his boss. The big man's face was impassive. Behan could just make out the outline of the bandages under Cooney's shirt where Newill had shot him in the shoulder during the gunfight at HSI's offices a week earlier. It struck him as slightly odd that he owed this man his life, yet still barely knew him. Before the attack on his home, he'd seen Cooney once or twice at HSI headquarters, but had never had cause to speak with him. Now he considered just how lucky he'd been that Cooney had been on the call roster that night. The rest of his team had been wiped out by one man, but Cooney? He'd refused to give up, and shown a tenacity that was all too uncommon.

That was a quality that Behan appreciated in a man, especially one in this line of work.

"Anything?" Behan asked in greeting.

Cooney shook his head and sat down in the chair opposite Behan's bed. "Nothing. The guy's a ghost. The car he stole from the Shell Plaza parking garage turned up in College Station, but I seriously doubt he went any farther north than that."

"You think that was misdirection?"

"That's what I'd do," Cooney said. "But the only play that makes any sense for him would be to get out of the country, and the quickest way to do that is to go south. I'm betting he switched cars in College Station and reversed course, crossed the Mexican border somewhere between Laredo and the coast."

Behan nodded. "Then where, do you think?"

"Anybody's guess. I sent a couple of guys over the border yesterday. They're gonna do some sniffing around down there, see if anything turns up. But I gotta warn you - Mexico's a free-for-all. We go asking around about stolen cars, faked IDs, or passing out descriptions, anything that we'd normally try to use to track somebody down? That might get our guys killed, just for the asking. Besides, Newill could have gone down there and stolen the Mexican president's car, and nobody'd report it. If we find any leads, it'll be out of sheer luck."

"HSI doesn't have any people based in Mexico, anyway," Behan said. "Last guy we had there got killed in a kidnapping attempt. Do you have any local contacts down there?"

"I can make some calls," Cooney said. "I know a couple of guys who might help, maybe hook up with the two I already sent down. But like I said, it's a free-for-all. Cartels don't appreciate outsiders sniffing around. It'll cost a fortune to convince anybody to do it."

Behan nodded. "I don't care what it costs. We need to tie this off. Newill didn't get all of our assets, and I'll use whatever we have left to make sure he doesn't get the jump on us again."

"All right, then," Cooney said, heading for the door. "I'll ask around."

J. Edgar Hoover Federal Building
Washington, D.C.

The tall, thin man walked purposefully to the security checkpoint. An armed guard barred his way when he reached the metal detectors.

"Identification, please." The thin man handed over a military ID. The guard looked at it, cocking an eyebrow. "How can I help you… General?"

"I have information regarding the murder of President Galen Tolliver," the man said. "I also have reason to believe that because of that information, my life is in imminent danger. I demand protection."

The guard looked from the man back to the ID in his hand. "Step to one side, sir." He leaned over his console and picked up the phone.

General Franklin Pope had to force himself not to turn and run. He could feel the eyes of the several people who'd come in behind him boring into his back, and he couldn't shake the thought that one of them might just be waiting for an opportunity to kill him. He'd been under enormous pressure for weeks, trying to deal with the fallout from the bungled mission to take out Tolliver, followed by the murder of Defense Secretary Coleridge. Then the press had leaked video of a man in the act of shooting Tolliver fifty miles from the crash site, and the nation had seemed to lose its collective mind.

For once, the conspiracy theorists were not the only ones claiming to see nefarious plots in every relationship in Washington. Pope had known that his involvement as Coleridge's Air Force liaison for HSI would come to light sooner or later, especially after Coleridge was killed. Now he hoped that he could confess everything he knew to the FBI in exchange for protection. He looked up as the guard put the phone down.

"Take a seat over there, sir." The man indicated a some chairs placed to one side of the entrance. "Someone will be right out to meet you."

The White House
  Washington, D.C.

"I know you have a lot on your plate, sir, but I thought you would want to know." Will Beckerdite looked at his boss, trying to see an indication that anything he'd just said was registering with the man. But President Reese just sat there, staring at the surface of his desk, eyes barely blinking. "Mr. President?"

Reese kept staring, but opened his mouth slightly, as if he wanted to answer. Then he raised his hand off the desk and gave his chief of staff a dismissive wave. Beckerdite stared at him for another long moment, then turned and left the office.

He was halfway back to his own office when he almost ran into Secretary Black going the opposite direction. Beckerdite nodded in greeting. "Mr. Secretary."

"Mr. Beckerdite," Black replied. "I'm on my way to speak with the President. I assume he's in the Oval Office?"

"He's in there," Beckerdite said. "But I wouldn't bother, if I were you."

Black's eyebrows went up. "Well, you're not me, young man." He turned to go.

"Mr. Secretary." Black stopped and half-turned as Beckerdite stepped closer and lowered his voice. "I think he's lost it."

Black stuffed his hands in his pockets. "Meaning what, exactly?"

"You saw him in the Situation Room earlier. He's been like that all week, and getting worse. His temper flares up, and then he just deflates, like he did just now. But lately, it's gotten worse. It's like he's pulling back into a shell - hiding, if you like - and every bit of bad news pushes him deeper. When he comes out of it, he's usually raving about something, or attacking anybody in the room. But just now, I couldn't even get him to respond when I tried to give him his daily brief. He just *sat* there. It's like he's in a waking coma."

Black leaned forward slightly. "Are you telling me you think the President is incapacitated?"

"I'm not qualified to make that call, sir. But it seems to me that a president who is completely unresponsive to the day to day requirements of the office -" Beckerdite stopped, then took a breath and gathered himself. "Now, we're at war on top of everything else? I don't know what to do, Mr. Secretary. But this scares me."

Black ran a hand through his graying hair, then looked sharply at the younger man. "Come with me." He turned back the way he'd come and started to walk away, stopping after a couple of steps to look back. Beckerdite hadn't moved. "Well?" Black said. "You say the situation scares you. Don't you think we should go and do something about it?"

Beckerdite hesitated for another moment. His sense of loyalty recoiled at the idea of doing anything behind Reese's back, but he didn't know what else he could do. He fell into step behind Black and followed him out of the building.

Texas Medical Center
Houston, Texas

"You did the right thing by calling." Behan was sitting up in bed, talking into his cell phone when Cooney came back into the room. "Yes, I do want it dealt with," Behan continued, motioning Cooney into a chair. "No mistakes. Get it done immediately. No. I'll contact you." He ended the call and looked at Cooney. "We need to move."

"Move? With respect, sir, the doc said it was a miracle they saved your foot. He said you're gonna need at least another week of physical therapy before you can even put weight on it."

"I'll be the judge of that," Behan said, swinging his legs off the bed and sitting up straighter. He winced and sucked in a breath as the blood flowed to his wounded foot. "Get me my clothes, then go find a wheelchair. "We're not safe here."

"What's wrong?" Cooney was instantly on alert. He lowered his voice. "I thought you said your story was watertight."

"It *is*," Behan answered. "As far as the police know, we both got shot when we surprised some looters in my home during the storm, and then you drove me here afterward. But one of HSI's assets inside the Air Force just showed up at FBI headquarters in Washington. If he finds a sympathetic ear there before our people can deal with him, they'll start asking a lot of very pointed questions. Then it's only a matter of time before somebody connects us to Coleridge, and then Tolliver."

"But you have people inside the FBI, right?"

"Not enough to be sure we're safe."

Cooney swore, then grabbed Behan's clothes from the wardrobe and tossed them onto the bed next to him. "I'll go get that wheelchair."

U.S. State Department Headquarters
Harry S Truman Building
Washington, D.C.

"Sit," Black waved Beckerdite into a chair. Beckerdite reluctantly took it, sitting on the edge and looking like he regretted getting into Black's car in the first place. Black didn't mince words as he took his seat behind his desk. "You agree with me that he's incapacitated."

"Honestly? I don't know what to think."

"Don't temporize. You're no idiot, Mr. Beckerdite, but if you'll forgive my saying so, you've attached yourself to one."

Beckerdite clenched his jaw, but said nothing.

"It's no reflection on you," Black continued. "Not necessarily. As little as a year ago, Reese seemed to have a very clever political mind. I disagreed with almost all of his policies, but he seemed intelligent enough. To be honest, I thought he was more qualified for the office than Tolliver."

"Yet you supported Tolliver over Reese when it looked like the primary would be inconclusive."

"That was a matter of expediency. I'm a realist, Mr. Beckerdite. At that time, neither I nor Reese had the kind of support necessary to win a national election. Tolliver did. The office of

Vice President, as you well know, is about the least desired position in Washington, except for the fact that it can serve sometimes as a springboard into the Oval Office. But that's only if a person is patient, and if that person's running mate doesn't completely poison the political well while they're waiting."

"You took State because it gave you distance from the White House." Beckerdite said. It sounded like an accusation.

Black nodded. "I did. I didn't want to have to appear too supportive of Tolliver. The man was an arrogant, elitist fool, but he had the reins of the party, and the rest of us were just along for the ride. Taking the position at State was the only way I could retain some level of autonomy without being completely shunted aside."

Beckerdite nodded, accepting the explanation even though he disapproved of the reason. "So now you have the opportunity to step in and pick up the pieces."

Black leaned back in his chair. "I'd say this situation has gone from opportunity to necessity."

Beckerdite sagged slightly. "I have to agree." He looked like all the air had gone out of him. "I don't know what you think I can do about it, though."

"Are you familiar with the Twenty-fifth Amendment?"

Beckerdite paled. "You want to declare him unfit?"

Black's eyes were steady. "That would be one avenue, yes. In cases where the president is declared unfit to carry out his duties, the vice president becomes the acting president until such time as the president is able to resume."

"But Reese still hasn't named a vice president."

"Which adds considerable complications," Black admitted. "But they aren't insurmountable."

Beckerdite was confused. "What does that mean? Reese isn't going to simply hand over the presidency to the first person who asks nicely. Have you *met* the man?"

Black snorted. "I know. Look, Will. The way I see it, we have a couple of options here. First, we can go through the process of getting a majority of the cabinet heads to declare him incompetent in accordance with Section Four of the Twenty-fifth Amendment. Now, while I don't think we'd get much pushback, that would still effectively leave Reese in office - the vice president would only be the acting president until Reese declared himself fit again."

"Which would take him all of two seconds."

"Precisely. He needs to be *completely* removed from office, so he has no basis for returning."

"How?"

"He could resign."

"Ha!" Beckerdite scoffed. "He's been less than a month in the office he's wanted all his life - there's no way he'd resign."

"Nixon resigned with one sentence in a typed letter. It was that simple."

"But Nixon wrote that letter of his own free will!" Beckerdite shook his head. "Reese won't do that, not ever."

"He's completely out of it, Will. How many things do you get him to sign every day, without him reading them?"

Beckerdite smiled as if he'd just heard a really stupid joke. "You think if I drop a resignation letter on his desk, he'll just sign it without noticing? Really, Mr. Secretary, that's ridiculous."

"In any other circumstances, I'd agree with you. But you've seen his behavior lately." Black rapped his index finger against his temple. "He's not right, and you know it. The last two conversations I had with him before today were like I was talking to a crash test dummy. He just stares at his desk and mutters. You give him a pile of documents to sign, and he'll do it without coming out of his little trance."

"That still doesn't solve your particular problem. Even if he does sign a resignation letter, you realize that without a vice president, power would devolve onto the speaker of the house."

Black let slip a thin smile. "Which would be less than ideal, since Norton is in the opposition party."

"And if for some reason *he's* unable, it goes to the President pro tem of the Senate -"

"Who is ninety-two years old," Black finished his sentence.

Beckerdite paused, staring hard at Black. "And then after him, *you're* next in line."

"You catch on quickly." Black got up and walked around the desk. He leaned against the edge of the desk and looked down at Beckerdite. "I'm currently two steps too far removed from the position to do anybody any good. The only way to avoid a messy succession would be to have Reese name a vice president, *and* get that person confirmed by Congress before Reese resigns. Then when he resigns, succession will be quick and painless."

"Painless for whom? This is going to cause even more chaos. The country has been invaded; people are rioting all over - you think another leadership crisis is going to make them feel *more* secure about the future of the country?"

"What's the alternative, then?" Black asked quietly. "Leave him in office? Seriously, Will. He's at the heart of the current chaos, and you know it. He wanted that office all his life, as you said, but now that he's got it, it's broken him. Some people just aren't up to the task, and the fact that Aron Reese is one of those people is happening at the exact worst time in this country's history. We have to get someone in office who can right the ship of state, before it's too late. You know that, I think."

Beckerdite lowered his head into his hands."I know. I *know*. Norton would probably be worse than Reese and Tolliver combined, and Durber is too old." He looked up. But still, neither of them would just walk away from the opportunity, any more than you would."

Black's eyes widened. "You think this is about me?"

"Please. Politics are always about the politician, Mr. Secretary."

Black nodded. "I understand why you feel that way, but my personal ambition has nothing to do with this. The country is falling apart around us, Will. Something dramatic needs to be done, and quickly, or we're going to lose everything."

"And the dramatic event just happens to involve *you* taking over the government? Pardon my cynicism, sir, but that seems just a little *too* convenient."

"Look. You're right - I have no shortage of confidence in my own abilities, but I'm also a realist. The two men ahead of me in the line of succession are unacceptable because one is a self-serving narcissist with absolutely no moral compass, and the other has had one leg in the grave for the last twenty years. Neither of those two men are what the country needs at this moment in time. We need a leader who will put the survival of the country ahead of his personal ambition, and who won't drop dead of old age twenty minutes after taking the oath of office."

"Political correctness is not exactly your strong suit, is it?"

"Political correctness is part of the problem, but let's focus on the most pressing issues, shall we? If we don't get things turned around, the country as we know it will come apart. Can we afford that? Do you want to be a citizen of a Russian satellite? Or maybe of one of the newest third-world countries in the world? The ship is sinking, Will. We have to do something besides just listening to the band play."

"You're advocating a coup."

Black didn't flinch. "I am. And I need your help to pull it off."

J. Edgar Hoover Federal Building
Washington, D.C.

Pope had been waiting almost fifteen minutes when a man in a plain suit emerged from behind the security checkpoint and opened a door next to the metal detector.

"General? Will you come with me, please?"

Pope stood, then glanced reluctantly back at the revolving doors leading out to Pennsylvania Avenue.

"General?"

Pope looked back at the man. He felt trapped. To leave now

would certainly raise questions, but if he stayed there would certainly be more questions than he was willing or able to address. The guard shifted his position, moving to Pope's right as he lowered his hand to rest on his holstered pistol. The agent in the suit took a step toward him, his own hand subtly moving to his hip as he did. Pope suddenly realized he'd made a terrible mistake. He turned and ran for the door, and the agent shouted after him.

"DROP THE GUN!"

Pope's last thought was that he'd been a complete fool.

The White House
Washington, D.C.

"Mister President?" Beckerdite leaned through the Oval Office door, almost hoping that Reese would scream at him so he could go away and forget this ridiculous idea of Black's.

But Reese looked up, smiling. "Come in, Will. Close the door." Beckerdite did as he was told, then took a position standing in front of Reese's desk. "You look tired, Will."

"It's been an exhausting few weeks, sir. For all of us."

"It has. What's on your mind?"

Beckerdite fidgeted. "Well, sir…"

"I owe you an apology, don't I?"

"Excuse me, sir?"

"You were in earlier, trying to brief me on the riots, or something. I wasn't giving you my undivided attention, was I?" He rose from his chair and came around the desk, standing uncomfortably close. He took Beckerdite's hand and shook it. "I'm sorry about that, Will. I hope you realize that I'm here for you, no matter what."

"Uh… thanks." Beckerdite felt himself recoiling, physically leaning backward away from Reese's smiling face. Reese abruptly let go of his hand and walked over to the window. "We have such an opportunity here, Will. I think we can really get this done!"

Beckerdite blinked. "I'm sorry, sir - get *what* done, specifically?"

Reese turned, looking at him with a bemused expression. "The country, Will! We can make it right! We can turn it around - revive the American Dream, get people back to work! When we implement my programs, we'll completely revamp education, health care and Social Security! This is the opportunity of a lifetime - we just need to reach out and take it!"

Beckerdite had the unsettling feeling that he'd stumbled into a campaign commercial; then he realized with a shock that he was exactly right; Reese was quoting one of his own campaign speeches from three years earlier, when he'd been running in his party's presidential primary. That contest had ended in a hotly contested convention, where Reese, Tolliver and Black had all gained followers but failed to attain the clear majority of votes needed to win the nomination. Eventually Reese and Black had held their noses and agreed to put Tolliver at the head of the ticket, with Reese as the Vice Presidential nominee and Black contenting himself with the promised position of Secretary of State.

Now, here was Reese, president by default as a result of Tolliver's murder (which many people suspected him of planning), reciting old stump speeches as if he were still a candidate, while the country was coming apart around him. *The man is delusional,* Beckerdite thought. He noticed that Reese had abruptly gone silent. He looked over at the president, only to find him glaring back at him.

"What are you waiting for?" Reese snapped.

"Sir?"

"I told you half an hour ago that I wanted to talk to Senator Tolliver, Tommy! Now get him on the phone!"

Beckerdite gaped. "*Senator* Tolliver, sir?"

Reese waved a hand at him as he picked up the phone on his

desk. "Oh, you're completely worthless. Get out! I'll call him myself!"

"Yes, sir." Beckerdite backed out and pulled the door closed behind him. The staff in the outer office avoided his eyes when he turned around. He ignored them and retreated to his own office, still in shock.

Secretary Black's assistant connected Beckerdite's call immediately. *"Will. How did it go?"*

"Sir, I'm at a loss for words. The president is even worse than he was earlier today."

"What happened?"

"He thought I was his old campaign manager, Tommy Morton. He thinks he's still campaigning in the presidential primary. He also thinks Tolliver is still alive. He told me to get *Senator* Tolliver on the phone. Sir, he's completely lost it."

"Wonderful," Black said, his voice dripping sarcasm. *"Bad enough dealing with a partial lunatic, without him becoming a total lunatic before you can get to grips with him."*

"Sir, what can we do at this point? I was going to float the suggestion that he should start considering a vice-presidential appointment, like you said, but he just... he just snapped. I mean, he's been erratic before, but this?"

Black cut him off. *"All right, Will, calm down."*

"Calm down? I'd love to, Mr. Secretary, but seriously? My wife and I have a little girl. What kind of country is she going to grow up in? We're at war, the economy is wrecked, the President of the United States is a drooling lunatic, and there's no clear line of succession to replace him. And you're telling me to calm down?"

Black put Beckerdite on speaker and punched the intercom button. *"Katie? Get in touch with Senator Durber. He's probably at home in the middle of a nap, but don't let his nurse put you off. Tell the senator I'd like to meet with him right away, and I'll come to his home if necessary."*

"*Yes, sir.*" The line clicked off, and Black switched Beckerdite back to his handset. "*I need you to meet me back at my office right away, Will. We need to talk to Durber before this goes any further.*"

CHAPTER THIRTEEN

Invaderet

Chugach Mountains
Five Miles East of Elmendorf AFB

Broome stumbled out of the trees into a large, gravel covered clearing. Looking around, he realized he was standing in a staging area for loading tanks and other tracked vehicles aboard heavy transports during mobilizations. At the moment, it was deserted. There was a large, elevated loading ramp where low-boy transports could move alongside to pick up or drop off their cargo. There were no vehicles or people around, but the place gave Broome an uneasy feeling anyway. He looked back and forth, checking for signs of life, then hobbled the several hundred yards across the clearing as fast as his leg would allow.

Broome knew the Glenn Highway was still between him and the airbase, and though he wasn't exactly sure how far he'd come, he knew it couldn't be much further ahead. Re-entering the trees on the far side of the loading area, he could hear occasional sounds of traffic in the distance. He quickened his pace, hoping to flag down a motorist and find a place to lay low until he could better assess his situation.

Then he heard gunfire.

Broome pulled up short behind a clump of trees and listened. The thick trees made it difficult to pinpoint the sounds, but he could tell there were several large caliber weapons mixed with small arms fire, and it sounded close - less than half a mile away. He could hear multiple engines as well, and tires screeching on pavement. He couldn't hear any voices yet, so he figured he was still at a safe enough distance for the moment. Slowly, he started moving toward the sound of the fighting. If the gunfire was coming from an American ground unit, he might be able to hook up with them and reconnect with his own unit in time.

As he moved to the west, the noise of the battle grew louder. He could almost make out the highway through the trees when there was a deep *crump* followed by a fireball that rose above the trees in front of him. The staccato of automatic gunfire increased momentarily, then tailed off to nothing. He moved closer, only stopping when he was fifty yards from the edge of the trees.

Now he could see through the undergrowth well enough to make out what had exploded. A Humvee was turned on its side and burning fiercely, one wheel still spinning. Broome could see several bodies around the wreck, as well as one dangling awkwardly out the roof turret. None of them were moving. A diesel engine revved nearby, and Broome shifted his eyes to the left. A large armored personnel carrier came into view, driving on the east shoulder of the road, with what looked like a 30 millimeter auto cannon mounted on the roof, pointing at the wrecked Humvee. The vehicle resembled an American Stryker, but the prominent red star on the side made it obvious that it was Russian.

A garbled voice boomed out over a loudspeaker as the vehicle lurched to a stop several yards from the Humvee. Broome couldn't make out what they were saying, but then he noticed someone moving on the ground on the far side of the Humvee. Through the smoke he could just make out a pair of legs, but the rest of the body was obscured by the vehicle itself. The loudspeaker command barked again, and then Broome was stunned as the big 30 mm cannon on the roof of the Russian vehicle came to life, sending a spray of heavy bullets into the wounded man.

Broome drew back further into the trees, stunned. It was clear the Russians had won this exchange, and he wouldn't find any help here. He'd have to give this area a much wider berth, until he could be certain how far the Russian cordon stretched around Elmendorf and Richardson. He couldn't afford to be captured, especially if this was how they were treating prisoners.

He backtracked several hundred yards into the stand of trees. When he was confident he couldn't be seen from the highway, he turned to the north and set out again, going as fast as he could manage on his injured ankle. He had no idea where he should go, but he knew he needed to get away from the Russian patrol as soon as possible.

Earlier in the day he'd thought about making his way to his own apartment in southeast Anchorage, but now he saw the impossibility of that idea. The Russians had clearly cut the Glenn Highway northeast of the city, and he had no illusions about being able to cross their lines to the south on foot - especially not while he was hobbling around like this.

His best choice, he decided, was to head north toward Eagle River, and hope that the enemy hadn't extended their lines quite that far yet. He knew several people in his squadron had homes there, but he'd never visited any of them. *Should have accepted those barbecue invitations,* he chided himself.

He was frustrated at how helpless he felt. When he was in his Raptor, he'd always felt in control of things, right up until the Russian pilot had proved that his confidence had been somewhat misplaced. Broome didn't like being on the losing end of anything, and he was determined to set that right as soon as possible.

He was racking his brain, trying to remember the layout of

things to the north of his position, when he stepped over a log and into a hole with his already sprained right leg, dropping eighteen inches before his forward momentum slammed his knee against the side of the hole and snapped his torso over double. The pain shot through him like a bolt of lightning, and it was all he could do not to cry out. Very carefully, he sat back on the log and dragged his leg free of the hole, then collapsed off the back of the log into the dirt and pine needles, just focusing on his breathing.

Broome was about to roll over and try to stand again when he heard voices. They were coming from the south, close enough that he could tell they weren't speaking English. He knew that he had no chance of outrunning anyone in his present condition. His only hope was to hide.

Looking around, he realized that the fallen log he'd stepped over was raised off the ground several inches. It was laying across and almost parallel to a smaller log beneath it, but the slight difference in angle left a small gap between the two. Brush growing against the backside of the log to Broome's left enclosed a small recess; he just had to crawl through the gap between the logs and lie flat, and he'd be hidden from all but the most careful inspection.

He craned his neck to try to see if anyone was within view, but he couldn't see anything. The voices were drawing dangerously close. Biting his lip against the pain, Broome quickly dragged himself across the smaller of the two logs and slithered into the gap. He shoved his legs as far under the logs as he could manage, and found that there was just room to conceal his whole body. He had a slightly obstructed view to the south from his position. He tried to slow his breathing as he waited for the patrol to catch up.

Slowly, Broome pulled his sidearm from its holster. Now more than ever he wished he hadn't lost the larger survival kit and the rifle in it when he'd punched out. He had no illusions about his chances even if he'd had the more powerful Rattler compact rifle with him; if it came down to a firefight, he figured that either way he was as good as dead. Even if he somehow managed to outshoot two or three of the patrolling troops, his damaged leg meant he'd never get far before the others caught up and took him out.

The rifle would have been more comfort than utility at this point, he had to admit. He wasn't a particularly good shot with either weapon. The pistol seemed pitifully small in his hands, but he braced it on the log and tried to hold it steady anyway. If he was going to get killed today, Broome thought, he might as well make the enemy regret it on his way out.

Movement in the trees now, about forty yards away. Broome shrank as far back as possible, certain that his pounding heart was going to give him away. He could just barely make out the silhouette of legs moving, just one pair at the moment, but there were raised voices and laughter, so there were at least two soldiers coming, maybe more. Broome's breathing sounded like a hurricane in his ears, and he felt a terror rising up inside him in spite of his best efforts to keep it at bay.

There was a sudden flurry of movement to his left, followed by a shout. Then two shots rang out and Broome's heart leaped in his chest. Dirt exploded ten yards in front and slightly to the left of his position, and something rustled in the pine needles, but he couldn't see what it was with the log blocking his view close to the ground. Should he return fire? Maybe they were just trying to flush him from cover, trying to get him to give himself away?

Then, softly at first, but quickly increasing in volume and pitch, came an eerie, keening wail from the brush close by. It made the hair stand up on the back of Broome's neck as it increased in urgency, a panicked, screaming noise full of anguish.

Broome gripped his pistol tighter as two armed men emerged from the brush. One was laughing, playfully shoving his companion, while the other grimaced in discomfort at the horrible screeching sound coming from just a few yards to the left of Broome's hide. He watched as they approached, close enough that he could make out the color of their eyes. Broome held his sights steady on the closest one. He was slowly squeezing the trigger back toward its breaking point when the laughing man bent down and picked something out of the underbrush. Broome stopped himself.

The man was holding a large rabbit - an Alaskan Hare. The animal screamed louder, and the man slung his rifle and used both hands to wring its neck, finally putting a stop to the horrible racket. The man laughed again, shaking the dead animal in his friend's face and saying something in Russian that sounded less than complimentary. The other man brushed him off, turning back to retreat the way they had come.

Broome held the pistol steady on the log until the men disappeared from sight. Then, finally allowing himself to relax, he lowered it to the ground in front of his face and dropped his head onto his outstretched arms.

He didn't stop shaking for a long time.

Los Angeles Memorial Hospital
Los Angeles, California

Karly Bynum parked her car in the drive-up to the emergency room entrance, afraid she wouldn't be able to walk the distance from the parking lot. A nurse came through the automatic doors and was about to wave her away when Karly opened her car door and fell out onto the pavement at her feet, unconscious. The nurse keyed a radio and called for a gurney, then turned Karly over and started checking her vitals. Her pulse was racing and her blood pressure was falling rapidly, and she was burning up.

The doctor on duty came outside and knelt on the pavement next to Karly as the nurse quickly filled him in. "Pulse is one-sixty, BP is fifty over thirty. Temp is... *wow*. One-o-eight."

"Any sign of trauma? Head injuries?"

"None so far."

The doctor felt Karly's pulse himself, nodding as another pair of nurses wheeled a gurney up. "Let's get her inside." As they hoisted the young woman onto the gurney, the doctor noticed blood starting to seep from her nose, ears and eyes. His heart dropped. "Hang on, everybody. Debbie, call upstairs and get an isolation ward set up. We're all on quarantine as of right now. Have them clear a path for us - I don't want anyone else exposed to her or us until we figure out what's going on here." The first nurse got back on her radio and started making calls.

One of the other nurses, a woman in her late fifties who had spent time in rural clinics in Africa treating Ebola patients, looked across the gurney at the doctor. "What are you thinking?"

The doctor met her gaze, then looked down at Karly, who was convulsing slightly. More blood was showing at the corners of her mouth and her breathing was coming in rasps. He shook his head. "I'm *hoping* it's just a really nasty drug overdose. He looked over at the nurse again. "But if it isn't, I think we're all in serious trouble."

She nodded. "I hate to say it, doctor, but this *is not* an overdose." They all started moving toward the doors.

"Ebola?" The first nurse asked, her voice shaking.

"Not necessarily," the older woman said. "Could be that, or Marburg, or some other type of hemorrhagic fever. Doesn't much matter. They're all bad."

Alexandria, Virginia

Black sipped at his whisky. "So, you can see our problem, Senator."

Lloyd Durber was sitting in an electric wheelchair, chewing furiously on a toothpick and alternating his condescending glare between Black and Beckerdite. He finally settled on Beckerdite.

"So you claim he said all this just today?" He raised a finger and shook it. "And don't even think about embellishing any of this to make yourself look better, young man, because I will roast you alive if I find you've lied to me. This is *not* the time for story telling."

"Ease up a little, Lloyd." Black looked almost amused. "There were plenty of other witnesses in the Situation Room, if that's what you want."

"Don't you 'Lloyd' me! Durber snapped, inadvertently spitting his toothpick into his lap. "If you'd taken my advice three years ago and *fought* at the convention, rather than rolling over and taking that worthless job at State, you would have been president, and neither of those two idiots would have ever set foot in the Oval Office for so much as a *photo op!*"

Beckerdite looked wide-eyed at Black, who shrugged. "He makes a point." He looked back at Durber. "But as I said then, *Lloyd*, if I'd have contested it any further than I did, the entire party would have fractured, and the other side would be in the Oval right now, so shall we get past the past and just deal with our current nightmare?"

Durber snorted, patting the blanket on his lap in a vain attempt to find his toothpick. "'Nightmare' is the understatement of the century, Sidney. You know we'll never get anything past that snake Norton. He craves the presidency more than he does his next breath. We try to get you in, he'll smell a rat and scream bloody murder. International media will be crowing about another 'American coup'. It'll never fly."

"I disagree."

"Oh you do, do you? And why might that be?"

"Because like everyone else in this town, Norton has skeletons, and I happen to have the key to closet where he hides 'em. He'll stay in line, for the good of the country, or I'll turn those considerable skeletons loose."

Durber cocked an eyebrow. "You'd better have something airtight, Sidney. Some illicit affair from thirty years ago isn't going to cut it. People just don't get excited about that sort of thing these days, not like they used to."

"Don't worry. You may not be aware, but Norton and I go way back. We went to Yale together; same fraternity." Black leaned forward. "He was involved in the death of a young girl while he was a student there. Drunk driving. The school looked the other way because he was an ambassador's son. But I couldn't ignore it. I saw the police reports."

"And how did you manage that?"

"It wasn't hard. See, his dad got the police to hand them over, wipe the whole thing clean. But then Norton made the mistake of showing the reports around the fraternity, bragging about how he got away with it."

Durber sighed. "That's all hearsay at this point, Sidney. Ancient history."

"It's not hearsay if you have the reports." He fixed a level stare on Durber. "I made copies."

"You're kidding."

"No, I'm not."

Durber scowled. "That's a pretty calculating move for a college student. Why would you copy them? Did you have a grudge against him for some reason?"

"Not anything specific," Black said. "I just hated the way he was gloating about the whole thing. He didn't care about the victim, not even a little. It was all a game to him. I just didn't think it was right."

"Then why didn't you tell someone at the time?"

"I was an idealist, Lloyd. But I wasn't stupid. I asked my father what to do. He was the police chief in Houston at the time. He made some anonymous inquiries through friends of his, and word came back to leave it alone. Norton's father had some powerful friends, and they weren't about to let his son screw up his entire future. We found out that the lead detective on the case refused to look the other way, and was fired on some trumped up pretense. He turned up dead a few days later, reported as a suicide."

Beckerdite slumped in his chair, while Durber made a face.

"My dad told me to let it go," Black continued. "So I let it go. But I never forgot it. I kept the copies of the police reports. I figured that someday, somewhere, they might be of some use. Seems I was right about that."

"You're going to blackmail him into accepting you as the Vice President?" Beckerdite's voice was barely audible.

"I'm going to play a card that I've held in reserve for decades, Will. Norton deserves to be punished for what he did, even if it was forty years ago. I doubt he'll want to contest the appointment, if it means digging up the dirt that he's kept hidden all these years."

"I don't know…"

"Secretary Black is right," Durber said. He'd stopped searching for his toothpick, and was sitting upright with a determined look in his eye. "Norton is a snake. As soon as word gets out that Reese is incompetent, he'll be pushing for him to be diagnosed, so he can step into the office. As long as there's no vice president, he's next in line, and he knows it."

"As far as word getting out," Black said, "it's already common conjecture around Capitol Hill. The only thing keeping people from looking into it more closely at the moment is the fact that Reese cancelled all his press briefings. He hasn't made a public appearance since then, and that's probably the only thing keeping the wolves at bay."

"What's wrong with him, do you think?" Beckerdite asked. "He's changed so quickly, it's unreal. I mean, just last month, he seemed completely normal, and now it's like he's got dementia. He reminds me of my grandmother, to be honest. She couldn't remember anything from day to day - she'd forget she was married to my granddad, forget where she lived… It was terrible to watch, but it took her a couple of *years* to get as bad as Reese seems to have gotten in just a month. Is that even possible?"

"Anything's possible, young man." Durber finally found his

toothpick and jammed it back into his mouth. "We need a professional opinion, though. We need to arrange to have him examined, *in private.*"

"I don't see how that would be possible," Beckerdite said.

"I do," Black cut in. "Let me talk to the head of the Diplomatic Security Service. He's a friend. He should be able to coordinate discreetly with the head of Secret Service, let him know that the President needs to have an off-the-books medical exam, get his detail to cooperate." He looked at Beckerdite expectantly. "You think you can convince Reese that he has a pressing need to go to Camp David?"

Beckerdite looked panicked. "How, exactly? I was in the Oval earlier today, and I half thought he was going to start barking like a dog! How do you expect me to convince him to do anything?"

"You're his Chief of Staff, aren't you?" Durber asked in an acid tone.

Beckerdite spun on the old man. "Yes, sir, I am. But the last time I checked, he thought I was his campaign manager - someone he *fired more than three years ago!*"

Durber was unfazed. "Well, if your diagnosis is correct and he is suffering from dementia, you'll never really know what he's going to do until you try, will you?"

Beckerdite rubbed his head with both hands. "I don't know. I don't really know what to do."

"Will, listen." Black leaned back in his chair. "We're in uncharted waters here, that's pretty clear. We cannot allow Reese to just run out onto the South Lawn tomorrow morning, 'barking like a dog', as you so eloquently put it. The country is on the brink of collapse. If *he* collapses, with no clear successor in place, the power struggle that follows could bring the country down for good.

"Now, if we do nothing, and Reese loses it in public, Norton *will* lobby to succeed him on grounds that he's incompetent and has no Vice President in place. He'll eventually win that argument, Will, but the necessary political wrangling to get him there will be too much for the nation to bear, especially considering the Russian invasion, terrorist attacks, vigilante reprisals and rioting in every town and city that we're dealing with already.

"But - and admittedly, this is a pretty big 'but' - if we get Reese to designate a VP *before* he publicly loses it, there can be a seamless transfer of power if and when he *does* lose it, and the nation will have one less straw on that shaky camel's back."

Beckerdite just stared at the floor.

"Face facts, young man," Durber said, his tone finally softening. "The country is dying, right in front of us. You need to decide, is it worth saving, or would it be better to put it out of its misery? Listen to me." He waited until Beckerdite finally looked up. "I've been a politician for almost seventy years, in one capacity or another, and I've never seen this nation in a crisis so serious as this. Reese continuing as president poses a threat to the continued safety and sovereignty of this nation; of *that* I am certain. If there's a chance that we can salvage something from the debacle of his short tenure, then I believe we need to at least try."

Beckerdite looked from one man to the other, finally focusing on Black. "What do you want me to do?"

Los Angeles Memorial Hospital
Los Angeles, California

Doctor Miguel Lozano rubbed his eyes, taking a deep breath before he picked up the phone and punched in the number for the Medical Director's office. The phone only rang once before someone picked it up and spoke.

"Kantner."

"Doctor Kantner, this is Doctor Lozano from the ER. We have a situation here, sir."

"A 'situation?' Be more specific, Miguel." Benjamin Kantner was a widely respected physician and researcher, but he wasn't known for his patience.

Lozano didn't waste time. "Ten minutes ago, we admitted a female patient, early twenties, showing all the signs of some type of hemorrhagic fever. She collapsed and lost consciousness right after she pulled up to the ER. We put her in an isolation unit, and we've taken some blood samples. The lab is looking at them now."

"How many of your people were exposed?" Lozano interrupted.

"Three nurses and myself. The patient died a couple of minutes ago."

Lozano swore under his breath. "You followed all the protocols, Miguel?"

"Yes, sir. As soon as I saw she was bleeding from her eyes and ears, I suspected it and took precautions right away. Nobody else got within fifty feet of us until we were all in the iso unit."

"You said she drove herself in? What about her car?"

"I had security send an officer to cordon it off, but told them to stay out of it. They noticed an asthma inhaler on the front seat, but we're not certain if it belonged to the patient. The officer is in a separate iso unit right now; we're monitoring his vitals."

"All right. Well done, Miguel. Sit tight until the lab gets the results back. I'll get on the phone with the CDC."

"Yes, sir."

Cook Inlet
Near Point Possession, Alaska

Rollinson and her crew collapsed as one on the beach at Point Possession. They were cold, but thanks to their survival suits, they'd all avoided frostbite, or worse. The two hundred yard swim from the wreck of their helicopter had been brutal, especially for Rollinson and Hulse, who were adequate swimmers at best. Taylor and Kennedy had buddied up with them, but by the time they'd reached the beach, they were all wrecked.

They immediately built a fire, then spent several hours on the beach trying to raise someone on their survival radios, but they couldn't get a response on any frequency. The few snippets of conversation they did pick up were weak and mostly blocked by static, and if anyone heard their calls, they didn't respond. Realizing they had little choice but to save themselves, they decided their best option was to move, so they set out to the southwest on foot.

They made it almost fifteen miles that day, following the Kenai Spur Road along the coast. It was more than twenty five miles from Point Possession to where the dirt road turned into pavement. So far, they had seen no traffic, nor even any fresh tracks in the hard-frozen snow that covered the road. When they came across a boarded-up summer home perched on a bluff overlooking the Cook Inlet, they decided to stop for the night. Rollinson had hoped to find people in the house who could help them, but the house was empty, and they were exhausted, so they had little choice.

They broke in.

The place's electrical power was provided by a generator that had no fuel, but there was a working wood stove in the main room, as well as an ample supply of firewood piled out front. There was no food, or running water, but after what they'd been through, it felt like the height of luxury. Hulse built a fire, and the others dragged mattresses and blankets into the great room from the three bedrooms, placing them in a semi-circle around the stove.

They all slept hard that night.

Glazkovskiy Bridge

Angara River Crossing
Irkutsk, Russia

Georgy Toporov coughed violently, a racking, wet cough that surprised him with its sudden violence. He had a stabbing pain in his chest, but he tried to convince himself that it was just another asthma attack. It felt much worse, though, and even Georgy had to admit that he was worried. All morning, he'd felt worse than he could ever remember feeling from his asthma. He'd tried to tough it out, but now he felt like he was on fire inside. Nothing felt right, and he was starting to get scared.

"That's a nasty cough," his passenger said from the back seat, without looking up from his cell phone. "You should take some honey in a glass of vodka. That'll set you straight."

Georgy barely heard the man, as another bout of coughing doubled him over so suddenly that he lost control of the car. The taxi drifted to the right and slammed against the Jersey barrier on the north side of the bridge. His passenger looked up from his cell phone in alarm as the car slid to a grinding stop against the barrier.

"Hey! Wake up! You can't just stop here, are you mad?" Georgy rested his forehead on the steering wheel, ignoring the blaring horns and shouted curses from passing drivers swerving to avoid his cab. There was no shoulder here, only the concrete barrier separating the traffic from the narrow sidewalk on the outside of the bridge deck, and now his cab was blocking most of the westbound auto lane.

The bridge had four lanes; two outside lanes for automobile traffic, and two center lanes fitted with flush mounted rails for electric streetcars. Georgy's cab was now forcing the heavy traffic to dodge onto the westbound streetcar track to get through.

Georgy gasped for breath as more coughs racked his body. His eyes watered with the pain, so much so that he found he couldn't blink them clear. He raised a hand to wipe them, but when he lowered it, it came away covered in blood. Terrified, Georgy looked down and noticed more blood spattered on the steering wheel where he had coughed. He panicked, throwing open his door to flag down help.

The driver of a tractor-trailer coming up behind him wasn't paying close attention, distracted by an argument he was having with his wife on his phone. He noticed the stalled cab too late. He yanked the wheel left, but the truck steered like a pig, and the oversteer took him across the westbound track and onto the eastbound one, where a streetcar was bearing down on him. Another oversteer to the right to escape, and the truck ran right into the panicked cabbie as he staggered away from his cab.

The impact threw Georgy twenty feet ahead, slamming him onto the concrete bridge deck in a broken, bloody heap. The truck driver stood on his brakes, bringing his rig to a sliding stop just a few feet shy of where Georgy lay.

Then a westbound streetcar bashed into the back of the truck, pushing it forward far enough to crush Georgy beneath its front tires.

Emergency services responding to the scene twenty minutes later had no way of knowing that the bloody corpse pinned beneath the truck was infected with a dangerous pathogen. The incubation period of a week to ten days predicted by the Chinese scientists had been reduced to three in Georgy's case, due to his severe asthma. Had he made it to a hospital, the bleeding from his eyes, nose, mouth and ears that had started just before the crash might have caused immediate concern and led to a quarantine, but under the circumstances, his body looked no more bloody than it should have, considering what it had been through, and no one bothered to investigate his death more closely.

No extra precautions were taken in handling Georgy's body, no caution for the virus that would surely have killed him if the truck had not. Even if they had known, authorities would still have had to track down all the people Georgy had come in contact with since he'd driven the Chinese man to the Marriott three days earlier. That man had already returned to China, after spending two days walking the most crowded public areas of the city, coming into close contact with as many people as possible.

Others who had been on the same flight as the Chinese man had also been exposed, and they had in turn come in contact with dozens of other people after they landed. Those people then exposed everyone in their own circles, and by the time Georgy was mercifully killed by the truck on the Glazkovskiy Bridge, the chain of exposure had already spread across Irkutsk and beyond. Georgy was only the first of the casualties. Those who fell sick after him might have envied him getting hit by a truck; it was a much quicker, much less agonizing way to go.

But in spite of its effectiveness in Georgy's case, the virus in Russia would not follow the pattern its creators had hoped for. Events had taken place there years earlier that would inadvertently diffuse the situation and allow the virus to quickly burn out, leaving one leg of the Chinese war plan severely crippled.

The Tattered Tam Pub
Credenhill, Herefordshire, England

All the men responsible for Tony Holland's rescue were gathered at the Tattered Tam as a means of winding down. This night was the first time they'd all been free to meet, since they'd spent the previous several days in debriefings and interviews with government officials and military commanders. The capture of Akhtar Khan had ensured that nobody was going to question too closely the real reason for their mission to Rud. Khan had great potential as an information source in the war on terror, and the British authorities didn't want to look that particular gift horse in the mouth. They'd look the other way where Boone's private invasion of Afghanistan was concerned. The ends, in this case, justified even the most unorthodox means.

Finally able to relax, Holland was feeling better than he had in years. His son had all but come back from the dead and they were together again, surrounded by good friends, men who understood them and spoke their language. He allowed himself to start thinking about what might come next. Thanks to the video of Newill killing Tolliver, he and Burdin were no longer suspects in the murder. There would still be questions, but at least now, Holland wouldn't have to answer them from a jail cell.

Maybe Tony would come home and stay with him in Idaho. They could spend some real time together, explore new places to camp and fish, and just savor the fact that they were both alive, and safe.

Their ordeal was finally over.

Holland was returning to their table from the bathroom, grinning to himself at the prospect of a normal life. He didn't notice the hush that had come over the entire room until he got to the table and Boone met his eyes with a look Holland knew all too well. The others' faces were all grim, and Tony was looking down at the table.

"What?" Holland had a sudden feeling of dread. Boone nodded up at the TV screen on the far wall of the pub. Holland turned to look. A news feed was running pictures of several explosions at what looked like an airfield, with descending parachutes clearly visible in the distance. A ticker scrolled across the bottom of the screen, summarizing what was happening.

WORLD WAR III?
RUSSIANS INVADE ALASKA / NO AMERICAN RESPONSE
UK PRIME MINISTER DECLARES NATIONAL EMERGENCY
* * *

Holland felt the air go out of his lungs. For a moment, he'd thought that the worst was over. He'd dared to hope that he could recover some sense of normalcy now that Tony was safe, but he'd been horribly wrong.

Nothing was over.

Not yet.

CHAPTER FOURTEEN

Eleison

Chugach Mountains
  Eight Miles South of Eagle River, Alaska

Day 19

Broome had spent the next twelve hours after his close call with the Russians trying to avoid anything that looked remotely like civilization. He spent the night hiding in a copse of trees and brush so thick that he had to get down on his stomach and wriggle his way into it. He'd barely slept, but at least he'd been reasonably sure nobody would trip over him.

Awake at first light, he listened for a long time, then carefully dragged himself out and continued hiking to the north. He didn't have far to go in a straight line, but trying to avoid open spaces and especially roads forced him to take a much more circuitous route than he would have liked. The area east of the Glenn Highway and Fort Richardson was peppered with small arms shooting ranges, ammunition dumps and tank parks. He carefully avoided them all.

He wanted to get out of the woods, but at the same time needed to stay hidden. His main problem at the moment was the cold, and lack of food. He'd nibbled on an energy bar the first day, but that was gone now, and his stomach kept reminding him of it. Like it or not, he was going to have to move into the open, risking discovery in exchange for finding shelter and a meal. His right ankle and knee were both badly swollen, making every step an agony.

Finally, he crested a low ridge and came in view of the outskirts of Eagle River. He stayed under the trees for a long time, watching the roads for signs of military vehicles, but didn't see much traffic at all. After an hour, his stomach was grumbling so much that he decided to risk it. He followed a shallow cut in the hillside, keeping to the brush as best he could, and headed down toward the scattered houses on the outskirts of town.

Greenwich, Blue Mountains
15 Miles East of Kingston, Jamaica

"I've *got* Percocet in my bag," Cooney said, looking sideways at Behan as he dropped a heavy rucksack on the living room floor.

"I said, no." Behan winced again, shifting his foot on the stool in front of his chair. "I need to be able to think straight."

"Nothing quite so distracting as constant pain," Cooney said. "But it's your funeral."

"I appreciate your concern." Behan's tone was anything but appreciative.

Cooney grinned. "I'm not gonna lie. I have something of a vested interest in your well being, if you get my meaning."

Behan forced a smile, trying again to make his foot comfortable, and failing. "And here I thought you were just a good Samaritan."

"I'm a mercenary good Samaritan," Cooney said. "You sign my checks, so I care."

"Remind me not to miss a payday."

"No problem." Cooney walked over to the broad expanse of windows overlooking the lush green foothills between the house and Kingston, with the Caribbean Sea in the distance beyond. "Not bad. Anybody else know about this place?"

"No one who can connect it to me. Nothing more valuable than a good accountant, if you want my opinion."

Cooney scoffed. "Al Capone might disagree." He turned around. "So? What do we do now?"

Behan picked up a remote and switched on a large TV on the wall. It was tuned to a 24-hour news channel. He muted the volume and watched the news chyron as it scrolled across the bottom of the screen.

"Checking stock prices?"

"Checking my back, Mr. Cooney." He watched for a few more moments. "There." Behan pointed at the latest item scrolling past.

DISGRUNTLED AIR FORCE OFFICER PULLS GUN AT FBI HEADQUARTERS/ COMMITS SUICIDE BY COP

Cooney looked at Behan as the older man switched off the TV. "Was that your 'asset' inside the Air Force?"

"It was." Behan returned Cooney's look. "Is that a problem?"

Cooney chuckled. "It's like I said. You sign the checks. I don't see a problem."

"Fantastic. What do you have on Newill?"

"Exactly what I expected," Cooney said. "Nothing, so far. I did contact one of my guys in Mexico and connected him with the two contractors I sent down from Texas, but it's going to take some time. Is this place secure enough for us to stay a while?"

"I don't want to retire here, if that's what you're asking," Behan said. "We'll stay until we're content that Newill is no longer a threat."

"We may both have to retire here, then." Behan glared at him, and Cooney raised his hands in surrender. "Or not. Like I said, I'm working on it. Give my guy some time."

Eagle River, Alaska

Broome pulled up in a stand of trees across a two lane road from a small, ranch style house, set back about twenty yards from the road. His leg was on fire, he was cold and he was starting to feel shaky from hunger. He wished the sky was darker, but at this time of the year, even after the sun went down, it was still light enough to see clearly almost twenty four hours a day. The darkest part of night was little more than a deep twilight, and that lasted less than three hours between midnight and three in the morning. He guessed it was about eleven in the morning now, and the sun was up and shining brightly. The last remnants of spring snow were rapidly melting away, and the mosquitos were already out in force.

Broome looked up and down the quiet road, weighing the danger of exposure against his need for food and medical attention. The area was eerily quiet. He listened and watched for a few more minutes, then made up his mind. He had to try.

Stepping from the trees, he hobbled across the narrow verge and stepped onto the pavement. Halfway across, the front door of the home opened slowly, and a young woman stepped out. She had a rifle low in her hands, pointing directly at Broome's chest. He stopped in the middle of the road and slowly raised his hands.

"What do you want?" the woman asked. There was an edge to her voice. Fear, anger, confusion - Broome couldn't tell.

"I'm sorry to bother you," he said, keeping his voice low. "My name is Ray. Captain Ray Broome. I'm an Air Force fighter pilot. I got shot down yesterday near Eielson. I'm hurt, and I could use some help."

"Can't help you," the woman said, waving the rifle barrel to one side. "Get on down the road."

"Ma'am, please," Broome said, taking a limping step toward

her. She responded by raising the rifle to her shoulder and taking careful aim. He stopped walking.

"I said I can't help you!" she repeated in an urgent voice. "Russians said anybody caught fighting against them or even helping our soldiers will be shot. I got a little kid to worry about, so you just get on down the road like I told you!"

Broome shuffled backward. "Ok. I'm going. Sorry to bother you. Sorry." He turned and limped back across the road, slowly disappearing into the brush.

Darcie Tanaka pushed the door shut behind her, but watched through the window until she was certain the Air Force officer was gone. Then she put her back against the door and slid down to sit on the floor, holding the rifle upright between her knees. She leaned her head against the forestock and closed her eyes.

"Mommy?"

Darcie opened her eyes to see her five year old daughter Arisu standing at her feet. "What is it, honey?"

"Was that a bad man?"

Darcie shook her head. "No, Ari. I don't think so."

"How come you pointed Daddy's gun at him if he wasn't a bad man? Daddy said you should never point a gun at someone unless you were really gonna shoot 'em."

Darcie smiled. Her husband Kenji had been killed six months earlier in a car crash, but Ari still talked about him every day, as if he was coming home any time. "Daddy was right, but it wasn't safe for that man to stay around here, honey. I had to scare him away, so the bad men wouldn't hurt him."

The little girl furrowed her brow for a moment, thinking. "If you hadn't scared him away, maybe he coulda scared the bad men instead."

"I don't think so, honey. If we would have helped him, the bad men would have wanted to hurt us. I can't let that happen to you."

"Mommy?"

"What, baby?"

"If the bad men are bad, why should we do what they say?"

Darcie winced. Her daughter had an amazing ability for simply stating the uncomfortable truth.

Cook Inlet
Fifteen Miles SW of Point Possession

Rollinson woke to the sound of her own stomach growling. "Jeez, Lieutenant," Hulse grumbled as he rolled back into his blanket on the mattress next to hers. "You wanna turn that down a notch?"

"Sorry," she said, sitting up and rubbing her eyes. She felt horrible. She'd swallowed a good deal of seawater in the crash and the swim to shore, and that combined with the exertion of the previous day had left her with a raging sore throat. Her thirst was almost overpowering, but even more than that, she was hungry. "What do we have for food?"

Kennedy rolled off of his mattress and stretched his back. "I feel like I died." He started digging in the pockets of his survival suit, finally pulling out a Meal, Ready to Eat. He opened the main pouch and laid out the various items carefully on the floor in front of him. Hulse walked over and added two energy bars to the small pile, and Taylor tossed in a squeeze pouch of protein drink. Rollinson had lost her MRE in the crash, and had nothing to offer. They all sat for a moment, looking at the meager supply of food.

"How far to Kenai, you think, boss?" Taylor asked.

Rollinson shook her head and tried to clear her throat without aggravating it. "Dan?" she rasped. "How far do you figure we made it yesterday?"

"Fifteen, sixteen miles, tops," Kennedy answered. "All those snow drifts we had to slog through really slowed us down."

"So that leaves us, what? Thirty miles to Kenai?"

"More like forty, if we follow the road, and that's really our only option. Nikiski is ten or fifteen miles closer, I'm not exactly sure, but we're bound to come across somebody before we get even that far. The beginning of the pavement can't be too far off now, and there are quite a few houses in the woods between here and Nikiski."

"So, another day of walking." Hulse didn't sound excited about the prospect.

"Yup," Kennedy said. "I'm not all that familiar with the area, just what we've seen from the air, but I know I've seen signs of life between here and Nikiski, maybe a third of the distance?" He shrugged. "I'm just guessing."

"All right," Rollinson said. "Looks like we're walking again, at least for today. Let's divvy this stuff up into thirds as best we can. Eat a third of it now, and another third tonight if we haven't been picked up by then. That'll leave us with one third as a reserve for tomorrow, just in case."

"What about water?" Taylor asked. "I'm totally dried out."

"Let's get some pots from the kitchen. We'll gather up as much snow as possible and melt it on the stove. Look around for some kind of containers to carry it in, too. I don't want to die of thirst with all this water laying around."

They all pitched in gathering snow, and spent a couple of hours melting it, nibbling at their food rations, and generally resting for the day's walk. When Rollinson figured they could wait no longer, she gave the order.

"Let's go, boys. We gotta get back to civilization." The three men followed her out of the house, after Taylor had stopped to write a note to the owners of the home, apologizing for the break in and listing off what they had used, and where they could be contacted to pay for it. He pulled the door shut behind him, but it wouldn't quite latch.

"That's a bummer," he said, frowning. "Critters are gonna get in there and trash the place."

"Nothing we can do about it now, Taylor," Rollinson said.

"Who knows if these people are even gonna make it back out here any time soon? There's a war on, remember?"

Taylor stared at the ground ahead of him as he plodded out of the barren yard toward the road. "You really think that's what's going on?"

Kennedy answered for her. "No other explanation that I can see. We pulled an armed guy out of the drink wearing a Russian uniform, and the ship that he fell off of was a disguised Russian amphibious landing ship, which then opened fire on us." He threw a stick he'd picked up into the woods. "Do the math. We're at war, all right."

Eagle River, Alaska

Ray Broome had never felt so vulnerable. In spite of being trained to thrive in chaotic situations, he felt completely out of his depth now. The Air Force had sent him to Survival, Evasion, Resistance and Escape school as part of his pilot training, and that course had given him a reasonable confidence that he could handle himself if he was ever downed in enemy territory.

But this wasn't enemy territory, was it?

Everything about the situation seemed wrong. His own countrymen were only a short walk away, but the only one he'd come in contact with since he'd bailed out of his jet had threatened to shoot him. Was no one resisting the invasion? Had America rolled over and died in just one day? It was unthinkable to him, but he couldn't imagine any other explanation. He'd expected to find no shortage of civilians out with their hunting rifles and personal vehicles, fighting back with vigor. But nothing he'd seen since he hit the ground had pointed to that. Everything was upside down.

He stumbled, tripping over some underbrush for what seemed like the thousandth time. He went down on his face, cursing. Exhausted and frustrated, he just rolled over and stared up at the sky, taking the opportunity to rest. He had to stop thinking about how this wasn't what he'd been trained for. Actually it *was*, it was just... different. He wasn't in a foreign country, but if he had been, the local population wouldn't have necessarily been any more reliable than this. He needed to think straight, and start treating this situation as if he *were* on foreign soil.

Food. That was the first thing, the *most* important thing. He would have to approach civilians with extreme caution. If what the woman with the rifle had told him was true, the Russians had somehow made everyone afraid to stand up to them. It made sense; he'd watched them machine gun a wounded soldier in the wreckage of his Humvee. They probably weren't interested in winning hearts and minds at this point.

He lay there, not moving, for a long time. His mind was spinning with what to do. He toyed with the idea of just walking out of the woods and into the first fast food restaurant he found, but the absence of civilians moving around freely made him think that most businesses would be closed anyway.

Where were people fleeing to? he asked himself. Any time that armed combat breaks out in an urban environment, large numbers of the local population will naturally run, seeking to put distance between themselves and sudden, violent death. *Probably north*, Broome thought. He was trying to remember the layout of the streets as he'd seen them from higher up on the hill when exhaustion finally caught up with him, and he slowly drifted off to sleep.

Kenai Spur Road
27 Miles NE of Kenai, Alaska

"Finally!" Kennedy walked from the gravel road onto the spot where the paved highway began. "Civilization!"

"'Bout time," Rollinson rasped. She was twenty yards behind, with Taylor and Hulse hovering protectively on either side. She sounded terrible. The exertion of two days worth of forced marching was aggravating what the seawater she'd swallowed had started. She'd developed a nasty cough over the course of their trek, and now she doubled over with her hands on her thighs, hacking and coughing.

"Here ya go, Ell-Tee," Taylor handed her a water bottle he'd taken from the cabin the night before. She caught her breath and looked up at him, nodding her thanks as she accepted the bottle.

Kennedy looked back. "Shouldn't be too much longer, Boss. Now that we're on the pavement, we oughta run into somebody sooner or later."

Rollinson took a long pull from the water bottle, then slowly swallowed as she handed it back to Taylor, wincing with the discomfort. "I sure hope so. I'd hate to have to drag you slackers any further."

Her three crewmen grinned back at her. They were all very loyal to her, she knew, having proved that they were a great team plenty of times before now. But this was something more than anything they'd faced to date. Normally their job consisted of patrol and frequent assists and rescues under difficult conditions, but losing their helicopter and ending up on foot wasn't something any of them had ever expected. Rollinson had been concerned that under the stress of the new reality, her tightly knit crew might not perform to their usual standard. She needn't have worried.

"We can pick up the pace if you like, Ell-Tee," Hulse said. "You go ahead and lead, and we'll do our best to keep up."

She shook her head. "I think if I lead, we'll never get there. Let's just all keep on keeping on. Dont worry about me, guys. I'm all right."

Taylor took a sip from his bottle. "You let us know if you need a break, all right?"

Rollinson nodded. "You got it." She straightened up slowly and forced herself to start moving.

Eagle River, Alaska

Darcie looked at her cell phone, wondering if it was safe to use. She'd left her daughter playing with her toys in her bedroom while she tried to figure out what to do. Her best friend, Blanca Trujillo, lived two miles to the north, but she hadn't heard from her since all this had happened. Blanca was a Stryker vehicle commander at Fort Richardson, but she lived in Eagle River with her husband, who was a paramedic and volunteer firefighter. Maybe Blanca would know what she should do about the pilot she'd chased away earlier. Mostly, Darcie just wanted to *talk* to someone, to get some encouragement. She was worried about how she would protect and feed Ari if the Russians started coming around.

They wouldn't bother tracking civilian text messages, would they? she thought. She looked out the kitchen window for what seemed like the thousandth time, into the copse of trees where the American pilot had disappeared, then made up her mind. She picked up her phone.

U OK? She hesitated a moment, then sent the text. The answer came back a few seconds later.

WHERE DID WE MEET?

That caught Darcie off guard. *What kind of question…* then she realized that Blanca was trying to verify that it was actually Darcie sending the text. She hurried to type the answer.

BREWERY TOUR. WHERE DID U SPILL BEER?

IN YOUR HAIR, LOL ;)

GLAD UR OK. CAN U TALK?

Darcie's phone started ringing almost immediately. "Hey, Blanc. It's good to hear from you!"

"You too, D," Blanca said. "I've been worried about you guys, but haven't had a chance to check on ya. Sorry about that. You OK?"

"So far. You think it's safe to talk?"

"Probably for a little while, at least," Blanca said. She didn't know for sure, but figured a short conversation would be safe for now. "You at home?"

"Yeah. I'm worried, Blanc."

"You seen any troops?"

"You mean Russians?"

"Yeah."

"From a distance. They drove a couple of trucks through the neighborhood down the hill with loudspeakers, telling people to stay home. They said if anybody helped American troops, they'd shoot them. You think they'd really do that?"

"I *know* they would." Blanca remembered the burning wreckage of *Frostbite Five*, and the grievously wounded driver they'd rescued from it. He'd died of his wounds several hours after their escape from the firefight at Eielson.

"I'm scared, Blanc." Darcie lowered her voice. "For me, but more for Ari. She's already been through enough, losing her daddy. I don't want her to have to grow up as a refugee on top of that."

"Might not have a choice in the short term, D," Blanca said. "You stay around there, things might get so bad that being a refugee will start looking pretty good."

"What are you gonna do?"

"Can't say yet. Not because I don't want to, but because I'm still not sure, you know? It's hard to tell where things are worse and where they're better. Might be better to make a break for Canada before too long."

"I'm starting to run low on groceries, Blanc."

Blanca paused for a moment, wondering if she should do what she wanted to do. Darcie was her friend, but she was a civilian. From what Blanca could tell, the front lines were very close to Darcie's neighborhood, but several miles from her own. She and Ari would be safer moving north, but for how long? But the alternative - a young single woman with a five year old child and no one else, stranded behind enemy lines? Blanca knew they wouldn't escape trauma of one type or another. Better to try to get to safety than to just sit around hoping safety will come to you. Blanca made up her mind.

"You need to get out, D. Come meet up with us. We'll figure something out for you two."

"Are you sure?"

"Positive. You can't stay there. No telling what they'll do to civilians if this occupation goes on for any length of time. You remember I showed you where Manny's side gig was? Just answer yes or no."

Darcie remembered. Just a few weeks earlier, Blanca had given her and Ari a tour of the volunteer fire department where Manny spent a lot of his time. "Yes, I remember."

"Good. You think you can get away from the house and meet me there without being seen?"

"Oh, man, Blanc. I don't know. How do I know I'm not gonna run into a roadblock as soon as I leave the neighborhood?"

"You don't, girl. But if you stay, they're gonna find you eventually. You gotta go out for food. As soon as you do, they're gonna key on you right away, that's just the truth. Better to leave early when things are still confused. Odds are better you'll slip through now than later after they've tightened their grip on things."

Darcie thought about it. "I could try staying off the main roads, I guess."

"That's your best bet. They can't have roadblocks everywhere, not yet. The closest one to you that I know of is on the Glenn Highway half a mile south of the exit for the landfill. You stay clear of that. They'll still be trying to consolidate things closer to the bases in Anchorage, figuring out where their vulnerabilities are. But after they do that, they'll start expanding their perimeter. You understand?"

"Yeah. They'll take my neighborhood when they expand. I get it."

"Ok, then. How soon can you leave?"

Darcie felt a wave of helplessness wash over her. The idea of running and leaving behind the only home her daughter had ever known was difficult to process. "I don't know. Twenty minutes?"

"That'll do. Only grab what you need to survive, nothing else. If you can't eat it, wear it or use it to buy food or protection, you leave it behind. Text me when you leave the house. I'll meet you at Manny's place, right?"

"Right. Thanks, Blanc."

"Be careful, D."

Blanca knew she'd done a pathetic job of hiding her concern, but she couldn't help worrying about Darcie's chances. Since Blanca's group had escaped the attack on Eielson, they'd ventured out in ones and twos in civilian vehicles, probing to the south to find the extent of the Russian occupation. She knew that if Darcie went north from her house on Eagle River Loop Road, she'd probably avoid being seen, but if she turned to the west and went directly toward the highway, she'd almost certainly attract unwanted attention.

"You all right, Blanc?" Blanca's husband, Manny, had come in without her noticing.

She got up and wrapped her arms around him. "Just talked to Darcie."

"She OK?"

"For now, yeah." Blanca looked at Manny, then looked down. "I told her to come up here."

"All right."

"You're not mad?"

Manny grinned. "Why would I be? She and Ari are like family. Only people gonna be upset by them coming is your Army buddies, I'm guessing."

Blanca slapped his shoulder. "Why would you think that? They're good guys."

"I know," Manny said, "but I know how they think. I used to be one of 'em, remember? Extra mouths to feed, non-combatants to worry about. You know the drill."

"Just 'cuz you think like that, doesn't mean the rest of us do."

"You know I'm right."

"That's what bothers me. You still think like a soldier."

Manny grinned again. "Oh, I'm still a soldier at heart. I'm just smarter than the rest of those guys, is all. Better looking, too." He dodged as Blanca tried to smack him again. "When are they coming up?"

"She said she'd try to leave in twenty minutes. I told her I'd meet her at the fire station."

Manny pulled a doubtful face.

"What, no good?"

"I'd just hate to have her followed there," Manny said. "If she's not careful, she could lead a Russian patrol right to it."

"You have a better idea?"

"Maybe we should meet her halfway, make sure she's clear."

She thought about it for a moment. "That's not a terrible idea."

"Oh, thanks. Your enthusiastic praise gives me wings."

She laughed. "Sorry, babe. I'm just thinking if you're right, I should go wake up the standby crew and run down there in the Stryker, just in case."

"There's the paranoiac I know and love. You want me to go with? Or you gonna ditch the smart, handsome civilian for a bunch of smelly grunts?"

"My relationship with the 'smelly grunts' is strictly professional." She gave him an appraising look. "You can give me a ride to the station, though."

"Whoa." He grinned. "I'm flattered, I guess. I'll get the keys. Text Darcie and let her know we're coming."

Kenai Spur Road

26 Miles NE of Kenai, Alaska

The four Coast Guardsmen had gone another mile or so when they heard an engine. A battered old flatbed pickup lurched around the corner toward them, the driver slowing as he came into view. They all stepped off the pavement, and the driver stepped on the gas, blowing past them without another glance.

"Hey!" Taylor yelled, waving his arms as the pickup flew by.

"Chivalry must be dead around here," Rollinson said, leaning over with her hands on her knees again, trying to catch her breath.

"Jerk." Taylor was glaring down the road after the truck.

"Give the guy a break," Kennedy said. "He probably heard about the invasion, and figured we were the bad guys."

"You kidding?" Hulse was incredulous. "Everybody in Alaska knows what Coasties look like. That dude just didn't want to get involved. Hope it was his house we broke into."

"That does bring up a couple of questions, though," Kennedy said, as they all resumed walking. "We haven't talked about what to do if we run across a Russian patrol, or maybe worse, what we do if we run across some armed locals that figure *we're* the Russians?"

Rollinson stifled another cough. "Well, if we run across Russians, we can't very well fight, since all we have is two pistols between us. Best bet is to stay out of sight. As far as trigger happy locals?" She looked at Hulse and raised her eyebrows in doubt. "We'd better hope they're not some of the few Alaskans who *don't* know what Coasties look like. Until then, next time we hear a vehicle, we should probably get off the road until we can ID it as friendly or not."

They walked in silence a while longer, then Kennedy fell into step next to Rollinson, well behind the other two. "How you feeling, Boss?" He waved a hand at her before she could answer. "And don't tell me you're fine, 'cuz I know that's a load of crap. How much farther do you think you can go on like this?"

Rollinson looked ahead at Taylor and Hulse, then lowered her voice. "Honestly? I'm about done in, Dan. I inhaled a ton of water yesterday. I can't seem to clear my lungs." As if on cue, she went into a bout of coughing that forced her to stop walking and double over again.

"Hold up, guys," Kennedy called out. Taylor and Hulse walked back to them, both men looking worried. Rollinson kept coughing, then spat a gobbet of blood onto the ground at her feet. Kennedy glanced at the other two men. "Maybe we need to take a break."

Rollinson shook her head and wiped her mouth on the back of her sleeve. Taylor handed her his water bottle again, and she drank gratefully. "You need to be in a hospital, boss," Taylor said.

"You're probably right," she said, her voice like a rasp. "But I don't see one around here, do you? Which means, we keep walking."

"Come on, Joy." Kennedy took her by the elbow and ushered her off the road to a fallen log, helping her to sit down. "I agree, the fastest way to get you help is to keep moving, but we're not moving fast enough this way, and you clearly can't move any faster." Rollinson looked like she wanted to protest, but she was forestalled by another coughing fit. "I rest my case," Kennedy said. "We need to split up."

She looked up at him then, her eyes flashing disagreement, but he held up a hand. "Just hear me out. We can't leave you by yourself out here; you'd be sure to end up as bear chow before we were half a mile away."

Rollinson grinned in spite of herself, then shook her head and patted the 9mm pistol holstered on her survival harness. "I bite back."

Hulse laughed. "A 9 millimeter is a pretty tiny bite, when you're talking about brown bears. You'd just make 'em mad."

"So we can't leave you alone," Kennedy went on. "But if one of us stays, the other two can make better time toward help.

Sooner we can get somebody's attention, the sooner we can get you to a hospital."

"I'll stay," Taylor said. "I've got more medical training than either of you two." He looked at Rollinson and smiled. "Besides, if a bear charges us, all I need to do is outrun the Ell-Tee."

"You guys are so sweet," Rollinson whispered. "Hard to believe you're all still single."

Kennedy smiled. "All right, then. Looks like it's you and me, Darnell. Leave them the rest of the food. If we push it, we should be able to find help within the next ten miles or so."

Hulse nodded and handed over what was left of their rations. Then he and Kennedy took off at a trot, leaving the other two sitting there on the fallen log.

Eagle River, Alaska

Broome woke after just a few minutes, but he'd been out long enough to lose track of time. He tried to gauge the height of the sun by the angle of the shadows in the trees, and figured he hadn't slept long. He felt a *lot* hungrier, though.

Rolling over in the dirt and pine needles, he forced himself to his feet. Going back deep into the trees wasn't going to be an option with his leg in the condition it was. He decided he'd have to go back to the road and follow it. If he heard a vehicle, he'd just have to dive for cover.

Slowly, he worked his way through the trees, angling away from the solitary house he'd approached earlier. He wanted no part of a nervous mother with a loaded rifle. He came back up on the road about a quarter mile past the house, and started working his way to the west. Several hundred yards farther on, the road bent around to the north. Broome was getting tired again, and the pain from his leg was almost blinding. As he walked, he gradually drifted away from the shoulder and closer to the center of the road, but he was too worn out to notice.

The car came around the corner behind him suddenly, the dense vegetation on both sides of the road masking the sound of its approach until it was too late. Broome tried to run for the brush on the west side of the road, but as soon as he pushed off with his right leg, it buckled under him. He slipped in the loose gravel and went down hard.

I guess that's that, he thought, as he dragged himself from one knee back up to a standing position. *I'm done.* He turned to face the vehicle, and was surprised to see the young woman from before behind the wheel. For a brief moment, he thought she might just run him down and keep going, but then she brought the car to a skidding stop a couple of yards away. She sat there, staring at him over the top of the steering wheel. He raised his hands palms out, and started to back away, but she pulled the car closer and rolled her window down.

"I probably shouldn't do this, but we're getting out of here. Going north to stay with some friends. You want a ride, you can come along." For the first time, Broome noticed the child in the back seat.

"You sure?"

"No," the woman said. "But my daughter thinks we should help you, since I told her you weren't one of the bad guys."

"Well, I'm not. And I really would appreciate the help."

"Come on then. But you should know, I'm armed and I know how to fight." She looked embarrassed. "Just on the outside chance that you're lying."

"I'll keep that in mind, thanks." Broome shuffled painstakingly around to the passenger side and clambered in. "Thanks so much," he said as he pulled the door closed behind him and Darcie accelerated. "I was running out of gas."

"No problem. I'm sorry about before; I just couldn't risk letting you in. Now that we're leaving, though…" her voice trailed off. "I'm Darcie, by the way. This is my daughter, Ari."

"Hi," Ari said in a small voice from the back seat.

"Hi," Broome said. "Nice to meet you both."

"You mean, without me pointing a rifle at your head?"

"Yeah," Broome let out a tired laugh. "I could do without any more of that today."

"Are you a soldier?" Ari asked.

Broome half turned in his seat. "No, Ma'am. I'm a pilot. I fly an F22 fighter. At least... I did, until I got shot down yesterday."

Ari's eyes were wide. "Was it scary?"

Broome looked at the little girl and smiled. "You ever been on a carnival ride?"

"Just a merry-go-round."

"Well, it was like a really big, really fast merry-go-round, and it exploded before I could get off."

"That doesn't sound very fun."

He laughed again. "No, I guess it doesn't." He looked across at Darcie. "So, what changed your mind?"

"About you?" She jerked her head toward the back seat. "That was all Ari. After you left, she asked me why I was chasing away the good guy and doing what the bad guys told me to do. I felt guilty about it, but I'd already chased you off. Then we almost ran over you, and I figured it was another chance to do the right thing."

"I'm grateful you listened to her."

"My dad used to tell me that you could learn from anybody, no matter how old, educated or experienced they were. You just have to know when to listen."

Broome nodded and looked out the windshield. They were approaching an intersection.

Darcie pointed to the left. "My friend told me the Russians have a roadblock on the highway over that way. We should go right and try to stay away from it. She's gonna meet us in town, anyway."

"Sounds good to me," Broome said, looking both ways. "I'm just a passenger."

Darcie pulled the car forward and turned to the right. She didn't notice the Russian truck rounding the corner from the left until she was out on the road and glanced back into her mirror. "Oh, no." Broome caught her looking in the rear view, and twisted in his seat to look. There was a Lynx scout vehicle about five hundred yards behind them, coming up fast. As Broome watched, the top hatch opened and a soldier's head and shoulders appeared above the roof. He had a rifle, and was aiming it in their direction.

"Floor it!" Broome shouted, "GO, GO!!"

Darcie let out a shriek, but she stomped the accelerator to the floor at the same time. The Russian fired off a couple of rounds that went high. Darcie's Acura SUV was several years old, but it was light and had a powerful engine. The Lynx didn't have the acceleration to keep up for very long, so all they had to do was survive long enough to outdistance them.

"What should I do?!?" Darcie shouted, as the Russian let loose another burst from his AK-15.

"Just keep it pegged! We're pulling away!"

Then one of the Russian's rounds smashed through the back window, going between the two front seats and embedding itself in the dashboard. Darcie swore as the engine revved and their speed climbed through seventy miles an hour. Ari was crying and screaming in terror in the back seat.

Broome decided he'd had enough.

He reached up and opened the sun roof, then twisted around in his seat, planting his injured right knee on the center console as he drew his M18 from its holster. "Keep it straight for a sec, but keep going as fast as you can." He gritted his teeth against the pain in his leg, poked his head out of the sun roof and laid his arms flat across the roof, taking steady aim at the slowly receding Lynx. It was about two hundred yards back now. Broome knew the pistol didn't have the range or the killing power of the Russian's rifle, but he didn't care. He elevated the sight to a point about three feet above the shooter's head and squeezed the trigger.

The bullet smashed into the left side headlight on the Lynx, surprising the driver enough that he jerked the wheel slightly just as the soldier with the rifle fired again. The sudden jolt caused him to miss wildly. The driver braked hard, the nose of the Lynx dipping as the front shocks absorbed the weight of the truck. Broome adjusted his aim higher and fired again, but they were too far away now for him to tell if he'd hit anything. He could see the man in the hatch pounding the roof of the Lynx in exasperation before Darcie roared around a bend in the road and the Russians temporarily disappeared from view.

"Ari!" Darcie shouted. "Are you okay, honey?"

Ari was in hysterics and could only sob in response. Broome dropped back into the car, then wedged himself between the front seats so he could reach Ari. He quickly checked her over, releasing her seat belt so he could lean her toward him and check her back for bullet wounds. He was relieved not to find any. "It's ok, Ari. You did great," he said, re-connecting her belt and sagging back into his own seat. He looked over at Darcie. "She's fine. You ok?"

Darcie's eyes were huge and filled with tears. She was clearly terrified, but she was still doing a good job of holding it together while keeping the car on the road. "I think so."

They were coming into the outskirts of Eagle River. Subdivisions and strip malls cropped up along the road on both sides. The trees thinned out as they entered the built up area, and they could see more around them. There still wasn't any civilian traffic to speak of, but more importantly at the moment, there wasn't any military traffic either. It felt like they were driving into a ghost town.

They passed the high school and continued north. As they approached an intersection, they saw a police car speeding off to the west. "Should I follow him?" Darcie asked, her voice still shaking.

"I don't think so," Broome said. "Not sure where he's going, but if your friend said she'd meet you in town, we should probably just keep heading that way. Where exactly is she gonna meet you in town, anyway?"

"Next to a coffee shop we go to. We're almost there; it's only another block or two."

"Ok. Let's just stick to that…" He was cut off by the bark of an AK-15 close at hand, and looked around in time to see the Russian Lynx coming at them from a side street to the west. "Hit it, Darcie!" Broome fell back into his seat as Darcie stomped on the gas pedal. The SUV slewed crazily from side to side as she wrenched it around a corner to the right, trying to put distance between them and the Russians.

The soldier in the hatch of the Lynx was firing wildly now. Broome looked over his shoulder and could have sworn the man was laughing, but Darcie yanked the car into another turn, and he couldn't be sure. As they came around another corner, Darcie screamed again, yanking the wheel so hard to the right that the Acura slid sideways before the wheels impacted a curb and the car rolled over onto its driver's side, sliding several yards before grinding to a halt. As they came to rest, Broome saw a flash of movement as something big passed quickly through the intersection behind them. The deafening report of a large caliber machine gun ripped the air.

"Darcie?!?" Broome had to shout to be heard above the shooting. "You okay?"

"I'm not hurt," Darcie shouted back. "Ari, stop crying, honey! Are you hurt?"

Ari was wailing from the back where she was hanging sideways in her booster seat. Broome reached back to try to release her, but couldn't quite get there. Darcie released her own belt and clambered between the seats, trying to calm her daughter, but the heavy barrage of gunfire so close at hand had her inconsolable.

The shooting abruptly stopped, and Broome risked a glance out the rear window. An American Stryker had interposed itself between their vehicle and what was left of the Lynx. Two soldiers had dismounted the Stryker and were approaching the destroyed Russian vehicle, weapons raised, while the Stryker's roof mounted .30 caliber machine gun pointed at the wreckage, searching for a target. As Broome watched, a female soldier emerged from the back of the Stryker and ran toward their car.

"D?" she called out. She was a stocky Hispanic woman who looked like she'd be a match for any Russian, armed or otherwise. Darcie was too busy checking on Ari to notice, so Broome climbed up out of the passenger side of the car and raised his hands.

The soldier had her sidearm out in a flash, pointed at Broome's head. Without changing her aim, she leaned to one side, trying to get an angle to see inside the Acura. "D! It's Blanca! You okay?"

To Broome's relief, Darcie heard her. "We're ok, Blanc. Just scared. Don't shoot this guy, okay?"

Broome did his best to grin at the woman with the gun. "Captain Ray Broome, US Air Force," he said. "She's right, Sergeant; I'd really appreciate you not shooting me right now."

"Staff Sergeant Trujillo," she said, still not lowering the pistol. "What're you doing with them?"

"Got shot down, first night. Wandered around in the woods and came out in front of their house. Darcie ran me off at first, but then she picked me up off the side of the road a few minutes ago."

One of the soldiers trotted up. "All clear, True. We'd better get gone, before somebody calls in an airstrike or something."

Trujillo finally lowered her weapon. "D! Is Ari okay?"

Darcie was handing Ari up and out the passenger window to Broome, who'd climbed out and was crouched on the side of the car. "She's scared, but she's not hurt."

"All right, you guys are coming with us. We need to leave, right now. It isn't safe here."

"There's an understatement," Broome muttered.

Trujillo ignored him as she holstered her pistol and reached up to take Ari from him. "Hey, Ari. It's Auntie B. You want to go for a ride in my big truck?"

Ari kept sobbing as Trujillo turned her to face away from the now burning Russian truck. "I'm happy to see you, Blanc," Darcie asked, as Broome helped her to climb out of the wrecked Acura.

Trujillo was already heading for the Stryker with Ari. "Manny got me to thinking it'd be better to come get you. He was afraid you were gonna run into trouble before you could get out of town. Looks like he was right."

"You have fantastic timing, Sergeant," Broome said. "Thanks for bailing us out."

"I'm just glad we weren't late." She handed Ari to Darcie. "Get her strapped in." She looked at Broome, whose limp was obvious. "You hit, Captain?"

He grinned. "I fell out of my plane, fell out of a tree, and then fell into a hole."

Trujillo nodded, looking at him skeptically.

"Uh-huh. Well, try not to fall out of the truck, all right?"

Broome nodded and smiled again, following Darcie and Ari up the rear ramp into the Stryker. "I'll do my best."

As the big combat vehicle turned around and headed north, Broome looked down at Ari, sitting in Darcie's lap. Darcie was speaking softly, trying to console her daughter, who sounded like she was hyperventilating. "Ari, look at me," Broome said, just loud enough to be heard over the noise of the Stryker as it picked up speed. "Can you look at me?" After a moment, the little girl raised her eyes to his. "Remember what I told you about my jet exploding?"

Ari nodded, her eyes wet with tears.

"Well… What we just did? That was *way* scarier. So, what that tells me, is that you're a pretty tough little girl, you know? You made it through something even worse than I did when my plane got shot down. That's pretty impressive, if you ask me. I know a lot of grown men who wouldn't have been as brave as you were just now."

Ari took a couple of ragged breaths before answering. "But… but… you did it with us, too."

Broome nodded, stealing a glance at Darcie before answering. "Yeah. You're right. We all did it together. I think that makes us a pretty good team, don't you?"

Ari leaned her head against her mom's chest and nodded, keeping her eyes fixed on Broome's. She took a deep, shuddering breath. "I'm glad mommy didn't shoot you."

Broome couldn't help but laugh as he stretched his injured leg in front of him. "So am I, kiddo. So am I."

CHAPTER FIFTEEN
Estus Maximus

British Army Garrison - Stirling Lines
Credenhill, Herefordshire, England

"How's he doing?" Boone thrust a disposable cup full of steaming coffee at Holland as he opened the apartment door.

"He went out for a run," Holland answered, taking the coffee. "Come on in."

Boone followed Holland inside and glanced around. "You shouldn't get too used to this place. You stick around here much longer, you're gonna start sounding like a Brit."

"It'll make me seem cultured." Holland sat down on the arm of the couch and sipped his coffee. "I would like to get Tony home, though. This is decent, but it's still just someplace else."

Boone nodded. "The Japanese surrendered today," he said. His voice was expressionless. He could have been commenting on the weather.

Holland looked up. "What? The Russians invaded Japan, too?"

"Didn't have to," Boone said. "The Japanese saw the writing

on the wall. The Russians bypassed 'em to the north on their way to Alaska, but it doesn't take a rocket scientist to figure out they'll have Japan surrounded on three sides as soon as they consolidate their gains. The Japanese Prime Minister announced a 'non-aggression' pact with the Russians this morning, if you can believe that."

Holland scoffed. "The last time the Russians signed one of those, it didn't go so well for 'em."

"Yeah, well. Modern Japan isn't exactly Nazi Germany. I don't think the Russians are too worried about it this time around."

Holland shook his head. "Any other little rays of sunshine you're holding back?"

Boone took a deep breath. "Well, let's see. Taiwan's under a full invasion alert. They think the Chinese are finally gonna try to take the island back by force. Hard telling if the Chinese have the stomach for that yet, but you never know. My guess is they'll wait and see what the Russians do, but with Japan out of the way and Alaska looking like it won't last long, you couldn't really blame the Chinese for getting nervous. Sino-Russian border relations have never been exactly rosy."

"You think North Korea'll stay out?"

"They'll stay out, unless the fathead with the bowl cut gets an itchy nuclear trigger finger. I think the Chinese can keep him in check, at least in the short term. Shoot, if Russia wins in Alaska and starts looking to their own southern border, the Chinese and Koreans might feel like they have to join forces. That wouldn't be too much of a stretch." Boone set his coffee down and walked over to the window, hands jammed in his pockets. "Whole world's lost its mind."

Holland watched his friend. "You want to know what I think?"

Boone half turned, grinning. "No."

Holland ignored him and answered anyway. "I think we have bigger fish to fry at home. We need to get our own house in order, before we worry about the rest of the world."

"The rest of the world might not give us that kind of time."

Holland looked down at the floor. "Don't give up the ship, Boone."

Boone almost smiled at that. "It's already going down, brother."

"I disagree. America's been through plenty of trouble before, and come through all right. We just need to consolidate... get the different factions working together..."

"Might be better to just let it die, Law."

There was a long silence. "You don't mean that."

Boone turned around. "No? You're a history buff, so answer me this: If Rome could have survived - if they'd been able to fight off the barbarians and then flush the rot out of the Senate and off of the throne - do you *really* think it would have ever gotten better? Or just kept on trucking down the slippery slope to extinction?"

Holland sighed. "The Rome/America comparison has been done to death, man."

"Yeah, and with good reason. There's plenty of similarities, but it isn't just Rome and America, Law. That's too simplistic. I'm talking about great civilizations in general; *all* of 'em. They all fall, every one. America is like Rome in that they were both wildly successful *in their time*, but just like every other culture that made it to the top of the dung heap of history, there comes a time when it just can't fight off its own collapse."

"Wow."

"'Wow', what?"

Holland shook his head. "I never took you for a cynic, brother."

"No? And I never took you for a starry-eyed optimist, Law! Honestly, who are you to talk about the potential of western civilization, when you moved yourself out to the backside of Idaho and all but shut the whole country out because you were sick to death of the direction it was going? You told me yourself that you quit watching the news because it was too depressing, but now you're trying to defend the same bankrupt society the news was reporting on!" Boone flopped into a leather chair and scowled out the window.

Holland stared at his coffee cup. "I just can't see quitting, that's all."

Boone shook his head, then smiled. "I know. You wouldn't know the meaning of the word."

"I didn't think you did either," Holland said. "You serious about giving up?"

Boone got up. "Nah, man. Forget I said any of that. I'm just frustrated that it's come to this. I made the mistake of letting it get to me, is all."

"Totally understandable."

"But I still think you're wrong."

"You're giving me whiplash, Boone. Quit switching positions, would ya?"

"I'm not," Boone said. "You think America can bounce back, but you said we need to get our own house in order first, right?"

"That's right."

"And I said it might be better to just let it die. That was mostly out of frustration, but it had a grain of truth in it, too."

Holland scowled. "What *are* you talking about?"

"Look, man. American society is fractured, right? We can both agree on that, at least?"

Holland nodded.

"OK, then. Look at it this way. You're laid up in bed with a broken leg, and half a dozen armed robbers kick your door down. You gonna wait for the leg to heal before you defend yourself?"

Holland sighed. "That's a little overly simplistic..."

"I'm tailoring my message for my audience."

Holland chuckled. "So you think if we don't deal with the outside threat, we'll be dead before the internal threat has time to matter."

"Winner, winner, chicken dinner. Domestic protests,

crumbling economy, bad leadership - all that stuff will end up being the Russians' problem if we let them keep a toehold on our territory. You know how it goes, Law. Somebody establishes a beachhead, you gotta throw 'em back in the water quick-like, or before you know it, they'll use that beachhead to overrun the whole country."

"I get it." Holland shook his head. "But you can't deny that all the internal chaos is gonna make dislodging the Russians that much harder. Domestic problems tend to force people to lose focus on everything else."

"Nobody said it'd be easy," Boone said with a shrug. "Which brings me back to the original question you avoided. How *is* Tony?"

"I'm not sure," Holland sighed. "He seemed pretty fragile, like he was on an emotional roller coaster, you know? Up one minute and crash the next. Overall though, I thought he was doing great, considering everything he'd been through. But when he saw the news last night about the invasion, it just seemed like it ruined him. He got low and hasn't snapped back yet."

"Not surprising. He's a tough kid though. He'll get through. Just needs time, I'm betting."

"Yeah, well. It doesn't look like the world's gonna stop long enough to give him that time. Here I was hoping to get him home to some peace and quiet so he could recover, and now this happens."

"Yeah, the world does keep on turning. You can't ever tune it out completely, no matter how hard you try."

Holland scowled. "You think because I'm concerned about my son, that means I'm 'tuned out?'"

Boone held his hands up. "Don't get yer knickers in a twist, Law. I'm saying that having your only child return from the dead after two years is bound to make anybody want to forget the rest of the world for a while. You're *allowed* that much, brother."

Holland shook his head. "Sorry, Boone. I guess I am a little on edge. I'm beyond thankful that we got him back, but the fact is, he's changed. He mostly alternates between angry and withdrawn. Can't say I blame him. He's locked away for two years, and then when he gets out, he finds the whole world has turned upside down. I'd be withdrawn, too."

Boone raised an eyebrow, but decided not to comment on how withdrawn Holland had become himself over the past couple of years. "You gonna get him some help?"

"General Reardon called this morning and offered to let him stay here, talk to some SAS shrink."

"I believe the accepted term these days is 'therapist'."

Holland scoffed. "Look at you, all politically correct."

Boone grinned, but cocked his head to one side, looking carefully at his friend. "How're *you* doing, Law?"

Holland put his cup down. "I'm fine."

"*Everybody* says that."

"Yeah, well - just 'cuz it's a cliché doesn't mean it doesn't apply."

"Ok." Boone took a long sip of his own coffee.

Holland smirked. "You don't believe me."

"Hey man, I *know* you, remember? You were always the one who was rock solid, no matter how much of a fur ball we got caught up in. You never seemed to show any kind of stress from it. I always admired that about you, especially because *I* always had to cover up exactly how much the job got to *me*."

Holland's eyebrows went up. "*You* were faking, all those years?"

Boone chuckled. "'Fake it 'til you make it,' they told me. I guess when I couldn't make it, I just kept on faking it. I knew I was fooling myself, but I'm surprised I fooled you. Anyway, I always thought you were this super-human character, because none of what bothered me so much ever seemed to bother you at all."

"Aw, what a load of nonsense."

"No, it was true," Boone said. "For a while, anyway. But then after Lexie passed, I started to re-think it. I *saw* you change, brother."

Holland's face clouded at the mention of his late wife. He shook his head. "No way not to change, once you lose somebody like her."

"I know." Boone sprawled in the armchair and stretched his legs out. "It was the same with me and Mags." He watched his friend, tracking the discomfort in his face. "I think if she'd survived, I might have had something close to what you had with Lexie. Me and Mags just weren't together as long as you two, is all."

"I don't know if I ever told you how sorry I was about her passing, Boone."

Boone waved that off. "Of course you did. You and Lexie were the ones who got me through it, as much as two friends could do. But my point isn't about my losing Mags. We were only together nine years. Don't get me wrong - it was the best nine years of my life, but you and Lexie had decades together, and when she passed, you changed. I could see it. The job held me together after Mags died. That and raising Cece."

Boone's daughter Cèlia was married now with three kids of her own. Boone had made superhuman efforts to raise her as a single father in a job that demanded his near-constant absence, and father and daughter adored each other.

Holland smiled at the memory. "You did good with her, Boone."

Boone scoffed. "I had good material to work with. Cece's a carbon copy of Mags. But don't change the subject - we're talking about you, here. Since you took early retirement to take care of Lexie, you didn't have the job to come back to after she was gone. I think the only thing you had left to hold you together at that point was Tony, only he was a grown man by that time. Cece was little when her mom passed, so we still had each other - whenever I wasn't working. Tony was already out of the house when you lost Lexie, so you were left mostly alone."

Holland was staring straight ahead now, eyes fixed on a spot on the carpet.

Boone pressed ahead. "Then, when you thought Tony was gone too, you changed again. You sorta withdrew. It was like watching an armadillo curl up into a ball."

"If you're talking about Idaho, I moved there *before* Tony was captured."

"Idaho's just a place, brother," Boone said. "I'm talking about your state of mind. When you lost Lexie, it was like you were hollowed out. I remember thinking you'd better not go outside in a high wind, else you'd blow away."

Holland chuckled and shook his head.

"But then when Tony disappeared, it got worse," Boone went on. "You just sorta, you know - *died*. Without actually dying, if that makes any sense."

"Yeah," Holland said, his voice catching. "It makes perfect sense."

"It's understandable," Boone said. "Like I said, you and Lexie had something most people only dream about, and Tony's the type of kid most parents can only wish for. You lost *both* of them, in less than two years. That's gotta hurt, I don't care if you are Superman."

Holland sensed Boone was going someplace he didn't like. "That's all true enough, Boone. But I've got Tony back. I'm good now - never better. I'm just worried about his future, you know?"

Boone nodded. "I know. You think he'll take Reardon up on his offer?"

"I doubt it. I brought it up to him earlier, and then he got the sudden urge to go out for a run."

"Maybe you should go with him."

Holland blinked. "Go where? For a run?"

"No, stupid," Boone said, sitting up and propping his elbows on his knees. "Go see Reardon's shrink, with Tony."

"I believe the appropriate term these days is 'therapist'."

Boone grinned. "Whatever. He'll appreciate you being there, and if we're honest, you could use some help, too."

That made Holland tense up. "You think *I* have PTSD?"

Boone sighed. "Law, I think that after everything you went through over all your years of service, losing Lexie, losing Tony, then getting Tony back; if you don't have just a *little* bit of PTSD, then you must be some kinda cyborg sent back through time to kill us all."

Holland laughed, and the front door suddenly opened. Tony was standing there, with a nervous, hunted look on his face. Boone got up and walked over.

"Hey, Younger," Boone said, wrapping Tony in a bear hug.

"Hey, Uncle Boone." He broke the hug awkwardly and looked at his dad. "What's so funny?"

Boone answered for Holland. "I was just telling your dad that he'd make a terrible Terminator. His Austrian accent sounds more like somebody with a bad head cold."

"Huh." Tony didn't see the humor. He looked back at Boone, who had his keys in his hand. "You're not leaving just because I came back, are you?"

"Nope," Boone said, walking over to embrace Holland, who looked confused. "The Brits cooked up a plan to save the world from Russian cyborgs, apparently. General Reardon asked me to come along."

"You're leaving just like that, huh?" Holland said.

Boone smiled. "Just like that. Somebody's gotta try to stop the Red Menace."

"Boone." Holland gripped his friend's hand. "I… I don't have any words." He looked at Tony, then back to Boone. He had tears in his eyes. "What you did… finding Tony, helping to get him back… Thank you, brother."

"No worries." Boone clapped a hand on Tony's shoulder. "This kid's one of the good ones. I'm glad we could *all* help."

Holland took a deep breath and collected himself. "So,

speaking of help…"

"*No*, Law," Boone cut him off. "You two just got your lives back." He shook his head. "No way I'm gonna ask you to separate again so soon."

"What, did you forget what you just said about dealing with the armed robbers first?"

Boone grinned. "My advice is case-specific. In your case? Good grief, man, take a break for once in your life."

"I must have missed something," Tony said, looking from one man to the other. "*What* armed robbers?"

"He's talking about the Russian wolf on the Alaskan doorstep," Holland explained. "I offered to help, but…"

"We could go together," Tony interrupted.

Holland looked at his son and smiled, eyes welling with pride.

Boone looked at Tony from under knotted eyebrows. "That's good of you, kid. But here's the thing." He wrapped a beefy arm around Tony's shoulders and drew him aside. "See," Boone said in a stage whisper, "your old man has been through a lot, so he needs to stay here and talk to some folks to help get his head straight. It'd probably go a lot smoother if he had you here with him while he does that."

"I can hear you," Holland said.

A faint smile crossed Tony's face. "*He* needs *my* help, huh?"

"More than you know, kid. If you're here with him for his treatment, they might even be able to save him from a life of sitting in a chair and drooling all over himself."

"I'm standing *right here*," Holland protested.

"My point is," Boone said, still ignoring Law, "that the best medicine for your dad right now is your company. In all seriousness, he could use you here with him. The Brits are using some kind of rapid eye movement therapy that's supposed to help people get past the emotion of traumatic experiences without losing the facts of what happened, or something like that. General Reardon said it works incredibly fast, too."

"You knew about Reardon's offer?" Holland asked.

Boone grinned. "It might have come up."

"Ok, then. Since you seem to be better informed than I am, how fast is this therapy supposed to be?"

"Reardon said they've seen people get better after one session."

Holland snorted. "Oh, come on, Boone. PTSD isn't something you just get over like that."

Boone raised his hands, palms forward. "Hey, I didn't believe it at first either, but Archie vouched for it. Said he's done it, and so have a bunch of his buddies - guys with pretty severe cases. He said the average is about three sessions with the therapist, but some of them were completely functional after just one."

"That's pretty hard to believe."

"I know," Boone said. "But maybe that's just because we've been conditioned to have low expectations. You and I both know most PTSD therapies don't work, or they take years to do any good at all, so when something comes along that claims to be this effective, we're just naturally suspicious of it." He looked intently at Holland. "Do me a favor, man. Go. For just one session." He winked at Tony. "Then, if it doesn't kill you, I might even try it myself."

"You'd need a lot more than one session," Holland said, grinning. "You've never been quite right in the head."

Boone glared at Holland, but spoke to Tony. "Maybe the 'therapist' can teach your old man to use words that help, not words that hurt." That made Tony and Law both laugh. "Besides," Boone went on, "if it does work, you two can always catch up to us."

Holland looked over at Tony. "What do you think? Want to take a shot at 'curing' your old man?" Tony shook his head and looked down at the floor, considering. Holland watched him, afraid he might leave again.

"You know," Tony said slowly, "you guys are both *terrible* at encouraging people." He glanced up, and the hint of a smile was back. "Maybe *I* should go with Reardon, and you two can stay here for couples' therapy."

Boone looked at him, feigning shock. "Such insensitivity! Clearly, you're a chip off the old block."

Kenai Spur Road
26 Miles NE of Kenai, Alaska

"C'mon, Ell-Tee," Taylor pleaded softly. "Just try to relax, and breathe."

Rollinson was sitting with her back against a tree, gasping for every breath. She sounded like she was drowning, and Taylor felt helpless, knowing that he couldn't do anything for her. In all likelihood, she was suffering from secondary drowning as a result of all the sea water she'd swallowed when they'd ditched their helicopter the day before. The exertion of hiking as far as they had in an attempt to find help had probably made her condition worse.

Taylor was the newest member of Rollinson's crew, having transferred from Boston seven months earlier. At first, he'd been unsure of the soft-spoken pilot's ability to take charge when necessary, but she'd shown right away that she was a born leader. She just wasn't loud about it. Since then, Taylor had joined Hulse and Kennedy in their devotion and respect for their pilot. The four of them made an exceptional crew, and any of them would have given their last breath to help any of the others.

But now, when breath was what Joy Rollinson needed most, Taylor was helpless to give it to her. He had no medical kit, and no way of easing her breathing. He knew that her lungs, irritated by the ingested seawater, were inflamed and producing excess fluid in addition to the water she hadn't been able to cough up. All that fluid was restricting her ability to get enough oxygen, and the longer she went without proper treatment in a hospital, the more likely it was that she would simply suffocate and die.

The young woman who had impressed him with her professionalism, skill and friendship was dying right in front of him, and there was nothing Taylor could do to stop it.

Camp David, Maryland

"Try to relax, Will," Black said. The two men were walking down a tree-lined road between Camp David's main lodge and the skeet shooting range, where they'd landed in Marine One several hours earlier. "You did well getting him here, by the way."

"Can't help feeling like I lied to him," Beckerdite said. "I just told him there was a summit meeting with the British Prime Minister that Tolliver had been putting off for months. I told him that he'd promised to make time for it. He looked at me like he was trying to figure out if I was serious, and then he just shrugged and said yes like it was no big deal." He stopped walking and faced Black. "How did you get him to agree to the physical?"

"Doctor Oldenbourg did that. Just came into the room this morning, said 'Good Morning, Mr. President, are you ready for your physical?' and Reese just followed him out like a puppy."

Beckerdite shook his head in wonder. "What do you think his problem is?"

Black shook his head and resumed walking. "I'm not a doctor. I agree with you, though, for what it's worth. It looks to me like Alzheimer's, but I've never heard of that advancing so fast. I really have no idea."

Beckerdite's phone pinged in his pocket, and he stopped again to take it out. Black took his phone out as well. "I guess we'll find out soon enough," Beckerdite said. "Doc's done with him."

Back in the main lodge building, Black and Beckerdite met the

Physician to the President, Colonel (Dr.) Oldenbourg, in a private office adjacent to the President's quarters. Black shook the doctor's hand and got right to the point. "Well? What did you find?"

Oldenbourg wagged his head back and forth slightly. "Nothing good, I'm afraid. Based on a *very* preliminary investigation, as well as what you gentlemen and others in the White House have told me, I believe the President is suffering from Sporadic Creutzfeldt-Jakob Disease. I'll need a brain MRI, an EEG and possibly a spinal tap to be certain, but I've seen it before. He has all the classic symptoms, especially considering the speed of the disease's progression. That's usually what tips us off, is how fast this thing takes hold."

"What's 'Sporadic Crites...'" Beckerdite trailed off.

"Creutzfeldt-Jakob Disease," Oldenbourg corrected him. "It presents in two main forms most commonly. If it's the familial form, then it's caused by inherited mutations in the prion protein gene that damage the brain of the victim. That form typically progresses more slowly than what we're seeing here, which leads me to believe that isn't the case. If in fact, it's not the familial, but the sporadic or 'classic' form, then we really don't know what causes the mutation. Either way, the prognosis is grim. The 'classic' form, or what we refer to as sporadic CJD, progresses with alarming speed, and the condition is usually fatal within months of the first onset of symptoms."

"Months?" Beckerdite had gone pale. "He's been acting strangely for at least a month already. If it's what you say, then he really doesn't have much time left."

The doctor shook his head. "This isn't my specific area of specialization, you understand, but I did spend fifteen years as an infectious disease specialist at USAMRIID. The condition is uncommon, but I have studied it in connection with the Mad Cow Disease outbreaks in Britain years ago; and I've treated patients with it several times. I'm as certain as I can be without further tests."

"So," Black cut in, "in your professional opinion, is the President capable of carrying out the duties of his office?"

Oldenbourg sighed. "That would depend on the day. Victims of sCJD can have extended periods of complete lucidity - however, the longer the disease progresses, the fewer and further between those periods will become. He seemed perfectly lucid when I examined him just now, though he was very fatigued. I gave him something to help him sleep. But to be honest, he doesn't have much time left before it becomes completely impossible for him to carry out even the simplest task, much less the duties of his office."

"Does he know?" Beckerdite asked.

"Not yet," Oldenbourg glanced at Black before answering. "I told him there were several possibilities that could explain his symptoms, but I want to be certain before I tell him anything definitive. I can do the EEG and a spinal tap here, but for the brain MRI, we'd have to check him in to Walter Reed."

"And we cannot afford to do that at the moment," Black said. His tone hinted that there could be no argument on the subject. "When can you do the other tests, Doctor?"

"I'll let him sleep for a few hours, then I can see him again in the clinic here and get the tests set up. Should have some definitive results back by later this evening."

"All right. Thank you, Doctor. Please let me know if you need anything at all."

"Yes, sir, Mr. Secretary." Oldenbourg's cell phone buzzed, and he fished it out of his pocket, looking at the screen. "If you'll excuse me, gentlemen, I need to take this." He didn't wait for a response or look up from the phone as he left the room.

Black watched him go, furrowing his brow slightly.

After the door had closed, Beckerdite looked at Black in disbelief. "Oldenbourg is in on it," he said in a flat tone.

Black was forced to put Oldenbourg's odd departure to one side for the moment. "'In on' what, exactly, Will?"

"You really need to ask that question?"

Black lowered his head, then raised his eyes to glare at the younger man. "You think this is a conspiracy."

"What would you call it?" Beckerdite shot back. "You convince me to get the President up here under the pretext of finding out his medical condition, if any, and all along, you had the Physician to the President in your back pocket! Reese could have had a nasty hangnail, and you still would have had him diagnosed as critical before lunch! Do you have your inauguration speech already written, too?"

"You need to settle down, young man."

"No! I'm tired of being told to settle down! I don't want to be a part of this any more, *at all*. It isn't right, what you're trying to do."

"Not right?" Black got up and stepped in front of Beckerdite's chair, looming over him. "Not right? Please explain to me exactly what about this isn't right, Will!" He waved an arm in the direction of Reese's quarters. "That man very likely was involved in the *killing* of his former boss, just so he could have his job! And now, because that same man failed to appoint a vice president, we're staring down the barrel of a full-blown constitutional crisis the moment his condition gets so bad that a dead man couldn't help but notice it! Norton will come gunning for the presidency when that happens, you mark my words!"

He took a breath and continued, moderating his tone. "Now, whatever else you may think about me, Mr. Beckerdite, I am a patriot. I love this country, warts and all. Reese is crooked, but that fact is likely to be rendered moot in a few weeks when they haul him off to a home to live out what little time he has left. Norton is just as bad if not worse. I will *not* stand by and allow him to step into the presidency or destroy the nation trying, just because Reese was too paranoid, reckless or ignorant to nominate a second in command!" He walked back over to his chair and sat down.

"I'm not perfect, Will. I'll be the first to admit that. But too often, the presidency goes to the one who's most able to win a surface level popularity contest with the voters. I couldn't compete on that field, because as you pointed out, political correctness is not exactly my strong suit. I'm abrasive, rude and insensitive. But if you want someone who is willing to work themselves to the bone to put the country's best interests ahead of their own gain, then I'm the only one on the field at the moment. If we allow Norton to take the office, we lose the country. I'm certain of that."

Beckerdite was trying to think of a response when Dr. Oldenbourg came back into the room. His expression was grim.

"Was there something else you needed to tell us, Doctor?" Black asked.

"Things just got a lot more serious, Mister Secretary," Oldenbourg said. "I just got off the phone with the Centers for Disease Control. They think we may have an outbreak on our hands."

"An 'outbreak'? Of *what?*"

"It's apparently too early to tell, but it seems to be a type of hemorrhagic fever. Could be Ebola, or Marburg. They're waiting on test results."

Black glanced over at Beckerdite, who had buried his face in his hands. "Where?"

"First patient showed up yesterday in Los Angeles. White female, twenty-six years old. She died an hour after she got to the hospital."

"One patient doesn't seem like much of an outbreak to me, doctor." Black said.

Oldenbourg shook his head. "She's not the only one. She just appears to have been patient zero."

"Exactly how many more people are we talking about?"

"In the past twenty-four hours, forty-three similar cases in Los Angeles alone, sir. Fifteen in the San Francisco Bay Area, twelve in Seattle, nine each in Portland and Las Vegas. Various other cities all along the West Coast are reporting single digit numbers as well. All the patients have underlying asthma in common, but they're presenting with hemorrhagic fever."

Black scowled. "Asthma? Is it possible somebody laced a batch of inhalers with a virus?"

"That's a possibility. They're running tests on all the inhalers the patients had in their possession, but it's still too early to tell with any level of certainty. I'll need to brief the President, sir."

Black looked at him. "You think that'll make any difference?"

"My opinion is irrelevant at this point, Mr. Secretary. I have a job to do."

Black nodded. "Then you should probably go wake him up, Doctor." Oldenbourg nodded and left the room. Black eased himself into a chair, sighing.

"This is probably where you say 'I told you so,'" Beckerdite said bleakly.

"Not really my style, Will. But I'm sure it's completely obvious to you now why we need to finish what we came here for."

Beckerdite raised his head. "'Obvious' doesn't make it any more palatable." He got up and headed for the door.

"Where are you going?"

"I have no idea, Mr. Secretary," Will answered, without turning around. "All I know is that this whole thing makes me sick and terrifies me at the same time. I just want to be someplace else."

Black nodded as the younger man left the room. *I can certainly understand that,* he thought.

Kenai Spur Road
  NE of Kenai, Alaska

"C'mon, c'mon!" Kennedy urged. "They should be right up here someplace!" the driver of the pickup they'd flagged down just stared out the windshield, not sharing the same sense of urgency at all, much to Kennedy and Hulse's exasperation. The pickup rolled around a bend in the road, and Kennedy's heart jumped as he saw a lone silhouette walking toward them half a mile away. Then his heart dropped again.

It was Chris Taylor, and he was carrying a body.

Taylor's eyes kept filling with tears as he walked. Joy Rollinson had fought for breath as long as she was able, and when she finally stopped breathing altogether, Taylor had worked himself to exhaustion giving her mouth to mouth in a vain attempt to force air into lungs that were full of liquid. Rollinson had died looking into his eyes as he leaned back to take another breath, and he'd immediately felt like he'd failed her.

Unable to sit with her and wait, and unwilling to leave her, Taylor had slung her body across his shoulders in a fireman's carry and set off down the road. When the pickup carrying Hulse and Kennedy came around the corner, his feelings of abject failure came rushing back. He just stood there in the road, waiting for the rest of his crew.

As the truck drew alongside, Kennedy couldn't tear his eyes away from Taylor, holding the body of their friend and pilot. He and Hulse had run for several miles before finding the man driving this battered old truck, and they'd both chafed at the lack of urgency the man displayed in getting them back. Now, that didn't matter any more. They were too late.

In the back seat, Hulse was in shock. He wanted to think that maybe Rollinson was just unconscious, but one look at Taylor's face, and he knew. The old man brought the truck to a stop, and Hulse followed Kennedy as he got out.

Taylor looked exhausted. He started to lower Rollinson's body to the ground, then staggered as he lost his balance. Kennedy grabbed him as he fell, easing his burden by gathering Joy into his own arms and gently laying her out on the road. Hulse came up and laid an arm across Taylor's shoulder, and they all just looked down at her, stricken by their loss.

"You still wantin' a ride back to town, then?" The old man had come up behind them, unnoticed. "Better load 'er in the back. I ain't got 'nuff gas to be sittin' around here idling all day."

CHAPTER SIXTEEN

Mollis Sub Ventre Sunt

**Queen Elizabeth Hospital
Birmingham, England**

Day 20

"Accelerated Resolution Therapy, or 'A-R-T'," the doctor said. She was in her early sixties, and looked more like a dowdy grandmother than a cutting edge clinician. "It works through what we call memory reconsolidation, which is basically replacing negative images and sensations in the memory with positive ones.

"Essentially, what we will do is have you bring up the traumatic event in your mind and walk through it, just as if it was happening again. The difference between ART and traditional treatments is that we don't require you to verbalize anything about the experience. You can say nothing to me whatsoever, if that's what you prefer; but you do go through the event mentally.

"As you're doing that, I will be moving my hand from side to side in front of your eyes, which gives your eyes something to follow, and replicates the eye movements we see during REM sleep."

"So, you're a hypnotist." Tony's voice was flat and skeptical.

"Not at all," the doctor said. "Hypnotism actually presents entirely different electrical patterns in the brain than we see through A-R-T. I will not be hypnotizing you, no."

Holland cut in. "So, that's all you do, is wave your hand? Ma'am, forgive me for saying so, but that seems a little far-fetched."

"I understand your skepticism, Mr. Holland," she said. "But no, that's not all that's involved. As I move my hand, you will bring up an alternative, positive outcome to the situation; how you might have liked to see it turn out, for example. You will mentally watch that outcome as you continue to follow my hand, and the bilateral eye movement will help to store your traumatic memories in such a way that they no longer have primacy in your mind. You'll be able to recall the memory without the emotional stress that was previously associated with that memory."

Holland glanced sideways at Tony, who was slowly shaking his head. "I don't know, Doc," he said. "I've always sort of believed that if something sounds too good to be true, it probably is."

"That's a fair statement," the doctor said. She folded her hands in front of her. "Let me try to explain it in a different context. If you had suffered, say, the loss of a limb in combat; you might expect to have some sort of physical therapy as part of your treatment, to help you learn how to function with your injury, correct?"

"Sure."

"Of course. So now imagine that you have that same injury, and your doctor offers nothing but endless prescriptions of Percocet or OcyContin - with no physical therapy whatsoever. What do you suppose your potential for recovery would be?"

"Pretty slim," Holland said. "Potential would be a lot higher for addiction than anything else."

"Precisely," she said. "A-R-T is like physical therapy for your memories. The treatment itself seems unorthodox, but the actual effect it has is remarkable. We're treating the underlying cause rather than just putting a bandage on the symptoms. A-R-T is a healing process, not just a painkiller."

Holland looked at Tony, who was leaning forward, no longer shaking his head. "What do you think, son?"

Tony blinked, then looked at his dad. "I'm not sure what to think."

"How 'bout I go first, then?" Holland asked.

Tony shook his head. "You don't have problems, Dad - I'm the one that's messed up."

Holland laughed. "You don't know me very well, bud. I started having nightmares as soon as I heard you were missing."

"*Really?*"

Holland nodded. "Really. A lot of times, I'd see you out in public - at least, I'd imagine that I saw you. Across the street, passing me in another car, all kinds of places." Tony was staring at his dad now, his jaw slightly open. "All those years in the military, I never had that kind of thing happen to me, but as soon as I thought I'd lost you, I felt like I couldn't control my own imagination. Then, when we found you, I hoped that once we brought you back, that stuff would go away, but it hasn't. Night before last was the worst nightmare I've ever had."

"I didn't know, Dad."

"Doesn't matter." Holland reached over and squeezed his son's shoulder. "If you don't want to do this, that's fine. But I'm gonna give it a shot, no matter what you decide. I don't want to live with this fear constantly jumping out at me when I least expect it. And if it doesn't work out for me, you'll know not to waste your time." He looked up at the doctor. "When can we start?"

She smiled and rose to her feet. "Right now, if you'd like."

* * *

An hour and a half later, Holland emerged into the waiting room. Tony saw him coming and stood up. The expression on his dad's face was completely changed. Tony thought he saw some of the old playfulness there again, in spite of obvious signs of fatigue.

"Well?"

Holland said nothing, just grabbed Tony and crushed him to his chest in a hug.

"Uh, Dad? You wanna let me breathe a little, here?"

"You gotta give this a try, son," Holland said, pulling back and holding Tony at arm's length. He shook his head, smiling. "It's crazy, but I can't believe how much it helped in just that one session."

"You're serious?" Tony asked.

Holland nodded. "I'm telling you, bud - it works. At least, it seems to work. I haven't ever been able to think about the time you were a prisoner without feeling like I was suffocating; but now?" He spread his hands. "I can't explain it. It feels like I'm still fully aware of everything that happened, but I'm just not being crippled by it any more."

Tony nodded, watching his dad carefully. He'd been surprised by how serious the man had been when they'd reunited just a couple days ago - his dad had always been reserved, but he'd also been a loving, happy man who gave his wife and son all his love unconditionally. But there, under fire in Afghanistan, Tony had seen someone different. Holland had displayed a kind of barely controlled but intensely focused violence that Tony had never seen in him before, and now, it was like someone had thrown a switch and turned that part off. In spite of that, Tony still wasn't fully convinced.

"I just don't see how it could help that fast."

"Well, you'll never know if you don't at least try it. Look, son. I've been around guys my entire career who've struggled with PTSD. For whatever reason, I've been fortunate enough not to have to deal with it until you went missing, but now that I've had a taste of what it feels like?" He shook his head. "I don't want anything to do with it. I certainly don't want to be fighting those demons for the rest of my life, and I don't want you to have to do that, either. I know this seems weird at first glance, but if it can get us better?" He spread his hands. "I think we should give it a chance."

Tony stared at his feet for a long moment. When he finally looked up, there was a determination in his eyes that hadn't been there a moment earlier. "All right," he said. "If you think it's worth it, I'll give it a shot."

"Atta boy." Holland put a hand behind Tony's neck and drew him close, pressing their foreheads together. "I'm proud of you, son, you know that?"

Tony reached up and clasped his hands behind his dad's head. They stayed like that for several moments before he managed to speak. "There's nothing to be proud of, Dad. I let everybody down."

"*That's not true.*" Holland's voice was quiet, but emphatic. "You did everything you could, and when you couldn't do any more, you still *stayed alive*. That's the most important thing. You survived it, son. You didn't quit, you hear?"

Tony's eyes were clamped shut, and he was clearly struggling. "Do you ever feel like you're just gonna explode?"

"You bet I do. When the government refused to help find you, I was so full of rage, I scared myself. I thought I was gonna hurt somebody. Or worse."

Tony released his grip on Holland's neck and straightened up. "That's how I feel, Dad. *All the time.*" He had tears in his eyes.

"Then let's try to change that." He waved to the receptionist, who nodded and picked up her phone, speaking into it briefly.

The doctor emerged from her office, smiling. "Mr. Holland? Shall we begin?"

Lawson wrapped an arm across his son's shoulders and led him forward.

Skagway, Alaska

Kevin 'Beast' Burdin followed Boone off the plane and onto the tarmac. It was freezing outside even though it was fully spring. Burdin pulled his coat tighter around himself and hunched his shoulders against the wind blowing off one of the dozens of nearby glaciers.

Skagway lies at the end of a deep fjord eighty-five miles north-northwest of Alaska's capital of Juneau. A destination for cruise ships on whale watching and glacier tours before the economy crashed, it was also a convenient place for Boone to stage a covert insertion into Russian-held Alaska.

Just over five hundred miles east of Anchorage, Skagway was also a little too far out of the way for the Russians to have bothered with just yet. Still focused on consolidating their gains in and around Anchorage, Fairbanks and the North Slope oil fields, the Russians had so far been content to leave the towns and villages on the Alaskan Panhandle alone. They were strategically insignificant to an occupying force trying to control resources and commerce, but they were critical to a clandestine opposition force.

Boone had planned this operation on the fly with help from General Reardon. Intended as an area reconnaissance, he, Burdin and other employees of Gallowglass Tactical would infiltrate occupied Alaska along with some British Special Air Service commandos. Working in teams of two to four men, they would insert into various locations across the state to gauge Russian troop dispositions, strengths and weaknesses.

The two men walked into the passenger terminal and stopped to look around. There were about a dozen people in the small building besides the ten who had just got off the plane with them. Boone scanned the room, his eyes finally coming to rest on an older man with a massive grey beard near the front doors who was staring right at him. Boone walked over.

"You haven't changed much, Louie," he said, sticking out his hand. "Except for that road kill clinging to your chin."

Louie grabbed Boone and hugged him, slapping his back so hard he almost knocked the wind out of the younger man. "Jealous. You wish you could grow a beard like this."

"I wish you hadn't had salmon for lunch," Boone said, reaching out and tugging on Louie's beard with a grin. "You left half the fish in there."

Louie grinned. "Who's the youngster?"

Burdin stepped up and offered his hand. "Kevin Burdin."

"AKA 'Beast'," Boone added, as Louie enveloped Burdin in a hug. "Beast, meet Armstrong."

"Nice to meet you," Burdin squeaked. Louie let him go. "I can see where you got that nickname." Louie just gave him a quizzical look, and Burdin laughed. "You almost cracked my ribs."

"Not sure what that has to do with it," Louie said. "I got the nickname because I look exactly like Louis Armstrong." Burdin looked at him blankly for a moment, then glanced at Boone and raised an eyebrow. "You know," Louie offered. "The trumpet player?"

Burdin shook his head. "I'll have to take your word for it."

"Way before his time, Louie," Boone said. "So, you got a ride, or are we walking from here?"

"Kids these days," Louie said, winking at Burdin. "Always want to be driven everywhere."

"I'm only ten years younger than you," Boone protested.

"You look ten years older. I bet I could outrun you right now."

"Shouldn't we find your walker first?"

"Jeez," Burdin said. "You two are like a couple of teenagers."

"Ya gotta laugh at life, son," Louie said, leading them to the parking lot. "Because without a doubt, it's gonna laugh at you."

"*How* far?" Burdin was incredulous. They were gathered around

Louie's dining room table.

"Nine hundred miles or so, by boat," Louie said again.

"Why can't we just fly closer first?"

"Because we don't know how tight the Russians have the airspace locked down. Lots of rumors flying around about Russian jets shooting down just about anything that flies. They're strangling the little villages out in the bush, and we can't take the chance that some combat air patrol wouldn't see you and splash you without so much as a tip of the hat."

"But they're not cracking down on commercial boat traffic?"

"Even Russians gotta eat, son. As far as we can tell, they're leaving the fishing fleet mostly to its own devices, which is why we're sending you in a trawler. You get a nice ocean voyage from here to Anchorage, get to do a little fishing while you're at it. Everybody wins."

"How long will this trawler take to get us there?" Boone asked.

"Sixty, seventy hours," Louie said. "Figure in at least a day for fishing en route - four days, tops."

Burdin shook his head in disbelief. "Fishing? We don't have time to be screwin' around, fishing!"

Louie cocked his head and looked like he was about to say something, but Boone cut in. "Yes, we do. We're going in as crew on a fishing boat, right? We get stopped and have no evidence of actual fishing on the boat, you think that'll prompt more questions, or less?"

Burdin looked at him, then sat back and nodded. "Right. Sorry. It's been a long couple of days. I'm not thinking straight, I guess."

"No worries, younger," Louie got up and moved to the ancient coffee maker on the counter. "I wish we had a better option at this point, but the Russians have the upper hand, for the moment. They've completely locked down the economic infrastructure in the state. We have to imagine they're working their way out from the cities. I've heard rumors that there's at least one nosing around here in Skagway already. Best to act natural until we know for sure where we stand."

"You think there's anything to those rumors?" Boone asked.

"There's always *something* to a rumor," Louie paused to hand Burdin a cup. "There's always new people in this town, so it's impossible to know for sure. I'm constantly seeing new faces at the docks; guys looking for work, tourists wandering around. Mostly guys looking for work the last couple of years, though."

"Anybody new show up recently, that might be an informant?" Burdin asked.

Louie grinned. "Just you, *comrade*."

Alexandria, Virginia

Nikki Nikkanen tossed her keys on the counter, then fished her ringing phone out of her pocket and answered it. "This is Nikki."

"*Nikki, it's Charley.*" Nikki's boss at Net News Daily, Charley Carter, had taken to calling her at all hours of the day and night since she'd managed a personal interview with the Lemhi County Sheriff more than a week ago. That interview had led NND to break the story on Lawson Holland, who at the time had been the suspected murderer of President Galen Tolliver. Shortly after that, it had also led to NND breaking the rest of the story, which was that Holland *wasn't* the murderer, but an apparent Good Samaritan who had almost saved Tolliver's life. Since *that* story broke, Carter had leaned heavily on his newest reporter.

"What's up, Charley? If you're wondering about me talking to Holland yet, I'm sorry, but I still haven't been able to track him down. Guy's a ghost, and I -"

"*That's not why I called,*" Carter cut her off. "*You haven't had any contact with anyone at the White House since you left, have you?*"

That caught her off guard. "No. You know they basically froze me out after I quit. I mean, Will Beckerdite called me the day I left to say he was sorry it happened, but that's it. Why?"

"You think Beckerdite might be willing to give you some inside baseball?"

"I doubt it, Charley. He's worried about his own job. I think Reese scares him. Will has a wife and a kid; he doesn't want to screw up his gig, even if his boss is a loon."

"Funny you should use that particular term."

"What term? Loon? That isn't funny - everybody knows Reese has been acting like he's a couple sandwiches shy of a picnic."

"It may be more than just occasional erratic behavior, Nikki. I want you to dig around, see if you can sniff anything out."

"What, you think he's certifiable? So do a lot of people, but I don't think there's much anybody can do about it. What have you heard?"

"I have a couple of my own sources in the White House," Carter said. *"More than one has mentioned Reese being absent from just about every staff meeting for several days. He's there, in the White House, but he's not there, if you get my meaning. Then today I hear that he suddenly left yesterday to go up to Camp David, but there was no press release, no scheduled statement from the press office, nothing. We almost always get something when a sitting president goes up there, even if it's just the standard 'flew to Camp David for a working weekend' nonsense."*

"I'm not sure what you're thinking is happening here, Charley. Reese doesn't follow any of the norms at all. Abnormal *is* his normal. You sure a trip to Camp David is worth getting excited about?"

"Let's just say I have reason to believe Reese isn't driving the bus any more. Call it intuition, call it sixth sense, whatever you like, but it feels to me like when Kim Jong-il disappeared in 2009. They didn't admit he was dead until two years later. They just kept on like nothing had happened."

"Come on, Charley. You don't think Reese is dead?"

"Not dead, no. But I think something's going on that somebody in government would rather keep a lid on. Ask around, Nikki. See if you

can catch a whiff of anything."

Nikki was skeptical of the whole idea, but she agreed to do as Charley had asked. He'd been very good to her, hiring her on the spot after she'd quit her job as Reese's press secretary less than three weeks earlier. He was a good boss, but he did have a flair for conspiracies that Nikki didn't always share. She shook her head as she scanned the contacts on her phone. *Maybe I just don't want to go anywhere near the White House again,* she thought. She found Will Beckerdite's contact, swallowed hard, and placed the call.

He picked up on the third ring. *"Beckerdite."* Nikki could hear birds in the background.

"Will, hey. It's Nikki Nikkanen. How're things?"

Beckerdite's voice was atonal and clipped. *"Things are crap. You know that."*

"Uh, yeah, I guess I do. I'm really sorry about that."

"What can I do for you, Nikki?" Beckerdite sounded tired and low on patience.

"Well, I just wanted to say that I really appreciate how you treated me while I was working at the White House, Will. It wasn't the best work environment."

"It still isn't." He paused, and she heard a car door slam, blocking out the bird noise in the background. *"But I'm guessing that's not why you called, and I have to tell you, I can't talk to you about anything regarding the president specifically or the White House in general. You're sort of a pariah around the administration, you know."*

"I believe that, and I understand the difficult position you're in."

"I really doubt that." Nikki sensed something more in Beckerdite's statement than just dissatisfied sarcasm. She decided to go for broke.

"Will, you know I'm working for Net News Daily now, right?"

"Oh yeah. Everybody was talking about how fast you landed on

your feet. I wouldn't show my face around the press office any time soon, if I were you."

"I didn't plan to," she said, chuckling. "Look Will, the real reason I called you was that we're hearing some rumblings coming out of the White House that everything isn't exactly running smoothly, and I was wondering if you could maybe give me a little insight into what the problem is?"

There was a long silence before Beckerdite finally answered. *"Nikki, if you want my honest opinion, I think you did a great job in the short time you were the acting press secretary. You had an impossible to please boss and a hostile press, and you handled it better than anybody expected."*

"Thanks -"

"And I consider you to be a friend, seriously I do. But if you think I'm going to comment on anything in this administration and thereby jeopardize my own position, you've lost your grip on reality. Goodbye, Nikki."

With that, he hung up, leaving Nikki staring at her phone and wondering if he'd been trying to tell her something without actually looking like he was.

Now I'm *starting to think like Charley,* she thought.

Nikki sat at her kitchen table for several minutes, trying to put a finger on Beckerdite's behavior. She knew things at the White House were a mess, but there had been something else in Will's voice; something unspoken, just bubbling beneath the surface. He'd seemed frightened, almost.

She picked up her phone and called Charley again. He picked up right away.

"What'd you get?"

"Nothing, I think."

"'You think?' I'm not sure if I should be disappointed or intrigued."

Nikki described her conversation with Will, including his tone and what mannerisms she'd been able to detect over the phone. But what got Carter's attention was her assessment of

Beckerdite's unspoken fear.

"Frightened?" Carter asked, clearly curious. *"Does he strike you as a timid person, under normal circumstances?"*

"Not timid, no. More like… careful. Cautious. Don't get me wrong, he knows his job, but working for Reese makes it almost impossible to be good at it. I think that maybe Will just came to the point where he was overly cautious about everything he did, just to get by. He never seemed scared, though. Just cautious."

"But today, he seemed frightened?"

"That's what it felt like to me."

"Okay. So what would frighten a normally cautious man who works for a completely unpredictable boss?"

"I don't know, Charley. Reese is already a loose cannon. I don't see how he could get any more off-putting than he already is."

"So, what if what's bothering Mr. Beckerdite is coming from someone or something other than Reese?"

Nikki scoffed. "Take your pick, then. There's any number of reasons for somebody to be terrified at the moment."

"Do you have any other contacts you could try?"

She thought about it for a long moment. "There might be one. But don't get your hopes up - this is the longest of long shots."

The phone rang twice before someone picked up. *"Ethan Pellegrini."*

Nikki had to stop herself from cringing at the voice on the other end of the line. "Ethan, good afternoon. It's Nikki Nikkanen."

Pellegrini's tone turned icy. *"What do you want? Calling to see how the knife wound is healing?"*

"I'm sorry?"

"You should be. That little stunt of yours, telling the president that I'd sent you out to interrupt his golf game right before you quit. You almost got me fired."

"Look, I'm really sorry about that, Ethan, that wasn't my

intention."

"You could have fooled me."

"Honestly, though - can you blame me? You seemed to be doing your best to make my job impossible."

"Hmph." He paused. *"Well, maybe I was, just a little. I might have been getting a little too territorial for my own good."*

"Sounds like we were both a little out of line. I am sorry about that, seriously."

He brushed the apology off. *"Doesn't matter. I doubt I'll have any territory to defend in a few days, anyway."*

"Oh? Why do you say that?"

"Isn't that obvious? 'Director of Oval Office Operations', when there are basically no operations going on anywhere in the White House, much less the Oval Office? But I suppose I shouldn't be telling you that, should I?"

"Why not?"

He laughed. *"Because you're the enemy, now! You're part of the press, and are therefore not to be trusted!"*

"Well, coming from my previous job, I can see how that might be the wisest course."

"I bet you can. So is that what this is about? You trolling for inside dirt?"

"You might call it that," she admitted. "What with the president cancelling all of his pressers, it's getting hard to get a read on what the executive branch is doing."

Pellegrini laughed again, rueful this time. *"I'm still in the executive branch, and I don't know what we're doing, either. You shouldn't feel bad about it."*

"Well, since we're back on speaking terms, would you mind talking about that? Completely off the record, of course. 'Anonymous source', and all that."

"There's no such thing," he scoffed. *"But why not? You ask, I'll decide if it's worth answering. Or more likely, I won't have the first idea what the answer is, and you'll be just as out of the loop as I am. Fire away."*

"Thank you, Ethan. I appreciate it." Nikki's mind was racing. She'd expected Pellegrini to hang up on her; now she didn't want to press him too hard for fear of scaring him off. She decided to start with something small. "For starters, what can you tell me about the daily press briefings? Are they going to come back any time soon?"

"I doubt it," Pellegrini said. *"Reese is paranoid - even more so than he was when you were still here. No way he's going to stand up and let the press take shots at him in person. As far as the press office doing it, they still haven't replaced you, so I don't think the daily briefs are a top priority at the moment."*

"Wow."

"Yeah. Anyway, he spends most of his time drifting off topic no matter what he's talking about, so it's probably better for the public image if he stays out of sight."

"Is he?"

"Is he what?"

"Staying out of sight? On purpose, I mean?"

"I don't know if it's intentional or not, but based on what I've seen, I think it's good policy."

"So he's still conducting day to day business, he's just not keeping the press in the loop."

"That's putting it mildly. I don't see a lot of day to day work getting done, though. Between you and me, they had an emergency meeting in the Situation Room the day before yesterday, because of the invasion I'm sure, but Will Beckerdite had to go and drag Reese out of the residence to get him to the meeting. He was watching cartoons or something, can you believe that?"

She couldn't, but she wanted to keep Pellegrini talking, without appearing to focus on Reese. "So, did they come up with a plan for dealing with the Russians?"

"Not as far as I know. Reese went to the Situation Room, yelled at everybody for a few minutes, then acted like he had someplace else he needed to be. Walked out and left them to play army men by themselves."

"That's pretty incredible, considering the circumstances. I'll bet you're pretty swamped trying to handle the fallout from all that?"

"You might think so, but no. There haven't been too many requests for the president to clarify or follow up, or really to do anything, if I'm honest. That's why I say I don't have any territory to defend."

That was odd. Normally, the president's schedule was full from dawn to dusk and beyond, with dozens of requests coming in every day for him to do more. Pellegrini should have been extremely busy under the circumstances.

"So, how is his schedule being set up and run, if you're not doing it?"

"I don't know," he answered, obviously frustrated. *"Will Beckerdite does some of it, but the rest is just random, seat of the pants type stuff. You know what it reminds me of? In junior high school, when the teacher just randomly didn't show up to class, and everything just turns into chaos. You ever have that happen?"*

"Yeah, once or twice."

"That's what it's like here. The inmates are running the asylum." Nikki was about to comment, but Pellegrini kept going. *"And to top it all off, yesterday, Beckerdite came in here and told the president that he had a summit meeting to attend with the British PM at Camp David, and Reese bought it! He left with Beckerdite and the White House doctor in Marine One first thing yesterday morning."*

"Why'd the doctor go with them? Is Reese sick?"

"I don't know. You know how he usually travels with the president on longer trips. Maybe he's depressed, I have no idea. But that's not the weird thing - the weird thing is that there is no summit meeting. The British PM is on a diplomatic visit in Australia."

"You sure that's what Will told him?"

"Well, it's second-hand information; some of the executive assistants overheard them talking about it when they came out of the Oval Office, but they all told me they heard the same thing."

"And you have no idea why he'd need to go to Camp David?"

"No idea."

"Interesting. Anything else you want to share, Ethan?"

"Not at the moment. But I may need help finding a job after I get fired from this one; maybe I'll use you as a reference."

"Let's hope it doesn't come to that."

"You can hope all you want," Pellegrini laughed. *"With all the crazy going on in the world, you add in Reese's behavior, and it doesn't take a rocket scientist to figure out that something's gotta give, one way or another. I'd lay even money that I'm out of work in a month. I never should have gone into politics. For what it's worth, I'm sorry for how I treated you while you were here. You deserved better."*

"Thanks for saying that, Ethan. If you need anything, feel free to call, all right? I don't know if I'll be able to help, but I'm willing to try."

"I might do that," Pellegrini said. *"In the meantime, don't forget, I'm anonymous."*

"I won't forget. Thanks again, Ethan."

Nikki put her phone down and stared out the window. It wasn't at all unusual for a sitting president to travel with the White House physician if he was going any distance from Washington, but taking the doctor along on a trip to Camp David did seem a little off. It seemed even more off when she considered the trip was made under a press blackout. People who had nothing to hide usually didn't act like they were hiding something. Or was she seeing a conspiracy under every rock, now? She picked up the phone and dialed Charley again.

"That was quick," he said in greeting.

"Would you think it was unusual for the president to take a doctor along on his trip to Camp David?"

Carter thought about it. *"Not if there was a medical reason for it. If the president was sick, then yeah, it'd be perfectly normal. Why?"*

"My source told me that's what happened yesterday. The White House doctor went along with Reese and Beckerdite to Camp David."

"Which would indicate that Reese is sick."

"There's something else. My source said that Beckerdite told Reese that he needed to go to Camp David for a summit meeting with the British Prime Minister."

"*So?*"

"So, the British PM is in Australia at the moment."

"*That might explain Beckerdite's unease,*" Carter said.

"You think he lied to Reese?"

"*Think about it. You said yourself that Beckerdite isn't normally timid, just 'cautious'. Right?*"

"Yeah…"

"*Well, ask yourself why such a cautious person would lie to the president? That puts that cautious person in the middle of something really serious that they would normally avoid. We already have a seriously unstable president in office during the middle of the worst existential crisis this nation's seen since the Civil War. Then, Beckerdite somehow finds himself in the position of having to lie to the president to get him away from Washington. You think being involved in something like that might scare him?*"

"It might, yes. Will doesn't strike me as the deceptive type."

"*So. We have reports of Reese abruptly leaving for Camp David, with his personal doctor in tow. Beckerdite was with him, and Beckerdite was behaving strangely when he spoke to you afterwards. Now you have corroborating information from this other source of yours indicating that Beckerdite lied to Reese in order to get him to go to Camp David. That lie can be explained one of two ways: Either it was to mask their real reasons for going from the people in the Oval Office -*"

"No," Nikki said with finality. "The staff in the West Wing would see through that right away."

"*- or, the intention all along was to deliberately deceive Reese.*"

"You think they're trying to hurt him?"

"*No, I don't. Oddly enough, it sounds to me like someone's actually trying to help the man. Look, he's been acting crazier than an outhouse rat lately. What if there's a medical explanation for it?*"

"Like what? He's been eating paint chips in the Oval Office?"

"I'm thinking more like Alzheimers, based on his behavior. What if they're trying to treat him for something like that, trying to keep it under wraps?"

"Oh, man," Nikki said. "Are you thinking what I'm thinking?"

"I might be. If you're thinking about what happens if the president is mentally unable to do his job, but he still hasn't appointed a vice president yet."

"Yeah. That's exactly what I was thinking."

CHAPTER SEVENTEEN
Dum Spiro, Spero

State Capitol Building
  Salem, Oregon

State Senator Mark Wyvern blew into his office like a hurricane, startling his aide into spilling her coffee.

"They actually did it!" Wyvern said, slapping a manila folder down on her desk. "They've lost their collective minds, and now they're in there *congratulating* themselves over it!"

Amanda Hiller looked up, ignoring the spreading puddle of coffee on her desk. "They voted for secession?"

"That's just the start of it." Wyvern sagged into a chair. "They also voted to 'accept Russian aid and logistic support in forming a new independent government'. They voted for *annexation*, Amanda." He looked at her in disbelief. "They just willingly turned Oregon into another Crimea."

Hiller stared at him. Wyvern finally noticed the spilled coffee and grabbed a napkin off the side table, offering it to her. "I don't get it," Hiller said, taking the napkin and absently mopping at the spill. "I thought the closed session was just to discuss the *possibility* of seceding - nobody said anything about Russia!"

"The governor dropped it on us right at the outset. They started talking about whether or not it was even legal to secede, and she stood up and said, 'There's another option.' She claimed that the Russian government had been in contact with her, and made all kinds of goodwill promises and assurances of independence, as long as the State of Oregon places itself under the 'administrative umbrella' of the Russian Republic."

"'Administrative umbrella?' What's that supposed to mean?"

"It's a fancy way of saying 'Russian boot heel,'" Wyvern said. He shook his head. "I can't believe it's come to this."

"So what happened after that?"

Wyvern sagged into a chair and let out a long sigh. "The governor asked for a referendum on secession *and* alignment with the Russian Republic. The Russians apparently sweetened the deal with a bunch of trade incentives that they'll never make good on, but most of the senators acted like that was as good as money in the bank. They passed it. Twenty-three to seven."

Hiller was stunned. "This can't be happening."

"It already happened, Amanda. They set up an impromptu committee meeting right there, and drew up a bill on the spot. It was a complete farce - they must have had everything prepared before we even called for the closed session last week - but the governor picked up this 'spontaneous legislation', as she called it, and waved it over her head, crowing about how Oregon is taking the lead in a 'new era of American liberty.' All her cronies were clapping and fawning all over her."

"Didn't anybody protest?"

"All seven of us who voted no protested, but they shouted us down." He shook his head. "Oregon doesn't have a representative government, Amanda. Dissenters are marginalized, ignored or brow-beaten by the majority until they lose the will to resist. People on the east side of the state may as well have no representation in government, for all the good we do 'em in this town."

Hiller leaned back in her chair and looked at the ceiling. "So? What do we do now?"

Wyvern shook his head. "We go home. There's nothing left here for us to do here - we lost. The people of this state lost, if you ask me. But I know that at least the people I represent don't want any part of what happened here today, so I'm going to suggest something else. It's time people on the east side have a government that's responsive to their needs."

Hiller raised an eyebrow. "*You're* talking about splitting the state? Didn't you always say the 'State of Jefferson' movement was just a bunch of wackos?"

"I did, but that was then. Face it - either we split and go it on our own, or we work something out to join with Idaho or Eastern Washington; it doesn't matter. We can't stay part of Oregon - not if Oregon's going to be a Russian satellite. I can't be a part of that, and I'm sure a majority of the folks east of the Cascades will agree with me."

Rukha, Afghanistan

Daoud paced the floor, impatient as always, his temper barely contained. "He should have been here by now, Ayoub. Why this delay?"

"He said he would come." Ayoub looked nervously at the third man in the room, who shook his head and made a calming motion with one hand.

"Please sit down, Daoud. You are beginning to make me nervous as well." The man was old, and carried himself with the bearing of someone who had been through a great deal in life, yet had somehow managed to emerge unchanged. "They are new to this country. Perhaps he became lost."

"Lost," Daoud snorted. "These people cannot even find their way to a simple meeting, and you wish to ally ourselves to them? Really, Yunus. I do not see the advantage here."

Another man came into the room and addressed Yunus. "Malik-sayb? He is here."

Yunus nodded. "Thank you, brother. Please bring him in." The man nodded and hurried out. Yunus turned to Daoud. "You see? A little patience, Daoud, is all that is required."

Daoud scowled. "We are wasting our time. These people have nothing to offer us."

"On the contrary, Daoud," Yunus said. "They have a great deal to offer. Our only task is to find out what they require in return. If that is acceptable to us, we will do business."

"And what if it is unacceptable, Malik-sayb?"

"As I said, brother. Patience." Yunus looked up as a stranger was ushered into the room. Yunus gestured to a seat across from him. "Welcome. Please, sit." The man replied with a thin smile and sat down.

"Thank you for meeting me, Malik-sayb," he said, his Dari nearly flawless.

Yunus cocked his head to one side. "It is nothing. You speak our language well, sir. Yet I cannot imagine that you have been long in this country."

The man smiled again. "I have been longer in study, than in practice. It is refreshing to be able to use what little I have learned."

"Ayoub," Yunus said. "Tea for our guest, please."

"Yes, Malik-sayb."

"You are gracious," the visitor said, nodding. I am pleased we can meet face to face, as friends."

"You *presume* that we are your friends," Daoud growled.

Yunus held up a placating hand. "Forgive him please, my friend. He has spent his lifetime amid broken promises and the continual deceptions of foreigners. I mean you no offense, sir, but it is in our nature to be suspicious of outsiders. You understand, I am sure."

The man nodded. "Of course." He looked up and smiled as Ayoub handed him a cup of tea. "My thanks." He dipped his head over the tea, slowly inhaling the scent, in no apparent hurry.

Yunus flicked his eyes from the foreigner to Daoud, whose scowl had only deepened. He looked back at their guest. "How is it that we can help you?"

The man sipped tentatively at the tea, then nodded in appreciation. "An exceptional blend." He lowered his cup. "But where are my manners? I have not made a proper introduction. My name is Han Jiayi. I am sent by my government on a diplomatic mission of great importance to my country, and to yours as well, I think."

"What do we have to do with China?" Daoud wanted to know.

"Afghanistan is a crossroads," Han said. "It has been so for centuries, but its strategic position has only ever been exploited by outsiders, rather than used by Afghans to better their own positions in life."

"*You* are an outsider." Daoud's eyes flashed as he spoke. "Just like the English. The Russians. The Americans. You expect us to believe that your country will be any different?"

Yunus again raised a calming hand. "We will hear him out, Daoud."

Han inclined his head. "Again, my thanks." He looked Daoud in the eye. "I understand your suspicion. But unlike those imperialist nations, China has no desire to exploit the Afghan people. We offer infrastructure - roads, airports, bridges, modern farming equipment. We offer you prosperity and a brighter future for your children."

"Why do you not bring this proposal to the government?" Daoud asked. "Why come to us? The Hazara are but a small faction, and we have many enemies. Why come to us?"

"If you were in my position," Han asked calmly, "Would you go to the Afghan government?"

Daoud barked a laugh. "Of course I would not. There is not a bigger nest of vipers anywhere in the world."

"Which is why I come to you."

Yunus leaned forward slightly. "Forgive me, but I fail to see what you want from us. As Daoud pointed out, we have very little power here in our own country. Perhaps you should have approached the government."

Han shook his head. "With respect, your government does not interest us. Peace interests us. Prosperity for your people. Progress. These things interest us. But we have no desire to force these things on anyone. We wish to work with agreeable parties within Afghanistan who share our vision for the future. We had hoped that the Hazara might be among the first of those agreeable parties."

Daoud shook his head in disgust. "You want power."

Han's eyes flashed slightly. "As do you, Mr. Farouq."

Daoud flinched at that. "How do you know my name?"

Han sipped his tea again. "We know a great deal. We know that the Hazara were allies of the Americans once, hoping to use their strength as a defense against your countrymen who hated you. We know that when the Americans began peace talks with the Taliban, you took offense and began to oppose them - even attack them where it was possible."

"We did what we felt necessary for our survival," Yunus said.

"Of course. No one could fault you for it. We do not judge you for casting your lot with a person such as Akhtar Khan; you needed a patron, and he was a willing benefactor." Han leveled his gaze at Yunus. "But now that benefactor is dead and gone. His money, and his father's money, have been seized. You will no longer benefit from their largesse."

Daoud's face was reddening. "How do you know all this?" He took a step toward Han. "Who is your informant?"

"Daoud!" Yunus snapped. "You forget yourself." Daoud was almost shaking with rage, but he forced himself to step back, bowing slightly to the older man.

Yunus regarded Han through narrowed eyes. "My young friend's manners are lacking this morning, but he asks a valid question. Perhaps you have an answer?"

Han spread his hands. "We have no informant, I assure you. What we do have, is one of the largest and most far-reaching intelligence and surveillance networks in the world. We do not miss much that interests us. We know that Khan planned to use the American Marine you captured to get back in the good graces of the Americans once their military forces returned to your country, which you hoped they would do in response to the attacks you planned and subsequently blamed on ISIS and the Taliban." He glanced at Daoud, whose jaw was now hanging slightly open. "Yes, my friend. We know that the Hazara were behind the spate of attacks in the U.S. I must say, that was an ambitious plan; one that you almost brought off. If Khan had not been taken and killed, you might have accomplished more."

"We may still," Daoud said. He didn't sound convinced.

"I doubt that," Han said. "You must be realistic. The Americans attacked your compound in the mountains because they had intelligence linking you to the attacks. They executed a surgical strike to capture and eliminate Khan, because they knew he was behind it all. There is no other explanation."

He looked from Yunus to Daoud and back again. "The fact is, your plan to ingratiate your tribe to the Americans by offering to 'repatriate' their Marine backfired. There really was little chance of them ever being interested, had you had time to make the offer before he was stolen from you. Now that your deception has been exposed, you will most certainly find no help from them." A thin smile crossed his face. "They have other worries at the moment that are infinitely more pressing, after all."

Yunus leaned back, folding his hands in his lap. "You seem to have us at a disadvantage, my friend," he said. "You know all about us, yet still we know nothing of you, or of what interest you have in us. If you know so much, what need have you for us?"

Han shook his head. "You speak wisely, Malik-sayb. In truth, we do not *need* you, necessarily." Daoud scowled, but Han pressed ahead. "We could proceed as the Russians and Americans did, with blunt force and little understanding of or concern for your people, but we all know how those tactics work in the end."

He sipped his tea. "But as I said, we want peace, not another endless, unwinnable war. Afghanistan is a failed state, gentlemen. I did not approach your government because it is a government in name only - it governs nothing. It is to the various tribes that leadership in this country must devolve, if things are ever to change. We propose to facilitate that change, and we propose that your tribe, the Hazara, should be among the first tribes to accept their new leadership role."

"Ridiculous," Daoud said. "This has been tried. You will never get all the tribes to work together. There is too much hatred, too many long memories."

Han smiled again. "I said nothing of 'all' the tribes, my friend. Those who choose to work with us will have the full support of the Chinese government and people. Financial, medical, commercial infrastructure, military intelligence; you will share in all of it as China leads the world into a new era."

"And those tribes who choose otherwise?" Yunus asked.

"They will be... marginalized. They will fall from grace, as it were. Accepting the future requires letting go of the past."

"You would make us your vassals," Daoud muttered.

"On the contrary," Han said. "In return for your loyal help and local support, you would hold power in your own country. Tribal rivals will become friends, or they will be pushed aside. If you support us, we will ensure that your people are no longer marginalized and mistreated."

"And if we do not - you will ensure that our mistreatment continues?"

Han spread his hands. "I offer you the opportunity not only to survive, but to *thrive*. Of course, the choice is yours, but you must know that the offer will be made to the other tribes as well." He got to his feet and handed Yunus a card. "You may contact me at this number, but do not delay over long. There may be limited room at the table."

Yunus looked at the card as Han moved to the door.

"Wait."

Han turned, surprised that it was Daoud that had called him back.

"Yes?" He studied the younger man, whose eyes were dark with hatred.

"You spoke of support."

"I did." Han had to stop himself smiling. It always came down to money, in the end. "We are prepared to arrange payments on a regular basis..."

"I am not interested in money," Daoud snapped. "I am interested in information."

Han stepped away from the door. "What manner of information?"

"The team that took and killed Khan. Can you find them?"

"This is not important at this moment, Daoud," Yunus cautioned.

"Of course it is important! Do you expect us to simply look the other way at this slap in the face? These Americans come in and destroy our compound, kill our brothers, take what is ours and make us vulnerable to our enemies, and your counsel is to wait? No, Malik-sayb. It is too much. You may not see the need to hunt them down and punish them, but I do." He turned back to Han.

"I asked you a question. Can you find them?"

Han regarded Daoud with curiosity. "I am certain it can be done. It will be faster, however, if you can provide us with any information you may have discovered during the attack. Did the attackers have any identifying features - uniform insignia, specific weapons types, that sort of thing?"

"I have something better. The American Marine that was taken from us. His name is Tony Holland."

Han nodded. "That is a start. Is that all you require?"

"No," Daoud said, glancing at Yunus. "When you have found him and his rescuers, I want to deal with them myself."

"That is irregular," Han said, "but not impossible. Am I to understand then, that we have an accord?"

Daoud glanced at Yunus, who hesitated, then nodded slowly.

"We have an accord."

Camp David, Maryland

Beckerdite walked slowly back into the main lodge after ending his call with Nikki. He felt sick, and he was fighting the worst headache he'd ever had. He slumped into an armchair near the big fireplace in the main room and leaned his head back, staring up at the ceiling.

How had it come to this?

He wasn't the type for political intrigue, Beckerdite knew. He was more of a true believer, someone who thought that his service in the administration was a means toward doing something good for his country. He never imagined that would include a complex deception such as Secretary Black was advocating.

But on the other hand, he knew that if they allowed nature to take its course, Reese would suffer an embarrassing public breakdown, and there would be a bloody power struggle to follow. And Black was right about the fallout from such a power struggle.

Under the present circumstances, it would bring down the entire country. Add to that the news of a potential viral outbreak on the west coast…

Will lifted a hand and placed it over his eyes, desperately trying to shut out the world. He had nearly slipped into a fitful sleep when a voice startled him.

"You lied to me."

Will dropped his hand and opened his eyes. Reese was

standing in the doorway, hands stuffed in the pockets of a pair of flannel pajamas. He watched Will for a moment, then came closer and stood in front of the hearth. "I guess I shouldn't be surprised. Everybody lies to you, eventually. Comes with the job, I suppose."

"Sir, I -"

Reese waved a tired hand, silencing him. "What surprises me most isn't the lie, Will. It's that I *believed it.*" Reese swiveled his head to look at him. "That's what actually scares me. I don't know what I'm thinking from one moment to the next. Can you imagine what that might feel like?"

He turned his head back and stared into the fire. "I have moments of clarity, like right now, where I realize that the rest of the time, I'm trapped inside a brain that's short-circuiting. I can tell when it's happening, sometimes. When I'm in the middle of an 'episode'. I can recognize that my thoughts aren't straight, but it's like I'm just a spectator - I can't do anything about it. More often than not, after it's over, I forget that it happened, or that I even knew something was wrong." He looked back at Will, and the expression on his face was pure fear. "Who do you trust, when your own mind abandons you?"

Beckerdite was stunned by how much Reese had seemed to age, just in the past few days. Seeing him that way made him realize suddenly that he only felt pity for him. "I'm so sorry, Mr. President."

Reese ignored him. "Black thinks I should name him as my vice president, while I'm still sane." He scuffed a toe against the hearth. "I suppose you agree with him."

"Mr. President, I'm uncomfortable about the entire situation. I agree with Secretary Black that your not having a vice president in place casts serious doubt on the continuity of government. Your diagnosis only makes that concern more pressing, sir."

"Black and I don't exactly get along."

"Would you prefer to hand the office to Norton?"

Reese snorted. "I'd prefer being boiled in oil."

"The country needs strong leadership, sir." Beckerdite wasn't sure how far he could press Reese, but he was beyond caring now. "To be honest, your condition has left a lot of questions about your abilities, and with all the unrest and uncertainty, people are losing what little confidence they still had. I think if we don't restore some sense of order, and soon, the country could easily collapse." He let out a long breath, glad to have finally spoken his mind. Then he noticed that Reese was staring into space, unresponsive.

"Mr. President?"

Reese turned and looked at him, a quizzical expression on his face. "Bacon," he said, after a moment. "I think I'd like bacon with breakfast today, Tommy." Then he smiled broadly at Will, turned and left the room.

Will felt like a balloon with all the air leaking out.

He found Secretary Black eating his own breakfast on a covered porch overlooking the woods and the large outdoor swimming pool. Will stood there, looking down at Black's food and wondering how the man could eat anything.

"Sit down, Will. They'll bring you a plate if you like."

"I'm not hungry." He turned and looked out across the property. "I don't think I can do this any more."

Black put his fork down. "'Do' what, exactly?"

Will turned and pointed toward the building. "This! Leading a mentally impaired man around by the nose like a dancing bear at a circus! It isn't right, Mister Secretary, and I want out."

Black folded his hands on the table and sighed. "Fine. You can quit any time you like. Just know that as soon as you walk out, you've signed a death warrant for this country. We've discussed this, Will. Reese can't govern anymore - if he ever could in the first place. He's incapacitated, and the next man in line for the presidency is an unapologetically power hungry crook. At best, a Norton presidency might slow the national decline by a few months. *Maybe*. At its worst, it would bring it about sooner.

"So, you go ahead and leave. But in his present state, Reese isn't likely to listen to anyone but you. I discussed the situation with him last night after the doctor gave him his diagnosis, and I think it took everything he had not to jump up and choke me on the spot - even though he knew I was right. He hates me, Will. Even if he agrees that this is the best way forward, he's going to need you to walk him through the process. If it's just me he's dealing with, he'll refuse to go along out of pure spite. He needs you to keep him on track, before he comes off the rails for good."

Will turned around. "Do you think he had Tolliver killed?"

Black didn't flinch. "We'll probably never know, for sure. But since you ask - yes. I think he was involved in some way."

Will shook his head. "You're *all* crooks. Every last one of you. Tolliver was guilty of treason; Reese - he's a murderer, or at least an accessory to it. Norton was negligent in killing a minor, Durber's an extortionist." He looked down at Black. "So where does that leave you, Mister Secretary?"

Black returned his stare, unblinking. "You're right, Will. In the end, we're all stained by each other's sins. Guilt by association if you like, but guilt, in any event. Maybe I'm guilty of attaching myself to an administration that I despised, just to avoid being left out in the cold completely. I'll accept that. But if I'd decided to stand on principle at the convention years ago, I would have been completely unable to do anything about the present crisis we're in. Wouldn't that have been another sin, then?"

"I don't know," Will said, finally sitting down. "I don't know what's right and wrong anymore."

"Well," Black offered. "If it makes you feel any better, I'm not altogether certain about that, myself. I'm not deluded enough to think I've never made mistakes. I know I've made quite a lot. But I also know that if we have a chance to correct a mistake, we should take that chance. I don't want to live to see my country die, Will. I think we have this one chance to turn things around, and if we don't take it?" He shook his head. "That might be the greatest mistake of all."

Will was trying to think of a response when the door opened, and Reese stepped out onto the porch. The two men moved to stand, but he waved them back down. "Sit down, both of you." He walked over to the porch rail and rested his hands on it. "I hate this," he said, staring out across the landscape. Black and Beckerdite shared a look, but stayed quiet.

"I thought it was my destiny," Reese continued. "To hold this office. I always thought it was something that I deserved, somehow. I convinced myself that Tolliver stole it from me, that I'd been wronged by that deal we struck at the convention." He turned around, and they could see his eyes were red, with prominent bags under them. He looked exhausted, and at least ten years older than he really was. "I saw myself as bigger than the office. It was there to serve me. *My* ambitions." He raised his right hand slightly, watching in a detached way as it trembled slightly, out of his ability to control. "So much for destiny."

He lowered his arm and looked at Black. "I don't like you, Sidney. I don't think that's any great secret. But I'm inclined to think that you're right, at least about the future of the country. If I'm honest, I was probably out of my depth *before* I started slipping. Now, they tell me there's a viral outbreak out west…" He shook his head in disbelief and looked at Will. "Write up a letter for Congress, naming Secretary Black as my choice for Vice President. I'll sign it. But you'd better get it done now, Will, before I change my mind." He turned away and leaned on the porch rail again. "Or before my mind changes without me."

CHAPTER EIGHTEEN

Iter Bellator

British Army Garrison - Stirling Lines
Credenhill, Herefordshire, England

Day 21

"Dr. Nevelson tells me you've made incredible progress." General Reardon was standing in front of his window, looking out with his hands clasped behind his back. He turned around. "Both of you."

Holland nodded and looked at Tony, seated to his left. "That's mostly thanks to my son, General."

Tony allowed himself a slight smile. "Once I saw how well the therapy worked, I guess I couldn't wait, sir. Sorry if I caused the doc any problems by asking to double up on sessions. She was amazing, really, to put up with me and clear her schedule for me like that. I'm really grateful for what she did - for what you've all done, General."

Reardon waved a dismissive hand. "Think nothing of it, lad. A-R-T therapy has actually been around for more than a decade.

Many people dismiss it, but we've found that it has been invaluable in getting our lads right again. It seems that it's gone a long way toward doing the same for you two."

"It has," Holland said. "I think we're both ready to get back to work, General." He looked at his son again.

Reardon could see the pride in the older American's eyes. "I do appreciate that," he said. "But I want to be very clear, gentlemen. If you need more time, you must take it. I cannot compel you to do anything. If you do decide to work with us, it will be in the capacity of 'independent consultants'. You're not part of the British military in any way. Now, that is not to say you'll be completely on your own, but you know very well that many nations take a dim view of civilians on the battlefield. You could be treated as spies, if caught."

Holland studied his son's expression. "Tony?"

Tony met his dad's eyes. "I'm in, Dad. Hundred percent."

Holland smiled. "There you have it, General. You already have the rest of Boone's team on board. Might as well let us catch up to them."

Reardon nodded. "There is one other recent consideration of which you may not yet be aware."

"Which is?"

"Our government has been contacted by your Centers for Disease Control. It seems there is some type of outbreak happening on the American west coast. A type of hemorrhagic fever. It seems to have surfaced in Los Angeles yesterday, and there are multiple cases popping up in other locations every hour. I must say, it doesn't look good."

"Biological warfare?" Holland suggested.

"It is a distinct possibility, but much too early to tell with any certainty. More pressing to us at the moment is the effect this will have on transport. I have no doubt that air travel is going to become nearly impossible very soon, which means that if we are to do anything requiring the use of civilian aircraft, we need to do it now, else we'll all be stuck here under a quarantine."

"All the more reason to go," Tony said. "Dad?"

"No doubt about it," Holland said, giving his son a wink. "Get in the boat, right?" Tony grinned and nodded.

"Very well," Reardon said. "We're very grateful for your help, gentlemen. But make no mistake - even without factoring in the potential of biological agents, we will be heavily outnumbered in this fight."

Holland's expression hardened. "So were the Irish troops at Jadotville." He was referring to an Irish Army unit assigned to a U.N. peacekeeping mission in the Congo in 1961. A hundred fifty-seven Irishmen had fought more than three thousand mercenaries, tribesmen and settlers to a standstill.

Reardon nodded. "I'm quite familiar with the Jadotville operation, Mr. Holland. I'm also aware that the Irish troops ran out of food, water and ammunition, and were forced to surrender. They outfought their opponents at every turn, and still lost the battle. And after they returned home, the military, government and press all treated them as pariahs for surrendering."

"They only had to surrender because they had no support."

"An unpleasant situation you may well find yourselves sharing. Let me remind you, this operation enjoys only a very tenuous support from my government. What little coalition we've been able to cobble together from NATO nations so far could well collapse under the slightest pressure, and this latest news about a potential biological threat could easily provide that pressure."

"We understand that, General. But the bottom line is that *our* country has been invaded. Our friends are over there, or on their way, to try to do something about it. Whatever support you can give us will be greatly appreciated, but we're going - with or without your support."

Reardon nodded. "I thought you might feel that way. I only needed to make you fully aware of the situation." He stood and moved toward the door. "Now, then. There's an aircraft waiting to take me and a few others to Canada. I'm sure we can make room for two more."

Holland looked at Tony. The younger man was smiling.

"We're with you, sir."

Tampico, Mexico

The large yacht sat tied up to the Tampico Yacht Club pier on the Pánuco River, gently wallowing in the wake of a passing container ship. The main salon door opened, and two men walked out, both pointedly ignoring the armed guards standing on the aft deck and along both side decks. One of the men, dressed only in board shorts, sandals and several gold neck chains, watched as the other took out his phone and placed a call.

"*You have something for me?*" the voice on the other end sounded less than optimistic.

"As a matter of fact, amigo, I do." Hector Furtado glanced over his shoulder at his host and smiled. "I have a contact who knows where your man went, but the information comes with a condition."

"*Name it.*"

Furtado grinned again at the other man, this time giving him a thumbs-up as well. "He has a rival he'd like to have removed from the playing field. Do that, and he'll point you to your man."

"*Is this rival in the local area?*"

"He is, my friend. He is in the shipping business. He has caused various problems for my contact's employers. Removing him would be a show of good faith on your part, which they will reward with the information you need."

"*Fine. I have two men already in country. I'll send them to you, you give them their target.*"

"You don't want to know who the target is?"

"It doesn't matter who it is. Just tell them. As soon as the job is done, I'll expect an answer from your friend." He disconnected the call.

Furtado looked at his phone and shrugged, then looked at the other man. "They agreed, mi amigo."

The man in the shorts flashed a gold-toothed grin.

MOD Saint Athan Airfield
Saint Athan, Wales

The fifty mile helicopter ride from Credenhill to Saint Athan in Wales had taken less than twenty minutes. Now Holland, Tony and Reardon walked across the ramp toward a Boeing 737 painted in the livery of WestJet Airlines, the second largest Canadian airline behind Air Canada. Holland looked at the big jet, then turned his head to look at Reardon.

"The Canadians know you're borrowing their jet?"

Reardon smiled, stepping to one side of the air stairs so Holland and Tony could board first. "We have an understanding. Make yourselves comfortable. The rest of the crew is coming along now." He inclined his head toward the terminal building. Two dozen men were just exiting the building and heading their way, all of them carrying large rucksacks, bags and hard equipment cases. "Once they're settled, we'll be on our way."

Holland studied the group briefly before mounting the stairs. They all had the steady confidence and bearing of trained operators that he could pick out of a crowd from a mile off.

SAS or SBS guys, he thought. *So much the better.*

They were going to need all of their expertise and then some if they wanted to have any hope of pulling this off. He just hoped they weren't the only aces up Reardon's sleeve. He boarded the aircraft and took a seat near the middle next to Tony. His son looked up and smiled.

"It's funny," Tony said, turning to look out the window.

"What's that?"

"I always wanted to follow in your footsteps, Dad." Tony turned to look at him, smiling slightly. "I never thought I'd be walking beside you into a fight."

"You did all right for yourself in Afghanistan the other day," Holland said. "I think if we'd have shown up ten minutes later, you woulda been on your way down the mountain to meet us anyway."

Tony shook his head. "You're still a terrible liar, you know that?" He paused a moment. "But thanks anyway, Dad, seriously. I'd just about given up hope. Then you and Boone show up out of nowhere with a whole crew of snake eaters. I gotta tell you, that was the best day of my life. I'm just glad I got to help a little on the way out." He looked at his dad and grinned. "That was some Medal of Honor stuff you pulled, carrying me out under fire like you did."

"Nope." Holland patted his son on the knee. "That was just normal, every day dad stuff. No way was I gonna leave you there, my boy." His voice had become thick, so he stopped talking and just smiled at his son.

Tony was about to answer when Sergeant Major Alvin Deane entered the plane, saw the two Americans, and bellowed to the men behind him, "Ah, bollocks, lads - we're on the wrong plane! This one's full o' tourists!"

Tony looked up and grinned at the British NCO. The man had taken great pains to see to every need the Hollands had since they'd returned from Afghanistan, from driving them back and forth to see Dr. Nevelson to all but force-feeding Tony extra food with the fussy intensity of a mother bird.

Archie Foxall was right behind Deane. He grinned broadly at the two Americans. "They're not tourists, Sergeant Major," he said, holding his rucksack ahead of him as he walked down the aisle. "Can't you tell cabin crew when you see 'em?" He stuffed his ruck into the overhead bin and flopped into a seat across the aisle from Holland. "Miss, I'll have a bourbon, neat - as soon as you like."

"Good to see you too, Archie," Holland said. "Afraid I can't help you with the bourbon. Let's just say I owe ya, how's that?"

Archie shook Holland's hand. "That'll have to do for now, mate. Glad you both made it."

"So are we," Tony said. He looked at the line of men entering the cabin, his brow furrowing slightly as he didn't recognize anyone else. "What about the rest of our crew? Baga? Koz? Brady? Aren't they coming, too?"

"They're way out ahead of us, lad." Archie reclined his seat, drawing a complaint from the man who had taken the seat behind.

"Make yourself comfortable, why don't ya?"

"Pipe down, Alice," Archie said. He laced his fingers together behind his head and let out a contented sigh, then glanced across the aisle at Tony. "They buggered off right after Boone and Burdin left the other day. We keep screwing around here, they're gonna finish the war 'fore we get there."

"As long as they come out on top, I don't mind a bit," Deane said from his seat a row ahead. He turned and looked at Tony. "How you coming along, young gun? Need anything?"

"Quit yer fussing over him, Sergeant Major," Archie said. "We didn't bring along a pram for you to push him around in." He winked at Tony.

Tony chuckled. "No thanks, Sergeant Major. I'm all good."

Holland watched the exchange with satisfaction. Tony had called the other men involved in his recent rescue 'our crew'. That was a strong indication that he was already feeling part of something larger than himself again. Holland knew that was a significant step toward healing. Isolation after combat was a killer for many veterans. Being part of a team again at this point could be just as effective as the A-R-T therapy with Dr. Nevelson had been. Holland took a deep breath and relaxed, letting the banter wash over him. He was going back into combat, but neither he nor Tony would be doing it alone.

It was a very comforting feeling.

Greenwich, Jamaica

Cooney pocketed his phone and walked out onto the large covered patio. Behan was sitting at a table, picking at his grilled tuna steak. He laid his fork down and looked up.

"How much?"

"Just the cost of a bullet. That's a bargain, if you ask me."

"That depends on where the bullet goes." He looked at Cooney for a moment, but when the big man didn't offer anything more, he leaned back in his chair and folded his hands. "So? Where *is* this bargain bullet headed, exactly?"

"To end a rivalry in the drug shipping business in Tampico. Some low-level dealer trying to muscle into somebody else's territory, if I had to make a guess."

Behan's face clouded. "We," he said slowly, "are not in the business of *guessing*, Mr. Cooney. Do you mean to tell me that you agreed to eliminate a target without knowing the identity of the target? You gave them a blank check?"

The first hint of uncertainty started to show on Cooney's face. "You said you didn't care about the price…"

Behan exhaled sharply. "I meant that in terms of money only! For all we know, you might have just agreed to knock off the head of the Sinaloa Cartel in exchange for information that we don't even have yet!"

Cooney stiffened. "I trust my guy," he said. "He wouldn't let me stick my neck out like that."

"But you didn't bother to check, did you?"

Cooney clenched his jaw and looked away.

Behan shook his head. "Call your man back. Find out who the target is, *before* they get to him. I want to know what we've gotten ourselves into."

Cooney nodded, pulling out his phone. "No excuses, boss. It's my fault. I'll fix it."

U.S. State Department Headquarters
Harry S Truman Building
Washington, D.C.

"This is Secretary Black." He had been looking forward to this call all day. "What can I do for you, Mr. Speaker?"

"You can cut the crap, Sidney." Speaker of the House Andrew Norton didn't sound happy. "You know why I called. This appointment you coerced out of Reese is never going to hold up. I'll make certain of that."

"Coerced?" Black did his best to sound hurt by the accusation. "What a terrible thing to suggest, Andrew. I'm disappointed in you."

"I don't really care what you think about me, Sidney. I'm going to fight this. Reese is incompetent; everybody's suspected it for some time. He failed to name a VP, which means *I'm* next in line for the presidency, and I mean to have it. You'd better get ready for a messy Congressional inquest into this."

"No," Black said. "I don't think so."

"Oh, no?" Norton snapped. "Just watch me, Sidney."

"There won't be anything to watch," Black said. "Let me tell you a story, Andrew. You see, once upon a time, there was a certain spoiled frat boy at Yale. This frat boy got into an accident, driving drunk. Killed the young girl he was with, who just happened to be a minor. Now, our hero's daddy was connected, so he managed to get the charges to go away, but Daddy was stupid. He made the police surrender all their files on the investigation to him, but then he let his drunk, murdering son have access to those files. And the idiot son took them back to his fraternity, and showed them around to his buddies, *bragging*. This story ringing any bells?"

"That never happened," Norton said in a low voice that lacked the conviction of just a moment earlier. "You have no proof."

"Oh, but I do, Andrew. I do. You went out drinking and left the case files in your room. I made copies."

Norton spluttered in disbelief. "Wh- why? *Why would you do that?* We were twenty years old!"

"Simple. I didn't like you. I didn't like that you got away with it, and I especially didn't like that you showed absolutely no remorse about it. That girl was *fifteen years old*, Andrew. You should have gone to prison. It wasn't in my power to make that happen, but it's in my power now to make sure you go no further in life than you already have.

"Your political career is over. You will not say so much as 'boo' in Congress about my appointment to the vice presidency, or those case files *will* come out. It'll come out how you killed a little girl, then dragged her into the driver's seat and blamed her for the wreck. There's no statute of limitations on negligent homicide in the state of Connecticut. Did you know that, Andrew?"

"You're bluffing."

"Try me. You *will* lead the push in the House to confirm my nomination in record time, Andrew. And once I'm sworn in, you *will* quietly retire, for 'personal medical reasons.' Go live in Florida. Move to Paraguay. Go play in the highway, for all I care, but you will *disappear* from public life, or I will spare no effort to see that you finally *do* go to prison, and that you rot there for whatever's left of your worthless life. Do I make myself completely clear to you, Mister Speaker?"

Greenwich, Jamaica

"Tiburcio Velasco," Cooney said, opening a laptop and placing it on the table in front of Behan. "Low-level drug trafficker in the Jalisco New Generation Cartel, operating out of Pueblo Viejo across the Pánuco River from Tampico. Until recently, he's mostly been a gopher, without much status."

Behan looked at the file on the laptop. "Then why does your contact want him dead?"

"My contact doesn't," Cooney corrected him. "*His* contact does."

"I don't want to argue semantics." Behan rubbed his temple with his thumb. "Why does *this person* need to be liquidated?"

Cooney nodded, pulling out a chair and sitting down. "Hector - that's my contact - told me that this Velasco character is basically the new front man for a JNGC push to exert more pressure in the area. The Sinaloa Cartel has been looking to expand its own operations around there, and this guy Velasco is the point man running the counter-operation for JNGC."

"So the Sinaloa Cartel wants Velasco dead."

"Yes, sir."

Behan stared at the screen, eyes narrowed. "Then why don't they just do it themselves? They have plenty of hitters, and they don't normally care about being discrete."

"JNGC has Velasco under pretty tight security, according to Hector," Cooney said. "Maybe Sinaloa just wants it taken care of quick and easy, without having to make a lot of noise?"

"No," Behan said. "They aren't stupid. Why would they trust outsiders?"

"I don't know." Cooney leaned back in frustration. "What do you want me to do?"

Behan closed the laptop. "Call your contact again. Tell him your employer needs to speak with his contact, before we can proceed. We're not getting tied up in a turf war between a couple of Mexican drug cartels until I get some more information."

State Capitol Building
Olympia, Washington

"The passage of this referendum marks the third of its kind in just two days along the west coast of the United States. First Oregon, followed by California, and now finally, the State of Washington have all passed measures aimed at beginning the process of secession from the United States of America.

"Although many argue this move is against the law as established by the Civil War and explained in the Supreme Court decision in *Texas versus White* in 1868, others point out that the American Revolution would have been considered illegal on similar grounds - had the American colonists lost the war. But the fact that the rebels *won* the war ultimately rendered the question of legality irrelevant.

"The leaders of the three states that are now being collectively referred to as the 'Coalition of the Pacific' - as well as their would-be Russian sponsors - are no doubt banking on a similar outcome. Whether or not recent rumors of a deadly viral outbreak along the west coast have pushed these three state legislatures more eagerly into the arms of their Russian 'benefactors', however, remains to be seen. This is Nikki Nikkanen in Olympia, Washington, reporting for Net News Daily."

Nikki waited for the cameraman to cut the feed, then blew out a tired breath. She'd only arrived in Olympia fifteen minutes earlier, after Charley Carter had insisted she get on a chartered business jet and fly across the country on no notice. Charley had smelled a story the previous day when the Oregon legislature had voted to align that state with the Russian Republic. While Nikki had been airborne, California had quickly followed suit.

Nikki's pilot had then changed their destination from Salem, Oregon to Olympia, Washington at Charley's insistence. Charley had known that the west coast states were likely to stick together, even if it was in what he referred to as 'a fit of governmental madness'. If Nikki had arrived at the state capitol in Olympia just fifteen minutes later than she did, she would have been too late to break the story.

It seemed that like Oregon and California, the Washington state legislature couldn't jump into bed with the Russians fast enough, and as she and her cameraman had climbed the capitol steps, they'd been met by politicians and staffers coming down, most of them glowing about what they claimed was a bright new future, while the unhappy minority fumed at what they saw as a treasonous betrayal of the public trust. Nikki agreed with the latter group, but for the life of her, she couldn't see a way out of the hole the country seemed to be falling into. It made it more difficult to stand in judgment over these who had made a terrible choice when faced with nothing but terrible choices.

"What do we do now?" Ike, her cameraman asked as he stuffed his gear back into his bag.

Nikki looked around at the people on the capitol steps. Several of them were waving hastily drawn peace signs on scraps of cardboard. Another group was clustered around several other reporters, who were trying to keep the group's red and gold communist flag from fouling their camera shot. Her eyes finally came to rest on a group of disabled veterans gathered on the far side of the parking lot, flying a large American flag above them.

Their flag was upside down.

"Back to the airport, Ike," Nikki said. "Let's go home."

"You think there'll be anything left of the country by the time we get there?"

"Hard telling. But it looks to me like this part the country at least is already too far gone. I always thought I'd be covering this sort of thing in some third-world country someday, not here." She shook her head. "I guess we're in the third-world, now."

U.S. House of Representatives
Capitol Building

Washington, D.C.

"Ladies and gentlemen, this country is facing a crisis unlike any it has faced since the Civil War. In times like these, it is imperative that the people of the United States have confidence in the ability of their government to weather any storm. Insuring the continuity of government is part of instilling that confidence." Norton held up the letter, signed by Reese, nominating Black for the position. "With that in mind, I move for an immediate vote on the confirmation of Secretary of State Sidney Black in the position of Vice President of the United States of America. As you all know, the Senate already approved the appointment this morning, so I urge you, my colleagues, to put partisanship aside and join me by voting in favor."

Seventy-two representatives had been killed just three weeks earlier in the terrorist attacks that had swept across the nation, and so far none had been replaced by the state governors. That left only three hundred and sixty-three representatives to vote. After just twenty minutes of verbal arguments that offered nothing more than token resistance, Secretary of State Sidney Black was overwhelmingly confirmed as the new Vice President of the United States by a vote in the House of Representatives of three hundred forty-nine to fourteen.

West Building, Zhongnanhai
Beijing, China

General Ma was waiting in Zhao's office. Zhao ignored him as he entered, moving directly to the liquor cabinet and pouring himself a drink. Ma shifted his feet nervously, waiting to be acknowledged. Zhao finished mixing his drink, took a slow sip, and turned.

"You have news for me, General."

"Yes, *lingxiu*. Some of it is very auspicious."

"I would prefer it were *all* auspicious, but perhaps we must content ourselves with half measures for the moment?" He watched as Ma squirmed under the criticism, then sighed. "Proceed, my friend."

Ma cleared his throat. "Sir, as you requested, we have mobilized our ground forces near the border with Russia."

"What of our navy?"

"Multiple ships are already on station in the Sea of Japan. We have two submarines off the coast of Alaska. The first is the *Yetaishan 7*, a Type 041 attack boat that was already on patrol in the Bering Sea. The second is the *Changzheng 21*, a Type 094 ballistic missile boat positioned somewhere to the south of Anchorage, well within range of its missiles. More surface ships are en route to the Gulf of Alaska, as you ordered."

"Any response from the Russians?"

"There have been overflights of the surface force by Russian surveillance aircraft. They know we're coming, but they have done nothing."

"What about our northern border?"

"We put out an announcement through diplomatic channels that we are deploying troops in northeast Heilongjiang province to deal with local civil unrest. Russian forces in the Amur, Khabarovsk and Primorsky regions are on alert, but there has been no major movement toward the border as yet."

"What of the Koreans?"

"They have mobilized their Army Group out of Chongjin and moved up to the Tumen River, under the guise of mobilization exercises. They assure me they are ready to cross the river at a moment's notice."

"Excellent," Zhao said.

"Sir," Ma continued, "although this seems on the surface to be good news, I believe it should be taken with caution. The discovery of our naval forces moving toward Alaska must certainly make the Russians suspicious that we are deceiving them about our ground forces near the border, and the North Koreans moving at the same time can only serve as confirmation of that suspicion."

"If they were so convinced," Zhao said, "they would be mobilizing troops. Don't you agree?"

Ma hesitated. "Of course, *lingxiu*. Unless…"

Zhao looked at him, raising his eyebrows.

Ma hesitated, then forged ahead. "Unless the Russians have no additional troops to commit?"

Ma's uncertainty only made him seem more pathetic. "You should know that is extremely unlikely, General."

Chastened, Ma lowered his eyes. "Yes, *lingxiu*. In honesty, I find it perplexing that they have done nothing. I expected them to respond unequivocally. I confess that this lack of action is puzzling."

Zhao smiled. "It is not a case of the Russians having no troops, General. As I told you several days ago, they do not wish to provoke us while they are entangled with the Americans. They are gambling that we are only going to observe, and not interfere. Soon enough, they will know the truth. They have made a fool's wager."

Greenwich, Jamaica

"Standby." Cooney turned and handed Behan his phone.

"Good evening," Behan said. "Who am I speaking to?"

"You may call me 'Jefe'. And what shall I call you?"

Behan didn't hesitate. "You may call me 'Boss'."

The man on the other end bellowed in laughter. *"You are a funny man, señor Boss! I like funny people, as long as they know when to* stop *being funny. Shall we get down to business?"*

"I'd like some clarity first, if you don't mind."

"Clarity? I'm disappointed. I rely on my people to be very clear in all our dealings, but it seems they have failed me in this case. What

exactly is causing you confusion, Boss?"

"I know who you work for," Behan said. "So I also know that you are not without resources of your own, people who would be perfectly capable of doing the task you are asking me and *my* people to do. So what I'm not clear on, *Jefe*, is why you need us in the first place?"

"We don't." Jefe sounded almost amused.

"Then I'm wasting your time. You have my apologies."

Behan was about to disconnect the call, but the man was speaking again. *"That is to say, we don't need you, if we want to lose more of our own people."*

"Now I really don't understand."

"Your man asked for information about a certain person - a gringo. I believe that gringo has taken employment with a rival of mine."

"You have evidence to back up your suspicion?"

"I have a ten year old boy who was on board a fishing boat that was stolen more than a week ago from our fueling dock. The boy's uncle and father were on board. The man who stole the boat probably came aboard while they were at the dock, and stowed away below decks in the engine room. After they got under way, the boy was working in the hold alone. He was coming up when he heard gunshots. He stayed hidden, but saw the gringo throw the bodies of his father and uncle overboard, about two miles offshore. Luckily, the gringo did not see him. The boy waited until the murderer went up to the flying bridge, then he slipped over the stern into the water. He swam until he was picked up by another fishing boat returning to port."

"I don't see how that helps me."

"It helps you, Boss, because the boy's description of this killer gringo matches the description your man gave for the person you are seeking. It helps you, because the stolen fishing boat later turned up in Campeche, four hundred miles to the southeast. Campeche is a stronghold of Los Zetas, one of our many rivals and an ally of the Jalisco New Generation cartel. Two days after the boat turned up, we lost one of our most important and best protected lieutenants to a sniper. The man got to within three hundred meters, made the shot, and

escaped without ever being seen. Now, as you say, we are not without resources of our own, but this level of skill? This is beyond even what we can counter, on short notice."

"And you think I can counter it?"

"Of that, Boss, I am not yet convinced. That is why you will deal with our friend Velasco, in much the same way as this mysterious gringo dealt with our lieutenant. This will serve as your bona fides to us. Velasco is very well protected. Your man will kill him and escape without being seen. When that is done, we will help you to find your gringo."

"I could just go down to Campeche. Look around for myself."

Jefe laughed again. *"And I would give you my blessing! But Los Zetas would find you out and kill you before you checked into your hotel. Your man got lucky, Boss. He happened to ask the right question of the right people at the right time. If he had come sniffing around even a week ago, we would have killed him and dumped his body in the ocean. But we need Velasco dead, both to send a message to Los Zetas and to prove to us that you are a worthy ally. And you need our help if you ever hope to find the man you are hunting. It is a perfect solution, no?"*

"No," Behan said. "But it is a solution, of sorts. If I agree, your people will guide us to the gringo?"

"Of course! A deal is a deal, mi amigo. Whatever else we may be, we are businessmen first. Our word is our bond. To do otherwise, that would be bad for business."

"How soon do you need our part?"

"As soon as you like. But be warned, if this gringo you're hunting is working for Los Zetas, the longer you delay, the more difficult it will be to find him. A man with his... skills, would be in much demand anywhere in the world. I doubt he will remain in Mexico for long."

Behan knew the man was right. If he ever wanted to get to Newill, it had to be now, while the trail was at least warm. "Very well, Jefe. We have a deal."

"We have nothing, Boss," Jefe said, all the humor gone from his voice. *"Nothing, until Velasco is gone. Do not delay, mi amigo. Our*

offer will not stand forever."

"Fair enough." Behan ended the call.

"Well?" Cooney asked, as Behan handed his phone back.

Behan looked at him. "You any good with a long gun?"

Cooney half-grinned. "Better than most."

"Good. You can forget about using your men for this job. I want you to do it, personally."

CHAPTER NINETEEN

Mare Crura

FV In Decision
Gulf of Alaska
250 Miles WNW of Juneau

"It'll pass after a day or two. Just need to get some real food in you." Boone was leaning on the rail, grinning as Burdin continued to be violently sick over the side of the boat.

"You keep saying that," Burdin gasped. "But I don't think I'm gonna live that long." He retched again, but nothing came out; his stomach had been thoroughly emptied hours before, and the idea of putting anything back in it only made him feel worse.

"Nah," Boone said, slapping him on the back. "You'll be fine. Just look at me. First time I went to sea, I thought I was gonna die, too. An old Master Chief I worked with forced me to eat a steak dinner, and after that I was fine. Speaking of that, we really should rustle you up a burger or something..."

"Oh please... No..." Burdin moaned as he was wracked by another dry heave.

"Do you mean to tell me that in all your time in Delta, they never made you do any open water training?"

Burdin wiped his mouth on his sleeve and gratefully accepted the bottle of water Boone held out. "Sure they did." He took a tentative sip, rinsing out his mouth. Then he abruptly leaned over the rail and heaved again.

"Looks like it didn't quite take," Boone said, still grinning. Burdin straightened up, offering the bottle back to Boone, but he waved it away. "Ugh. No thanks, man. That's my little gift to you."

"Thanks a lot." Burdin took a deep breath, staggered a little, and grabbed the rail harder. "I was gonna say, we did open water training, but nothing like this." He pointed with his chin at the huge rolling swells all around them. "This is just ridiculous."

"This is nothing," Boone laughed. "Try getting picked up out of twenty foot seas by a submarine at night. That's a *lot* more fun."

"I bet." Burdin leaned on the rail and took several long breaths. "I'd go below, but that just makes it worse."

"I'm telling ya, you need a good thick steak or something. I don't know what it is, but protein seems like the best cure for it. If you eat a bunch of sugary crap, for some reason your body just can't wait to feed it to the fish."

Burdin turned another shade of green. "Did you really get this sick your first time out?"

"No." Boone's grin was even wider now. "Not really."

Twenty minutes later, Burdin was stuffed into a cramped booth in the tiny salon below decks, eyeing the steaming portion of meat loaf the captain, Theo, had just dropped on a plate in front of him.

"Tuck in, brother." Theo said. "It'll cure what ails ya." He grabbed a pan off the cook top and shoveled three fried eggs on top of the meat loaf. "Fried in bacon grease. For seasickness, the greasier the food is, the better." He frowned when Burdin's only response was to press himself further back in his seat, eyeing the plate like it was a snake.

"Sorry, Theo. I don't think I can do it." The color was draining from his face again.

"Got to, brother." Theo looked at Boone. "You want something, chief?"

"Whatever you got left in the pan'll do me."

"You got it." Theo dumped three more eggs onto a plate and added a slab of meatloaf, then plunked the steaming mass down on the table. "I gotta get back up and relieve Boyd," he said. "He's a menace behind the wheel."

"What?!?" Burdin looked up. "Doesn't he know how to drive the boat?"

"It's not that he doesn't know how to," Theo splashed coffee into a mug and headed for the companionway. "He just doesn't know how *not* to." He stopped and glanced down at Burdin. "Don't worry about it, man. I only let him drive when we're too far from land to run into any of it. Enjoy your food."

Burdin picked up his fork and gave the meatloaf a noncommittal poke. "I don't know how these guys do it. I feel like I'm rolling around inside a clothes dryer, but he just whips us up a big mess of food and grabs a cup of coffee like it's no big deal."

"It's not a big deal, to them." Boone carved off a big piece of meatloaf and inhaled it. "Everybody has their own kind of normal," he went on, his voice muffled by the food. "This is theirs." He wagged his fork at Burdin's plate. "You gonna eat that, or what?"

Burdin watched him chewing and wrinkled his nose, fighting down another wave of nausea. "Not eagerly." He took a breath and cut a thin piece from his fried egg. He stared at it for a moment, then jammed it in his mouth and closed his eyes, willing himself to keep it down. Boone poured a cup of coffee and slid it across the table.

"Atta boy. Wash it down and do it again." He speared one of his own fried eggs and waved it at Burdin. "Theo said he'll need our help on deck in about an hour."

Burdin's eyes widened. "What for?"

"He said we're coming up on their first longline. We need to help 'em haul it in and reset it."

"I almost forgot we still have to actually fish on this trip."

"You'll love it." Boone happily chewed another huge mouthful. "Theo said this line we're coming up on is set on the bottom for cod and halibut. Cod are great, but you wouldn't believe how big some of the halibut can get. You ever seen one?"

"Are you kidding? I'm from Texas, remember? The only thing that comes to my mind when you say fishing is large-mouth bass. At least they live in lakes, where sensible people go fishing."

Boone chuckled. "Just wait. I went fishing on a charter just south of here years ago and caught a halibut that weighed more than two hundred pounds. Flat as a pancake, both eyes on the same side of its head - goofy looking thing, but it was a great time. They really fight when you get 'em to the surface." He stuffed another bite in his mouth. "C'mon, boy! Eat up - you're gonna need your strength if you're gonna be any help slinging fish that size into the hold. We still gotta earn our keep, ya know."

Burdin looked doubtfully at the mass of greasy food still on his plate. He had to admit, in spite of his nausea, he was starting to feel hungry again. He set his jaw and carved a piece of meatloaf.

"Can't wait."

"Just ease up next to it." Theo was standing next to Burdin, who was seated at the helm, guiding the boat slowly toward the buoy that marked their first longline. Theo had called Burdin to the bridge, reasoning that he might recover faster if he had something to concentrate on besides the motion of the boat. He was right. Maneuvering the eighty foot vessel in the swell demanded concentration, and Burdin seemed to be enjoying himself now. As the *In Decision's* bow came alongside the buoy, Theo nodded with satisfaction.

"All right, give her a touch left rudder. Now reverse the engines just enough to stop our forward motion - that's it, all stop." He watched as the two deck hands worked to snag the buoy and thread the attached line to the winch. Within moments it was winding in the mile-long line and more than a thousand individually baited hooks attached to it.

"Nice job. You put us right on that buoy."

"Thanks. What do we do now?" Burdin wanted to know.

"Now, we see what we caught. You go down on deck and let Jerry know you're not dying anymore. He'll tell you what to do."

Burdin nodded, giving the captain's chair back to Theo. He was definitely feeling better, though he wouldn't have believed eating a greasy meal like he had would have done anything but make his condition worse. He still felt a little off, but figured he was past the worst of it. He stopped at the companionway and pulled on his rain gear, then stepped out onto the broad deck.

It was like walking out from under a cliff into a waterfall, as a wave broke over the bow of the boat and the spray parted around the superstructure, enveloping the aft deck in a cloud of mist. Burdin instinctively pinched his shoulders and moved to the rail, where Jerry, the mate, was running the winch. Jerry grinned.

"Thought we were gonna have to bury you at sea, brother!"

"I wondered about that myself," Burdin said, returning the grin. "Not today, though. How can I help?"

Jerry inclined his head toward a large tub on the deck against the rail. "Bait bucket. As each snood comes up to the block, your buddy Boone will gaff the fish on the hook, and pass the line to you. You bait the hook and let the line run back over the side."

Burdin looked at the bloody mass of bait in the tub and felt his stomach clench again. "I'm pretty sure I know what a hook is, but the rest of that stuff is Greek to me."

Jerry laughed. "Don't worry about it. The block is the pulley the line is wound through. The snoods are the short lines attached to the main line; they all have baited hooks on 'em. Gaff is the long pole with the hook on the end of it. You got it?"

Burdin nodded. "Well enough, I think."

"Good. Look at the bright side - if you can get through baiting this line without puking again, you'll be cured for good!"

"Great." Burdin shuffled over to his place on the rail, relieving the third member of the crew, a big Norwegian named Einar. After giving him a few pointers, Einar slapped him on the back and stepped back, where he could keep an eye on the entire process. Jerry engaged the winch again and the line started coming in.

The first several snoods had nothing but empty hooks on the end, so it was just a matter of re-baiting them and letting them run back over the side. Then one came up with a halibut on the hook. Burdin was stunned at the size of the fish - it had to be five and a half feet long. He gaped as Boone hooked the fish with the gaff and wrestled it onto the deck.

"Whoa, look at that!" Burdin had completely forgotten his seasickness now.

Einar laughed. "That's nothing! Only a hundred, hundred and twenty-five pounds, maybe. Just wait 'til we get a really big one!"

"Quit gapin' and get that hook baited!" Jerry hollered, all his recent good humor gone. He'd had to stop the winch to keep the line from pulling the now empty hook back over the side while Burdin stared at the fish.

"Sorry." Kevin lowered his head and quickly baited the hook, allowing the process to keep moving. The same pattern was loosely repeated as they worked their way down the longline. Several empty hooks would pass, then they'd pick up a halibut or cod, then several empties again. Burdin found he was enjoying himself as the hours passed. Halfway through the line, they switched places, and he had to learn how to quickly gaff the big flat fish and get them inboard quickly so as not to slow the line. He quickly learned that Jerry was happy as long as things were moving, but the slightest delay would set him to cussing a blue streak.

Burdin had been on the gaff for half an hour when Theo's voice boomed over the loudspeaker attached to the rear of the wheelhouse.

"Big airplane coming in low, dead ahead!"

Burdin looked, but Boone cautioned him. "We're fishermen, remember? Just keep on fishing."

Burdin knew that was the best thing he could do, but the urge to look was almost too much to resist. He forced himself to pay attention to the large cod that was coming over the side, and only looked up when the noise of the jet was impossible to ignore. As he raised his eyes, he saw that the aircraft had four engines, a massive horizontal radar dish mounted on two pillars just aft of the wing, and a large red star prominent on the tail.

"Looks like an IL-76," he shouted at Boone over the noise as the big jet passed close off the port side, barely a hundred feet off the water.

"Same airframe," Boone answered, raising an arm and waving. "But they retrofitted it with airborne radar and renamed it. That's a Beriev A100."

"Are they armed?"

"Don't think so. It's like our AWACS - meant for early warning and air battle control. Not sure why he's screwing around down low like he is but I doubt anybody's gonna report him out here."

"He'll report *us*, though."

"That's the idea. And all he'll have to report is a bunch of guys hauling fish out of the water. By the time we show up in Anchorage, our cover story'll be well established. We just gotta keep on playing the part." He looked over at Burdin. "Hey. You're not green anymore."

"Cured by adrenaline and greasy protein." He busied himself getting the next fish off the hook and sliding it across the deck that led to the hold below, where it would be packed in ice for the trip to Anchorage. "I hate this."

"It's not that bad," Boone said. "You'll get used to the blood and guts after a while."

"Not the fishing. The *waiting*. I just want to get there already, and *do* something."

"Sometimes, the best thing you can do is take your time. We can't just go charging in to Anchorage, guns blazing. We don't have the numbers or the firepower for that. But if we can slip in unnoticed, and move around without them knowing what we're up to, we stand a better chance of finding some weak spots that we can exploit. Until we get a lot more backup, it's gotta be a guerrilla war for us."

"I get all that," Burdin said. "I just seems like if your house is on fire, you should *run* for a hose, not walk."

Starshiy Two Seven
Russian A-100 Airborne Early Warning Aircraft
Over the Gulf of Alaska

"Another trawler," the copilot said, his voice laden with contempt. "Sometimes I think we're here to enforce fishing treaties, rather than fight a war."

"You should keep opinions like that to yourself, Artem."

The pilot's rebuke had little effect. "I don't care. We both know we'd be better used up north, where the fighting is. Not out here in the middle of nowhere, watching fishermen wave at us! If they would have allowed us to go in with the first wave, we could have helped the fighters kill the Americans without taking any losses. This is a disgrace."

"You have no way of knowing what we could have done, Artem. We weren't there."

"Which is exactly my point, Grisha! *We weren't there.* We're the only airborne radar platform in theater, and they put us out here, where there is no threat. We are wasting our time."

"We are following orders, Artem. You should remember that. High Command is concerned about American bombers coming from the south, so we patrol to the south. That allows us to keep eyes on the American fishing fleet at the same time."

"'Following orders,'" Artem scoffed. "Do you expect me to believe that you agree with our orders completely? You have no complaints?"

"I have complaints, yes. But unlike you, I keep them to myself."

"Counting fishermen," Artem grumbled. "I'm sure my grandchildren will be very proud of me."

Grisha laughed. "If the Americans manage to get any fighters in the air," Grisha said, "the first thing they'll come after will be us. When that happens, you may wish we were back counting fishermen."

CHAPTER TWENTY

Cancri in Ollam

Comox Valley Airport
Comox, British Columbia

Day 22

General Max Reardon stepped off the WestJet Boeing 737 MAX and walked across the ramp to the civilian terminal. The original plan had been to arrive on a military transport and deplane at Canadian Forces Base Comox on the other side of the airport, but intelligence had indicated there was an informant among the 19 Wing personnel. Flight schedules for the Canadian CP-140 anti-submarine patrol aircraft based at Comox had been leaked, and two of the planes had been ambushed and shot down by Russian fighters in international airspace south of the Gulf of Alaska. So Reardon and his staff had decided they would still stage out of Comox, but they would have to do it from the civilian side and keep the Canadian Air Force in the dark.

This added a significant degree of difficulty to what they were planning. Getting small teams of special forces operators into occupied Alaska wasn't impossible, but it got more difficult with each passing day. The Russians had all but eliminated resistance in and around Fairbanks and Anchorage by destroying or capturing what little military resources remained there. Some of the American Army and Air Force personnel had put up a fight on the first night, but the amphibious landing at the Port of Anchorage of what amounted to a slightly under-strength Russian mechanized brigade proved to be more than enough to win the day.

Most of the military equipment stored at Fort Richardson outside Anchorage was taken intact. The massive drawdown of forces instituted by President Tolliver two years earlier had left just over twenty-five hundred active duty military personnel in the entire state of Alaska. It didn't surprise Reardon that the Russians had won the battle in less than forty-eight hours. They had achieved near-total surprise, they had the advantage of greater numbers, and they attacked with battle-hardened troops against a weakened, inexperienced and unmotivated garrison force.

All of which simply meant that Reardon had his work well cut out for him. It galled him to see how far the United States had fallen in two short years. It was like watching a massive bull shackled to a post, then left to the mercy of a pack of wild dogs. Reardon wanted to cut the bull loose again. He just hoped it wouldn't be too late.

Entering the terminal, Reardon looked around and located the rest of the crew who had come with him from England. Holland and his son were standing easy next to the luggage carousel. Sergeant Major Deane was chatting with a pretty woman standing in the queue for the rental car counter, and several of his other men were wandering around the baggage claim area, looking for all the world like tired travelers just wanting to get their bags and get out of the airport. Reardon made a mental note that all his men were present before he headed outside and hailed a taxi. The others would follow in ones and twos. Once they were all settled in their various hotel rooms, they would meet and figure out their next step.

Reardon just hoped they weren't too late.

Avenue Bistro
Comox, British Columbia

Thirty Minutes Later

"Things are unravelling faster than we expected." Lawson Holland handed Reardon a pint glass full of a locally brewed ale and pulled up a chair as the general switched off the news program on his laptop.

"I won't argue with that, lad. Have you heard anything beyond what that report said?"

"Only that the secession referenda weren't even close to unanimous, contrary to what the legislatures are claiming. There are huge portions of all three states that are firmly against this, but those areas are mostly rural and under-represented in the various state houses."

"So, you think it's going to happen?"

"I think there's the potential for all three states to fracture along political lines. Eastern Washington and Eastern Oregon are ideologically and politically more aligned with Idaho and parts of Northern California than they are with the western parts of their own states, and they have been for decades. It's been a bone of contention for a long time in those areas, so I don't see the people just standing by and becoming Russian citizens without doing something about it."

"You know, this may be an opportunity," Reardon said, staring into his ale.

"How so?"

"If the Russians are supposedly supporting these secessions, but are faced with armed uprisings from within those very states, that might present a critical drain on their resources that they could otherwise do without."

"Except for the fact that all three of those states are resource rich," Holland said. "Taking them by main force might have been in their long-term plan all along. I think they only tried this diplomatic angle as a long shot, and they got lucky - but if they get pushback, they still might think it's worthwhile to go ahead and bring the pain."

Reardon smiled. "You have a unparalleled gift for expression."

"I'm not as genteel as you, sir," Holland said, "but I do know which way the wind's blowing. If I was the Russians, I wouldn't want to miss the chance to pull the entire west coast of America into my sphere of influence. Alaska's one thing. It's big, but it's *really* empty. Pretty easy to hold onto the few population centers there. Oregon, Washington *and* California? That's another ball of wax entirely. Ivan's gonna have to commit a lot more people to holding those three states than he will in Alaska. I'm not saying he won't - just saying it'll cost him more - and that might make him a little desperate."

"You mean reprisals."

Holland nodded. "I think we're way past things returning to normal without an incredibly high cost in human terms. When the Russians invaded the Crimea a few years back, they at least had the thin claim that it was historically part of their territory. They can't make that claim here. They're sticking their necks way out, and that means they're gonna be coming at this with a much higher level of commitment. This is gonna get a lot worse before it gets better, sir."

"Mmm." Reardon drummed a finger on the counter. "We don't have enough firepower to answer the Russians on two North American fronts, lad. If we contest their moves on the west coast, we'll never get them out of Alaska. If we contest Alaska, they'll try to take the west coast, but at least there's the chance of more organized local resistance coming to our aide in those states."

"Maybe," Holland said. "It's gonna be dicey, either way."

"Have you heard from Boone's team?"

"Not yet."

"What about Holland the Younger?"

Holland grinned. "Tony's out chasing supplies with Sergeant Major Deane. The Sergeant Major mentioned something about stealing a truck. A 'tactical acquisition,' I think he called it."

"Sergeant Major Deane is ever resourceful," Reardon said, as if the idea of his aide committing Grand Theft Auto was perfectly normal part of his day-to-day operational duties.

"You think they'll be able to find what they need?"

"If I know Sergeant Major Deane, he'll not only find what we need, he'll have the owners volunteering to give it away free of charge."

Holland chuckled. "An army without good NCOs is an army in retreat."

"Very true." Reardon looked at Holland over the rim of his glass as he took a drink. "We should discuss your role, Lawson."

"All right."

"This potential for hostilities and unrest in the west coast states puts us in a quandary, to put it lightly. We can't openly fight on two fronts, but we will need people on the ground there soon, as well as the teams we're moving into Alaska. If the Russians are able to shift their resupply south, to the port facilities in Seattle or even Portland, it'll be all but over for us."

"Agreed."

"I'll give you the option, then," Reardon said. "We have very few contacts in Oregon and Washington. We'll need to set up several guerrilla teams in both states - try to steal a march on the Russians around the major port cities. If they shift operations there, we go into sabotage mode - blowing up port facilities, hitting shipping, et cetera. Tie them up and grind them down. You can have one of those teams, or you can stay with us on the northern front. Going south would be a bit closer to home for you, would it not?"

Holland nodded. "My house is in Idaho, yes, but I don't have anything else there to go back to at the moment. My only family is here, and it seems to me that the most critical fight is gonna be up here, too. I'll stay."

Reardon ran a finger around the rim of his glass. "I thought you might. Perhaps we should discuss your next move, then."

"Before you start, sir, if it's at all possible, I'd like to work with my son."

"I wouldn't think of separating you," Reardon said. "He's a capable young man, and I'm sure you're in no hurry to part ways after only recently getting him back."

"No."

"That's fine. Tony will be part of your team, as will Sergeant Major Deane and Mr. Foxall. I'm sorry that I can't spare more manpower for you, but you understand we are in a difficult position, and speed will tell more than numbers at this point."

"What did you have in mind?"

"How familiar are you with Fort Greely?"

"I know it's an Army base in Alaska," Holland said. "Apart from that, I'm clueless."

"Greely is an anti-ballistic missile battery. We can't guarantee that the Russians won't be able to re-task its missiles to use against our submarine launched missiles, so we want the facility either captured or destroyed."

Holland's eyebrows went up slightly. "How many missiles are we talking about?"

"Between thirty and fifty in underground silos, according to our best estimates."

"And how big is Greely?"

"The entire base? Not very large. The missile battery itself is the only part that concerns us, and it's less than three square miles."

Holland leaned back in his seat. "Less than three square miles."

"That's correct."

"Now I see why you apologized for not giving me more men. How are four guys supposed to take and hold a missile base that's three square miles -"

"*Less* than three," Reardon corrected him.

Holland shook his head. "Less than three or more than two, it doesn't matter. There's no way a four man team can hold that much territory for longer than about thirty seconds against even a mildly determined opponent. You should know that, General."

Reardon nodded. "I do. And I will grant that taking the battery intact is a lofty goal, but if it can be done, it would be exceedingly beneficial to our long term goals."

"Okay, so it's one of those things that'd be nice to have, but everybody knows is never going to happen?"

Reardon shrugged. "If you like, yes."

"Then let's stick to reality. Your second option is to destroy the missiles?"

"That's correct."

"Then why not just hit the battery with a couple of Tomahawks? You said you weren't sure if the Russians *could* re-task the missiles - that would imply that they haven't done it yet. If that's true, then they don't have a viable defense for a missile attack yet, right?"

"Our missile assets that we have in theater at the moment are severely… limited," Reardon said. "We have to prioritize what we do have, and the priority right now is the softer targets that will limit the Russians' mobility. Airfields, fuel depots, pipelines and the like. Besides which, if we simply throw missiles at it without getting first-hand intel on the place, we'll never know if we *could* have taken it intact."

Holland nodded. "So, because you have no proof that the Russians *can* use the Greely missile battery, it becomes a lower priority target - "

"But not low priority enough to ignore altogether," Reardon finished the thought for him. "We're spread incredibly thin here,

Lawson. We must employ our resources very carefully."

"Begging your pardon, General, but sending four men unsupported against a fixed position of unknown strength doesn't sound like a very careful plan to me."

"I agree with you, believe me. We have a paucity of assets set against an abundance of targets. The passage of time will not turn that equation in our favor if we do nothing. We must take some risks. If you wish to decline, I understand, but please know that I don't have anyone to take your place. I'm organizing dozens of missions similar to yours all across Alaska. To be honest though, this mission is probably the most difficult of all of them."

"Why not send your own guys then? Why send us?"

Reardon grinned. "Remember, half of your team will be 'my guys', as you say. The other half will be you and your son. You come very highly recommended, thanks to Boone, and if your son is anything at all like his father, I like your overall chances."

Holland tried to scowl, but couldn't help grinning. "Flattery will get you nowhere, General."

"Can't fault a bloke for trying."

"I guess not." Holland took a deep breath. "So, how are we getting in?"

"Well, I would have preferred to use Comox as the staging point, but if our intel is correct, it's not secure. We got in on one of the last commercial flights, anyway. Canadian government is grounding all commercial jet traffic in the western provinces 'out of an abundance of caution'. That means we'll need to rustle up ground transport from here, and each team will have to drive to a smaller local airport where they can charter a plane to take them further north.

"If Sergeant Major Deane and your son are able to complete their 'tactical acquisition', you'll have the first leg of your transportation sorted. I've managed to run down a private charter service for the four of you in Boundary Bay, but it's at least four hours away by car, plus a ferry ride. You'll need to take the charter as close to Greely as you can, but you may have to break the journey up into different flights, depending on how far the pilot is willing to take you. If you can manage a flight across the border into Alaska, so much the better, but I'm not confident of your chances there. I'm sure the Russians are going to be very touchy about air traffic in and out of the state."

"Shouldn't be a problem, sir. There's gotta be a bush pilot between here and Greely that's willing to take us in under the radar."

"Yes, that's the hope. Once you're on the ground, transportation will be up to you. I wish I could do more, Lawson, but I'm afraid you'll have to improvise as best you can."

Holland swirled the dregs of his ale, staring into his mug. "What about getting out again?"

Reardon looked at him for a long moment. "I'm sorry, lad. I just can't see that far ahead at the moment."

Holland nodded. "No worries. Seems like improv is my middle name lately."

"Does that mean you'll go?"

"I guess it does." Holland held his mug out toward Reardon. "Here's to bad ideas and flawless execution."

Boundary Bay Airport
Delta, British Columbia

Five Hours Later

"Just pile your gear there," the pilot said, indicating a spot on the pavement next to the airplane. "I'll stow it for you." He'd said his name was Shorty, but that must have been a joke, because he looked to be at least six foot six. He had a shock of red hair on his head that grew wildly in all directions, making him look like a slightly crazed scarecrow.

Holland and his team busied themselves unloading all their gear from the stolen van while Shorty carefully stowed it in the cargo pod attached to the belly of the big single engine Kodiak bush plane. While none of Holland's team were in uniform, it was impossible to disguise their gear - it was clearly not hunting equipment. Shorty stuffed a tactical rifle case into the pod, followed by a rucksack full of body armor. He smiled slightly.

"You boys must be goin' after some seriously big bears."

Holland stopped what he was doing and looked over at the Canadian. "In a manner of speaking, yeah. Is that gonna be a problem?"

"No, no. Not for me, it isn't. I don't like 'bears' much anyway. But depending on how far you need to get into 'bear' country, it could be a big problem - if you take my meaning."

"Do you have a suggestion?"

The man straightened up and stretched his back. "Well, like I say, everything depends on how far you need to go. The fella I spoke with on the phone before you got here said you'd probably need a multiple leg flight, but he didn't really elaborate beyond that."

"If that was a concern, why didn't you tell him no?"

Shorty laughed. "Because his credit card went through!" He went back to stowing the gear. "But if you want my help, you're gonna have to be a little more specific about your destination. Unless you just wanna fly around in circles until your friend's credit runs out."

Holland studied the man's face for a moment, then looked over at Sergeant Deane. Deane gave a curt nod and went back to unloading the van.

"Just outside Fairbanks," Holland said.

The pilot whistled. "When you said you needed to go north, you weren't kidding around."

"Nope. Can you get us that far?"

"Well, I can get you part the way, bud, but not all. Just lemme finish up here, and I'll make a couple of calls before we take off, see if I can find you another ride further on. Can't guarantee nothin', though. From what I hear, the further that way you go, the hairier things get."

After they finished loading the gear into the Kodiak, Shorty went into the charter office and made several calls. Holland and Deane waited outside while Archie and Tony ditched the van in the long-term parking lot at the civilian terminal. Deane was leaning against the tail of the Kodiak, hands stuffed in his pockets, watching Holland pace back and forth.

"You trust this bloke, Law?"

"I'm not sure. Reardon set it up. You're Reardon's guy, so you tell me."

"The general has excellent instincts, but I'd be lying if I told you any of this was orthodox enough to give me warm happy feelings."

"He did say we'd have to improvise."

"Improvisation is one thing. Willingly sticking your arse into a steel trap is another."

"That's true. Problem is, we don't have a lot of options at the moment. Sooner or later we're gonna have to trust an outsider or two."

"Mm. I'd feel better about it if I knew who he was ringing up in there."

"We'll know soon enough. How do you feel about running from the Mounties?"

Deane grinned. "They're bound to go easy on me; I'm a British citizen. Fellow subject of the Queen."

"I thought the Canadians got their independence?"

"They did, but they still love the Royals. You're an American, which they're not all so fond of at the moment. Besides, aren't you still a fugitive in the States as well?"

"I lost track," Holland said. "Why, you thinking of turning me in?"

"If there's a substantial reward involved, you never know. I would like to fatten my pension a bit."

Holland laughed, then turned as the charter office door opened and Shorty came out. "Any luck?"

"Well, that depends on what you call lucky," Shorty said. "I got a buddy up in Whitehorse that's willing to take you as far as Dawson City."

"Which is where, exactly?" Deane asked.

"Yukon Territory. Right up near the Alaskan border, but it's still about… two, two hundred fifty miles short of Fairbanks."

"That's a long walk," Holland said. "Any idea about the status of the border crossing in that area?"

Shorty shook his head. "Nope. My buddy told me there're some rumors about bush planes being shot at in that area, and I imagine the roads aren't a lot safer. But he does know another guy with a charter service outta Dawson City. He couldn't get a hold of him just now, but he said he might be crazy enough to take you over the border. He'll keep trying to get him while we're en route to Whitehorse; at least, that is if you want him to."

"What do you think?" Holland asked Deane. "Worth a try?"

Deane spread his hands. "We play the hand we're dealt, I suppose. If we wait around for perfect, we'll miss all the fun." Archie and Tony appeared from around the corner of the hangar, back from disposing of the van. Holland gave them a thumbs up.

"All right," he said, turning back to Shorty. "We'll try it. If your buddy can't get a hold of his friend, we'll just have to take our chances hitchhiking."

Shorty laughed. "No offense, but you four fellas look like the type of hitchhikers normal folks would want to avoid!"

The flight to Whitehorse was rough, to say the least. Shorty kept them traveling up steep river valleys and canyons the whole way, careful to avoid climbing above the surrounding terrain unless the weather closed in too thick around them. He wanted to keep them below the coverage of any ground based radar, and the ground clutter from the rugged terrain would help to mask them from airborne radars as well.

The result was a very bumpy ride that was sometimes shockingly close to the surrounding mountains, but Shorty seemed unfazed by it. Holland had had his doubts when they boarded the plane and watched Shorty fold his gangly frame into the pilot's seat, but once they were airborne it was obvious the man knew his business. They'd stopped once for fuel at a tiny backwoods airstrip along the way.

"Better safe than sorry," Shorty had explained. "I coulda probably got us all the way in one leg, but I'd rather have too much fuel than not enough." Looking down at the formidable landscape all around them, Holland couldn't help but agree.

They finally landed at Cousins Airport, a single strip north of Whitehorse next to the Yukon River with no hangars or services. They were all stiff and sore from the bumpy flight, and looking forward to getting back on the ground. Shorty taxied the Kodiak to a gravel ramp adjacent to the south end of the runway and pulled off. There was another Kodiak waiting for them on the ramp. As they taxied up, a diminutive man climbed down out of the pilot's seat and stood waiting for them. He couldn't have been more than five feet tall.

"You sure you didn't steal yer name from this bloke?" Archie shouted from behind Shorty's seat.

Shorty laughed as he cut the engine. "Nope. But I gotta warn ya, don't make fun of his height. He's sorta touchy about it."

"What's his name?" Tony asked.

"Red."

The four men exchanged glances, looking from the red-haired giant who'd brought them this far to the gray-haired little man waiting for them alongside their next ride.

"*He's* Red, and *you're* Shorty?" Archie asked, incredulous. "You blokes need to take a look in a mirror once in a while."

As it turned out, Red was more touchy about his height than

Shorty had let on. He also seemed to be touchy about every other topic as well. He grumbled and groused while they transferred their gear, he complained while he said his farewell to Shorty, and he muttered under his breath for the entire first hour they were airborne on their way to Dawson city. Before they had taken off, Holland had convinced Deane to take the front seat this time, after Red had complained long and loud about 'dang Americans running around playing Rambo.'

Deane had tried small talk several times, but after being rebuffed again and again he'd finally given up. Now he was slumped in his seat, staring out the side window, while Archie peppered the irascible pilot with a series of increasingly inane questions from the seat behind him. He ignored every rude answer and insult that Red dished out, and pressed on with barely contained glee.

"So how much did you say this plane cost, mate?"

"I didn't," Red snapped. "And I'm not your dang 'mate', either."

"I bet it's easy to fly. When we get to Dawson City, what say you let me have a go?"

"Not a chance!"

"What does this do?"

"Don't touch that!"

"Can you do a barrel roll?"

"NO!"

Law and Tony used the time to try to catch up on sleep, but the back and forth between Red and Archie made it impossible. After what seemed like the thousandth time Red had barked at Archie, Law realized that Tony was struggling not to laugh.

Tony saw his dad looking at him, and jerked a finger in Archie's direction. "He's gonna get us kicked off the flight."

Law grinned back. "I doubt it. I think Reardon paid enough to make it worth putting up with even this amount of stupidity."

Archie was still going. "Can I have a little set of metal wings?"

"NO!" Red responded by putting the plane in a steep dive and banking hard to the right with the bend of the canyon they were following.

"WOOOHOO!" Archie hollered. "That's the stuff, mate!"

In frustration, Red banked hard back to the left and pulled the nose up abruptly.

"Hey Red, what do I do if I need to puke?"

Red finally gave up and just glowered out the windscreen for the remainder of the flight.

When they finally touched down at the Yukon Dawson airport east of Dawson City, Archie was grinning, Deane was just waking up, and the Hollands were both ready to be done flying. Red was equally ready to be done with his passengers, as his hurry to unload their gear made abundantly clear. He'd radioed ahead and told their next pilot to meet them, but when no one was waiting at the little airstrip, Red didn't seem to mind.

"I appreciate you putting up with us, Red." Holland offered the pilot his hand, but the little man ignored it.

"You boys shouldn't be rockin' the boat, goin' into Alaska like this." Red tossed a pack on the ground at Law's feet. "Gonna get yourselves killed, and then you're probably gonna get a bunch of other people killed, 'cuz all you're gonna do is make the Russians mad. You shouldn't go provoking 'em, if you ask me."

"The case could be made that they provoked us," Holland said. "We didn't invade Russia."

"Maybe not." Red dropped the last case and straightened up. "But you Americans are always causing problems. Never leave well enough alone." He pointed with his chin at another plane tied down fifty yards away. "That's your next ride, anyway. You can drag your bags over there and wait for your pilot. He should be here soon."

Holland looked at the other plane, separated from them by a hundred yards of empty ramp that Red could just have easily taxied across before unloading their gear. Now they'd have to drag everything by hand. He shook his head. "Well, thanks for getting us this close, anyway."

Red missed the sarcasm completely. "Oh, don't thank me," he said as he clambered back into his own plane and fired up the engine. "You're all gonna get yourselves killed, take my word for it." He slammed his door, powered up the engine, and taxied off in the direction of the fuel pumps.

"He was a cheery sort, wasn't he?" Archie stood next to Law, watching the man go.

Law looked sideways at him. "He might have been more cheery if you hadn't been antagonizing him for the last hour and a half, Archie."

Archie shrugged and grabbed his pack. "Not my fault he was born with no sense of humor. Guy had it coming. All full of righteous indignation at what we're doin', but not quite righteous enough to turn down our money. If we end up winning this thing, he'll be the first one to brag about how he heroically flew the troops into combat. Pinhead."

Holland grunted as he shouldered his own pack and grabbed a rifle case in each hand. "Oh, I don't disagree - but maybe next time you could hold the teasing until we get all the way to where we're going?"

"Nah," Archie said, grinning. "Small price to pay for watching that bloke squirm."

Tony walked past them, headed toward the other plane with a load of gear on his back. "Let's just hope the next guy has a better sense of humor. I'd rather not end up dropped in a river someplace."

CHAPTER TWENTY-ONE

Antiqua Mariner

FV *In Decision*
   Gulf of Alaska
   175 Miles S of Anchorage

Day 22

"We should do this again," Boone said, staring wistfully over the bow rail. He felt Burdin staring at him and turned his head. "After the war, I mean. We should get a bunch of guys and charter a boat, spend a few days trophy fishing in the Caribbean."

"You're nuts," Burdin said, talking through a mouthful of ham sandwich. "I've had enough deep sea fishing to last a lifetime. I'm never gonna eat another fish as long as I live - provided I live through this goat rope we're heading into."

"You gotta admit, this has been an experience of a lifetime."

"It's been an experience, I'll give you that." He stared at the waves ahead. "How long 'til we get into Anchorage, you think?"

"Theo said we should get in sometime tomorrow. I'm a little

surprised we haven't run into any Russian naval patrols. Seems we oughta be pushing up against their defenses by now."

"Careful what you wish for." He flicked the last bite of his sandwich into the air, where a following seagull swooped down and caught it before it hit the water. "I'm about done with seagulls, too, come to think of it."

Boone smiled. "What do you think Tony and Law are doing about now?"

"Sitting in a pub, chatting up a couple of waitresses, if they're smart."

The two men looked at each other, then said in unison, "But they're not that smart."

"You think Reardon's psychiatrist did Tony any good?"

Boone leaned over the rail, watching the bow wave. "I sure hope so. He's a good kid - and he's tough, too. Archie and his buddies couldn't say enough good about that therapy, so…" he shrugged. "I hope for his sake it gets him through. That much time in captivity messes with your head."

"You ever been a prisoner?"

Boone shook his head. "Nope. Lucky, I guess. Law was, though."

"Really? When?"

"1992. In Sudan."

"What was he doing there?"

"We. I was there with him. Louie, too. You'll meet the fourth guy that was on our team tomorrow; he's our contact in Anchorage."

"Ok. So what were the four of you doing in Sudan in 1992?"

"Hostage rescue. Bunch of militants took some missionaries hostage; there were three Americans in the group, so we got the call. We got 'em out, but Law got separated and captured in the firefight. We spent almost a week trying to find him, chasing these guys all over this massive swamp. By the time we got him out, he was in pretty bad shape."

Boone had an uncharacteristically serious expression on his

face. "I thought we'd lost him, to be honest. I tell ya, the idea of having to tell his wife that he was never coming home almost drove me crazy. It was a good thing Monty and Louie were there with me, 'cuz I was seriously not thinking straight by the time we found Law."

"That doesn't seem like you, if you don't mind me saying."

Boone chuckled. "Nope. I know, I'm usually the guy who can't be serious, no matter what. But we all have our moments, right? I found out then that losing my best friend, the husband of my wife's best friend? That was my tipping point.

"That's why I'm hoping Tony gets better, man. Him and his dad are more than just my friends; they're my family. I can't stand the idea of them going through life wrecked by something that happened to 'em in the past."

"Which explains why you did so much to put together Tony's rescue."

"Yeah, I guess it does." He grinned at the younger man. "But I'd probably do the same for you, too. You're not quite immediate family yet; you're more like a distant cousin. But that still counts for something."

"That's comforting." Burdin grinned back, but it was forced. "I know what you mean, though. About finding your tipping point."

"You found yours, I'm guessing?"

"Almost. Holland actually kept me from going past it. If he hadn't shown up when he did, I'm sure I'd have killed Tolliver myself. I can't help thinking how close I came to being the next John Wilkes Booth or Lee Harvey Oswald."

"Never would have happened," Boone said.

"You don't think so?"

"Nah. You only have one last name. All the *really* crazy ones have at least two."

"You shoulda been a sociologist, Boone."

"Oh, I am. I just don't get credit for my work." He watched the seagulls wheeling and diving alongside the boat. "You *really* think you would have offed the president?"

Burdin's eyebrows went up. "Why? Don't you?"

Boone shook his head. "Nah. I haven't known you very long, but you don't strike me as the assassin type."

"You'd be surprised. I was."

"What do you mean?"

"What you were saying about getting to a tipping point - that's true. I never would have pegged myself as the assassin type either, but when Tolliver got elected and gutted the military, and then left so many of our guys to the wolves overseas …" He paused, shaking his head as if to force the memory away.

"Anyway, that would have been more than enough to make me hate the guy. But my brother was one of the ones Tolliver abandoned. That made it personal." His voice wavered as he went on.

"When I saw the video of his execution, Boone, something died inside of me. Call it decency, or morality, call it what you like, but I just wasn't the same after that. I went to work for HSI, and when they called me with a mission and I found out Tolliver was the target, I didn't hesitate. I *wanted* to kill him."

"But you didn't go through with it."

"No. Holland stopped me."

Boone looked at him. "That's not exactly what he told me."

"Really? What'd he tell you?"

"He said you were arguing with your team about it. Said one loud mouthed guy was taking a little too much pleasure in the idea, trying to goad you, and you took issue with that."

Burdin thought about it. "That's close enough to the truth. But we weren't arguing about whether we should kill Tolliver or not. We were arguing because Skeet was just a little *too* into the killing. He *liked* the idea, and I guess that just annoyed me."

"Which is why I say you're not the assassin type. You saw the moral wrong, and when that guy tried to push it on you, you pushed back. You're not a murderer, kid. You might be capable of killing when the situation demands it, but you're not a murderer. There's a big difference."

"I don't know. I used to agree with that, but when I look back at how easily I almost made the jump from one to the other, it scares me. I guess that's why I feel like I owe Holland so much. If he hadn't stepped in when he did... I'm not sure I coulda come back from that." He looked at Boone. "Holland gave me my life back. Gave me a chance to move on without burning everything down around me." He took a deep breath. "Hard to put a value on that."

"Which is why you came with us to get Tony out."

Burdin nodded. "Tony being the last survivor of my brother's unit made it that much more compelling, but yeah, I think I would have done the same regardless of who were getting out."

"Another reason why you're not the bad guy here," Boone said. "I look at you, and I see a guy who's trying to do the right thing under pretty messed up circumstances. That's all any of us can ask of anybody else, really. It's easy to go with the flow, do the wrong thing and pretend to have no regrets. It's a lot harder to take risks for the greater good, and have to pay a heavy price on top of it."

"You're making me feel all noble inside, now," Burdin laughed.

"All part of the service. Look, man. All we can do is separate right from wrong and do our best to stay in the right. When everything turns a shade of gray that you can't figure out, you go with your best judgment and let the chips fall where they may. Then you learn from it and move on."

"Is that what we're doing? Moving on?"

"*You* might be. I think *I'm* still in the 'learn from it' phase."

Pueblo Viejo
Veracruz, Mexico

Cooney had always loved Mexico, and he found that he

especially liked Pueblo Viejo. The city had a certain lawless, Wild West sort of vibe to it that he appreciated. True, it was wracked with crime, poverty and chaos on the best of days, but he had always thrived in that kind of environment. Not exactly the type of place he'd want to buy a vacation home, but it was perfect for his purposes at the moment.

Pueblo Viejo had a large population of foreigners coming and going, many involved in working the offshore oil rigs that dominated the view from its beaches. That allowed him to blend in to the crowd with a minimum of notice. Just one more gringo in a constantly changing crowd of gringos. That suited him just fine.

He was sitting just inside the window on the third floor of a run-down house that fronted along Independencia Road. Across the narrow dirt track north of the house was Cementerio Del Arbol, a huge old cemetery crowded with headstones, old crypts and broken down family monuments that looked as if they had been randomly stacked in a mad jumble rather than carefully planned out. The place looked more like a scrapyard for marble and granite cast-offs than a cemetery. Cooney wondered at the lack of order in the place. Cementerio Del Arbol was far from a peaceful place, unlike cemeteries he was familiar with in the States. Instead of wide, spreading shade trees and acres of orderly markers, this place was a pastiche of dirt, mud and blowing trash.

In spite of all that, Cooney had found that the locals still revered the place. People whose relatives had recently been laid to rest there would come and faithfully lay flowers on their headstones, paying their respects in silent grief. Most of the mourners could be found on the north half of the cemetery, however, where the newer and more ornate headstones stood. The south side, which was laid out inside a six foot concrete wall just across a dirt alley behind Cooney's hide, was a collection of much shabbier monuments. This was where the poorest of the poor laid their loved ones to rest.

Tiburcio Velasco had been one of those poor - until recently, when he had risen in prominence in the Jalisco New Generation drug cartel. But years before that had happened, Velasco had buried his grandmother in the poor section on the south side of Cementerio Del Arbol. The old lady had struggled to raise him since he was a baby, doting on him in spite of his wild mood swings and constant trouble with local gangs.

As a young man, Velasco had seldom listened to his grandmother, but he had loved her dearly in spite of that. When she passed away three years earlier, Tiburcio had had to rob several bodegas just to be able to afford the cheapest plot at the back of the filthy cemetery, and he'd always felt that he had let his grandmother down by not doing more for her. He told himself that someday he would have her remains moved to a better place, but in reality, now that his lot in life had drastically changed, he couldn't be bothered. He settled for visiting her grave every Sunday, replacing the wilted flowers from the week before and spending a few moments remembering the kind old woman who had tried so hard to raise him right, only to fail.

His success in life, if he was honest, had come from doing the *opposite* of what the old lady had always told him to do. His propensity to seek out trouble rather than avoid it had caught the attention of the Jalisco New Generation drug cartel, and the cartel had taken him in as a gopher shortly after his grandmother's death. He had been nothing more than an errand boy at first, making deliveries and collecting protection payments from local businesses, but it was a steady income and it gave Tiburcio something to feel proud of.

He finally gained his step when one of the 'clients' he went to collect from had refused to pay. The bodega owner had claimed that he had no money; some story about a sick child. The discussion turned violent, and Tiburcio had shot the man in the middle of the road in front of his store, in broad daylight in front of a crowd of witnesses. Rather than land him in trouble, the killing had caught the eye of his superiors. He had done well, they told him. He had acted decisively. As a reward, they put him in charge of JNGC's drive to expand further in the local area, and Tiburcio jumped at the chance.

The expansion of JNGC's operations that followed was anything but acceptable to the Sinaloa cartel, which had until that time enjoyed little opposition or competition in Pueblo Viejo. Behan's new contact within Sinaloa had suggested that Velasco's sudden death at the hands of an unseen sniper would send an unmistakeable message to JNGC leadership that Sinaloa was not to be trifled with. In exchange for sending that message, Sinaloa might be willing to help Behan and Cooney find Justin Newill.

The possibility that Newill had recently hired on with allies of JNGC in Campeche was tantalizing, in that it was the only lead Behan and Cooney had. Newill's continued existence made it problematic for Behan to resurrect HSI from the mess it had become following the hit on President Tolliver. Behan wanted Newill neutralized, and Cooney knew he was willing to do just about anything to see that done. Accepting a contract on Tiburcio Velasco was a small price to pay to get them on Newill's scent again.

Trade a cow to get a cart, trade a cart to get some grain, trade some grain to get a cow, Cooney thought, looking through his rifle scope. *It's all just business, one way or another.*

Velasco's devotion to his grandmother's memory - and his predictability in showing that devotion - was what brought Cooney to the vacant house overlooking the Cementerio Del Arbol. Behan's contact had told him about Velasco's habitual weekly graveside visit. The man had said that Velasco never came at the same time of day, but he did show up at some point almost every Sunday. All Cooney needed was patience, and a high powered rifle.

The rifle in question was a Ruger Precision Rifle chambered in .338 Lapua Magnum, with an eight inch long Banish 30 Gold suppressor fitted to the end of the barrel. The Ruger was inexpensive as far as precision long range rifles were concerned, and heavier than many other rifles, but it was still exceptionally accurate and reliable.

From a well prepared position, Cooney had no doubt that he would hit whatever he aimed at within fifteen hundred yards, nine out of ten times. Velasco's grandmother's headstone was only three hundred yards away, so this would be little more than a chip shot. Hidden in the shadows of an upstairs room in the derelict building, Cooney had a perfect view of the cemetery while he waited to get down to business.

Cooney had started watching the grave as soon as the sun had risen that morning, and he hadn't left his spot in the four and a half hours since. Now the temperature in the room was already climbing well above a hundred degrees, and he was sweating heavily. He stretched his back and took a long pull from a bottle of water. A family of four shuffled into view, pausing at a shabby looking grave about fifteen yards from Velasco's grandmother's plot.

Cooney was slightly distracted by the family, but it would have been impossible to miss Velasco when he arrived. He was dressed in expensive clothes that somehow managed to still be in poor taste, and he was flanked by two obviously armed guards, who walked slightly behind and apart from their boss. One of them peeled off and roughly herded the family away, his hand gestures leaving no doubt about what would happen if they stayed.

Cooney watched in irritation, his own somewhat jaded sense of honor taking issue with this rude behavior. His mission was Velasco, but at that moment, he decided to add to the target list slightly.

He waited while the two bodyguards spread out, giving Velasco some space to be alone at the graveside. They were about fifty yards apart, with Velasco roughly halfway between them and slightly farther away from Cooney's position. The American settled behind his rifle and waited. Velasco had his back to him, while the two guards were facing roughly in his direction. Clearly, they thought that any threat to their charge would come from the south side, perhaps through one of the rickety gates in the concrete wall.

Cooney controlled his breathing and relaxed. He decided to take the guard on his left first, not because he had harassed the young family, but because he was farthest away. His first shot would be the only one he could take his time with, and if he was in a hurry, he'd rather save the closer targets for his later, more hurried shots. He slowly took up the very slight amount of initial pull in the trigger, and when a loud truck horn blared from somewhere nearby, he added just enough pressure to break the shot.

Tiburcio Velasco swept last week's flowers from the headstone, gently laying the new bouquet in their place. Then he knelt down, careful to place a cloth on the ground first. He didn't want to stain his new jeans, even if the gesture made him look weak in front of his men. He was still slightly self-conscious, imagining their eyes on his back as he paid his respects, but he was growing used to it. These two men had been with JNGC much longer than he had, and he knew they probably resented his rise above them, but he didn't care. He was the man, now. They were just the help.

He bowed his head, making what he thought was a convincing show of grief for the men - *his men*, now - to properly appreciate.

The first bodyguard dropped in the dirt and lay still. The second man caught the movement out of the corner of his eye and started to turn, but Cooney had already cycled the bolt and swung the crosshairs onto him. The man had time only for a look first of disbelief, then a brief flash of recognition just as Cooney's second bullet slammed into his chest. He spun a half turn to his left and collapsed, his body crumpling against a decrepit monument. Cooney cycled the bolt again and quickly swung the crosshairs back to his left to focus on Velasco.

But Velasco was gone.

Cooney's heart jumped for a just a moment, wondering how the cartel thug had vanished. Then he settled back down and scanned the area around the grave Velasco had been visiting. *He's just a druggie, not a magician*, Cooney reminded himself. The only possible cover was a tall headstone with a statue of some kind of a saint on top, only a pace or two left of where Velasco had been standing a moment before. Cooney drew a bead on it. Through the scope, he could just make out an irregularity in the shadow cast by the headstone.

There was someone crouched behind it.

Velasco had been on one knee in an affectation of grief when the truck horn blasted, making him jump. He had always been a nervous person; always looking over his shoulder, always wondering if this strange noise or that strange shadow was somehow a threat to him. When the horn sounded, he flinched and glanced involuntarily in its direction, and saw instead one of his bodyguards collapsing to the ground like a bag of dirt.

Instinct took over.

He was on his feet in a flash, moving to the paltry cover of a moderately ornate headstone holding up a two foot tall statue of the Virgin Mary. As he moved, he heard the unmistakable snap of a suppressed weapon of some kind, just loud enough to be identifiable. He dove behind the headstone and looked back toward his other lieutenant, but the man was no longer there. Velasco's view was blocked by a row of tightly packed headstones and statues, but he knew - the second man was dead as well.

Sniper.

The thought chilled him. He wasn't afraid of anything that he could see well enough to fight, but a hidden killer with a long gun was terrifying to him. Tiburcio tried to bring up a mental picture of the surrounding area. All he could remember was the row of tenements and dilapidated houses that faced the cemetery along its south side. He couldn't recall any important details other than that several of the buildings were tall enough to overlook the cemetery's south wall. He was pinned down, and he knew it.

He'd been in plenty of dangerous situations in his life, and the fight or flight instinct, for him, had always manifested itself as *fight*. But now, knowing that the only thing between him and an unseen sniper intent on killing him was a three foot by four foot piece of two inch thick granite, he knew he had to get away. He glanced up at the statue. The Virgin offered nothing more than a beatific smile.

Desperate, Tiburcio pulled his 9mm Glock 17 pistol from behind his back. He was going to have to make his own way out of this. He bunched his leg muscles in preparation, and looked around for another spot of cover. The only thing close enough was a good sized tomb to his right. There were several people crouched behind it; at least two of them were children.

There. If he could get to the tomb, the people might distract the sniper, or make him hesitate long enough for Tiburcio to get further away. He dug his toes into the hard packed earth, and broke from cover.

Cooney didn't want to stick around any longer than absolutely necessary. The family that Velacso's thug had chased off had only gone a few dozen yards, waiting for whoever the important person with the bodyguards was to pay his respects and move on so that they could do the same. Now they were cowering behind a large tomb in the center of a little grove of dead trees, the father chancing the occasional peek from behind the granite wall as his wife and children cried and wailed in fright. They had seen both bodyguards die, and now they feared for their own lives.

Though Cooney bore them no ill will, witnesses were always a bad thing in his line of work. He'd been content to eliminate the man who had mistreated the family, but now they had become nothing more than a potential complication to his own safety. He needed to move things along and get away, before whatever passed for authorities in the area started sniffing around. He focused on the headstone where Velasco was hiding. He couldn't allow the criminal to simply cower there all day, so he aimed at a point in the center of the stone and fired.

Velasco moved just in time. As he started to run, the face of the headstone he'd been sheltering behind exploded an inch behind his head in a shower of broken granite and dust. He stumbled and half fell, but regained his feet and kept moving, raising the Glock and firing several rounds blindly in the direction he thought the shot had come from. The family behind the tomb crouched further out of sight, and the children screamed all the louder.

Cooney swore under his breath as he recovered from the recoil and saw his quarry squirting out from behind the headstone. He rapidly cycled the bolt and swung the barrel to reacquire his target, but he hurried the next shot and missed, the bullet smacking into another grave marker and showering Velasco in more dust and debris. Velasco had a pistol out and was shooting wildly, but none of his rounds came remotely close to Cooney's hide. The American took a breath as he cycled the bolt on the Ruger one more time, swinging the barrel more smoothly now to match Velasco's pace. He wasn't going to miss again.

Velasco flinched as a bullet smashed a headstone slightly ahead of him, making his eyes sting with the dust it threw into his path. A couple of stone fragments slashed into his cheek, but he ignored the pain and just tried to move faster. He was almost there...

Something crashed into his ribs, just under his left arm. The impact was incredible, but Velasco thought it odd in that it caused him no pain. Had he run into a gravestone? But no, now his legs had seemed to stop working, the world reeled and spun, and he was suddenly falling. There was a rushing sound in his ears as the ground came up. He didn't feel the impact when he hit, but strangely he could taste the dust in his mouth, mixed with the coppery taste of his own blood.

He slid to a stop in the meager shade of a dead tree, five yards short of the tomb he had hoped to shelter behind. He could see his own right hand stretched out before him, still holding the Glock, which was now at an odd angle, barrel jammed down in the dirt. Beyond that, he could only make out the blurry shapes of the young family as they fled away to the west in terror.

Their cries were the last sound he heard.

Cooney knew Velasco was dead as soon as he broke the final shot. He watched the man fold up and slide to a stop in the dirt, saw the unnatural angle of his arms and legs splayed around him, and he knew the bullet had at least severed his spine. A quick look through the scope at the rapidly spreading pool of blood beneath him was all the further confirmation Cooney needed. Velasco's back was broken, but he was bleeding out so fast that he'd be dead in a few seconds.

No need for another shot.

Cooney quickly folded up the Ruger's butt stock and bipod, reducing the overall length of the rifle by almost a foot. He stuffed it into its case, which was designed to look like it held surveying instruments. A quick look around the little room revealed all of his spent brass, which he stuffed into a pocket on the side of the case. He picked up his water bottle, took one last look outside at the body in the cemetery to be sure it hadn't moved, then left the building through the front door, out of sight of the cemetery.

It was a short walk to his rental car half a block away, where he stowed his bag in the back before pulling the car out of the alley where he'd hidden it and disappearing into traffic. He waited until he was several miles away before calling Behan, who answered without preamble.

"Well?"

"It's done," Cooney said.

"Any complications?"

"No. Your boys should be happy, though. They got three for the price of one."

"What are you talking about?"

"Turns out it was a table for three, not just one. It wasn't a problem, though. Everybody got served."

"I didn't ask for that," Behan said in a tight voice. *"It was supposed to be just the one."*

"Trust me," Cooney said, maneuvering the car through a knot of pedestrians shuffling across an intersection. "The message was sent. The people who asked us to send it aren't gonna care how it got there."

"They'd better not," Behan said. *"This is the only lead we have."*

"Don't worry about it. I'm on my way back now. Anything else you need here?"

Cooney could hear Behan taking a deep breath. *"Stay there,"* he said. "If they keep their end of the bargain, you should have a location as soon as I talk to them. No sense you wasting time coming back here first."

"There's going to be a little heat here for a few days. It'd probably be best for me to leave."

"You should have thought of that before you improvised then, shouldn't you?" Behan snapped. *"Stay put. I'll get back to you within the hour."* He broke the connection.

Cooney shook his head. He had no desire to stay here any longer, now that he'd dealt with Velasco. The longer he hung around, the greater the chance that some JNGC flunky or crooked local cop would key on him. He'd left no evidence at the scene of the shooting, and to the best of his knowledge no one had seen him leave the tenement, but he didn't want to take any more chances. He needed to get off the street.

He had flown in late the previous night on a plane Behan had chartered. They had taxied to a private hangar, and a well placed bribe had kept customs officials from inspecting the plane or its contents. The original plan had been to do the job, then return to the airport and leave the same way he'd come, but Behan's response to his report was making Cooney wary. He didn't like the idea of waiting around, and lacking any place better to wait, he headed back toward the airport.

He parked in a hotel lot half a mile from the executive terminal, then strolled inside the hotel and took a seat in the bar next to the lobby. His car was relatively safe for the moment, and he decided he could do with some food while he waited to hear back from Behan. He was coming down off an adrenaline spike from the shooting, which always made him ravenously hungry. By the time the waiter brought him the menu, he's already put Velasco permanently out of his mind.

CHAPTER TWENTY-TWO

Mortem Conscientiae

The Oval Office
  The White House
  Washington, D. C.

Day 23

"So help me, God." Sydney Black said, lowering his right hand.

"Congratulations, Mr. Vice President." Supreme Court Chief Justice Gallatin said in a low voice, shaking Black's hand.

"Thank you, Mr. Chief Justice. And thank you for getting this done under the unusual circumstances."

"My pleasure, sir." Gallatin took a step to the side, out of view, as Black turned to face the camera.

"My fellow Americans," Black began. "I accept this appointment with my oath, with deep gratitude, and with a profound sense of the danger facing our country at this moment in its history. We face immense challenges both at home and abroad, and I am honored that President Reese has placed his confidence in me to help him in meeting those challenges. I will not rest until I have given my utmost to preserve, protect and defend the United States of America from all enemies, foreign and domestic. I ask you all to join me in working to restore order to our nation, and to put it back on the path to greatness that it once blazed for others to follow. Thank you. May God bless you all, and may God Bless the United States of America."

Will Beckerdite watched the inauguration ceremony from his office, fighting a sinking feeling in the pit of his stomach. He knew that the swearing in was unique in two very subtle ways. First, it was done in the Oval Office, rather than the East Room or some other location, a not-so-subtle indication that Black was closer to the immediate position of power than the average vice president. Second, Reese himself was nowhere to be seen during the ceremony. The absence of the sitting president during the inauguration of a new vice president indicated very clearly that all was not as it seemed in the White House. Will wondered how obvious that was to people on the outside looking in.

As Black finished speaking, Will switched off his computer and started clearing out his desk. He'd had enough. Done enough. He couldn't shake the feeling that he'd been complicit in setting events in motion that would inevitably supplant Reese, and although on a certain level he knew that it had needed to be done, he still couldn't ignore the fact that he'd stained his own integrity by taking such an active role. He knew that Black would waste no time in pushing Reese aside and taking the presidency, probably in the next day or two at the latest. Will didn't want to be around when that happened. He'd had enough of politics to last a lifetime, and more.

Rukha, Afghanistan

"You know my feelings on the matter, Daoud." Yunus looked at the younger man sadly. "I appreciate all that you have sacrificed for our tribe, but I cannot help but think this is going too far. The Americans are collapsing. They are no longer a threat to us. And if what this emissary from China says is true, we are in a better position now than we were when the Americans first supported us years ago. We can move on. Forget the Americans. You do not need to do this."

Daoud was staring out the window at the mountains. "I killed my own brother, Malik-sayb." He turned slowly. "Did Akhtar tell you that?"

Yunus nodded, lowering his eyes. "He did not, but I suspected it. When you told me he was dead, I feared that you might have had a hand in the killing."

"Mine was the *only* hand in it." Daoud turned back toward the window. "I justified it, because Jahangir had betrayed his tribe - our tribe - to join that *Daesh* scum. I told myself that he was already dead, that it didn't matter. But he was still my brother, Malik-sayb. I killed him, so that Akhtar's plan could be carried out. I have made my peace with that choice. But then the Americans came, and took Akhtar, and with him any hope we had of seeing his plan through. Now, it is as if I killed my brother for nothing. I will put that right, if I have to kill each one of those commandos with my bare hands."

"And if Han cannot find them?"

Daoud shook his head. "I think he will. The Chinese are better even than the Americans at every manner of surveillance. He will find them."

Yunus frowned into his tea, nodding slowly. "And you will go after them? In their own country?"

"Theirs is a country in chaos, Malik-sayb. I will blend in. I will find them."

The door opened and Ayoub stepped through. "He is here, Malik-sayb."

Yunus nodded. "Show him in." He waited for Ayoub to leave, then turned back to Daoud. "Do not expect overmuch, my friend."

"I am too familiar with broken promises for that, Malik-sayb." He broke off as the door opened again, this time revealing Han Jiayi. Han bowed to both men as he entered, then waited as Ayoub backed out and pulled the door shut.

"Good afternoon, my friends," Han said. "I trust you are both well?"

"We are." This time, Yunus brought Han's tea himself. "Please, sit."

Han inclined his head in thanks, settling himself on the cushions. "I believe I have good news for you."

"Oh?" Yunus said, doing his best to show little more than mild interest.

"First, my government wishes to express its pleasure at your acceptance of our offer of cooperative support. As a sign of goodwill, we have placed certain funds in an account for your immediate use." He slid a card across the low table to Yunus. "You will find all the account information there. My government will be sending additional representatives to the area soon, and we look forward to your support in their efforts."

Daoud's natural suspicion got the better of him. "What 'efforts', exactly?"

Han showed his thin smile. "We require local knowledge. Tribal boundaries, both disputed and accepted. Rivalries, feuds, differences and allegiances. Names of those most likely to assist us in our construction projects, as well as those most likely to oppose us. You will be our local liaison, serving to facilitate our various efforts in the region. Is that acceptable?"

Yunus fingered the card Han had given him. "Yes. It is acceptable."

"Excellent. Now, to your specific request, Mr. Farouq."

Daoud's heart jumped, but he held his tongue, instead simply raising an expectant eyebrow at Han.

"We have learned rather a great deal about your Marine, my friend. His name is Tony Holland."

"It was I who told you that!" Daoud snapped in disgust.

Han nodded. "So it was. But did you know that his father is apparently a retired U.S. Navy SEAL?"

Daoud shook his head. "No. We did not know that."

"I trust you are familiar with them?"

"*Too* familiar."

Han nodded. "Yes. Well, it seems that the father was actually under suspicion for the murder of the American President Tolliver, though that accusation has since proven false. However, he has associates who are actively involved in mercenary work. One of those associates owns a company that appears to have assisted the senior Holland with the operation that freed his son, and resulted in the capture of Akhtar Khan. They were working in collaboration with British Special Forces, to what extent we are not yet certain, but the connection is indisputable."

"Where are they now?"

Han spread his hands. "Our information is inconclusive, but we believe the entire team is now in Alaska, fighting against the Russians. Their exact whereabouts is unknown at the moment, but when they use their credit cards or cell phones next, we will be able to pinpoint their location with much greater accuracy."

"I will require transportation," Daoud said.

"I beg your pardon?"

"Transportation," Daoud repeated. "I will need to get to them somehow."

"Ah." Han shook his head. "No, as I mentioned in our earlier meeting, that would be highly irregular, my friend. Our operatives can eliminate these men much more efficiently -"

"I am not concerned with efficiency! I am only concerned with justice, and honor. I must be the one to carry out this task. I will not send another person to do what honor demands of me."

Han sighed and glanced at Yunus. "Do you agree with this, Malik-sayb?"

"I fear Daoud is right." Yunus said. "This is a point of honor. Respectfully, we request your assistance, but if you will not provide it, I assure you - he will find another way."

Han looked at Daoud with disapproval for a moment before relenting. "That will not be necessary. It is not ideal, mind you."

"I understand. Thank you." For once, Daoud's tone softened. "When can I leave?"

"It will take some time, but I should think within the week." He rose to leave. "I must arrange transport and contacts... you will have to enter through the southern border, I think..." He moved toward the door, already lost in thought.

"Wait, my friend." Yunus stood. "You have been most generous, but you have not asked for a great deal in return. What more do you require from us?"

Han paused before turning to face Yunus. "We only require loyalty, Malik-sayb. And that, I believe, is a trait you are very familiar with."

White House Physician's Office
  The White House
  Washington, D. C.

"I imagine congratulations are in order, Mr. Vice President."

"Thank you, doctor," Black said as he took a seat. "But under the circumstances, I'd rather just get down to business. How is he?"

"Sedated. He had another episode while you were being sworn in. I warned you that might happen. Trying to have him do too much all at once only aggravates an already over-stressed mind. He scrambles, tries to understand everything at once, and it only results in more confusion."

"I understand. And I hope you understand why I needed to try. The country just can't wait much longer."

"I need to consider my patient's well being, over the needs of the country, Mr. Vice President."

"Of course. But at the moment, your patient's well being is directly tied to the country's need. The sooner he resigns, the sooner he can ease his mind."

Oldenbourg nodded. "I know. I know that staying in the job is only exacerbating his condition. I also know that pushing him to surrender that job also exacerbates his condition. It's like a Gordian knot."

Black nodded. "I agree. But Alexander proved the best solution to the Gordian knot was to just cut the rope. That's what we're doing here, Doctor."

Oldenbourg sighed. "Right."

"Look, I get it." Black rose. "Give him tonight to rest. We'll get it done in the morning."

"There's one more consideration." Oldenbourg ran a hand over his face. He looked completely worn out. "As much as I'd like him to be rested, it looks like events are going to dictate otherwise."

"What do you mean?"

"That virus the CDC has been watching?"

"Let me guess - Were the asthma inhalers tampered with?"

Oldenbourg shook his head. "No. First non-asthmatic victim showed up today in San Diego."

Black sat back down. "I have to confess, I had hoped this would be limited to asthma patients. You're saying it's in the general population as well?"

"Apparently so. These new cases all show the same symptoms as the others. Looks like asthma is just a complicating factor. It may allow for a shorter incubation period in asthma sufferers…"

"Hang on - you said new *cases*, plural. *How many* new cases?"

"In excess of three hundred."

"You're kidding. In just one day?"

"That's in San Diego alone."

Black's eyes widened. "In… Wait. How many are we talking about, then, overall? Nationwide, I mean?"

Oldenbourg shook his head. "We just don't know, sir. CDC is completely unable to even keep up with the reporting. Those were the numbers they gave me ten minutes ago, but it's a very volatile situation. It just exploded. At this rate, the hospitals in San Diego will be overwhelmed in a matter of hours…" his voice trailed off for a moment as he rubbed his eyes with one hand. "Sir, we have a serious problem. I really need to brief the president, regardless of his condition, but I just can't see how briefing him will do any good at this point."

Black stood up again. "Come on, I'll go with you. If he's coherent, so much the better. If not, then at least you'll have done your job, and we'll just have to press ahead as best we can from there."

Hacienda Puerta Campeche
Campeche, Mexico

Cooney sat in the shade of a palm tree next to the hotel pool, slowly sipping a coffee and looking for all the world like a tourist enjoying a vacation. The pool, surrounded by weathered stone and adobe walls reminiscent of an ancient Catholic mission, was abandoned this early in the morning, which was perfect for his purposes. Behan had made the arrangements; all Cooney had to do was sit there and wait.

He didn't have to wait long. He was barely halfway through his coffee when a waiter came around the false mission wall that bisected the pool, carrying a tray stacked with fresh pastries. "Buenos días, señor." The man leaned down and proffered the tray.

Cooney waved him off. "No, gracias." He wanted the man to go away in case his contact was waiting to approach.

"Buena elección," the waiter said, ignoring Cooney's refusal. He selected a croissant from the tray, wrapped it in a thin piece of waxed paper, and placed it on Cooney's plate. Cooney was about to protest, but stopped himself when he realized the man's eyes were fixed on his as he served the pastry. "Más café, amigo?"

Cooney smiled and held out his half-full cup. "Sí, por favor." He waited while the man filled his cup, then bowed slightly and excused himself. Cooney waited several more minutes, sipping his coffee before he leaned over and picked up the croissant. As he lifted it, he could see that the wax paper the man had used to serve the pastry had faint writing on it. Cooney took a leisurely bite, then sipped his coffee again. He leaned back in his chair and allowed his eyes to slowly scan the pool area one more time.

Sure that he was still alone, he picked up the rest of the croissant with the wax paper, popping the flaky pastry into his mouth. With a deft motion, he crumpled the paper into a ball in his left hand as he reached for his cup with his right. He took a last sip of the coffee, then wiped his hands with a napkin, stuffing the wadded wax paper under his watch band as he did so. Then he picked up the magazine he'd been pretending to read, stood up and walked across the pool deck, through the lobby and back to his room.

Once upstairs, Cooney went into his bathroom and started the shower, turning the water to its hottest setting and filling the little room with steam. He waited until the mirror and windows were completely covered in steam before removing the wax paper from beneath his watch band. Satisfied that any hidden cameras in the room would also be fogged over, he spread the paper carefully on the counter and studied the writing on it. There was an address and a series of numbers that he recognized as a lock combination.

Cooney committed all the details to memory, then struck a match from a hotel matchbook and lit the wax paper, letting the ash and the burnt match fall into the toilet. He flushed it away, then turned off the shower and left the room.

He spent the next half hour driving his rental car randomly around Campeche, executing a surveillance detection route to ensure he wasn't being followed. He drove to the west first, as if he was heading out of town, then he doubled back and pulled into a gas station. He went inside and bought a coffee, then came out and continued back to the east again. After several more misdirections, he'd seen no people or vehicles that looked like they were matching his moves. He pointed the car east again and joined Highway 180, following it for twenty minutes to the little town of Hampolol.

The address he'd been given was for a run down storage facility that fronted along Calle 7 near what passed for a town square. There was a brick mission church in the center of the square and several people were milling about, but it was mostly quiet. Cooney parked the car around the corner and got out.

There was no attendant at the facility, just a keypad on a grated door that led to the interior. Cooney keyed in the sequence he'd memorized earlier, and the door clicked open, revealing a dark single hallway with a line of doors along either side, spaced about four feet apart. He pulled the door closed behind him and walked down to the third door on the right. Another sequence of memorized numbers, and this door clicked open as well.

Stepping inside, Cooney found a wall switch and flicked on the overhead light. The room was about four feet wide by six feet deep. Shelves lined the wall along the left side, and a stack of crates lined the right, leaving a narrow walkway between. He opened the backpack he'd brought along and studied the labels on the crates and shelves. There were enough weapons and ammunition to outfit a heavily armed squad of men, with plenty to spare.

It would be more than enough for his purpose.

CHAPTER TWENTY-THREE

Ursus Patriae

Over the Robinson River
50 Miles SE of Fort Greely, Alaska

Day 24

Over the course of his long military career, Holland had been a passenger in just about every imaginable type of aircraft, and had parachuted out of most of them. He'd been in helicopter and plane crashes, had to fix a malfunctioning parachute during free fall - twice - and had the wing shot off of one aircraft he was in as it rolled down a remote dirt runway in Africa trying to take off.

None of those experiences had prepared him for this flight.

The pilot of the big, single engine Cessna 208B Grand Caravan seemed incapable of climbing higher than five feet above the nearest trees, and he nimbly maneuvered the aircraft through narrow mountain passes and above remote river beds as if he was playing a frighteningly realistic video game. At first Holland tried to focus on the scenery, but it was flashing by the window so fast that looking out the side of the aircraft was disconcerting.

His eyes were drawn instead to a bloody set of moose antlers and a large game bag full of meat the pilot had lashed to the right side wing strut while the four men had gone inside the little terminal to get something to eat. He'd lashed another set of antlers and meat to the strut on the other side as well. Once they'd eaten, the pilot had hustled them into the plane in such a hurry to depart that they hadn't bothered to ask about the extra cargo, but now curiosity and the need to focus on something besides the trees whipping past outside almost at arm's reach got the better of Law.

"Somebody decide they didn't want their moose?" he asked the pilot, whose name tag read *Punch*.

Punch shook his head. "Those are actually road kill," he said. "I just figured that having antlers and meat hanging off the wings would make us look like an actual backcountry flight, ferrying hunters back in from the bush." He jerked his thumb skyward. "Less chance of gettin' shot down by some trigger happy Russian fighter pilot, ya know?"

"Makes sense to me."

"Charter service out of Tok had a plane shot down two days ago about fifty miles from here. No warning at all. Sucker just dove on him out of the north and started shooting. And he was only carrying mail and groceries. Not a bunch o' crazy snake eaters, like I'm doing." He grinned. "We'll be lucky if we don't end up at the bottom of a smokin' hole before we land."

Holland gripped the overhead handle hard as the pilot dove over a small rise and into the river valley beyond. "Optimistic much?"

"Realistic," Punch said with a chuckle. "That guy that got shot down? Friend of mine. He was lucky. He was flying a Super Cub - a lot smaller plane than this, and you can land one in less than a hundred feet if you know what you're doing. He had most of his vertical stabilizer shot away, but he still managed to put the plane down on a sand bar in the middle of the Tanana River. Russian pilot circled him a few times and then just flew off. Couple of locals in a boat picked him up three hours later. This is a great plane, but it's a much bigger target, and if some Russian decides to start taking pot shots at us, it'll be a lot harder to finesse this thing onto a sand bar someplace."

"You know anything about their numbers up this way?"

"Nah. Being based outta Dawson City across the border, we haven't heard much. Just what the other pilots pass back and forth, which is how I heard about my buddy getting shot down. Your boss did some pretty serious convincing to get me to take this flight at all."

"He's a convincing sort."

Punch barked out a laugh. "Yeah, he paid me almost enough to buy a new airplane, so even if we do get shot down, I'm covered!" He leaned over toward Holland and lowered his voice. "Don't tell him I said this, but I woulda done it for nothing. I don't wanna have to learn to speak Russian." He leaned back and smiled.

"Then, when Red called me and bent my ear about how you boys were gonna get us all killed and how you shouldn't be running around provoking the Russians, I knew I *had* to take you in." He winked and then banked the plane without warning hard to the right, following a smaller tributary of the Robertson River upstream through a deep cut between two snow capped mountains. Holland glanced out the window at the peaks along both sides, threateningly close to the aircraft.

"We definitely got the impression that Red wasn't too thrilled to help."

"He's a good fella, actually," Punch said. "He's just got a lotta chips on his shoulder, mostly about his height. Ferryin' you four big boys up here to go put a hurt on the bad guys, probably just makes him feel smaller. He's been that way ever since I've known him. But he's not all that bad."

"Well, maybe that'll make Archie sorry for acting like an eleven year-old kid on a family vacation for most of the flight." Holland faked a Birmingham accent. "'Are we there yet? I need to pee!'"

"Ha!" Punch laughed out loud. "I'da liked to have seen that!"

"That's awful, Law," Archie protested. "You made me sound Australian!"

"Y'all sound the same to me," Law said, stifling a laugh.

"Two minutes!" Punch bellowed suddenly, making Holland jump. They all looked out the windows, trying to see their destination better.

Punch angled the plane closer to the right side of the canyon and continued his climb to match the rapidly rising terrain. Holland could see the flat rim of a plateau looming through a gap in the higher peaks, getting closer with nauseating speed. Punch leveled the wings and pulled back on the W-shaped control yoke, bringing the nose higher as they approached the rim. Holland didn't think it would be enough, and he couldn't help it as every muscle tensed in anticipation of slamming into the side of the mountain.

They cleared the rim with barely feet to spare, and Punch immediately chopped the power and allowed the plane to settle onto the relatively flat grassy surface of the plateau. He rolled a hundred yards to the northwest, then added power and kicked the rudder, bringing the plane back to face the way it had come. He cut the engine and hurried to unclip his safety harness.

"Welcome to the Macomb Plateau, gentlemen! Everybody out - I'm leaving in three minutes, so if there's anything you don't want me to sell as military surplus to my buddies back in Canada, you'd better shift it in a hurry!"

Holland clambered out of the plane, joined by Tony, Archie Foxall and Sergeant Major Deane. All of them looked slightly nauseous and very grateful to be on the ground. Punch scuttled around the aircraft, opening cargo doors and dumping their kit on the ground all around the plane, seemingly without a care for damaging it or not.

As they unloaded the last bag, he offered Holland his hand. "If I make it back to Dawson, I'll let your fancy British boss know you made it this far." He nodded toward the north lip of the plateau. "Alcan Highway's about six miles that way. Sorry I can't get you any closer, but I really don't feel like getting blown up today."

"Sorry we couldn't come in after dark," Holland said. "I don't envy you the flight back in broad daylight."

"Doesn't get completely dark around here for another month at least. You're in the land of the midnight sun, remember?"

Holland nodded. "I have a feeling that's gonna be hard to forget, before we're finished."

"You might be right." Punch threw a wave at the other three men and clambered back into the plane in a hurry. "Good luck to you fellas."

Holland barely had time to back away before Punch had throttled up the engine and was roaring back down the plateau to the southwest. The plane had only just got airborne when it shot off the edge, and then dropped abruptly over and out of sight, Punch using gravity to help build airspeed as he raced down the river valley and away, back toward Canada and home.

Holland turned to look at his small crew. "Well, I'd tell you guys that daylight's wasting, but that's gonna be one problem we don't have to worry about this far north. So I guess 'let's get a move on' is gonna have to be it for inspiration."

"Gonna need some kinda motor transport pretty quick like, Long Arm." Archie hefted a bulging rucksack onto his back and picked up a rifle, quickly checking the action to be sure it was loaded. "This is a lot of kit for the four of us to shift any distance on foot." All together, they had about four hundred pounds of gear to carry between them, not including weapons. "Not to mention the fact that on foot we stick out like a buffalo in a baby carriage."

"We're just gonna have to cowboy up, at least as far as the highway," Holland replied, shouldering his own pack. "We can find a rig down there." He watched as his son struggled with his own pack, which they'd packed slightly lighter than the other three. "Here, son." Holland grabbed the top of the pack with one hand and tried to help him lift it, but Tony spun away, sudden irritation on his face.

"I got it, Dad!" Tony snapped, but his annoyance melted away almost as fast as it had manifested. He lowered his eyes, embarrassed. "Sorry. Look, I appreciate you wanting to take care of me, Dad, really. But you gotta let me do it. You can't be babysitting me when things go sideways." Deane and Archie busied themselves with their gear, pretending not to notice the exchange.

Holland looked hard at his son. "You sure you're strong enough?"

"Why? Because it's been less than a week since I was wasting away in a hole in the ground in Afghanistan? If that's the case, then no, I'm not sure I'm strong enough yet. But this has got to get done." He cycled the bolt on his rifle, then looked his dad in the eye. "And you always taught me that the best way to do something hard is to just put your head down and push through it. So that's what I'm doing. Besides, you're the one took a bullet in the butt, not me. I can at least walk without a limp."

Holland nodded and grinned. "All right then, funny man. Let's both push through it then." He looked at the others. "You girls ready?"

"We've already left, in our minds," Deane cracked. "You two'll need to catch us up."

"Fantastic. Tony, take point. Hold up right after we drop down off the top of this plateau, and we'll take a look at the highway from there. Anybody hears any engines or anything else doesn't sound right, get under what cover you can right away. I don't want to get caught out in the open by a random patrol or some passing scout chopper. Let's motor."

They set off toward the north end of the plateau, Tony in the lead, followed by Deane and Archie at fifty yard intervals, with Holland bringing up the rear. He'd given Tony point partially as a way to show confidence in him, but also as a means to ensure they travelled at Tony's pace to start out. He knew his son was still very weak from the poor treatment he'd received at the hands of his Afghan captors.

Holland found himself wondering what the Brits had planned for Khan, the terrorist who had been holding Tony captive just a week earlier. He hoped the man would spend a very long time in a very dark place. Forcing that thought down, he scanned the top of the plateau and the surrounding mountains as they walked. The scenery wasn't nearly as dramatic as Afghanistan, but it was still shocking in the immense emptiness of the place. He knew there were plenty of little settlements and larger towns within a hundred miles of them, but he also knew that the wilderness that separated those pockets of civilization was as remote and unforgiving as any on earth. It wasn't going to be easy, fighting a guerrilla war against an entrenched enemy in this environment.

Their first objective was to find transportation. Then they needed to establish a reasonably secure base of operations, and if possible link up with any potential resistance in the area. About forty miles to the northwest of the plateau was Fort Greely, a smallish U.S. Army base tasked with a potentially large mission: intercontinental missile defense. Greely had roughly thirty Ground-Based Interceptor anti-ballistic missiles stored in underground silos. Those missiles and their control systems were Holland's main objective.

His team was tasked to find a way to either retake or destroy the missile site. Ideally, they would eliminate what they hoped would be a small skeleton force of Russian troops guarding the site, and then return control of the missiles to U.S. Army troops. The problem was, they had no solid intelligence on the composition or strength of the Russian forces at Greely, nor the availability or numbers of any American personnel in the vicinity.

Holland thought the mission had about a twenty percent chance of success, and that only if they managed to destroy the site and safely evacuate after. He knew that sending a four man team against a fixed facility with an alert defending force in place was reckless at best, but they really had no choice. If other thrusts across the state were successful, the Russians might choose to launch ballistic missile attacks in retaliation. In order to prevent that, Greely had to be retaken. Destroying it would prevent the Russians from using it to defend against British submarine launched ballistic missiles, but it would be better if they could take the base intact.

They had received reports that Russian airborne troops had descended on Eielson Air Force Base outside of Fairbanks, about seventy miles northwest of Greely. Mechanized troops had then rolled into Greely several hours later, taking the smaller base without much resistance. After that, the reports had stopped coming in altogether. Holland had no way of knowing if the Russians had reinforced the base or left it in the hands of a small unit for the time being.

All of which contributed to his unease, walking exposed across the top of a plateau a few miles from the main arterial highway in the area, within easy flying distance of Fort Greely. It would be all too easy to be spotted up here, and if the Russians were shooting down bush planes as Punch had said, they certainly wouldn't hesitate to fire on four heavily armed and unidentified men walking around loose like they were. He silently willed Tony to pick up the pace.

The Macomb Plateau rises above the Alcan Highway just south of the little village of Dry Creek. As Tony led the way, the team dropped over the north rim of the plateau and into a steep defile that followed a creek due northwest toward the town. They had to keep going another two miles in that direction before the mountains on either side opened out wide enough to give them a view of the village, with the Alcan Highway and the Tanana River beyond. Tony finally called a halt behind a forty foot high projection of rock that gave them cover from view below. The men all dropped their packs without a word and dropped into positions around the rock, each man scanning the valley below with binoculars.

"That highway's way too exposed," Deane said. "No cover at all, unless we're laying on our bellies in the berry bushes."

"The town doesn't look like much, either," Archie said.

"We're better off grabbing a truck in the town than trying to hitch a ride out on the highway," Tony said, staring intently at the half-dozen buildings in Dry Creek.

"I don't see anything worth grabbing, though." Holland was looking hard as well, but all he could see was a couple of old sedans up on blocks in front of two ramshackle houses, and three snowmobiles parked next to a shed that looked like they hadn't been used in more than a decade.

"I don't see any traffic out on the highway," Deane offered. "We go down there, we're gonna be out in the open for a while."

"What d'ya say, Law?" Archie asked, rolling to one side to look over at Holland.

Lawson took a long time to respond, scanning the town and the half mile of open ground between it and the highway before finally fixing on one house. It was farther south than the rest, and looked to be in better shape. It was also the only house in town with an attached garage.

"Red house, south side of town," he said. "I bet there's a pickup or something in that garage." He lowered his binoculars. "You're right, Sergeant Major. I don't like how exposed that highway is either. All it'll take is one patrol rolling up on us while we're thumbing for a ride, and that'll be all she wrote."

"Let's reconnoiter the garage then, shall we?" Deane lowered his binoculars and hefted his pack.

"You volunteering to take point?"

"With pleasure." Deane started off down the right side of the defile, using the terrain to mask their approach as much as possible. The slope was covered with chest high underbrush, mostly cow parsnip, thimbleberry and red currant, with various ferns and shorter blueberry bushes mixed in. As they descended, the brush got thicker and taller, reducing visibility to a few yards.

The relative silence was shattered by the sudden crashing of a large animal fleeing downhill away from the four men. Deane held up a fist, calling the men to a halt, and turned to look at Tony a few paces behind him.

"Bear?" Deane mouthed the question, his eyes slightly rounder than normal. Tony held his palms out and shrugged. He raised two fingers to his eyes, then pointed to the ground and raised his eyebrows. Deane nodded and moved ahead cautiously. Tony looked back at Holland and mimed a four-legged animal with his hand, followed by a shrug indicating he didn't know what kind. Holland nodded and passed the signal along to Archie as they waited for Deane to investigate. Deane crept back several moments later.

"Bloody big bear," he said, dropping to knee. "Or a small one with bloody big paws. Track was half again the length of my foot." He looked up as Holland and Archie came up. How big would a bear with that size paw be, do you think?"

"Big enough," Holland said. "The good news is it's probably in the next county by now. Bears don't like the smell of humans, and unless it was a mother with cubs, it's probably long gone. We just need to stay sharp and try not to surprise it if it's hanging around."

"You *want* me to make noise?" Deane clearly thought this was a bad idea.

"We don't want to make enough noise to alert anybody in the village that we're coming," Holland said. "But we do want that bear or any others in the area to know we're here. The wind just shifted downhill right before that one spooked, so that's in our favor now as well. Go ahead and talk out loud as we go, just until we break into the open again. Let's press on."

Deane shot a skeptical glance at Tony. "You stay in my hip pocket, you hear, lad? If I end up looking like a walking snack cart to some starving bear, I'll need you to bring the pain, quick."

Tony grinned. He'd spent enough time in the wilderness with his dad to know that bears deserved respect and distance, but he didn't fear them. "Don't worry Sergeant Major. I'll start shooting before he eats anything important."

"Marvelous," Deane said. "Easy to joke when you're not top of the menu." He set off down the slope again, much more tentatively than before.

As Tony walked past the spot where Deane had found the track, he let out a low whistle. "You weren't kidding, were ya? That thing's gotta be the size of a truck!"

"You're not helping, lad," Deane grumbled. "Let me guess; lorry-sized bears only eat people, right?"

"Pretty much."

"Brilliant. You ready to take point again, then?"

"I'm good back here, thanks."

Behind them, Holland paused for a moment, tilting his head to one side and listening. Archie stopped next to him. "I heard it too. Can't tell which direction though."

"Everybody hunker down," Holland said into his headset. "Jet engine."

They all dropped lower in the undergrowth and burrowed into it alongside of the little stream they'd been following, all of them holding their breath and trying to pinpoint the growing noise of an approaching aircraft. Holland had moved to the right of the stream, allowing a better view downhill and to the west-northwest, so he spotted it first.

"SU-57," he said. "Looks like he's patrolling the highway toward the Canadian border."

"Good thing he didn't run that route an hour ago," Archie said. "You think Punch had time to get back across?"

"Depends," Holland answered. "If the Russian's just

following the highway, he'll miss him. Punch would've gone as straight northeast as possible back to Dawson, and it's only about a hundred miles to the border that way. Highway 2 goes southeast from here, so if that was just a quick out and back patrol, Punch'll be well clear."

The insectile silhouette of the Russian fighter quickly passed to the north of their position, following the highway to the southeast and moving so fast it would have been a miracle if the pilot had spotted them. Still, they held their position for another ten minutes after the jet noise had subsided completely.

"You wanna stay hunkered here a while longer, see if he comes back?" Archie asked.

Holland looked at his watch. "Nope. Fast as he was moving, he'd almost be at the border to the southeast by now. But I'd bet he either turned north along the border to cut Highway 5 and follow it back down from there, or he turned south at Tok to follow Highway 1 toward Valdez. Single aircraft, lot of territory to patrol, I doubt he's coming back on the same route. Let's keep moving."

They hoisted their packs and continued down the slope for another half mile, where the underbrush finally started to thin out, giving way to a line of spruce and aspen trees that shielded their approach for the last quarter mile. When a last quick scan through the trees with the binoculars turned up no movement, they set out again, covering the remaining distance at a jog. Holland held them up just inside the tree line where he could see the red house they'd spotted from higher up.

"This is weird," Tony said as he scanned the buildings. "Where is everybody?"

"Dunno." Holland was looking intently at the area, systematically checking every building in his view. "Archie, you're with me. Let's bracket that place and take a look inside the garage. Tony, Alvin, go wide and back us up. Move."

Tony and Sergeant Deane broke in opposite directions, running parallel to the tree line for about twenty yards, where they stopped and looked back. Holland waved them forward, and they exited the trees and worked their way toward the property, keeping low and using scattered bits of brush and construction materials for cover. When they stopped behind a couple of outbuildings within ten yards of the house and garage, Holland and Archie moved up the center.

Holland stopped against the rear wall of the garage, covering the east side of the building while Archie moved up to a door on the south wall. He was reaching for the knob when a shot rang out, the bullet smashing into the wall a foot from Archie's head.

"You scum have taken enough already!" An elderly woman stepped out of a breezeway on the west side of the garage, pointing an ancient bolt-action rifle at Archie's head. "Now you just get on back to Mother Russia, and leave me alone!"

Holland stepped around the side of the building, his rifle trained on the woman. Before he had a chance to say anything, Deane's rifle barrel emerged from the breezeway behind her, coming to a gentle stop with the muzzle resting against the back of her head.

"Now, my Nan," Deane said softly. "I'd like you to lower that weapon. Bad enough you insult my friend there by calling him a Russian; let's not make it worse by actually hurting someone, shall we?"

The woman swiveled her eyes as far as possible without turning her head. She kept the rifle pointed at Archie. "You don't sound Russian."

"'Course I don't," Alvin said. "I'm from Twickenham."

"I dunno where that is." She slowly lowered the rifle. "But you *sound* like James Bond."

Holland moved up as Deane gently took the rifle from the woman. "Anyone else in the house, ma'am?"

She turned to look at him. "And you *almost* sound American."

Holland smiled. "I'm from Idaho, ma'am. Is there anyone else here? We don't want any surprises."

She ignored the question again. "What you doin' here?" She

paused as Tony stepped out from behind an outbuilding and approached the group. "And who's that?"

"It's all right ma'am," Holland said. "That's my son, Tony. My name's Lawson." He nodded at the two Brits. "These are our friends Archie, and Alvin."

She looked at Tony and sniffed. "He don't look much like you. What kinda name is 'Lawson', anyway?"

Archie smirked. "I think I like her."

She swung her attention to Archie. "*You* sound like Benny Hill."

Deane broke out laughing, but Holland was getting frustrated. "Ma'am, please. We're not Russians. We're the good guys. Americans and Brits. We're here to help. Now, please, is there anyone else on the property?"

The woman jerked her head sideways. "No. Just me. You're too late for anybody else." She turned on her heel and headed for the house, seemingly no longer concerned by the four armed strangers in her yard. She stopped at the door and looked back. "Well? Come on, then. Far as I can tell, all the 'good guys' turned tail and ran days ago. If you boys are who you say you are, then you're on your own. You stay out here, the real Russians are likely to show up and find you." She disappeared inside.

Holland looked at the others. "All right, then."

He turned and followed the old woman inside.

Club Náutico de Campeche
Campeche, Mexico

Club Náutico de Campeche was a private country club on the beach southwest of the city. Situated on a slight rise overlooking the Gulf of Mexico, it offered its residents some of the best views on the Yucatan Peninsula. Cooney had done his research, aided by leads sent from Behan's intelligence network, and learned that the head of the local chapter of the Los Zetas cartel lived in a villa at Club Náutico.

Estéban Serracana's home was a ten thousand square foot mini-palace on eight acres of land at the extreme southwest end of the grounds. It had four smaller residences arrayed around the main house for servants and guests, and was only approachable via the main drive, which was blocked by two gates; one at the main club entrance, and another at the end of Serracana's driveway. The entire compound was ringed by an eight foot stone wall and patrolled by armed guards day and night.

Cooney was watching one of those guards from his vantage point, hidden in the branches of a massive ceiba tree on a thickly wooded hill four hundred yards outside the compound wall. He'd climbed the tree the previous night, sleeping astride a large branch with his torso strapped to the trunk. He couldn't remember when he'd been so sore, or gotten so little sleep. In addition to the discomfort, he'd been harassed all night by an endless procession of bats flitting among the tree's flowers, their wings fluttering unnervingly close to his ears and making the hair stand up on his neck. He was not in a good mood this morning.

He'd chosen his perch carefully. From the large branch he was sitting on more than eighty feet above the ground, the foliage opened just enough to the northeast to give him a clear view of the compound while still keeping him well hidden. He'd studied the guards' patrols and shift rotations and learned that there were always at least six guards patrolling the perimeter of the compound. They each pulled two hours on patrol, with the rest of their eight hour shifts spent guarding the main house or providing vehicle security when Serracana left home. Cooney figured there must be at least twenty-four guards working inside the compound, in addition to household staff, groundskeepers and Serracana's family and hangers-on. It was a busy place.

Jefe had told Behan that his sources had overheard Serracana bragging about the new killer he had working for him; throwing

Newill's prowess around as a badge of honor as well as a not-so-subtle warning to rivals and enemies alike. Cooney figured if the reports were true, Newill would be somewhere close to Serracana. He didn't have to wait long to see if his hunch was right.

Serracana emerged from the house onto the patio facing the infinity pool and the view of the Gulf beyond. Cooney could see he was with someone, but he had stopped walking just as he exited the house and was blocking Cooney's view of the other person. Cooney shifted to the left, straining to get a better angle.

Then Serracana moved his head.

It was just a subtle shift in balance, a slight movement that gave Cooney a glimpse of the second man's face in profile.

It was Justin Newill.

CHAPTER TWENTY-FOUR

Canem in Odorem

Dry Creek, Alaska

Holland looked around. The interior of the house was dimly lit and cluttered with a mad jumble of knick knacks on every flat surface. It smelled musty. An old Labrador retriever cracked one eye open from his position on the living room floor next to a space heater. After eyeing the four strangers for a moment, the dog closed his eye, let out a long sigh, and went back to sleep.

"Good job, Harvey," the old woman grumbled. "You're still the worst guard dog in the world." She moved into the smallish kitchen and dug a can of beer from a battered old refrigerator. "S'pose you boys are thirsty. Ya wanna beer?"

Deane didn't hesitate. "Kind of you, Nan." The woman tossed the can to him, then took out another and tossed it to Archie.

"No, thank you, ma'am," Tony smiled and held up the end of the drinking tube attached to his CamelBak. "I'm good."

She looked at Holland. "You?"

"I'll pass, thanks."

"Suit yourself. This is the only stuff the dirty Russians didn't find." She cracked the top on the beer and took a long pull.

"Ma'am," Holland started, but the woman interrupted him again.

"Call me Aanaq. Everybody else does. It means 'grandmother,' but I don't have no grandkids." She took another drink of her beer. Holland noticed her hand was shaking.

"All right, Aanaq. As I was saying outside, we're here to help…"

"Don't see how four of ya can help much with anything. Not now."

"We do all right for ourselves, Aanaq. But if you could tell us whatever you might know about the Russian forces in the area, we'd really appreciate it. Number of troops, how often they patrol and where, that sort of thing?"

She shook her head. "Don't know much about that. Heard on the radio 'bout a week ago that they'd attacked Eielson. You know the air base, up in Fairbanks? Anyway, two days later, a couple of trucks rolled in here. 'Bout a dozen Russians got out, stole everything wasn't nailed down." She finished the beer and tossed the can in the sink. "Then they shot twenty people and left." She turned rheumy eyes on Holland. "So, like I said, I don't see how just four of you're gonna be much help. Those folks are gonna stay dead, no matter what you do."

"Aanaq," Tony cut in. "We saw a Russian fighter go by earlier. Is that a regular thing, do you know?"

Aanaq shrugged. "They been flying up and down the Alcan pretty regular since they first showed up. I dunno how often, but I've only ever seen one plane at a time. Heard they shot down a bush plane out of Tok the other day, though."

"We'd heard that, too."

"So what you all planning to do about it, huh?" Her tone had hardened. "You're gonna need a lot more people, you ask me. Emergency broadcast channel says they've got Fairbanks locked up tight. You go up there, you're gonna get slaughtered, just like they slaughtered those folks here the other day. If I'da been down here, I'd at least taken one or two with me."

"You weren't here when it happened then, Nan?" Deane asked.

Aanaq shook her head. Her eyes were welling up, and she turned away, looking out the window. "I was up on the mountain, picking berries. Heard the shooting. Time I got back, it was all over." She took a sharp breath. "They shot my husband."

Holland lowered his head. "I'm really sorry to hear that, Aanaq."

Archie stepped closer to the old woman and laid a hand on her shoulder. "I'm sorry to have to ask this, Aanaq, but what we really need is a car. Can you help us out?"

She waved a hand in the direction of the garage. "My husband's old truck's out there. It aint much, but it runs."

"That'll be fine, Aanaq, thank you." Holland leaned against the counter. "Is there anything you need? It's impossible to tell, but we might be back this way."

"Could use some more beer," she said. "But I doubt you're gonna even get two miles from here before some Russian guards pick you up or kill you."

Archie gave her a wolfish grin. "Aw, now, Aanaq," he said. "We may not look like much, but I promise you - by the time we get done, the Russians are gonna be needing protection from us." He leaned close to her ear, lowering his voice. "See, they don't know it yet, but *they're* the sheep here. You just shared a beer with the real wolves." He offered her his hand, which she took cautiously. "We'll make 'em pay for what they did."

Aanaq looked at each of the men in turn. "I was married to Ellis forty years. At least, it woulda been forty, this winter. Plenty of times I thought I wanted to shoot him myself, but I didn't never mean it. Now he's gone, it's too late to tell him all the stuff I never said." She turned back to the window. "You're all nutty, if you ask me. No point you all getting yourselves killed over Ellis. He's gone, and that's it. But if you're set on going after those fellas, I'm not gonna try to change your minds."

She dug her hand into a pocket and produced a set of keys. "If you're heading to Fairbanks, you got no choice but to stay on the Alcan as far as Delta Junction. That's about a forty mile straight shot, but it's forty miles of no place to hide from Russian patrols. It's just highway, surrounded by brush. Hardly anyplace to get off the road. You'll be lucky to get halfway there without getting caught. If you do get as far as Delta Junction, I'd get off the main highway there and use back roads into Fairbanks as much as you can."

"Thanks, Aanaq. We'll do that." Holland took the keys. "And we'll see if we can't make the Russians regret ever coming here."

"Yeah. You do that," Aanaq said. "I'm gonna go lie down. Close the garage door behind you. Don't need no bears rootin' around in there."

Club Náutico de Campeche
Campeche, Mexico

Estéban Serracana was a loudmouth. After only a few days, Newill was already beginning to regret signing on with the cartel. His first job had been simple, but Serracana had been disproportionately impressed by how easy Newill had made it look. He'd spent nearly every waking minute since then either slapping Newill on the back or talking about the things they would accomplish together in the near future.

As if Serracana could do any of it without him.

This morning, Serracana had called Newill to the main house to discuss his next job, but as soon as Newill had entered the main living room overlooking the pool, the cartel boss had started haranguing him about how together, they would rule the entire Yucatan Peninsula, all the while failing to get to specifics about the job at hand. Newill had been struggling to maintain a neutral expression, when in reality he just wanted to slap the jumped up little druggie. The only reason he said nothing and followed Serracana outside to the pool deck was that the man was paying him handsomely, and he'd given him a secure place to lie low for a while, following the chaos of Tolliver's assassination.

They stepped through the broad, double sliding doors together. Serracana stopped and waved his arms at the panoramic view. "You see, my friend?" he said. "All this, I built from nothing with my own sweat, my own blood. But the bosses, you see, my bosses, they still keep me down. They make me live in this backwater, because they do not appreciate true talent." He looked at Newill, standing beside him. "But I do. I appreciate skill when I see it, my friend. With your skill and my brains, we will turn this cartel around. We will be like kings!" He punctuated this by jabbing a finger in the air as he resumed walking slowly around the right side of the pool.

The house was built atop a narrow rise overlooking the Gulf. To allow the pool deck to match the level of the main floor, a large retaining wall had been built, which dropped off from the pool deck on the north and west sides. To the west was the infinity edge, terminating above a steep hill covered in underbrush and a select few trees that didn't interrupt the view. To the north, the wall bounded a ten foot drop to a manicured lawn bordered by the long drive leading from the gate to the front of the estate. The two men reached the north side, right atop the retaining wall, and changed direction slightly to follow the walk around that edge of the pool.

By the time Cooney had realized who the second man was, Serracana had already shifted back, blocking a clear shot. Cooney clenched his jaw in frustration, then settled in behind the scope, willing the cartel boss to move again. He didn't want to take another chance shooting secondary targets like he had in Pueblo Viejo. Behan had made it very clear that he was only here to kill Newill, so he waited for a clear shot.

He only needed Serracana to move six inches, and he'd have it.

Serracana was gesticulating, making sweeping hand gestures punctuated by stabbing the air around him with his finger. As he spoke, both men started slowly walking around the pool deck to the northeast. Cooney could see that in a few more paces, they would have to turn slightly, and he would finally have a clear line. He steadied his breathing and settled the crosshairs on the point in space where Newill's life was about to end.

Alcan Highway
23 Miles SE of Delta Junction, Alaska

Ma's pickup was a beat-up 1977 Ford F250 with an extended cab and four doors. The body seemed to consist of more rust than metal, and the muffler was little more than a vague memory. Even with the engine at idle, it sounded like a hundred chainsaws going at full throttle.

"Hard to sneak up on anybody in this thing," Tony shouted over the noise.

"WHAT?" Holland bellowed back, winking at his son in the rear view mirror.

Deane was in the front passenger seat, scanning the road ahead with binoculars. Archie was sitting in the back behind Holland, half turned in his seat to watch the road behind them. They'd made it almost halfway to the crossroads south of Delta Junction where they had planned to turn south toward Fort Greely and its missile silos, and so far they'd seen no other traffic.

"This thing have enough gas to make it to Greely?" Tony shouted.

"Hard telling," Holland yelled back. "Aanaq said it had 'some gas', but the gauge is broken. Just like most of the rest of the truck."

"Military truck ahead!" Deane shouted. "Looks like a Lynx." They all looked. The mostly straight stretch of highway gave way to a gentle right hand curve about a mile ahead of them. A truck the size of a large SUV had just rounded the corner and was bearing down on them rapidly.

"Everybody hunker down," Holland said.

"I can see two in the front," Deane said. He had slouched well down in the seat so that he could just peer over the dashboard with his binoculars. "Can't see in the back, though. Could be three or four more Ivans back there."

"Archie?" Holland shouted. The Russian truck was within a quarter mile now. Archie had his rifle rested on the left side of Holland's seat, pointing at a shallow angle out his side window, between the left side-view mirror and the roof support. It would only be difficult for the Russians to spot him for a few more moments.

"Standby," Archie answered. The Russian truck started to slow as they drew closer. If it continued on past the Americans, the Russian driver would be exposed to Archie's rifle in just a few dozen yards...

But the Russian driver either sensed the danger or recognized it in time, and responded by wrenching the steering wheel to his left, bringing the Lynx across the road with the passenger side facing the Ford, effectively blocking its path. At the same time, the roof hatch on the Russian vehicle swung open, and a trooper popped his head up. He had a rifle in his hand, but he'd made the mistake of standing up before he raised the muzzle through the hatch. Now it was pointing down, and he was struggling to get it clear of the hatch. He was too slow.

"Contact front!" Holland wrenched the wheel to the right and jammed on the brakes. The Ford had barely come to a stop when Archie's rifle barked once, then again in rapid succession. The man in the Lynx's center turret dropped back through the hatch as Archie's first bullet impacted the side of his head. His second bullet punched through the windshield, killing the driver, whose foot then relaxed and came off the brake, allowing the vehicle to start slowly rolling toward the north shoulder of the road.

Deane and Tony came out of the right side of the Ford as one. Deane covered behind his open door and fired a burst across the hood into the front passenger side of the Lynx as Tony stepped around the open doors and covered behind the fender, adding his own burst to Deane's.

"Moving!" Holland yelled. Archie held his fire as Holland exited the truck and ran to his left, covering the Russian vehicle as he went. Another helmet started to emerge from the center turret, and Archie fired at it before it cleared the lip of the hatch. The helmet pirouetted into the air and fell off the back of the truck, but its wearer didn't emerge.

"Moving!" Tony split away from the Ford and ran up the right shoulder of the road to the driver's side of the Lynx, aiming his rifle through the punctured windshield. From his new position he could see into the interior of the vehicle. "Three down, one still rolling around on the back seat!"

"You got him?" Holland asked as he approached the rear passenger door.

"I got him."

Holland yanked the door aside and pointed his rifle into the back seat. "*Vylezay iz mashiny!*" he yelled at the wounded trooper, but the man just groaned and held his head. Holland aimed over the back seat into the rear cargo area, but there was no one else in the vehicle. Satisfied that the man didn't pose a threat, Holland slung his rifle and reached inside, grabbing him by the back of his collar and yanking him out onto the pavement. Archie appeared at Holland's elbow as the Russian hit the ground, and he was on the wounded man in an instant, pinning him to the ground and searching him quickly for any other weapons.

"You think they got off a radio call, boss?" Archie asked.

Holland glanced into the cab, where the radio handset was still attached to its hanger on the dashboard. "I don't know." He listened for a moment. The radio crackled with intermittent conversations in Russian, but none of it seemed agitated or directed at them. "My Russian's way out of practice. Hard to tell what they're saying, but it doesn't sound like anybody's demanding answers. They would be, if these boys had called in before we hit 'em."

Archie finished putting a set of Flex Cuffs on the wounded Russian's wrists and rolled the man onto his back. He had a deep gash running from the top of his forehead across the crown of his head where Archie's bullet had grazed his skull, and it was bleeding heavily. The man's eyes had rolled back, and his breathing was ragged. "I think I mighta punched his ticket, boss," Archie said. He opened the first aid kit attached to his vest and clapped a bandage onto the man's head. The man's combat helmet had apparently slowed Archie's bullet just enough to prevent it killing him outright, but even a glancing blow from a thirty-caliber round is potentially deadly, especially when that blow is to the head.

Deane and Tony had run several yards up the road in opposite directions and established covering positions, waiting to see what their next move was and watching for other vehicles approaching, but so far the highway was empty. Holland knelt down next to the Russian and took his chin in one hand, turning the man's head to face him.

"*Vy govorite po-angliyski?*" Holland shook the man's head gently from side to side, trying to bring him around again, but the soldier suddenly arched his back and started convulsing. "He's seizing, Archie! Do you have anything…" He looked at Archie, who simply shook his head and frowned. Holland reached down and put a hand on the man's shoulder, but the convulsions abruptly stopped. He checked for a pulse, but there was nothing.

"Sorry 'bout that, Law," Archie said.

"Nothing to apologize for, Arch. I would have liked to ask him some questions, but it doesn't matter now." He looked at the man's rank insignia. "Just a corporal - he probably knew less than we do about what his people are up to." He looked around, assessing. "All right. Let's police up this mess and get gone before somebody else comes along." He let out a shrill whistle and waved the others back to the Lynx.

Club Náutico de Campeche
Campeche, Mexico

Newill was struggling to pay attention to his boss as the man's verbal diarrhea continued unchecked. He glanced to his right at the drop over the north edge of the retaining wall, and toyed with the idea of tossing Serracana over it. Maybe landing on his head after a ten foot drop would serve to shut the arrogant little man's mouth.

Cooney watched as the two men continued walking, their pace maddeningly slow.

Ten feet now.

Five.

Cooney's finger took up the play in the trigger.

Three feet.

They stepped into his line of fire. Serracana's head was still partially blocking Newill's, but the angle was slowly changing in Cooney's favor. He started his exhale, relaxing and anticipating the break of the trigger. He'd timed it perfectly.

Then a sudden breath of wind off the Gulf took hold of the ceiba tree, shifting Cooney's position slightly just as the trigger broke. At the same time, Serracana laughed at something, throwing his head to the rear in a show of overacted humor and putting it directly in the line of fire.

The 175 grain polymer tipped bullet struck the side of Serracana's head an inch behind and above his left ear. The bullet retained almost all of its original weight, but expanded to almost twice its original diameter on impact. The bullet's trajectory also changed dramatically, and that alone saved Newill's life. The impact against the left side of Serracana's skull caused immense overpressure inside, shattering the bone and vaporizing most of his brain. The bullet then deflected slightly from its original path, angling up and to the rear, just missing Newill's head as it disappeared in the direction of the lawn on the north side of the pool.

Newill's world suddenly exploded around him. Something struck a hammer blow to the side of his head, and his vision was momentarily obscured by a cloud of gore. He didn't realize that he'd been hit in the head by a silver dollar sized chunk of Serracana's skull, which left a six inch laceration across the left side of his own head, and almost knocked him off of his feet. But even as his mind registered the alarming impact, his subconscious instinct kicked in. He just managed to shift his weight and throw himself off the north side of the pool deck, falling behind the retaining wall to the lawn below, out of sight of the shooter.

Cooney recovered quickly from the recoil, but when he brought the crosshairs back onto the target area, Newill had vanished. He scanned the scene quickly, noting the body of Serracana and the mess that a moment before had been his head. Cooney swore, knowing that somehow he'd missed Newill, again. He made another quick scan of the area to be sure he couldn't see the killer anywhere, hoping he might emerge long enough for a quick shot. As he searched, two bodyguards burst from inside the house, looked at their dead boss, and started spraying the trees to the south of the house with AK-15 rounds.

Time to go, Cooney decided. He dropped off the limb and abseiled down his safety rope to the ground. He left the rope and his harness and sprinted south through the trees. His car was hidden at an abandoned construction site half a mile away, and he needed to get there in a hurry if he wanted to stay alive.

Newill hit the ground at the base of the retaining wall with a sickening thud. The impact knocked the wind out of him, and he was dizzy and already nauseous from his head wound. He groaned and rolled over, gasping for air. His head was covered in blood and his ears were ringing, but he could hear shouts and gunfire from above him on the pool deck. Whatever had just happened, it had to be all bad.

"*Mató al jefe!!*"

That was *definitely* bad. Newill blinked the blood from his eyes and tried to clear his head. Serracana must be dead, and now the guards suspected him for some reason…

A man peered over the edge of the wall. Seeing Newill on his back on the ground below, the man's eyes widened and he swung the muzzle of his AK-15 toward him. But even dazed as he was, Newill was still faster. He jerked his Glock 19 from his appendix holster and fired three quick shots as the man fired a burst of his own. The guard's shots spattered the lawn inches short of where Newill lay, throwing bits of sod and dirt over him, but at least one of Newill's rounds found its mark, and the guard reeled backward out of sight. More shouts came from above as Newill scrambled to his feet and started running parallel to the retaining wall, putting the house between him and the men on the pool deck and making for the driveway.

He caught movement out of the corner of his left eye and spun just in time to see another guard emerging from the trees twenty yards to his northeast, his AK47 already up and firing wildly. The burst went high, the bullets ripping the air above Newill's head. He dropped to one knee and fired another three rounds, this time connecting with all three. The man collapsed onto his face and Newill struggled to his feet again, forcing himself to move.

Cooney sprinted for several hundred yards until his heart rate spiked, then slowed to a steady run, reluctant to completely blow himself out without knowing that he was clear of the danger. He was moving mostly downhill through scrub and underbrush that was only thick in places, so he was able to keep up a decent pace. His rifle was slung over his left shoulder, and his pistol was in his right hand. He could hear cars occasionally pass on the two lane highway ahead, mixed with the fading sound of sporadic gunfire behind.

He pounded on through the brush, his mind working overtime. It was possible that the shot that killed Serracana had passed through and killed Newill as well, but Cooney doubted it. Contrary to Hollywood opinion, bullets don't cause human bodies to dramatically fly through the air as if they'd been hit by a speeding truck; in reality their reaction to gravity is more noticeable than the reaction to the impact of a bullet.

Serracana's case proved this - the bullet to his head had simply shut off the master switch in him, and gravity had taken over from there. He'd dropped straight down in his tracks. If the bullet had hit Newill in the head as well, it was likely he would have done the same, but by the time Cooney had reacquired his sight picture, Newill had vanished.

That would have only happened if he'd somehow survived the shot.

It was also possible that Newill had been mortally wounded and had then staggered off the edge of the retaining wall, and even now was bleeding out on the north side of the property. The third possibility was that he was uninjured or only slightly injured, either of which meant that Cooney had failed. If that was the case, he knew Behan would not be happy at all.

He had to find a way to salvage the operation, but going back to the compound was out of the question. It was stirred up like a kicked hornet's nest, and although he knew he hadn't been seen, he also knew that loitering in the area was bound to draw unwanted attention. He'd have to get back to his car and get clear, and come up with a different plan.

* * *

Newill rounded a corner of the house and flattened himself against the wall. The world was spinning around him and it was all he could do to keep his feet. He slid down behind a large bush and took a few deep breaths, then wiped the blood from his eyes again. His head was pounding and his nausea was getting worse, but he knew he couldn't stay there. The guards had obviously mistaken him for Serracana's killer, and it would be a fool's errand to stick around and try to convince them otherwise.

Forcing himself to stand, he looked around for a way out, but his head started spinning so violently that he sagged back against the wall for balance. He doubled over and vomited. Again he forced himself upright. A shout came from his left, and he launched himself from behind the bush, running on adrenaline alone. As he ran to his right, he trailed his pistol hand behind him and fired two quick rounds. Bullets slapped through the palms above and around him as he neared the main drive.

There were several cars parked in the circular driveway. Newill ran to the first in line, shooting out the driver's side tires of the three cars behind it as he went. More bullets whined overhead, and several smashed into the line of cars, puncturing windows and setting off alarms. Newill collapsed into the BMW M5 sedan at the front of the row. The vehicle was normally used by Serracana's bodyguards, and he was relieved to find they'd left the keys in the ignition.

The engine roared to life and Newill floored the accelerator, spraying gravel behind him as he maneuvered toward the main gate. Two guards at the gate opened fire as he approached, but haste and lack of training sent all their shots high. Newill accelerated toward them, weaving slightly as another wave of dizziness hit him. One guard dove out of the way, but the second was too slow, and the car clipped his legs as he jumped aside, spinning his body in a wild pirouette. His head slammed against the fender and he crumpled in a heap at the side of the driveway.

Newill kept his speed as he reached the gate, slamming it

aside. He overcorrected slightly as he turned right onto the main drive, and the car fishtailed wildly before he could get it under control. Several guards fired final bursts at the retreating vehicle, but only two rounds connected, spider-webbing the rear window before the speeding car rounded another bend out of sight.

Cooney waited for a car to pass, then sprinted across the highway after checking that no one was around to see him. He re-entered the trees and continued another hundred yards to where his car was parked. He could still hear sporadic gunfire in the distance, but he had no way of knowing what the guards were shooting at. All he could tell was that the shots were getting no closer to him. *Maybe the guards all turned on each other*, he thought with a grim smile, but he doubted it.

But then again, he thought as he climbed into his car, shoving the rifle into the passenger footwell, *what else would they be shooting at?*

He decided that finding out might be worth the risk. He'd just get on the highway and head back toward the main gate at Club Náutico. There was a chance it would be open, and then he could just drive slowly past Serracana's compound and see what he could see. It was an incredible risk, but he couldn't very well go back to Behan with nothing to show for the trip.

He pulled out onto the highway and turned east. An old farm truck was ahead of him, crawling along at less than fifteen miles an hour. He was frustrated with the pace, but it would do him no good to try to pass the truck on a blind corner, only to pull off a few hundred yards later. He forced himself to be patient, and dropped back a few more yards behind the truck.

They had almost reached the turn when a black BMW M5 rocketed onto the highway in front of them, overcorrecting as it turned to the southwest and going wide into the path of the truck. Cooney stood on his brakes as the truck driver did the same, and the BMW's rear left fender slammed into the truck's left front. The car bounced off in a shower of glass, and as the driver regained control he picked up speed. Cooney watched as he shot by.

The driver's face was streaked with blood, and he was slumped against the driver's door as if almost asleep. It was Newill, and he was injured.

Cooney stood on the gas pedal and cranked the wheel hard to the left in pursuit. He had somehow been given a second chance, and he didn't want to waste it. But as he pulled out into the westbound lane, his view was blocked by the farm truck and he didn't see the oncoming bus. It smashed into the passenger side of his car, sending it spinning. Cooney was showered in broken glass, and he felt a sharp pain in his back as his car spun fifteen yards and came to rest in a ditch. He looked up in time to see Newill's car disappear around the bend.

Kicking open his door, Cooney dropped into the ditch. He had no choice but to abandon his rifle; the truck driver and the occupants of the bus were already getting out of their vehicles and heading toward him. He clambered up to the side of the road as a man on a motorcycle approached from the southwest, slowing as he saw the wrecked car in the ditch. Cooney raised a hand as if to hail the man, and as the rider pulled abreast, he slapped his forearm across the man's throat, knocking him backward off the bike.

Cooney grabbed the handlebars and jumped on, goosing the throttle to spin the bike around. This time, he looked both ways, but he needn't have bothered. The bus that had hit his car was blocking traffic from the other direction. Cooney wound the throttle all the way to the stop and sped off in pursuit of Newill, leaving a crowd of confused and frightened people in his wake.

CHAPTER TWENTY-FIVE

Malum Impunitum

Alcan Highway
23 Miles SE of Delta Junction, Alaska

They took the Russians' uniforms and weapons, then dragged the bodies into the trees. After checking the Lynx to be sure it didn't carry any type of communications equipment that would allow them to be tracked, they continued on toward Fort Greely in the Russian vehicle. Tony and Deane followed in the Ford. Taking Ma's advice about getting off the main road, they found a gravel track leading to the west a couple miles before the main road turnoff. They followed the road through the forest for several miles, winding around through the thick trees and brush generally to the southwest. At an abandoned gravel quarry five miles off the main road, they abandoned Ma's truck, knowing that the Russians would be discovered eventually, and hoping the truck would be far enough away not to be associated with their killings. They didn't want Aanaq being the target of any reprisals.

A few miles further on, they came to a ford in Jarvis Creek, a glacial stream that ran to the north along the east boundary of Fort Greely. They were still about seven miles south of the base itself. Stopping in the trees on the east side of the creek, Holland checked his GPS.

"Go on then. Admit it," Archie deadpanned. "We're lost, aren't we?"

"Not quite. If this thing's right, we ford the creek here, and the road continues north all the way to the missile battery. Command and control building is on the north side of the battery; we should be able to blend in long enough to get to it."

"I think that phase of the operation bears a bit more discussion at this point, don't you?" Deane asked quietly. He'd finally spoken out loud what they'd all been avoiding. They were four men going up against an unknown number of enemy manning a fixed position. The enemy had landline and radio communications at their disposal with reinforcements only a call away. Holland's crew had nothing but themselves, and they were hundreds of miles from any kind of backup. Even worse, their intelligence about their objective had been so limited, they hadn't discussed a plan in any detail, instead opting to make a plan on the fly based on what intel they could gather once they were on site.

"You're right," Holland said, turning slightly in his seat. "Look, Reardon put me in charge of this goat rope, but he could have picked any one of you just as well." He looked at Tony. "Including you. I'm not gonna pretend to have all the answers, and if any of you has something to say, let's get it said, right now. Reardon wants us to either destroy that battery, or take it intact. The Brits have at least a couple of subs off the coast that are trying to make life hard on Ivan, but that counter-missile battery will nullify that as soon as Ivan gets it operational - if we don't do something about it.

"I don't see any better way to approach the battery other than from where we are right now - there's too much risk of being spotted or challenged the longer we screw around driving in circles out here in the weeds. So our approach needs to be through the woods from the south to avoid detection. Trouble is, that puts us on the opposite side of the battery from the command building. We want to take the command building intact, we gotta go across the battery, which is more than a mile of open ground that's bound to have guards and techs milling around everywhere.

"As of when we left England, the Russians still hadn't fired anything from Greely, which tells me they haven't cracked into the command network yet. But as soon as they do, they're gonna have a leg up on the British Navy, so we need to get this done." He looked around at the others. "Ok, let's hear it."

"Best chance to get close is to use the stolen truck and uniforms to bluff our way inside," Deane said. "But a bluff is only going to go so far. You said your Russian is out of practice; mine is non-existent. So unless you other lads are fluent, that's likely to be a problem."

Archie looked at Tony. "You didn't happen to pick up any Russian on that two year vacation of yours, did ya mate?"

Tony grimaced. "My Dari is passable, but I doubt that'll do any good here. And I don't exactly look Russian, either. Not like the rest of you Slavic-looking characters, anyway."

"Hang on, Law." Archie was already struggling into the Russian overcoat he'd taken from one of the dead soldiers. "How many launchers are there supposed to be at this site?"

"Forty. Give or take."

"We barely have enough explosives to take out half that."

Holland shook his head. "Which leaves us with just one option. We need to get inside the command bunker, and destroy the comm links to the missiles. No comms, no launch."

"Ivan'll have it back up in two or three days," Archie said. "Which means, we'll have gone and got ourselves killed for nothing."

Holland looked at Deane. "Sergeant Major? You agree with that?"

Deane looked skeptical. "Seems to me, Ivan will be able repair anything other than catastrophic damage. I don't think taking out a few computers is going to get it done."

"We can't be dallyin' around, though. Get in, get out," Archie added. "Just like we did last week with this young fella." He jerked a thumb at Tony.

"Son?" Holland gave his son a hard look. "You have an idea, now's the time."

Tony nodded. "I gotta agree, Dad. You guys got me out of that hole because you hit 'em hard and fast, and you pulled back as soon as you had what you came for. They never knew what was happening; they were totally outclassed."

"Correct me if I'm wrong," Deane said, "but didn't you lads have twice the men on that op as we have here - and you still came back one short?"

Archie's face clouded at the memory of Cal Hodge dying in the back of a stolen Afghan van, bleeding out from a grievous gunshot wound to the leg as the rest of the crew fought to rescue Tony from captivity. "Due respect Sergeant Major," he said quietly, "but you weren't there."

Deane nodded, looking at each man in turn. "No. That's a fact, lad. I wasn't there. I'm the last person to criticize a bunch of lads who did their best for a good cause. We're all grown-ups here. We're in the business of killing. Sometimes the other side gets their licks in as well. That's no reflection on you boys. All I'm saying is, we're the ones have to do this job. I want to see it done, but I don't want to see any of you die for something that makes no bloody difference in the long run."

The others fell silent.

"Look lads," Deane went on. "General Reardon is a top-tier officer. He's a true operator, but nobody can come out of the field to ride a desk for any great length of time without losing some of their edge. He's trying to cobble together a guerrilla response to a full scale conventional invasion, but essentially he's using school kids with pea shooters against the Death Star.

"As if that weren't enough, at the same time he has to babysit a bunch of politicians from twenty different countries, none of whom have any more backbone than a damp rag, preventing them from giving the whole operation away through stupidity or cupidity, or simply deciding to take their toys and go home. He's thinking more politically than militarily at this point. He sees the goal, not the game.

"So in the spirit of doing *something* being better than doing *nothing at all*, he's sent the four of us against a fixed position of unknown strength in broad daylight, thanks to the objective being this far north in summer. Add to that the very real possibility that we'll get trapped inside while Russian reinforcements envelop the command building?" He shook his head. "Not a good recipe for success."

"I thought you were Reardon's right-hand man?" Tony asked.

"I am, lad," Deane said, spreading his hands. "But I know when an operation stinks, even if it was planned by a man for whom I have the utmost respect. I just think he's wrong this time. If we stick around long enough to do any lasting damage to this place, chances are better than good that we won't be leaving under our own power."

Holland nodded. "I see your point, Sergeant Major, believe me I do. But there's two things to consider here. First, while we very well might get killed going in there, you said yourself that we're all big boys, and we're all in the business of taking risks. I'd argue there's nobody better at it. And second, even if there were somebody better at it, that somebody isn't here. We're it - there's nobody else coming.

"We all know the Allies don't have the numbers to repel Ivan by main force, so it's gotta be done surgically. Cruise missiles are gonna have to fill the role of heavy artillery, and if the Russians get this anti-missile battery operational, they're going to win that battle. Without some heavy bombardment, and soon, they'll be dug in all over the state and it'll all be over but the crying.

"I'm sorry we didn't have better intel at the outset of this, but things are just moving too fast, and with the U.S. being almost completely isolationist over the past two years, the Brits had very limited information for us to go on. Reardon's main contact in the American military is the Commandant of the Marine Corps, and he wasn't able to help with Army-specific data pertaining to this facility. So, there you have it. You all know as much as I do. This is just the best bad choice."

Deane tried to stifle a grin. "It's not like going in half-strength and fully blind is anything new - but you did ask for our opinions."

"Thanks, Sergeant Major."

"You might as well call me Alvin," Deane said. "If we're going to die together, we should probably do it on a first name basis."

"Right. Alvin it is. Archie? How 'bout you?"

Archie shrugged. "I'm a sucker for lost causes."

Holland shifted his eyes to Tony. "That leaves you, son."

Tony nodded. "This all really started when Tolliver abandoned all the guys like me overseas. He sent a pretty clear message around the world that America was weak. Russia's just now responding to that message. If I die doing this, at least I'll die trying to put things right again." He looked at his dad. "And at least now, I won't do it alone."

Holland reached back and clasped Tony's hand.

Deane raised his eyebrows theatrically. "You two finished with your tender moment? Good. Let's put our heads together then. We still need to figure a way to crack this nut without getting cracked ourselves in the process."

They had no way of knowing that as a result of the Russian high command cutting the amount of transports available to their invasion force, there was only a skeleton force of fifty Russian soldiers holding Greely at that time. Reinforcements had gotten caught up in the natural chaos of transporting large numbers of men and materiel between two continents during wartime. Reardon's focus on speed in lieu of comprehensive intel meant that the Russians were almost as unprepared to hold the missile base as Holland as his team were to assault it.

And they still had the element of surprise on their side.

Seybaplaya
17 Miles SW of Campeche, Mexico

Cooney slowed as he approached the outskirts of Seybaplaya. This was becoming a wild goose chase, and he knew it. But he also knew that if he didn't kill Newill now, while he was injured and vulnerable, his chance might just slip away forever. He'd followed the coast road from the scene of the accident, not bothering to turn off at any of the few minor roads or driveways along the route. He figured that Newill wasn't likely to hole up in the woods; he'd be in a rush to get as far away from Serracana's men as fast as possible, and Seybaplaya was the first town along the coast in that direction that had a decent sized port.

He pulled off at a Y intersection at the north end of town and checked the GPS on his phone. The town was straight ahead, with a small civilian port about a mile further on. To his right was a road leading to the industrial port, where several deep-sea oil exploration companies had maintenance and supply operations. There was bound to be some kind of offshore transportation there.

He pocketed his phone and turned the bike to the right.

Newill rolled up to the security gate at the port facility, slowing as the bored looking gate guard stepped out of his shack and held up a hand. The man carelessly leaned down toward Newill's window as he brought the BMW to a stop.

"Detener, amigo. No hay entrada."

"Estar tranquilo." Newill brought the muzzle of his Glock to within inches of the man's forehead. He nodded in the direction of the gate. "Abre la puerta."

The man gabbled nonsense for a moment, frozen to the spot.

"*Abre la puerta*," Newill repeated, more forcefully this time. His head was pounding, and he was still fighting dizzy spells. The dried blood all over the left side of his face gave him a manic look, and the guard was clearly terrified.

"Ahora!"

The man finally appreciated the danger. Hands raised, he backed away. "Sí, señor! Por favor, no dispares!" He turned his back and reached into the shack, slapping a button inside the door. The gate gave a shriek of un-oiled metal on metal and started to swing upward. As soon as it did, Newill steadied the pistol on the door of the car and shot the guard twice in the back. The man crumpled on the step of the shack as Newill put the car in gear and drove into the port facility.

"Gracias, mi amigo."

Cooney slowed as he approached the gated entrance to the port. He expected to see a guard, at least, but the gate was open and no one seemed to be around. He downshifted and slowed to a walking pace, then saw the feet sticking out of the guard shack door. He opened the throttle back up and rode on.

Must be in the right place after all, he thought.

The road inside the gate wound around a couple of low hills before the terrain opened up on a rise overlooking the port and the Gulf of Mexico beyond. The port was crowded with industrial equipment and parts for oil drilling rigs, as well as several dozen rig maintenance and construction barges. Each of the barges had its own helipad attached to the superstructure, making the port look like some sort of odd parking lot for floating heliports. To the right a large building holding offices and a smaller warehouse, while to the left was a jumbled scrapyard full of rusting hulks of unidentifiable equipment.

The road straight ahead wound down a steep hill and continued out onto a large breakwater enclosing an inner harbor. Several dozen boats and ships of varying sizes were tied up in the inner harbor, and several more were anchored in the outer road behind the long breakwater that jutted out into the Gulf more than a mile offshore. In the distance Cooney could see several offshore drilling rigs.

He slowed again at the top of the hill and took in the port. It was good sized, with any number of places that Newill could hide. But Cooney was certain that Newill hadn't come here to hide. He was looking for a way out of the country, which narrowed the search down to whichever vessels in the port looked like they were ready to put to sea. There were three in the inner harbor that were putting out exhaust fumes, so Cooney started down the hill in that direction.

Then he saw the helicopter.

It was about a mile offshore, probably inbound from the closest drilling platform on the horizon. It was heading for the helipad on a maintenance rig moored on the seaward side of the breakwater. Cooney had a feeling that wherever Newill was in the port, he was also watching that helicopter, and that he'd be making for it even now. If Cooney allowed him to reach it, the game would be up. The maintenance rig was almost half a mile away. Cooney cranked the throttle and sped down the hill toward the breakwater, bending low over the tank as he tried to squeeze every bit of speed out of the little motorcycle.

Newill drove slowly along the breakwater, eyeballing the exhaust fumes coming from the stacks of three of the ships moored in the inner harbor. He ignored a man in a hard hat who tried to flag him down and sped up slightly, deciding that the outermost vessel would have to serve his purposes. There was a gangway stretched from the jetty to the deck of the ship, and judging by the line of workers carrying boxes onboard, the ship was almost ready to depart.

The noise of an approaching helicopter made him look to his right. A red and black Bell 206 chopper was approaching from the west, lining up on the maintenance barge on the north side of the jetty. Newill immediately forgot about the ship and turned the car around, heading for the other side of the port.

The man who had tried to wave him down before tried again as he passed, but was lost in a cloud of dust behind the speeding car. Newill wanted to get to the helipad before the chopper touched down and the pilot had a chance to shut down the engine. He slid around a stack of shipping containers onto the main access road and pointed the car toward the maintenance dock.

Several workers at the dockside stepped out of the way in confusion, wondering who the lunatic was sliding to a stop in front of them in an expensive car. Newill opened the door and staggered out, waving his pistol to drive off the stunned workers. He weaved and stumbled as he made his way to the gangplank. One brave man shouted something, but Newill waved the pistol at him and he backed off. Newill kept on, boarding the barge as the helicopter flared to land on the helipad atop the superstructure thirty feet above the main deck.

Still dizzy, Newill ran drunkenly to the staircase leading up to the pad and climbed up. He could feel the swirling wash of the chopper's slowing rotors as he approached the top. Emerging onto the pad, he was met by three men who had just disembarked from the aircraft and were on their way to the stairs. They all went wide-eyed at the sight of him, covered in blood and waving his pistol, and they backed off to the edge of the pad, allowing him to continue.

Newill opened the cockpit door and shoved the pistol toward the pilot, who had been busying himself with a post-flight checklist. The pilot recoiled, hands raised, as Newill climbed in and sat down. He made a circular motion with his free hand while keeping the pistol aimed at the pilot's head. "Vamonos!"

The pilot pointed at the instrument panel, tentatively tapping one of the gauges while shaking his head. "No tengo suficiente gasolina!"

Newill glanced at the gauge himself, then shook his head.

"Tienes suficiente, amigo. Fly, or die." He planted the muzzle of the Glock against the pilot's temple to emphasize his point, just in case the man didn't understand the threat in English.

"Si, amigo, si." The pilot started flipping switches, reversing the checklist he'd just started, and the engine noise increased. Newill strapped himself in.

"Bien. Hombre inteligente."

49th Missile Defense Battalion
Fort Greely, Alaska

Two hours later, the stolen Lynx pulled out of the trees and onto a gravel access road that skirted the perimeter of the missile battery. The battery itself was a clearing in the trees more than a mile in diameter, dotted with several lines of missile silo doors, each door assembly protruding several feet above the ground, protecting the silo beneath. From above, the silos looked like giant plus signs set out in rows, with the arms of the plus signs formed by the concrete piers that supported the interlocking clamshell silo doors. The perimeter of the battery was ringed by light poles topped with powerful flood lights, which would illuminate the battery during the long Alaskan winter.

Tony was at the wheel of the Lynx now. They had watched from the cover of the trees as the Russian troops guarding the battery had made their rounds. A Lynx much like their own had circled the battery every fifteen minutes, following the irregular perimeter road just inside a ten foot high cyclone fence. There was a second road laid out in a rough square outside the fence. Between the two roads at the southeast corner of the installation was an immense asphalt equipment staging pad, with an access road leading to a locked gate at the southeast corner of the fence. It was the closest they could get to the fence without looking suspicious.

They'd watched the guards make seven circuits of the battery, and it was the same truck and crew each time. They figured the guards had to be on a shift rotation, but there was no way to tell how long the shifts were except to wait around for a new crew to show up, but they didn't have time to wait any longer.

Shortly after the guard truck had passed, Tony slowly pulled out of the trees and positioned the Lynx on the shoulder of the access road between the staging pad and the southeast gate, pointing away from the battery. Holland and Deane piled out and removed the spare tire from its bracket, leaning it against the front tire on the passenger side. Then they scattered several tools on the ground around the tire. With that done, Deane and Tony took cover behind a stack of shipping containers at the south edge of the pad. Archie and Holland stayed with the truck and waited.

Ten minutes passed before Deane called Holland on the radio.

"Tangos inbound. They'll have you in sight in ten seconds."

"Roger." Holland nodded at Archie, who dropped to his knees next to the spare tire and picked up a lug wrench. Holland started pacing back and forth, waving his arms in a show of agitation.

"They see you," Deane radioed. *"Slowing."* Holland responded by swinging a kick at Archie, connecting with his backside. Archie played it up, dropping the wrench and falling on his face in the gravel. There was a slight pause, then Deane said, *"They bought it. They're going to the gate."*

Holland didn't look up. He kept pacing around Archie and shouting every Russian curse he could remember, occasionally kicking him as Archie made a dumb show of trying to loosen the lug nuts on the front wheel.

Holland only turned to look as the other Lynx moved through the gate and he could clearly hear the tires crunching on the gravel. He gave the driver an exasperated look, throwing his hands up in an expression of frustration. The truck rolled to a stop twenty yards away.

"Same two blokes," Deane radioed as Holland walked slowly

toward the driver's door. *"I didn't see either of them use the radio."*

The two Russians got out of the vehicle, both grinning broadly at Holland, who they took for an older corporal, based on his rank insignia. The driver said something in Russian, but it was so quick that Holland didn't catch it. Instead he waved his left hand in Archie's direction and cursed him again. Tony's voice came over Holland's earpiece.

"Shift right."

Holland angled to his right, as if to come around the vehicle. He cursed at Archie again as he moved, drawing the driver's attention away from his movement. Tony's silenced rifle gave a muffled crack as Holland dropped to a knee, pulling his Sig Sauer P227 Tacops .45 from its holster and firing two quick shots, both taking the driver in the chest.

"Tango down," Tony reported, telling Holland that the passenger was no longer a threat. Holland jumped up and sprinted to the driver, who had collapsed behind the Lynx. He kept his pistol trained on the man until he was certain that he was also dead.

"All clear." Holland holstered his pistol and waved to hurry Deane and Tony back to the trucks.

Archie made a show of rubbing his backside. "D'you have to kick me that hard, mate?"

Holland grinned, swapping out the magazine in his pistol for a full one. He quickly inserted two fresh rounds into the other magazine and slipped it back into the sleeve on his belt. "Had to make it convincing, didn't I?"

Archie grinned back. "Oscar-winning performance, that was." He slung the spare tire into the cargo area on their Lynx, tossing the assorted tools in after it. As Tony and Deane ran up, Archie drove their Lynx closer to the other and started helping Holland to hoist the dead men inside. When the bodies were loaded, Archie drove the Lynx around behind the cargo containers where Tony and Deane had been hidden and left it there, trotting back to the others when he was finished.

"You moved pretty fast, Dad," Tony said. "Especially considering you got shot in the butt less than a week ago."

"You keep reminding me," Holland said, climbing into the driver's seat of the new Lynx. "I'm surprised I can walk at all. Still hurts."

"Sounds like 'Cry Me a River' pain, to me." Tony laughed as he got in the front seat next to his dad.

Deane scowled. "What are you two on about?"

"Inside joke," Holland said. He cocked an eyebrow at his son as he slipped the truck into gear and spun it around, driving through the now open gate and onto the inner perimeter road. Tony's change in attitude from earlier in the day, when he had snapped at Holland's small attempt to help him, was more than noticeable. Holland knew that combat often brought on dramatic mood swings in people caught up in it, brought on by the body dumping massive amounts of adrenaline to get through the dangerous part, followed by euphoria, depression or sometimes giddiness when the danger was suddenly past and all that adrenaline drained away.

He didn't want his concern for his son to color his own decision making, but he *was* concerned. He couldn't help it. Decades of training to detach himself from the crippling fear of potential harm to his buddies during combat operations seemed to make no difference now, when it was his son was facing the danger at his side. Tony was all he had left, and they had both risked everything by volunteering for this mission. Holland knew then, with a sudden implacable certainty, that he couldn't risk treating Tony with kid gloves. Taking his focus from the mission at hand and fixing it on protecting his only son was what his instinct as a father demanded, but he knew that doing that could jeopardize all of them.

He fell back on what he knew best - he had to treat Tony just like he would any other operator he worked with. Tony was his son, but he was also a warrior after all, just like the rest of them.

"Glad you can enjoy yourself at my expense. Next time, I'll

ride piggyback and you can get shot in the butt."

Tony laughed again. "No thanks." He stared intently out the windshield, eyes scanning the road ahead. "Honestly, I'm just glad to be here. I'd have gone nuts if you'd left me back in England. Feels good to be part of something worthwhile again."

Archie snorted from the back seat. "Let's just hope this isn't the last worthwhile thing any of us ever does."

Seybaplaya, Mexico

Cooney almost dumped the motorcycle as he rounded the corner toward the maintenance barge, sliding sideways in the loose gravel and only barely recovering. He jumped off the bike, dropping it next to Newill's abandoned BMW. Sprinting across the gangplank, he dropped onto the deck of the barge and ran across to the other side. The helicopter was already lifting off, so it was a waste of time to climb the stairs. He pulled his pistol from his holster and fired six shots at the fast retreating aircraft, and though he was certain he'd hit it, nothing happened. It continued to gather speed and altitude as it faded into the distance.

Cooney swore, then turned and re-crossed the barge to the gangplank. Several roughnecks were standing on the landward side, blocking his passage. One man held up a restraining hand.

"No queremos problemas, señor," he said.

Cooney raised the pistol and kept coming. "Bien. Fuera de mi camino."

The men backpedalled, running into and tripping over each other in their hurry to get away. Cooney let them go. He walked over to Newill's BMW and looked inside. The keys were still there, so he climbed in, started the engine and sprayed the men at the gangplank with a cloud of dust and gravel as he sped away.

He pulled out his phone as he drove and called Behan. He

didn't relish the coming conversation, but knew it couldn't be avoided.

"Behan." He already sounded irritated.

"Sir. We have a problem."

"Something tells me you're not referring to the problem of understatement," Behan sniped. *"From what I hear, Serracana's compound was like a war zone this morning. I expected you to kill Newill. I didn't expect you to kill him, Serracana and every cartel member within a five mile radius."*

Cooney bit back a retort. Behan didn't know, then. Somehow, he'd already heard about the shootout at the compound, but he was obviously assuming that Newill had been killed as well.

"Now you've gone and stirred up a hornet's nest down there," Behan went on. *"You need to exfil before the cartel finds you. Honestly, Cooney, I expected this to be a straightforward job. I give you credit for getting it done, but I would have preferred it being done a bit more quietly. You've got half of Mexico in an uproar already, and you've only been down there for two days… "*

"Sir." Cooney interrupted Behan's rant. "You're not getting the full picture."

There was an uncomfortable pause before Behan responded. *"What are you on about? What, exactly, am I not getting?"*

"Newill got away, Mr. Behan," Cooney confessed with an apologetic sigh. "He's in the wind."

49th Missile Defense Battalion
Fort Greely, Alaska

They drove across the battery, past ranks of subterranean missile silos, the slightly domed silo doors looking almost like giant pressure cooker lids in rows along the open ground. They didn't see any other patrols or personnel until they got within a quarter mile of the command building.

"Here's where it gets interesting," Archie said, as they passed three soldiers on foot heading in the opposite direction. At the moment, no one seemed at all alarmed, so they had to assume that their attack on the guards at the south fence had gone undetected.

Holland steered the truck around the back of the command building, parking on the far side of a six-wheeled Ural 4320 cargo carrier. "Tony, wait here and watch the approach from the north. Let us know if anybody gets close." Holland and the other two got out of the truck and walked toward the rear door of the command structure like they belonged there, stolen AK-15s slung over their shoulders.

There was no one else around the rear of the building. The rear door was windowless, and had a five-button cipher lock installed on the jamb beside it. Holland took a quick look around, then slipped his Halligan tool from his pack and approached the door, while Archie and Deane took up positions behind him. He was just fitting the pry bar end of the Halligan between the door and the jamb at the bolt when the door suddenly swung open.

Holland stepped back in time to avoid the door hitting him, and as he caught the pry bar, he looked up into the face of a very surprised Russian officer.

"*Chto ty delayesh?*"

In response, Holland flipped the tool over and thrust the flat adze-shaped end into the Russian's face, punching the man across the bridge of his nose and dropping him to the ground in the doorway. The man's head cracked on the floor and he went limp.

"Quick!" Holland hissed. "Help me get him inside!"

Archie and Deane stepped up and grabbed the man, dragging him back inside the building as Holland pulled the door closed behind them. They found themselves in a short hallway that ended in a T intersection about ten feet further in. There was a single door on the left side of the hall. Holland drew his pistol and pushed the door open, finding the small room on the other side empty. He waved the others inside, and they dragged the unconscious Russian with them.

Holland searched the room quickly. It was an electronic and utility maintenance room, little more than a large closet, but on the far wall behind a rack of electronics, Holland found a chart showing the layout of the building, as well as another diagram showing the entire missile battery. As he ran a finger over the schematics, he keyed his microphone.

"Tony, make sure you're clear, then get in here, and bring our own rifles with you. Archie'll meet you at the back door. Let us know when you're moving."

The reply was immediate. *"Moving now."*

"Archie, go let Tony in the back, I'll cover you."

Archie stepped over the unconscious Russian and peeked out the door as Holland moved up behind him. "Clear." Archie opened the door just enough to slip back out into the hall. Holland stayed inside the room with his pistol trained at the hallway intersection through the cracked door. A couple of moments later Archie hissed and Holland stepped back, allowing him back into the room with Tony behind him.

Tony glanced at the man on the floor, who Deane had already Flex-cuffed. He unslung the three extra SCAR combat rifles he'd brought in and passed them around. "What's the plan?"

Holland showed them the schematics. "There's underground access from this building to the entire battery through a system of tunnels. If we take out the control center here, there's a chance we can use the tunnels to get away to the south without being seen. It just depends."

"On what?" Archie asked.

"On how many people Ivan has roaming around in the tunnels," Deane answered. "Bound to be some tech types down in the missile silos themselves, checking systems and trying to figure out how to work the battery."

"Then how come we didn't see any activity topside?" Tony asked.

"That's a good point," Holland said. "Maybe they still haven't had time to get the right techs in country. Could be our lucky day."

"First time for everything," Deane cracked.

"Doesn't much matter, does it?" Archie asked. "We torch this building and try to escape, the missiles are still untouched, and we're trying to exfil from the middle of a fur ball. I like the idea of staying underground as far as possible. Get out of the tunnels at the south side, grab that first Lynx we stole and disappear."

"Which would allow us to set charges on each of the missiles as we work our way south." Holland said.

Archie shook his head. "Not enough charges. We only brought twenty-five detonators, and there's no way to set them off remotely underground - the signal wouldn't get through to half of them if we were at any kind of safe distance."

"We have basic timers?"

"Just ten."

"We could shoot 'em."

All of them turned to look at Deane. "Shoot what? The missiles?" Holland asked.

"Uh... Wouldn't that make 'em explode?" Tony asked.

Deane shook his head. "Not necessarily. Any of you have any kind of training in solid rocket fuels?"

"You're kidding, mate." Archie shook his head.

"Plenty of demolitions training," Holland said. "But that never really addressed rockets, specifically."

"Same here," Deane said. "But I've done some reading on the side, just scratching the surface, you understand. Always been curious about rockets, since I was a kid."

"Your point?" Archie urged.

"My point being that solid rocket fuels *can* explode as a result of overpressure or impact, but the reaction is dependent on mass and velocity of the projectile, as well as the type of fuel and the case material of the rocket itself."

"You lost me after the word 'explode'," Tony said.

"What I mean is, in general terms, the larger the mass and velocity of the projectile penetrating the motor housing, the greater the chance of detonation. So if I had to choose, I'd use a subsonic, smaller caliber pistol round rather than a high velocity rifle round with a heavier bullet. If we can puncture the solid rocket boosters, especially where the damage will go unnoticed, the rockets would still be able to launch, but they'd fail as soon as the fuel reached the rupture in the engine casing. If they didn't go up in a fire ball, they'd have control problems and most likely have to self-destruct."

"That's crazy," Archie said.

"I'm inclined to agree." Holland looked from Deane back to the schematic of the battery. "But if it's our only option, we need to figure out if it's workable at all. You say lower velocity is better - what if we puncture the casing with the pick end of a Halligan? It's a lot heavier than a bullet, but it's a lot lower velocity too."

Deane spread his hands. "As I said, what little I understand, I picked up from recreational reading. I'm not certain how close a Halligan and a pistol round would be on the curve of accidentally blowing yourself up. I don't even know what the engine casings on these particular missiles are made of. If they're aluminium or fiberglass, we should be able to penetrate them easily. If they're something heavier, such as steel, it'll take more mass and velocity to get through, which would then, in theory, put us closer to detonation." He shrugged. "That's just how I understand it, lads."

"'Recreational reading,' he says." Archie was shaking his head. "You're not normal, Sergeant Major."

"If I were normal, I wouldn't be here, now would I?"

CHAPTER TWENTY-SIX

Memento Mei

49th Missile Defense Battalion
Fort Greely, Alaska

After studying the schematics further, Holland had found the battery command and control room further inside the building. Trying to get there would without a doubt put them into contact with more Russian troops, so they decided to avoid it altogether. The stairs leading down to the silo access tunnels were around the corner from the maintenance room they were in, so they had agreed to take them in an attempt to remain unnoticed. Archie insisted on setting a timed charge on the main electrical control boxes in the room before they left. The damage to those wouldn't be permanent, but it would take time to repair and it would serve as a further hindrance to the Russians.

"Be a shame to leave a perfectly good target unexploded, now wouldn't it?" he'd said as he wired a charge and placed it out of sight near the main wiring trunk. "How much time, you reckon, boss - forty minutes?"

Holland considered it. "Forty minutes might be a little tight.

I'd like to be done in the silos and well away before that noisemaker goes off. Make it an hour."

"Right." Archie set the timer and stepped back. "We're on the clock."

"What about him?" Tony looked at the unconscious Russian on the floor.

Holland looked at the man, then fixed a level gaze at his son. "We can't risk him coming to while we're still in the tunnels."

Tony looked uneasy. "We're just gonna kill him?"

"If he wakes up before we're done, he'll bring the whole garrison down on us."

"I don't know…"

Deane stepped between Tony and the prone form of the Russian. "You lads move to the stairs. I'll take care of it, and bring up the rear." He punctuated the statement by pulling his combat knife out of its sheath.

"Dad…"

Holland took his son by the shoulders and leaned in close and lowered his voice. "We don't have time for this! That man, awake, means we die, got it? We don't know if he'll wake up on his own or not, but we can't afford that chance! He is *no different* than those others that we took out earlier - each one of them was a threat to our lives and the success of this mission. *And so is he.* We're at war here. You need to get your head around that, Marine. *Right now.*"

Holland let him go. Tony blinked a couple of times, then clenched his jaw. He didn't like the idea of killing a helpless man, but he'd had the concept of 'mission first' drilled into him a thousand times before in the Marine Corps. Until now, though, the enemy had always been shooting back, or at least capable of doing so. This man wasn't an immediate threat. He wasn't even conscious. It was a blurry line, and Tony wasn't sure he wanted to cross it, but he knew his dad was right.

Mission first.

He met Law's eyes and nodded.

Holland nodded back, relieved. "All right then. Archie, take point. Tony, stay in his hip pocket and I'll be in yours. Alvin - bring up the rear."

"Right behind you," Deane said.

The others stacked up at the door, Archie opening it a crack and peering out into the hall. "Clear." He pulled the door open and led them out. They turned left and stacked up at the tee in the hall. Archie stayed to the right side and looked left while Holland moved up to the left side and scanned right. "Clear," Archie said again.

"Clear," Holland replied. As he spoke, he felt Deane squeeze his shoulder, indicating he had caught up and was ready to follow. "Go," he ordered, and Archie immediately flowed out and turned to the right with Tony close on his heels. Holland and Deane followed, Deane keeping an eye on the hallway behind them as they moved. Ten paces further on they reached a door on the left side of the hallway with a sign that read, SILO ACCESS - AUTHORIZED PERSONNEL ONLY.

Archie tried the door and found it unlocked. He cocked an eyebrow at Tony, then opened the door fully, allowing Tony to leapfrog to the point position and cover his entry. There was a flight of stairs immediately on the other side of the door. Tony took a couple of steps down, then paused to wait for the others to get through the door behind him. As Deane brought up the rear, Tony caught his eye. He stared at the older man for a heartbeat, trying to determine if there was something different there, something that would differentiate a cold blooded killer from a normal person.

He was startled when all he could see was his dead friend Clay Bagley, shooting an unconscious Taliban fighter in the middle of that chaotic fight on an Afghan mountainside two years before. Bagley hadn't hesitated then; it had been understood that their situation was desperate and that leaving the man alive, while humane, would have also been suicidal.

Was that any different than this?

It only took Tony an instant to come back to himself. Deane was returning his gaze, and Tony blinked uncomfortably before the British man gave a slight nod. Reassured, Tony nodded back.

Then he led them off, descending into the semi-darkness toward the silos.

Presidential Residence
The White House
Washington, D. C.

"I don't remember." Reese's face was drawn, his tone bleak. He looked at Dr. Oldenbourg, then at Black, confusion written all over his face. He was sitting in an armchair with his hands gripping his knees in front of him, but the tremors were still visible. A persistent tic had developed in the muscles below his right eye. "What's this about a virus again?"

Black almost pitied the man's sudden vulnerability. What a difference a few weeks could make. A month earlier, this man had been plotting to overthrow the previous president, but now he was incapable of planning his own lunch menu. He looked weak, vulnerable and above all, frightened. "We briefed you on it last night, Mr. President," he said. "You were, ah… not exactly able to take it in at the time."

Reese shook his head. He looked to be on the verge of tears. "I can't… I don't understand why I can't remember."

"Memory loss is quite normal for this stage of your sickness, Mr. President," Oldenbourg said. "Your brain cells are gradually being destroyed by the multiplication of abnormal prion proteins in the brain tissue, and -" he stopped talking, finally noticing that Black was gesturing at him to be quiet.

"Mr. President," Black said. "You appointed me as your vice president. I was sworn in yesterday, shortly before we heard about the outbreak of the virus."

Reese looked up at him, then shook his head again. "There's a virus?"

"Mr. President," Black said quietly. "Sir. You're not well. You have been diagnosed with a terminal illness. For you to continue in your job now would be damaging to what health you have remaining, as well as being detrimental to the country. America needs strong leadership, sir. We're at war, and now it looks like we're dealing with a very serious viral outbreak as well. The people need to know that their government is capable of dealing with this crisis effectively."

Reese's tic grew more pronounced.

Oldenbourg stepped closer. "Mr. Vice President, I think we need to give him time to rest."

Reese cut in before Black could answer. "I can't do it, can I?"

"Sir?"

"I *can't* lead the country."

Black looked at Oldenbourg, then back at Reese. "I'm sorry, sir. But no, you can't. Not any more." *Not that you ever could,* he thought.

"What am I supposed to do now?"

Black glanced again at Oldenbourg, who sighed and gave a single nod of his head.

"Do you think you can read a statement, Mr. President?"

Reese seemed to shrink into himself as he finally accepted the inevitable. "I'll try."

49th Missile Defense Battalion
Fort Greely, Alaska

The stairs and corridor below were lit by utility lamps recessed into the concrete walls at fifty foot intervals, resulting in a succession of disconnected pools of light interrupted by intervals of near-darkness. As Tony led the way, he could see details in the distance closest to the lamps, but the dark spots between were nearly impenetrable until they were almost on top of them. It made his skin crawl, thinking that there could be someone crouched in one of those shadows, holding the crosshairs of a high powered rifle right on his chest. He strained his eyes, trying to force them to pick out details in the dark.

They'd traveled about a thousand feet down the arrow-straight corridor when they came to an intersection. Tony drew up to the opening and scanned the hall to the right as Archie scanned the other direction. They knew from the schematic that the corridor to the left led off to the easternmost of the battery's three launch arrays. The one to the east contained twenty silos; to the southwest, there was a smaller array with six more, and to the southeast, the final array held fourteen.

Here was where things would get even riskier. They couldn't possibly sabotage forty missiles in the less than an hour they had remaining before Archie's charge went off in the electrical vault. As soon as that happened, there was the very real risk that the Russians would lock down the entire base, including sealing off access to the very tunnel they were using right now. If they didn't finish before the explosive went off, they would end up trapped here underground, waiting for the inevitability of a last stand.

Their only hope was to separate. With three arrays to deal with and four men to do it, there was no easy or efficient method. Holland decided to split into pairs rather than send two men individually to deal with one array each while a pair dealt with the remaining one. They had forty missiles to sabotage, so each team of two men would have to deal with twenty missiles. He had suggested sending Tony with Deane, but the Brit had demurred.

"No, Law," Deane said. "You go with your boy. Good chance none of us make it out of here today, so you might as well spend your last few minutes with your own son, eh? Besides, this way we can make a friendly wager on who gets out first - bloody ungrateful rebel Yanks, or the Queens Own?"

"That work for you, Archie?"

"I dunno, boss. I might be handicapped if Ricky the Rocketeer here decides to stop and take snapshots."

"All I said, was that I read an article…" Deane protested.

Holland shook his head. "Good enough. Tony, it's you and me. We'll take the two smaller arrays, and you meatheads take the big one to the east. Fifty bucks says we have the truck running before you boys see the sunlight again."

"Make it fifty pounds," Deane said, grinning. "You forget - the American dollar's worth about as much as Monopoly money these days."

"Done. Good luck, boys. Our first launcher is closest, so if you hear a big boom, you'll know your bright idea doesn't work. If that happens, just get the heck out as fast as you can."

"Right. Same goes for you. Let's go." He and Archie turned and trotted off down the corridor to the left without another word.

"C'mon. Let's go break some expensive toys." Holland slapped Tony on the shoulder and took off down the right corridor. Tony noticed that his dad's limp was more pronounced than it had been earlier in the day. He was moving quickly, but it was obvious he was struggling.

"How's your butt, Dad?" Tony whispered when he'd caught up.

"Stiff as a board. I keep thinking it'll loosen up the more running I do, but so far, that's not happening."

"Coulda been worse, though. I'm glad it wasn't."

Holland paused in a dark patch and smiled back at him. "Me too." He raised his knee a couple of times, flexing his leg. "Should be coming to the first array in about a hundred yards. Let's cut the chatter. Probably gonna get some kinda contact pretty quick."

Tony slid the bolt on his SCAR partially back, ensuring he had a round chambered. "You'll want to sling that," Law told him. "At least until after we wake up the neighbors. You touch that thing off down here, and anybody on the other side of the array will hear it and sound the alarm. Let's stick to the sidearms, for now."

"Sorry." Tony dropped the rifle to hang barrel down from his chest sling, and pulled his own silenced Sig Sauer from his thigh holster, cracking its slide and checking the load. "Ready."

"On me." Holland set off at a fast walk.

They made it to the array access doors without running into anyone. They hadn't even heard any conversations from the tunnel ahead of them yet, which was good in itself, but still made them wonder. Where were all the Russians? The suspense was starting to make Tony jittery. He kept expecting someone to jump out of every recess and dark shadow, and when it didn't happen, he found himself almost disappointed. He was beginning to think that he'd almost prefer a gun battle to the tension of waiting for one to start.

Holland abruptly held up a fist as they passed through the access door. The corridor inside the door was lined with signs on either side, numbered twenty-one through forty. Of those twenty silos, they knew from the battery schematics that only silos twenty-one through twenty-five, as well as silo forty actually held missiles. The remaining silos had never been used, as the Tolliver administration had cancelled the funding to finish the battery's load-out. Holland took a long look down the main access corridor between the silos, then motioned Tony into silo twenty-one.

"Halligan, or .45?" he asked, eyebrows raised. He was standing on an annular platform surrounding a huge missile body that was almost five feet across and more than fifty feet high. Two thirds of the missile rose above them, with the lower third extending to the bottom of the silo, almost twenty feet below.

"You're asking me?" Tony had no idea which option was better.

"You know as much about it as I do."

"Which is exactly nothing."

"Sometimes, you gotta make a gut call. What's your gut telling you?"

"To run as fast and as far away from here as I can."

Holland chuckled. "Mine, too. All right, let's do this, then. I'll use the Halligan in here, you go across the way and use your .45. I'll give you sixty seconds before I swing."

Tony took a deep breath and stepped back to the corridor. "All right." He looked back. "Dad?"

"Yeah?"

"Thanks for trusting me enough to let me tag along."

Holland grinned. "Nobody I'd rather get blown up with."

"Love you, Dad."

"Love you, too. Shoot straight."

"*Swing* straight." Tony nodded and stepped out.

Holland pulled the Halligan and watched as the seconds ticked by on his watch. At fifty-eight, he squared his feet, blew out his breath, and swung.

Presidential Residence
The White House
Washington, D. C.

White House aides had set up a video camera and a teleprompter, aimed at Reese's chair. They'd decided to have him read his statement here in the residence rather than moving him to the Oval Office. Oldenbourg was finally convinced that his condition was starting to deteriorate faster, and they were rapidly running out of time.

Reese sat slumped in his chair next to the fireplace, staring sadly at the camera. An aide nodded at Black.

"We're ready, Mr. President," Black told Reese. "Just read from the teleprompter at your own pace, whenever you're ready."

"This isn't live?" Reese asked.

"No, sir. It's better this way, I think."

Reese nodded slowly, then looked at the camera. He scanned the teleprompter for a moment, then straightened slightly and began.

"My fellow Americans. For the past several weeks, I have been struggling to come to terms with physical difficulties…" His voice trailed off, and his head sagged slightly. He struggled to gather himself, and continued.

"My doctor has informed me that these… difficulties… are caused by a rare brain disorder, known as Sporadic Creutzfeldt-Jakob Disease. He tells me that it causes a rapidly progressing type of dementia." Reese looked more intently at the camera, and the tic under his eye flickered almost constantly. He stopped reading the teleprompter. "He also tells me that it's fatal." Again, he paused, seeming to steel himself enough to carry on.

"I *wanted* to be president," he said, staring bleakly into the camera. "I wanted to be a *good* president." His eyes wandered downward before he forced them back up with an effort. "I… I haven't been."

Black watched in grim fascination from off camera. *What is he doing?*

"Sometimes," Reese continued, "you want something so badly that you forget *why* you wanted it to begin with. I, ah… I don't really remember why I wanted this job. To be honest, I really don't even remember how I got it, but… well, I think… I suspect I didn't earn it." He looked straight into the camera, and a single tear slipped from the corner of his right eye, tracing a path down his face.

He paused, then continued with more conviction. "I *didn't* earn it. And now, I'm unable to carry it out." He took a deep breath, then plunged ahead, as if trying to get through the difficulty as quickly as possible. "As of this moment, I resign the office of President of the United States. I'm so very sorry." He lowered his head again.

Black motioned at the aide to stop the recording. "You did the right thing, Mr. President," he said, walking over to Reese.

Reese didn't look up. "Don't call me that." His head sagged lower, he drew a sharp breath and let out a single, ragged sob.

49th Missile Defense Battalion
East Missile Array
Fort Greely, Alaska

Archie and Sergeant Major Deane ran all the way to the battery entrance doors leading to the east battery without running into anyone. That changed suddenly when they opened the door and stepped into the long corridor running between the silos. There were three Russians in the corridor about forty yards ahead of them, talking as they walked away. Two were unarmed, but the third, trailing slightly behind, had an AK-15 slung across his chest. Responding to the sound of the door opening behind them, one of the lead pair half-turned to see who was there. The look of confusion that clouded his face caused the armed man behind to spin around as well.

The two Brits started firing, moving straight down the corridor toward the threat as they did. The man with the rifle was hit in the side as he turned, and one of the men ahead of him dropped with a bullet in his temple. Then the soldier got his rifle up and got off a sustained burst before he too went down in a fusillade of pistol fire from the Brits. He fell backward, getting tangled up with the yet unwounded man, who was cursing and struggling to get loose as Archie ran forward and shot him twice, ending the brief gunfight.

Hurriedly, Archie checked all three men for vital signs, but they were all dead. "Clear!" Then he turned, and saw Sergeant Major Deane slumped against the wall, one hand clutching his side. "Aw, bugger!" He ran back to his partner. "Where're you hit, Sergeant Major?"

"I'll live, lad," Deane said, grimacing with pain and

impatiently waving Archie off. His hand was covered in blood. "You've got to clear the battery! Make sure nobody heard all that commotion."

"Sure you're all right?"

"Go, lad. Make sure nobody else is down here." He struggled to his feet. "I'll get started on the missiles on this end, you can work your way back to me."

Archie ripped open his first aid kit and slapped a thick bandage into Deane's free hand. "Get pressure on that thing," he said. "I won't be a moment." Then he ran off down the corridor, quickly sidestepping into each silo and clearing them as he went.

Deane sucked in a sharp breath as he pressed the bandage against the wound. The Russian had got a lucky shot in that had clipped the edge of Deane's body armor, before smashing three ribs and punctured his left lung in the process. It was bloody and extremely painful, but not life-threatening. Not yet, anyway. Every breath was an agony, and Deane knew that if he needed to move fast, he wouldn't be able to. If his survival came down to a footrace, he'd be as good as dead.

He dragged himself into the first missile silo. With an effort, he raised his pistol and aimed at the solid fuel cell on the big rocket.

Don't blow up, you great dirty bugger, he thought. Then he squeezed the trigger.

Archie ran from one silo to the next, quickly clearing each before firing one round apiece into the rockets. He hadn't liked the idea of bypassing half of the missiles without damaging them - leaving them for Deane to deal with. He knew if something happened before he could come back for Deane, those weapons would still potentially be in play for the Russians. So he'd forced himself to move faster, zigzagging across the corridor from one silo to the next. He'd shot six of the big missiles before he even considered how mad this plan really was.

I'm shooting a bunch of bloody big missiles with a pistol from fifteen feet away, he thought. *One of these things decides to blow, there won't be so much as a memory left of me to scrape off the walls*. He knew he had little choice, though, so he pulled the trigger on the seventh missile and moved on.

Deane staggered from the first silo back into the corridor, and keyed his mic. "Four, it's Two. You copy?"

"All right, Two?" Archie's concern was obvious.

"I'm good," Deane lied. "Done with number two missile, heading your way. You leave any for me?"

"Negative, Two, sorry. Selfish of me, that. I'm halfway down the battery, no tangos in sight. I think we found all of 'em. I'll finish on this end and come back for you. If you need to rest, do it."

"Roger that, Four," Deane gasped through clenched teeth. He unkeyed and sagged against the wall, grateful for the rest.

Archie was pouring sweat. His pistol slide locked back as he fired the last round in the magazine, and he dropped the empty into one hand and slapped a full magazine into the well. He had seven missiles left. He checked his watch. Forty minutes had already passed since he set the charge in the electrical vault. Just twenty minutes until it went off, alerting the entire garrison to their presence. He ran to the next silo and fired into the side of the missile, then continued on to the next pair.

He wasn't sure he had enough time to damage all the missiles and still get Deane out.

49th Missile Defense Battalion
West Missile Array
Fort Greely, Alaska

Tony ran the thirty-five yards to the next silo, and got there with time to spare. He looked the missile up and down, trying to determine the best point of aim. With time about to run out, he followed his dad's advice and went with his gut. Raising his pistol, he pulled the trigger, unable to keep from cringing as he did. The report of the silenced shot was more a clack than a boom, more like an industrial stapler rather than a heavy caliber handgun. Still, it echoed briefly in the cylindrical space.

But that was all.

No explosion, no venting of toxic gases, no sudden death. Tony briefly considered putting another couple of rounds into the rocket, but thought better of it. They still had a lot more to go before they were done.

He emerged from silo twenty-two at the same time as his dad came out of number twenty-one. They both glanced up and down the long corridor between them, then Holland made a show of letting out his breath.

"You're not dead," Tony said, trying to hold back a nervous laugh.

"I'm only doing this ten more times, then never again. I feel like Bugs Bunny working in a bomb factory."

"We'd better go, if you don't wanna lose fifty pounds to the Sergeant Major."

"Oh, right." They took off down the corridor to the next pair of missiles, repeating the process. Then Holland took care of the missile in silo twenty-five, before they continued down the corridor to the end and silo number forty.

"Save your ammo," Holland said when they got there. He went in and punctured the solid fuel cell with the Halligan while Tony kept watch. When he'd finished, they had to backtrack halfway up the magazine to the auxiliary tunnel that led to the southeast magazine a quarter mile away.

They were jogging along with their pistols ready when somewhere ahead of them, a door slammed. They quickly stepped to the sides of the corridor, trying to dissolve into the intermittent darkness between lights. Although standing against the walls left them at a higher risk for catching a ricocheting bullet in a firefight, nobody was shooting at them just yet, and standing in the middle of the hall would leave them silhouetted in the lighting behind them. They had no real choice but to stand still and try to remain invisible.

They waited, catching their breath. Several moments passed before Tony spoke quietly into his mic, even though his dad was only six feet away. *Two hundred yards. Two of 'em."*

Holland strained his eyes against the gloom. "Stay put. Let 'em come."

They waited. As the two men drew closer, their voices became clearer, and it was obvious they were speaking Russian. They were armed with AK-15s, but the rifles were slung carelessly over their shoulders, and they walked and talked as though they had no concern at all.

"Let 'em get centered three shadows closer, then take 'em."

"Roger."

The soldiers kept coming. They were walking side by side, and as they stepped into the designated patch of shadow, Holland and Tony each fired twice. Almost simultaneously, the door clanged again in the distance. They froze. There was a long, nervous silence.

"Nikolai?"

Holland looked sideways at his son. "Get ready." Tony nodded. Then he jumped as his dad let out a sudden bellow of laughter. He looked over to see Holland moving into the light and walking toward the new voice. Tony quickly caught on, slung his SCAR behind him out of sight, and followed, adding his own forced laugh to the performance. He understood what his dad was doing - giving the newcomer confusing information. He would be expecting Nikolai and the other person, who had apparently entered the tunnel well ahead of him. Holland was simply making it seem as though they were laughing at a joke as they returned toward their friend.

As they closed the distance, both men continued to laugh. Holland interspersed his laughter with what sounded to Tony like random Russian words, like someone repeating a punch line in hysterics.

"Nikolai? Chto smeshnogo?"

The voice was closer now, still uncertain, but more relaxed.

"Follow my lead," Holland whispered as they passed through another pool of light and into shadow. Tony was wondering what he meant when his dad abruptly groaned and collapsed against the wall. If he hadn't cursed in Russian as he fell, Tony would have thought he was really in distress. "Crouch down right next to me," Holland ordered as Tony stepped closer. Then he continued swearing in Russian as he rolled onto his stomach and stretched his P227 out in front of him in a two handed grip, his forearms and the butt of the pistol firmly braced on the floor.

"Nikolai?!? Chto sluchilos?" The voice was urgent now, and followed by the sound of running.

"Shift left," Holland murmured. The footsteps were getting rapidly closer. Tony tried to relax as he moved to his left, but found it hard with his back to the enemy. He had an almost overpowering urge to turn and engage the man with his own sidearm, when Holland's pistol coughed twice with barely an interval. Holland was up and running before Tony could turn around. Tony stumbled getting up and ran after, nearly tripping on the bodies of the two men they'd shot first. He'd completely forgotten about them in the tension of drawing the third man in closer.

Holland was at least ten paces ahead as Tony regained his balance. He heard the third Russian cough, then the beginning of a cry for help, but that was cut short by another shot. Tony caught up to find his dad on one knee, searching the dead Russian's clothing. He looked back down the corridor toward the other two men, and mentally calculated the distance.

"That's almost seventy yards."

Holland looked up. "What?"

"You hit a moving target with a pistol, at almost seventy yards. Mostly in the dark."

Holland stood up. "He was moving straight at me. Hard to

miss." He put a fresh magazine into his pistol. "Lets move. I want to get out of this tunnel before the rest of the Red Army shows up." He stepped over the body and headed toward the east end of the tunnel at a limping trot.

Tony followed him, still a little bit in awe of his dad's ability to improvise in the face of complications. "So, what was all that you were saying back there - all that Russian?"

"You mean the joke?"

"Yeah. How many jokes do you know in Russian?"

"None. I just translated the punch line of a joke I knew from English, and repeated that like it was funny."

"What punch line?"

"The one from that old joke about what Washington said to his men before they crossed the Delaware River."

Tony was incredulous. "You said, 'Get in the Boat' in Russian, then laughed at it, and that guy believed it was a Russian punch line?"

"Think about it. How many times have you walked into a conversation right as somebody delivers a punch line, and it makes zero sense at all, because you didn't hear the whole joke?"

"Plenty, I guess."

"Well, that's what he thought he did. He *expected* to hear Russians in here. I didn't know what his name was or what Nikolai sounded like, so I couldn't exactly make conversation, but I *could* give him part of what he expected. He hears laughter, hears me repeating some nonsense phrase like it's hilarious, and his imagination fills in the gaps. Then I faked chest pains to get him to rush in closer. He'd have figured out earlier we didn't belong here if he'd have waited for us to come to him. My little charade wouldn't have stood up to any closer inspection."

Tony was incredulous. "You learn all that in the SEAL teams?"

"Some. Most of it's just from being a student of human nature. If you understand what people expect, you can use it to your advantage in a pinch."

"Geez, Dad. You should run for office."

"Ha. Not really the same thing. We use deception to gain the upper hand in a fight, and that's it. Politicians do it as part of a much longer game. To them, deception's a way of life. The truth isn't in 'em." He pulled up before a heavy metal door leading to the southeast missile battery.

"Look sharp now, here we go."

49th Missile Defense Battalion
East Missile Array
Fort Greely, Alaska

Deane sucked in a shallow breath and forced himself to stand. Staggering, he walked slowly south toward where Archie was working, his left hand against the wall to steady his progress, and his right clamped against his ribcage. Deane had been shot six times over the course of his career. The first time had almost killed him - a sniper in Bosnia had clipped him in the neck, partially opening his jugular vein. If it hadn't been for quick work on the part of a combat medic who'd dragged him out of the line of fire and treated him, Deane would have bled out in seconds.

That might have been better than this, Deane thought. No matter how he tried, he couldn't get a proper breath, and every time he breathed out, the next breath in got more difficult. He was almost certain that his left lung was collapsing. He'd always been tough, able to endure punishment without much effort, but this was pure torment. He felt as if he was slowly drowning and being crushed at the same time.

He managed to work his way past three pairs of silos, resting often, before he heard Archie coming back. He tried to take a few more steps, but couldn't manage it on his own. Leaning against the left wall, he concentrated on his breathing as much as possible.

"Sergeant Major!" Deane forced his eyes open to see Archie

bent over him. He barely managed a wince as Archie pulled his hand away from his ribs and checked the bleeding. Working fast, Archie pulled his knife and slit Deane's tunic up the side. The wound was ugly and ragged, with bruising surrounding it on all sides. Archie noticed some small bubbles at the center of the wound each time Deane breathed. He grabbed another bandage from his kit and placed it over the wound. Deane was in trouble, which meant they were both in trouble.

Archie wrapped gauze tightly around Deane's ribs, trying to hold the bandage in place and keep the wound from sucking more air inside his chest cavity. "We're running out of time, mate," he said as he worked. "Can you walk at all?"

Deane nodded. "If I can't keep up, you just leave me and bug out on your own, right?"

"You know better than that. Wouldn't be much of a mate if I did that, now would I?" He slid his hands under Deane's arms and muscled the older man to his feet. Deane groaned and almost collapsed to the floor again, but Archie pressed him against the wall until the pain passed and he was able to support his own weight.

"You're not much of a mate, not letting me die in peace." Deane said it with just a hint of a grin, but Archie could tell it took a lot of effort.

"No rest for the weary. Is your left arm hurt?"

"Don't think so. Hard to tell through the pain in the side."

"Perfect. That means you can hold your sidearm." Archie pulled Deane's pistol from his holster and pressed it into his left hand, then threw Deane's right arm over his shoulder, supporting most of his weight. Then he pulled his own sidearm and held it ready in his right hand. "All right?"

"All right."

"Let's go then. The Holland boys are gonna be waiting for us." Archie stepped off, allowing Deane to fall into step alongside him as they headed for the battery's south exit.

49th Missile Defense Battalion
West Missile Array
Fort Greely, Alaska

There were no Russians at all in the last battery. Holland and Tony made better time, running from silo to silo, puncturing the fuels cells and moving on. This battery only contained fourteen silos, unlike the one Deane and Archie were in, which had twenty. They had just reached the southernmost pair when they heard the north door open at the other end of the battery. Each man took cover in a silo doorway.

"Two, this is One," Holland radioed, his voice low. "Is that you, just entered the last battery?"

"One, this is Four," Archie's voice crackled in their earpieces. *"That's us. Hold your fire - Two's already been shot, and he'd like to avoid doing it again just now."*

"What's his status?"

"Pretty serious. He's ambulatory, but only just. Collapsed lung. I could use some help."

"Battery's clear, no tangos. Three's coming to you." He unkeyed and motioned Tony into the corridor with a jerk of his head. "Go. I'll finish these last two." Tony took off at a run.

CHAPTER TWENTY-SEVEN

Effugium

49th Missile Defense Battalion
Fort Greely, Alaska

Holland pierced the last rocket's fuel cell with the Halligan, then glanced at his watch.

Five minutes.

He stepped out into the corridor and looked impatiently to the north as he keyed his radio. "We need to get a move on, fellas!" Nobody replied for a second, then Tony's voice came on just as Holland saw them approaching in the dim light.

"We're coming, Dad. Be ready on the door."

Holland turned and ran for the south exit. He would have liked to help carry Deane, but in such close quarters, two men would probably be more effective at it than three. Better for him to clear the exit before the others got there. If there was a threat outside, the sooner they knew about it, the better. He carefully cracked the exit door open and scanned each side of the entrance tunnel. Walking up the ramp to the surface in a crouch, he scanned the entire battery from just above ground level. There was still no unusual activity. "Clear topside," he radioed. "Bring him out, I'm going to get the truck."

Deane was struggling mightily to breathe as Tony and Archie carried him between them toward the exit. No longer able to hold his weapon, he'd given it to Tony as soon as he got to them, and Tony had shoved it back into Deane's holster. They saw Holland go out the door, barely thirty yards ahead. They got to the door and stepped out into the tunnel, and as the door swung shut behind them, they heard a loud *whoomph* in the distance.

Tony trotted far enough up the tunnel ramp so he could look back to the north. His eyes widened slightly, then he ran back down to the others. "Your bomb just went off," he told Archie. "How much explosive did you use? It looks like you flattened the whole building."

"Waste not, want not." Archie grinned. Then an air raid klaxon started going off, the long wavering tone filling the air. Archie looked up. "I guess they finally figured out we're here."

"Let's hope Dad doesn't run into any trouble getting the truck."

Archie knelt down beside Deane and fussed with his bandage. "Gonna need to get a tube into his chest so his lung can inflate again," he muttered. Deane appeared to be unconscious.

The revving of an engine made them look up. Holland rolled up to the access tunnel in the Lynx they'd stolen on the highway. He slid the vehicle to a stop in the gravel and jumped out, limping around and opening the rear doors. "Let's go!"

The siren continued to wail as Tony and Archie hoisted Deane up between them and carried him to the truck, laying him gently in the back. Archie piled in after him. Holland was already back in the driver's seat, waiting impatiently. "C'mon, c'mon, c'mon!"

Tony ran around and climbed into the passenger seat, slamming the door behind him. "Go!"

Holland stomped on the accelerator and spun the vehicle around to the south, leaving the battery through the open southeast gate. As the missile base was swallowed by the thick trees crowding their rear view, he let out a long, tired breath.

Butch Lake
7 Miles South of Fort Greely, Alaska

Holland parked in thick trees fifty yards from the edge of Butch Lake. After re-fording Jarvis Creek, Archie had convinced Holland that if they didn't stop soon, Deane would have very little chance of survival. Now Archie was crouched over Deane in the cramped cargo compartment of the Lynx, examining the wound. Tony stood by, ready to help.

Archie carefully cleaned the area around the wound with alcohol. "Give me that clear tubing from my kit," he said. Tony found a length of plastic tubing and handed it over. "Cut me a few strips of surgical tape, about three inches each." As he said this, he wiped the tubing with an alcohol pad, then carefully inserted it into the wound, pressing it between two shattered ribs.

Deane flinched, then a hissing sound came from the tube as he took a breath, and his collapsed lung filled with air again, forcing the air out of his chest cavity through the tube. Deane's face relaxed, and his eyes fluttered, but he didn't wake up. Archie busied himself taping the tube into place so it couldn't fall out, then he replaced the bandage and wrapped gauze around Deane's ribs again. He sagged back on his haunches.

"Good to go, boss," he said. That should hold him until we get to..." He paused, scowling. "Where *are* we going next, anyway?"

Holland put the Lynx into gear and pulled back out onto the gravel road. "Back to Ma's place, I think. It's sorta on the way to the border."

Holland had been listening to the Russian communications on the vehicle's radio since they escaped from Greely. He'd been able to pick out enough chatter about a cruise missile attack to convince him that the Russians thought they'd been struck from the air. They still had no idea that a ground team had infiltrated the base. That couldn't last, though. As soon as someone went down to inspect the missiles, the hunt would be on. They needed to disappear. There was a slim chance that they could contact Punch, and arrange for him to pick them up on the Macomb Plateau, but as soon as the bodies were found in the access tunnels at Greely, the Russians would no doubt call in helicopters and fighters to help in the search. A single engine turboprop bush plane would be an especially tempting target. He figured they might be better off crossing the border on foot, as long as Deane could manage it.

The others fell silent as they retraced their route through the forest back toward the gravel quarry where they'd left Ma's pickup.

"We're not thinking about taking Ma's truck back to her, are we, Dad?" Tony finally asked, glancing around out the side window. "If we're spotted on the road in that pickup, we're just as likely to get into another gunfight. Won't we be less conspicuous in this?"

Holland considered it. "That depends. If - *when* - the Russians find those bodies in the tunnels, they're gonna expand the search to the entire base. They're gonna realize that they have people missing - the perimeter guards to begin with. But their truck was parked next to the command building where we left it, so they might think the guards went up in the explosion. That could buy us some time."

"But if they expand the search," Archie cut in, "and find their bodies behind those Conex containers outside the gate…"

"Which they will, before too long," Holland finished. "Then they'll know where to start. If the first group we hit on the highway was from Greely, they'll know they're missing before long, too. We can only hope that they were down from Eielson, and nobody's missed them yet. There's just too many variables. Driving around in a civilian truck could be good or bad, at this point."

"Think we oughta grab it, just in case?" Archie asked.

"No," Holland said. "As long as we're behind enemy lines, I'd rather look like the enemy than a civilian. I feel bad for Aanaq, leaving her truck way out here, but she didn't strike me as the type to be put off by a little inconvenience."

"Tough old bird was pure boot leather," Deane mumbled. They all looked at him, slumped in the back seat. His eyes were half open. "Sorta like me."

"She was a lot prettier than you, Sergeant Major."

"Nobody prettier than me, my boy." Deane forced a grin. "Just ask my wife."

"Tough old bird, indeed," Holland said, glancing at Deane in the mirror. "All right, then. I guess we're pretending to be Russians for as long as that keeps working for us. Their security was pretty lax back at Greely, so let's just hope that trend continues all the way to the border. I'd like to live long enough to make a report to Reardon about all this."

The Cannery Lodge
Kenai, Alaska

Following Joy Rollinson's death, the three surviving crew members of *CG6002* had found their way south to Kenai, hitching two more rides to get there. They'd turned Joy's body over to the police, then immediately set about trying to get back to their station on Kodiak Island. All of them had wanted to do something - *anything* - to avenge her death.

Getting back to work seemed like the most obvious way to do that, but as it turned out, it was also the most difficult. The Coast Guard Sector headquarters in Anchorage had gone silent after the invasion, and rumor had it that the personnel based there been rounded up and shot by the Russians shortly after they had landed at Elmendorf. When Kennedy finally got through to their duty officer on Kodiak, he'd been told to just sit tight until someone could come for them.

The only problem was, nobody came.

The three men had waited most of a day, and when it was obvious they had been forgotten, the chief of the Kenai Police had put them up at The Cannery Lodge, on the south bank of the Kenai River just outside town. The situation all over Alaska was extremely confused, and no one seemed to know how long it would be before the three men could get back to their duties.

Five more frustrating days had passed. The only traffic moving in and out of the port at Kenai was fishing boats; all air traffic had come to a stop. Landline communications had been mostly cut off beyond the city limits. Cell phones worked, but only sporadically. They were in the dark, and well out of the fight.

Finally, Darnell Hulse decided he'd had enough. He left the hotel early one morning without a word, leaving Taylor and Kennedy to wonder what he was doing. When he came back to the room an hour later, he didn't mince words.

"Pack your stuff. We're leaving."

Kennedy looked up. "Where've you been?"

"Getting us a ride," Hulse said.

Taylor stood up. "We don't have any stuff to pack. Where're we going?"

"Kodiak. Boat leaves in twenty minutes, with or without us."

Kennedy was on his feet now. "How'd you swing that?"

Hulse shrugged. "I walked up and down the pier, asking everybody I saw. Most of 'em wouldn't even look at me, but I found one crew that's making a run to Kodiak. Captain said the Russians have mostly left it alone so far. Said he even saw one of our helicopters working in and out of there a couple days ago. I figured since they aren't coming for us, we need to go to them."

Taylor was already on his way to the door. "Which boat is it?"

Alcan Highway

3 Miles From Tetlin Junction, Alaska

Holland had the Lynx at top speed as they rolled across the bridge over the Tanana River southeast of the village of Tok. They had seen no other Russian troops since they had got back onto the paved road. The bad news was that they'd heard several transmissions over the Russian radio about 'American ground forces' at Greely, which meant that the bodies in the silo access tunnels had been found. The only solution to that complication was to increase the distance between them and Greely as soon as possible - so Holland was driving as fast as the Lynx would go.

Three miles past the bridge, they came to Tetlin Junction, a wide spot in the road where the Taylor Highway meets the Alcan Highway. The Taylor Highway leads northeast to the Canadian border just west of Dawson. If they could cross the border there, they would be able to get in contact with Reardon shortly afterward, and figure out their next mission. More importantly, they could get Deane into a real hospital.

The Sergeant Major's condition had stabilized since Archie got the tube into his chest cavity, but he was far from comfortable, or even from being out of danger. Archie suspected the bullet had lodged somewhere in his torso, but he hadn't been able to do anything about it while they were bumping around in the back of a Russian military truck.

Holland cranked the wheel left, turning north onto the Taylor Highway. They passed a civilian pickup that quickly pulled off onto the shoulder when its driver saw the Lynx. The man watched them go by with a wary expression, apparently not sure if they were in a hurry to cause trouble for him, or some other unfortunate.

"Probably have as much chance of getting shot by a local as we do by the Russians at this point," Tony said.

"Maybe." Holland slowed as they went around a bend in the road, then stood on the brakes and pulled the wheel to the right, leaving the highway and taking a narrow track through the brush.

"What are you doing?"

"Take this," Holland pulled a satellite phone from a pocket on his sleeve and handed it over. "Hit redial, see if you can connect with Reardon. We need an exit plan for the border. Even if the Russians haven't locked it down yet, the Mounties probably have, and I doubt they'll be very welcoming to four armed men coming across in a Russian truck."

"Aw, I dunno," Archie said. "I hear the Canadians are a very tolerant lot."

"If they're that tolerant, the Russians would already be on the other side of the border, drinking beer and watching hockey," Deane growled. "We'll have to take a number at the pub."

Holland smiled in spite of himself. It was always amusing to see how men under the stress of combat would resort to humor at the most unlikely times. He often did it himself, without even thinking about it. Like a built in stress relief valve, he'd seen how humor helped people through some incredibly dangerous situations. Gallows humor, psychologists would call it. Whatever. Most of the psychologists he'd met could stand to lighten up a little, anyway.

He found a wide spot in the road and pulled off as Tony got a connection on the sat phone. "Six, this is Three. Request exit plan, route Bravo." He paused, listening. "All present, number Two is injured. Chest trauma with a possible punctured lung. Stabilized now, but we need help getting home." Holland watched as his son listened. Tony was fitting right in. His training as a Recon Marine had certainly helped him adjust to this strange new reality.

"Roger that, standby." Tony handed the phone to his dad. "He wants to talk to you."

Holland took the phone. "Go ahead, Six."

Reardon didn't mince words. *"What can you tell me, One?"*

"Just that holding the objective was a non-starter, sir. I think we all knew that going in. We had to settle for damaging the hardware."

"And?"

"And we decided to breach the solid fuel motors, make them unusable, at least in the short term."

"Did you get them all?"

"Affirmative. All damaged, plus Four set a charge in the command and control building big enough to break windows a mile away. There must be redundant controls, but that'll keep Ivan playing catch-up for a while, at least."

"Anything else?"

"Yes, sir - there weren't as many troops on site as we expected. One mounted patrol on the highway, one pair of mounted guards patrolling the site. In all, we only came across nine men inside the wire. There had to be more in the Command building, but we didn't go further in. I'd estimate they only had twenty or thirty covering the battery. More for the rest of the base, but no matter how you look at it, they're under strength. The patrol we took out on the highway may not have even been tasked to Greely; they could have been down from Eielson. My opinion, I think the Russians are operating on a shoestring - at least in this part of the state."

"That fits with our information as well," Reardon said. "RCMP has reported no cross border contact on your route - yet. They saw a truck yesterday morning, but it turned around a half mile from the border and drove away. Sounds as though Ivan is stretched thin, trying to cover a great deal with very little."

"That's good news, then," Holland said. "We need to get across the border and get number Two some medical attention. Can you smooth a path for us?"

"I believe so. Give me half an hour to talk to the mounties and the Canadian military attache. How long will it take you to get to the border?"

"Two hours flat out, maybe a little longer."

"Well enough," Reardon said. "I'll contact you when I have some *more information. Better get moving, Yank."*

"Wilco. Thanks, sir." Holland switched off the phone and stuffed it back into his pocket. "He said there's no Russian presence at the border yet, but they did have a single patrol approach yesterday. They didn't stick around." Holland put the truck in gear and spun it around, heading back to the highway.

"Could have been the owners of this thing," Archie said.

"Could have," Holland agreed. "Or it could have been just one of several patrols roaming around this side of the border that nobody's seen yet. It's more than a hundred miles from here to the border. That's plenty of room to run into somebody we'd rather not."

"If the Russians had time to shoot up Ma's little village, it's more than likely they'll have other patrols out. You don't typically stir up the locals when you're not feeling confident about the strength of your military position." Deane coughed violently and gasped for breath, the effort of talking almost too much for him.

"You might, if you're thinking you're in such a shaky position that intimidation is your best weapon." Archie reached over to check Deane's bandage, but Deane slapped his hand away.

"Quit your fussin', you're worse than my own mother."

Archie grinned and wagged his thumb at Deane. "If we do run into another patrol, we can just set this one loose on 'em. They'll be sorry they ever left the motherland."

Coast Guard Air Station Kodiak
Kodiak, Alaska

It was more than two hundred miles down the Cook Inlet from Kenai to Kodiak Island, and the trawler that carried them covered the distance at a maddeningly slow pace. The three men offered to help out on deck, hoping to pay for their trip as well as pass the time, but the captain wouldn't hear of it. His last boat had caught fire and sunk beneath him four years earlier, and the only reason he and his crew were still alive was that a Coast Guard crew much like this one had plucked them all out of the water. He owed the Coast Guard his life; the least he could do was to give these three a ride back to their base.

They arrived at three in the morning, the captain running his boat right up to the Coast Guard dock. A sentry with an automatic rifle tried to wave him off, but hesitated when he noticed the uniforms the three helicopter crewmen on deck were wearing. He looked uncertainly at Kennedy, but stepped into his path as he and the others disembarked.

"Halt! State your business, sir," the sentry barked.

Kennedy raised his hands. "Take it easy, Seaman. Bad enough to have the Russians shooting at us, without adding our own guys into the mix. Need to see the commander." He moved to step past, but the man backed up a step and brought the rifle to his shoulder, aiming at Kennedy's chest.

"I said, HALT!"

"Whoa, hang on!" Taylor and Hulse were about to rush the man, but Kennedy stayed between them.

"Knock it off, everybody!"

"You boys all right?" the trawler captain had stepped out of his wheelhouse and was watching the scene with a quizzical expression on his face.

The sentry swung the rifle toward him. "You need to get that vessel away from this pier, sir. This is a restricted area."

"Quit waving that thing around, junior," the captain answered irritably. You're gonna get somebody killed. "Look, these three are your missing helo crew. They got shot down the first morning, ended up stuck in Kenai, all right? They couldn't get any of your people to pick 'em up, so I brought 'em here."

The sentry looked closer at the three men. "That was you guys? We all thought nobody got out of that alive. Information's been kinda spotty."

"That was us," Kennedy said. "We all got out, but we lost our pilot the next day. We *need* to see the commander, right now."

The man looked uncertain for a moment, then finally keyed the radio at his collar, relaying the information to his command post. He nodded as someone responded in his earpiece. "Aye, aye." He looked at Kennedy again. "They're sending a car down for you."

"Thanks." Kennedy turned back to the trawler captain. "Looks like we're good to go, Cap. Can't thank you and your crew enough."

"Don't mention it. You boys watch yourselves, ya hear?"

They all waved as the man went back into the wheel house, and the big trawler slowly eased away from the pier and turned back down the channel toward open water.

"I'm sorry about all that, Lieutenant," the sentry said.

"I get it," Kennedy stopped him. "You're just doing your job." He smiled. "And we're just trying to get back to ours."

CHAPTER TWENTY-EIGHT

Spiritus Ante Mersum

Coast Guard Air Station Kodiak
Kodiak, Alaska

Day 25

The commander of Coast Guard Air Station Kodiak had been thrilled at the unexpected return of most of the crew of *CG6002*, and had assigned them a spot back in the shift rotation immediately. The station was understaffed, since another one of its helicopters had disappeared without a trace south of Kodiak on the first day of the war. The assumption was that the Russians had shot it down, but no one really knew for certain. That had left two operational HH-60s on the island, but only one complete crew.

The commander had been contacted by the Russians several days earlier, and informed that they could resume lifesaving operations and local patrols within a hundred mile radius of the station. Any other operations would be treated as hostile. But with just one operational helo crew, the station's readiness was seriously limited. Also, the possibility existed that not all Russian forces in the area were aware of the limited freedom that had been granted the Coast Guard. That made going back out an even greater risk than usual.

In spite of the danger, Kennedy and his men were more than ready to get back to work. The only reservations they held pertained to the new pilot they'd been paired with, a youngish looking lieutenant with a baby face and and a funny name.

Huey Loos had just transferred to Kodiak from Air Station San Diego two days before the war broke out, and he'd yet to fly a mission in Alaska. He also had the double indignity of having a name that closely resembled an '80s pop singer, as well as sharing his first name with a widely-used but mostly out of date military helicopter. It was a situation ripe for ridicule, and Loos, already quiet by nature, was now downright withdrawn. He was the new guy, and he'd shown up at his new duty station at the worst possible time. The unexpected return of Kennedy, Taylor and Hulse had given Loos an experienced crew, but they were less happy about the pairing than he was.

"What kinda name is that, anyway?" Hulse muttered, glancing over his shoulder at Loos, who was following a short distance behind as they walked out toward their new helicopter.

"Same kinda name as Darnell," Kennedy said. "Except it rhymes with 'news'. 'Darnell' doesn't rhyme with anything."

Hulse chuckled. "I just don't see how he has more flight hours than you, Ell-Tee. He looks like he's about twelve years old."

Kennedy shook his head. "Show some respect - he outranks both of us."

"*Everybody* outranks me," Hulse said. He looked back again. "Where's Taylor, anyway?"

Kennedy was about to say that he had no idea, when Taylor emerged from behind their new helicopter. He had a cloth in one hand, and stopped to polish something on the nose of the aircraft. "Guess he couldn't wait to get back to work."

When Taylor saw them coming, he straightened up and

turned his back to the helicopter, conspicuously blocking their view of the spot he'd been polishing. "Whatcha doing out here, Chris?" Hulse asked. "You missed the flight brief."

Taylor looked uncomfortable. "I just had to... check on something."

Kennedy stopped in front of their rescue swimmer. "You okay, Chris?"

Taylor nodded, but wouldn't meet Kennedy's eyes.

"What's going on?" Kennedy was starting to get concerned. Taylor wasn't normally given to erratic behavior. "You sure you're good to go?" He leaned to one side, trying to see behind him. "What is that?"

Taylor, eyes low, stepped away from the aircraft just as Lieutenant Loos caught up. Kennedy and Hulse both went silent. Taylor turned slowly and stepped back, and the four men stood there, looking at the black vinyl letters he'd stenciled onto the nose of their aircraft.

Loos looked uncomfortable. "Isn't... isn't that against regulations?"

Kennedy glanced at their new pilot, then put a hand on Taylor's shoulder. "That's nice work, Chris." He looked back at the lettering, then nodded and climbed into his seat.

Taylor and Hulse moved to the rear door without a word, Hulse clapping Taylor on the back as he climbed in.

Loos stood there a moment longer, looking uncertain, then walked around and climbed into the pilot's seat. He put on his flight helmet and keyed the intercom. "Who's 'Joy', anyway?"

Kennedy looked at him for a long moment. "You're sitting in her chair."

Loos' face fell. In the short time since he'd arrived at Kodiak, he'd only heard Rollinson referred to by her rank and last name. Now, his thoughtless comment made him feel like he'd just showed up drunk to a church picnic. "Uh, sorry, guys," he stammered. "I... I didn't realize..."

Kennedy was already checking the controls and going

through his portion of the pre-flight checklist. "Don't worry about it, Boss. Not your fault." He looked out at the clouds building over the mountains behind the air station. "Let's go save somebody, fellas. I think Joy'd like that."

Canyon Creek, Alaska
2 Miles NW of Little Gold, Yukon Territory

Holland and his team ended up waiting much longer than half an hour for Reardon to get back to them. While arranging the flight from Dawson across the border into Alaska had been a mostly simple thing, the attack on Greely had changed things dramatically. The Russians had increased their air patrols up and down the international border, and the Canadian government had ordered all border crossings, including the one at Little Gold, remain closed. They wanted to avoid the outward appearance of complicity in any resistance going on inside Alaska.

As a result, Holland's team was forced to lie low in the forest for a night, two miles west of the border. The Canadian government wanted to avoid overtly provoking the Russians by approving a cross-border extraction of the commando team responsible for destroying the missiles at Greely. Reardon had to work feverishly to convince them of the need to make a stand and assert their sovereignty in the region. If they didn't help, he argued, Dawson City would only be the first in a long line of Canadian border towns that would fall under the Russian heel. His argument worked - to a point.

Somewhat reluctantly, the Canadians agreed to provide air cover in the form of six CF-18 fighters operating out of CFB Cold Lake, Alberta. The fighters would patrol the border aggressively along a hundred mile front, from Little Gold in the north to where the Alcan Highway entered Canada in the south. The CF-18 pilots were aggressive, lighting up Russian planes with their missile radars and powerful electronic jammers every time they approached the border. The Russians had, as Reardon predicted, been reluctant to escalate tensions along the border when their gains in Alaska had not yet been completely consolidated, so they had backed down each time.

Some of the Canadian commanders worried that the aggressive use of jamming would make it plain to the Russians that the Canadians were hiding something; Reardon argued that any sovereign nation with an active armed conflict on its border would behave similarly, whether they were actively involved or not. It was a valid point. No one would reasonably expect the Canadians to be completely passive under the circumstances.

But Canada's willingness to participate seemed to end there. Rather than send in a regular army unit to help get Holland's team to safety, they sent a detachment of Canadian Rangers from the 1 Canadian Ranger Patrol Group to cross the border and escort them.

The Canadian Rangers are a reserve element of the Canadian Army, spread throughout remote areas of the country where it is not practical or possible to maintain standing army bases. The Rangers provide local security and support to Canadian Armed Forces units during domestic operations. While considered to be always on duty, their training is minimal compared to regular army troops, and their utility is more based in their local area knowledge and familiarity with the terrain close to where they live and work. When ten Rangers showed up at their hide west of the border, Holland and his team were unimpressed - at first.

But as they talked with the Rangers - most of them members of local First Nations tribes - they quickly recognized their professionalism and backcountry skill. They were all very capable woodsmen who took their mission very seriously. The fact that several were older than Holland and some were obviously overweight seemed to have no bearing on their ability to trek through difficult terrain over long distances without complaint - or much rest, for that matter.

The Rangers led the way through a narrow river gorge and across a knife-edge ridge, into a long, east facing valley that eventually sloped down toward the border well north of the Little Gold crossing. Four of the Rangers carried Deane between them on a collapsible stretcher, expertly keeping him as stable as possible the entire way.

They'd all crossed the border at a point that seemed at first glance to be impassable; a steep slope choked with thick brush. The Rangers wove their careful way through with little difficulty and no complaints. Once they were safely across the border, they continued through the woods another two miles to a logging road, where Reardon had arranged for ground transport to pick them up and drive them into Dawson City.

Deane was loaded into the back of a panel truck, protesting all the way. His wound had become infected while they waited for escort, and they were all concerned for his recovery, but he still resisted being taken out of the fight. Holland clasped the Sergeant Major's hand as the Rangers strapped him onto a gurney.

"Take care, Alvin. We'll check up on you as soon as we can."

"Don't blow sunshine up my skirt, lad," Deane groused. "You lot'll be a thousand miles away, gettin' yourselves shot to bits long before the quacks'll let me outta hospital."

Holland laughed. "Let's hope not." He backed out of the truck. Archie and Tony stuck their faces inside as he stepped down.

"Thanks for all your help, Sergeant Major," Tony said. "I'm glad that bear didn't eat you before we got to Aanaq's house."

"Cheeky bugger," Deane said. "Next time, you'll be on point."

"I look forward to it."

Archie reached in and squeezed Deane's foot. "Don't die, Grandad. I'd hate to waste all the effort it took to keep you alive."

"Dying might be better than listening to you brag day and night about saving me," Deane said, grinning. "Your head was swelled enough as it was." He looked at the others. "You lads go and give Ivan a stiff boot to the arse for me."

"We will." Holland raised a hand in farewell as one of the Rangers closed the rear door and the truck pulled away. The three men watched it go in silence, until the Ranger spoke up.

"You boys about ready? We should probably get you all loaded up and back to Dawson City. The war isn't over, yet."

Holland nodded. "No, it isn't. Not by a long shot."

They loaded into the remaining trucks and pulled out. Holland knew they'd won a small battle by taking out the missile battery. That victory had very nearly cost Sergeant Major Deane his life. As they rolled through the woods toward Dawson City, Holland couldn't shake the feeling that winning the war might carry a higher cost than any of them could imagine.

About the Author

M.P. MacDougall is an American historian and author of thrillers, humorous satire and fantasy. The youngest of twelve children, he grew up on a suburban farm, spending much of his free time chasing cows, perfecting bicycle stunts and playing in the dirt, and he never had to wear a helmet or use anti-bacterial soap. He was a professional Air Traffic Controller for more than twenty-six years, and a practitioner of the art of sarcastic banter and snide commentary for much longer than that. He holds a Bachelor of Arts in World Military History, because he's afraid he'll lose it if he puts it down. He lives with his very patient wife and kids in the Pacific Northwest of the United States.

This is his seventh book.

Also By M.P. MacDougall

Lawson Holland Thrillers
One Is A Warrior   - FREE Novella download at MPMacDougall.com
The Blood of Tyrants
The Blood of Patriots
The Tree of Liberty
The Calm of Despotism - Coming Soon!

How To Steer Your Kid Series (Humor/Satire)
Jet Screamer
Meat Sandwiches

Harvey Bennett Prequels (With Nick Thacker)
The Icarus Effect

Learn more about the author at
MPMacDougall.com

Thanks so much for reading!

Made in the USA
Coppell, TX
14 January 2022

71607166R00266